ALIEN SURROUNDINGS

The shaft was lit by orange-yellow light, with no sign of bottom. Warm oxygen-rich air pumped up from below. Juan took a coin from his pocket and dropped it in. It fell slowly, as if held by a force.

Rassmussen said, "It keeps a flat angle."

"An elevator?" Malachi asked, standing on the edge as he peered down.

"Hey!" a voice cried behind them. Juan started. The sound echoed through the passage. He turned to look back.

"Help!" Malachi shouted suddenly.

Juan spun around as his friend fell into the well. "Jesus," Lena said, dropping to her knees. She reached out with both hands, but Malachi was already too far down. . . .

"Together with his metaphysical imagination, his hard-earned understanding of science and technology, and his maturing skills as a delineator of character, his mastery of a distinctive prose style makes it impossible to regard Zebrowski as just another journeyman yarnspinner. . . . The strides he has made on a stylistic level—the increase in metaphorical aptness, in the beauty and simplicity of his images—cry out for applause."

—Michael Bishop

Other Books by George Zebrowski

NOVELS
Macrolife
The Omega Point Trilogy
Sunspacer
The Stars Will Speak

SHORT FICTION
The Monadic Universe

ANTHOLOGIES
Tomorrow Today
Human-Machines (edited with Thomas N. Scortia)
Faster Than Light (edited with Jack Dann)
The Best of Thomas N. Scortia
Creations (edited with Isaac Asimov & Martin H. Greenberg)
Synergy 1
Synergy 2
Synergy 3
Synergy 4
Nebula Awards 20
Nebula Awards 21
Nebula Awards 22

ESSAYS
Beneath A Red Star: Studies in Eastern European Science
    Fiction

ABOUT THE AUTHOR
The Work of George Zebrowski, An Annotated Bibliography
    & Guide, by Jeffrey M. Elliot & Robert Reginald

STRANGER SUNS

George Zebrowski

SPECTRA™

BANTAM BOOKS
NEW YORK · TORONTO · LONDON · SYDNEY · AUCKLAND

STRANGER SUNS

A Bantam Spectra Book / September 1991

A different version of the first third of this novel was serialized as
Stranger Suns in *Amazing Stories*, January and March, 1991, and
is Copyright © 1990, TSR, Inc.

A leatherbound hardcover signed First Edition of this novel was
published by Easton Press (MBI, Inc.), Norwalk, CT, 1991.

Grateful acknowledgment is made for permission to reprint the
following:
Excerpt from *The Seven Pillars of Wisdom* by T.E. Lawrence. Used
by permission of Doubleday, a division of Bantam Doubleday Dell
Publishing Group, Inc.

Excerpt from *The Two Sources of Morality and Religion* by Henri
Bergson. Translated by R. Ashley Audra and Cloudesley Brereton.
Copyright 1935, © 1963 by Holt, Rinehart and Winston. Reprinted
by permission of Henry Holt and Company, Inc.

ISBN 0-553-29175-0

Published simultaneously in the United States and Canada

PRINTED IN THE UNITED STATES OF AMERICA

RAD   0 9 8 7 6 5 4 3 2 1

To Janna, who did the right thing when other things weren't.

I

THE STRENGTH OF SECRETS

The eternal silence of these infinite spaces terrifies me.

—Blaise Pascal

I

INDUSTRIAL PARK

◑

Juan Obrion grasped the central guide bar and stopped his motion through the long tube leading from sleep quarters in the spinning wheel to the isolated work sphere, high above the hub. As usual, he had not slept well in the wheel's simulated half-g, waking up with the words *centrifugal sleep begets coriolis dreams* playing in his head, defying him to guess their meaning. They still seemed to mock him as he floated in place and peered out at the other components of the deteriorating industrial park orbiting a choking, warming Earth that would soon be able to support only the most obviously practical projects. Of the thirty bunched zero-g spheres, half had been empty since 2010. Four shuttles, abandoned six years later for lack of maintenance, drifted against the glow of early morning in the Pacific.

He feared the slow dying of devotion within himself, the loss of his feeling for the work of science, which he had once hoped would liberate him from the mill of power, greed, and survival that sooner or later enslaved most people; even on the high road of ideals, death still waited along the way. Liberation was beginning to look like an open grave.

He pulled up to a viewport so badly pitted by cosmic dust that it was impossible to see out. He tried to see a chaos pattern in the complex etchings, and was reminded of a letter by a Russian named Tasarov in a math journal, linking chaos and probability theory in a novel but untutored way. There's always a choice to do your best, he insisted to himself.

He pushed over to the other side of the tube, and watched the regular shuttle dumping its hundred-thousand-pound load of radioactive waste into the last containment sphere.

When it was sent on its way into the Sun, they would start filling the zero-g work spheres, which were now too old to renovate.

He grasped the center bar again and pulled himself forward toward the door to the control room. Get a grip on yourself, he told himself as he reached it and pressed his palm to the key plate. We're all good people up here. Hard workers, all ten of us. Better times may come.

The door lurched ajar, then slid open. He pulled himself inside, and tried to seem cheerful as he came up behind the stocky figure of his friend.

Malachi Moede turned from the control panel and said, "Just about ready to use again."

Juan smiled. Malachi floated up, slipped a smoke from the pack in his shirt pocket, and scratched the cigarette on the low ceiling. The tip glowed red against his black skin as he took a drag, then exhaled toward the ventilator intake. "I'm quite sure it will work perfectly," he said in his subdued British accent, which made even his most pointed remarks seem understated.

Juan recalled again how often he had been reminded that his detector was not relieving the choke below or opening Sunspace for industrial development. The complaints reminded him of his dead father, who would have said that his son had built a toy with other people's money for his own amusement. "Maybe we'll skip a few growing pains if this rig puts us in touch with our alien brethren." The bitter disbelief in his own voice disturbed him.

Malachi took a deep drag and held the smoke for a moment before releasing it toward the grille. "Possibly the tachyon beams are very tight and miss our rig. We'll have to search more of the sky."

"Or no one is sending."

"We couldn't say that even after searching the whole sky."

"Maybe it's the rig," Juan said, suppressing his desolate mood.

"I checked it from top to bottom today. Mind if I stay for part of your shift?"

Juan nodded, slipped into the control seat and strapped in, then opened the gyro controls. The screen's dark blue eye was blank as it came on; audio was silent. The magnetic field was a still pond waiting for a pebble to drop in. He reached out with a kind of lonely love and prayed for a faster-than-light particle to be absorbed, resonate with atomic particles in the field, and show up as an unmistakable jiggle on the display.

Malachi's hand touched his shoulder. "Don't take it so hard, dear chap. You stare at that thing as if expecting to see into the mind of God."

Maybe there was no one out there at all, Juan thought, and humankind was alone in the universe. His project had only added a tachyon silence to the radio silence of the universe. He had built a tachyon detector which did not detect tachyons, and that would be enough for Titus Summet to close it down.

He switched to a view of the shuttle pulling away from the dump sphere. As the orbiter dwindled, he found himself almost sympathizing with the ridicule that had been hurled against the tachyon project. Trying to eavesdrop on alien civilizations in the hope of picking up tech tips was like expecting to inherit wealth without knowing if one had rich relations. The basic scientific work for the detector was decades old; it would not yield new science without tachyons. A world fighting rising oceans, deforestation, ozone depletion, lack of clean air and water, and an increasingly better organized criminal class, could not afford altars to uncooperative gods. The cost of medical care for the aging, for the treatment of immune-system diseases, and the monitoring of the millions of drug-damaged individuals was increasing geometrically, as was the population. The only thing saving his project was its modest cost compared to the big ground-based projects.

"Maybe I need a rest," Juan said as he stared at the south polar icecap. It was bright in the sunlight. Clouds veiled the south Pacific. From a thousand kilometers out, no scars showed. A feeling of precariousness came over him. Something had dared to distinguish itself from the darkness—a vast planetary creature wrapped in gases, living on the Sun's streaming energy. What am I doing outside it, he asked, suddenly incredulous, even though he knew it was only his father again.

The audio monitor sang out a high, varying tone.

Juan switched back to the detector's blue eye. A twitching white line marched across the screen. "I'll get a fix," he said, not daring to hope.

"Look," Malachi said, "the ripples measure to our predictions for a tachyon mass running into the detector."

Sweating, Juan leaned forward against his straps—but his hopes died. "The signal's coming straight up from the Antarctic." He took a deep breath and switched to the main view of Earth, leaving the blue eye as a bottom-right insert. "Damn Summet, he's got a project of some kind down there!" He looked up at Malachi, who was scratching up another cigarette. "We've gone to a lot of effort to prevent anything else from triggering our detector. It's got to be an experiment generating tachyons."

Malachi coughed and slipped his cigarette into a wall slot. "If it's tachyons."

"What else could it be?"

Malachi nodded reluctantly. "At least we'll prove to Summet that our detector works, and be able to send out more than radio messages. We'll show those shining galactic cultures that we can do more than put up smoke signals. They might have a rule about replying to radio folk, you know."

The line continued to dance with the steady repetition of its sound analog.

"What are they doing down there?" Juan said.

"Maybe we're supposed to receive while they send. He planned to surprise us, and see whether we knew what we were doing. Time to call him and say we've caught on."

The director of UN Earth Resources Security stared blankly from the screen. "Juan, what are you talking about?" He ran a bony hand through his graying brown hair and scowled, bunching his thick eyebrows.

"You tell me, Titus."

Even though UN-ERS was responsible for the safe development of Earth's energy and resources, it too often became a forum for political intrigues. Summet wielded great power, especially when he invoked fears of new eco-disasters; but much of the time he simply caved in to national interests, while claiming privately that he chose the issues on which to give ground, to save his influence for more important ones.

Summet shifted his stocky frame in his chair, squinted, and said, "I don't know a thing about this, much as it would please you to think otherwise." He shook his head and smiled. "Are you certain?"

"All the physics I know says it's a faster-than-light signal."

Summet looked worried. "We do have teams down there, but nothing with tachyons."

"Maybe they're not telling you everything anymore."

"Impossible," Summet said. "You'll have to investigate."

"But you have people there already."

"This is still your project, Juan. The exercise will do you good. You don't look well to me. Three months of low and zero-g is not good for you."

"Could it be a private or national group?"

Summet shook his head. "I'd have known by now."

"Are you sure?"

"Go find out."

"It could be embarrassing to you. You might have to continue my project."

"Don't hope for too much. You and Malachi take the next waste shuttle down to Brazil. Your documents will be waiting. I'll get you some help."

The screen winked off. Malachi drifted up from below the screen and scratched a fresh cigarette on the underpanel.

"What do you think?" Juan asked.

Malachi puffed and said, "He doesn't like being puzzled."

"When's the next shuttle?"

"Three hours."

Juan switched back to the detector display. "We'll leave everything on feed to JPL." The white line on the blue screen still danced in step with the varying high tone. It had to be tachyons, he told himself, whatever the source.

2

A VOICE FROM THE COLD

◑

The Antarctic valley was a rocky bowl of snow and ice rimmed by mountains. Juan sensed a presence beneath his boots as he gazed up at the darkening blue sky. It was here, at the center of the fill, about forty meters down, according to the soundings. How long had it been here, and what had moved it to speak?

Summet had been prompt in sending both the tons of equipment and crew needed to set up base camp around the site, and in recruiting two scientists to help with the investigation. The camp, a semicircle of long huts around the site, had been ready when he and Malachi arrived two hours ago, three weeks to the day after the discovery, impatient to start work after a week's delay in Miami.

Juan retreated to the snow cab, climbing in next to Malachi, and they listened again to the radio relay of the signal from the detector. The audio analog of the tachyon stream was beginning to sound like an intermittent wail.

"Somewhere just below us," Malachi said.

Juan sat back. "Reminds me of an alarm. Nothing but a prearranged meaning. What do you think Titus makes of this?"

The Kenyan smiled from inside his parka hood and said, "There's a lot of guessing going on." He chuckled. "Makes you happy, doesn't it?"

The orange ball of the sun slipped below the peaks. The still landscape seemed ready for the six-month-long Antarctic winter night, now only days away.

Malachi said, "Let's set the markers for the diggers."

• • •

At twilight, the frozen continent seemed to draw its cold from the icy stars wheeling around the south pole. The semicircle of huts cast purple shadows across the azure-white plain as Juan hurried over to the snow cab. Downwind from the encampment, vapor from the smoke stacks was a fog bank rolling away across the snow. The industrial park was a swarm of bright stars rising in polar orbit from behind the molarlike mountains. He opened the cab door, pulled himself inside, and shut the door.

He pumped the sticky radio switch three times, and finally got the relay of the tachyon wail from Polar Sat One. The signal was unchanged—something proud crying in an empty auditorium where the house lights were stars. He felt apprehensive. After ten years of struggle to build the tachyon receiver, this message from home might turn out to be a cruel joke.

He killed the radio, shoved out through the door, and jogged back to quarters, trying to clear his mind of irrational suspicions. When he entered the antechamber to the large hut, he felt better. He took off his parka and went through the inner door.

Lena Dravic, Magnus Rassmussen, and Malachi were drinking coffee at the table in the center of the bare room, which was divided into bunk alcoves along the two walls. "Still there?" Lena asked.

"No change." He sat down and poured himself a steaming cup, admiring her high cheekbones and short, sandy blond hair. She made him feel anxious. "By the way, Lena, where did Summet steal you from?" He sipped slowly, wondering if she was attracted to him, or if he was only flattering himself; he had never been able to trust his feelings about women.

Her face flushed, and he realized that his question might be taken as an insult. She might be touchy about her work. He avoided her questioning blue eyes.

"Didn't he tell you?" she said with a slight accent. Summet had mentioned that she was Norwegian.

"No," Juan said, "and I don't go looking up someone's records without their approval. What were you doing?" He tried to sound sympathetic, then realized that her name was not Norwegian. Maybe she was using a husband's name.

"Drug biology," she said, "up in the orbital isolation cluster, making immune formulas so our leaders can stay in office

longer. I'd rather be researching, but it's not possible yet."
She gave a slight shrug. "I could be spared."

"I didn't mean to be rude," Juan said, glancing at Malachi
and Rassmussen.

"I know." She smiled, but for all he could tell she might
be hiding her dislike of him.

Rassmussen cleared his throat and sat back in his chair,
which was too small for his lean, wiry frame. "I pity Summet.
A failed scientist, he went into politics just in time."

"What do you do?" Malachi asked the older man.

"I'm just about retired, but I consult. Titus insisted I owed
him this one. I used to inspect electronics for the UN, mostly
weapons-monitoring gear." He scratched the white stubble
on his head and smiled apologetically. "I wanted physics, and
had quite a bit of it, with the chance for more, but adminis-
tration and straightforward applications of theory paid
better."

"What do you think we're dealing with here?" Juan asked.

Rassmussen shrugged. "Not tachyons."

"Why not?" Juan asked.

Rassmussen smiled. "I'd check your detector for spurious
input."

Damn technicians, Juan thought, and a burned-out one at
that. They always think they know more physics than anyone.

"What do you think we'll dig up?" Juan asked.

"It'll be something natural," Rassmussen said.

"Ah, but it will count for so much if it's tachyons," Malachi
said.

"Obviously," Rassmussen replied, picking up his cup.

"Summet has been threatening to close down the tachyon
listening project," Malachi continued, "and it hasn't been a
month since we got the equipment working properly."

Rassmussen smiled again. "In that case, let's hope." Juan
felt uneasy.

"I do hope it comes out right for you, Dr. Obrion," Lena
said. He looked directly at her, and she met his gaze.

"Summet can't be all bad," Rassmussen added, "if he supported your work at all."

Juan sighed. "It's crazy, receiving tachyons from a source
on Earth. It'll be embarrassing if it's something natural."

"But it does suggest that your detector works," Lena said
encouragingly. "A natural source of tachyons would be quite
a discovery by itself."

"If we're picking up tachyons."

"If your calculations say you are," Rassmussen said, "then stick to your data and don't listen to me."

"Thanks," Juan replied.

"What would you like it to be?" Rassmussen asked.

Juan did not reply. Lena said, "We'll know soon enough," still gazing at him with interest. He took a long sip of his coffee, feeling uneasy and full of doubt.

Malachi stood up. "We should get some sleep."

By noon, one heavy digger had gone down thirty meters and shattered its rotary blade against something harder than itself; by midafternoon the same thing happened in a spot seventy five meters away. Two big scoops were brought out from the copters and set to dig between the holes. Gradually, the site became one large excavation, with ramps leading down from north and south.

Floodlights were set up as the Antarctic night closed in. A second shift of workers replaced the first; backup equipment was readied. Summet had been both efficient and generous, Juan thought as he watched a small scoop roll down into the pit and pick at the hard ice, looking like a giant insect in the blue-white glare of the heavy lamps.

Malachi came up beside him. Suddenly there was an agonized grinding sound and the scoop stopped, its digger's claw poised over something dark. The operator looked up at them.

They went down the ramp, made their way around the scoop's giant treads, and squatted down for a close look. Juan felt the black surface with his gloved hand, restraining his growing excitement, then took out his geologist's hammer.

"A trapped whale?" Malachi said jokingly.

Juan struck lightly. "Seems metallic."

Malachi knelt down next to him. "This doesn't belong to anyone we know," he said, pulling the hood of his parka closer around her head.

"We'll widen the dig from here," Juan said.

"Juan, wake up!" Lena shouted, shaking him. He didn't remember coming inside to sleep, only that he had suddenly been very tired. "There's an opening."

She hovered over him, and seemed to float back as he sat up on one elbow. Malachi was drinking coffee at the table. His white cup resembled a huge tooth.

"What time is it?"

"You've slept five hours," Malachi said.

Juan shivered, wishing for sunny beaches and simple pleasures, then wondered what lay under the ice, and suddenly imagined a city locked in the cold, its cellars sunk deeply into the bedrock of the continent.

Lena was looking at him with concern. "Antarctic dryness affects some people strangely. You just about collapsed. How do you feel now?"

He sat up on the edge of the bunk and slipped on his boots. "What did you say before?" he asked as he got up and staggered to the table.

"They've found an opening," Malachi said as Juan sat down and poured himself a cup of coffee.

He gulped down the coffee and stood up. "Let's go."

Blue light streamed from the excavation, as if a strange sun were rising from the ice. A frigid breeze cut through the starry night as Juan followed Lena and Malachi down into the glowing pit. They found Rassmussen staring into a circular opening set at a shallow angle in a rising black surface.

Juan came up at his left and peered into the blue glare. His pulse quickened; the curved surface suggested a giant dome below the ice.

Rassmussen said, "The diggers say that the opening simply appeared. It was gone when I got here, then showed itself. If these five square meters of exposed curvature hold true, it's maybe two or three kilometers across, with this entrance somewhere near the top."

"So this is where the tachyons are coming from!" Lena exclaimed.

"It may well be," Rassmussen said, "that they are tachyons."

Juan threw back his hood and stepped up close. "There's a floor," he said, peering into the chamber.

"Wait!" Mal shouted as Juan entered an egg-shaped chamber filled with blue light. There seemed to be no other exit. Mal came in next to him.

Juan grabbed his friend's arm, pulled him deeper into the chamber and shouted, "Stand well back. I want to try something!"

"What are you doing?" Malachi demanded.

"I think I know!" Juan shouted, turning in time to see the opening glow red and disappear.

"We're trapped," Malachi said.

"No, wait."

Juan moved forward. The glowing red circle appeared again. "It's a lock!" Lena shouted from outside.

"Step back again!" Juan called out, retreating. "And stay back. I want to see if it's triggered from both sides."

Again, the opening glowed red and disappeared.

"I hope you're right," Malachi said.

They came forward. The circle glowed open and they emerged into the cold.

"But where does the lock lead?" Lena asked excitedly.

"A buried city?" Malachi said.

"So there was an advanced civilization in Antarctica," Lena added.

Juan said, "Let's look around before Titus drops a security lid. Are you all game?"

"Without a doubt," Malachi replied.

"This lock," Rassmussen said as Juan led the way back inside, "is impossible!"

From the middle of the small chamber, they turned and watched the exit glow red and blend seamlessly into the blue inner surface. "There must be an inner door," Juan said eagerly, moving toward the other end.

An orange glow appeared before him. "You've triggered it," Malachi said. Juan felt a gentle breeze as he went through the opening.

Overhead, yellow-orange squares of light curved away to the right, following the bend of a long passageway. The black floor reflected the lights as a dull streak.

"It spirals downward," Malachi said.

Juan led the way, examining the markings on the walls. Runs of concentric circles alternated with squares and triangles, joined by wavelets. For a moment he heard a strange whisper in his ears, but it stopped as he listened to it. He turned and looked back toward the lock. The others gazed back with him.

"It had better open when we leave," Lena said. "Maybe we should go back now."

"Let's look ahead a ways," Juan said, moving forward. Suddenly he was aware that all the surfaces of the passage seemed new, with no sign of wear. Not one light was out.

"A culture so advanced," Lena said, "existing long before us. Could they still be here?"

The passage continued to the right, its black walls displaying the same endless frieze of markings and oval, doorlike depressions.

Rassmussen said, "It's demoralizing. The lock back there implies a fantastically sophisticated power-handling capacity."

They entered a large oval area, with a large circular opening in the black floor. The spiral passage continued to descend on the far side. Juan approached and looked down.

The shaft was lit by orange-yellow light, with no sign of bottom. Warm, oxygen-rich air pumped up from below. He looked up and saw that the shaft did not continue through the ceiling, then took a coin from his pocket and dropped it in. It fell slowly, as if held by a force.

Rassmussen said, "It keeps a flat angle."

"An elevator?" Malachi asked, standing on the edge as he peered down.

"Heeeey!" a voice cried behind them. Juan started. The sound echoed through the passage. He turned to look back.

"Help!" Malachi shouted suddenly.

Juan spun around as his friend fell into the well. "Jesus," Lena said, dropping to her knees. She reached out with both hands, but Malachi was already too far down.

"Bloody stupid!" Malachi shouted, waving his arms. His figure dwindled.

"Mal!" Juan called, kneeling next to Lena.

"It's okay," Malachi answered faintly.

"I can't see him," Lena said.

Juan glanced up at Rassmussen. The older man seemed confused. "It wasn't a normal fall," he said, stepping back from the opening.

"We've got to do something," Lena said as she and Juan got up.

"Heeeeey!" the cry echoed again behind them.

"Over here!" Lena called back.

Juan heard footsteps. Two silhouettes came around the curve and stopped; a third dark shape joined them.

"Who are you?" Juan shouted.

The shadows came forward and became human figures. Juan recognized Florman, the tall, lanky excavation engineer, and Summet's stocky frame. The third man was a stranger.

"Obrion, what's going on here?" the director demanded.

"You know as much as we do. Who's this?"

"Inspector Ivan Dovzhenko, this is Dr. Juan Obrion. You've met the others, I believe."

Juan gave the Russian a quick nod. "We've just lost Mal, Titus. You startled us and he fell into this opening."

As Summet looked down the well, Juan glanced at Dovzhenko. Youngish with blond hair and gray-blue eyes, he seemed too stocky for his height. The usual second-rate Soviet scientist doubling as an ERS national observer. The best knew enough not to waste their time.

"You shouldn't have come in here," Summet said.

Juan said, "Mal went down slowly. He's somewhere below."

"Rassmussen, what do you think?" Summet demanded.

"I agree."

"And you, Dr. Dravic?"

"We all saw the same thing," she said.

Summet looked down into the well again and said, "I should order you all out of here right now."

Dovzhenko seemed nervous and wary. "Dr. Obrion, I must protest this—"

"We've got to find him," Juan said. "Down this passage."

Summet glanced at Dovzhenko, then nodded. "Wait here. I'll send down packs for you. You can't go bare-handed."

"Please hurry," Lena said.

Summet looked back up the passageway. "What in hell is this place?" He turned to Juan. "Is this where your tachyon beam is coming from?"

"It's still on?" Juan asked.

Summet nodded, then motioned for Florman and Dovzhenko to follow him out. "Stay put!" he shouted back as he hurried away.

3

THE SEEKERS

◑

Summet and Dovzhenko came back with six small packs, wearing their own, and carrying four others. "We'll leave one here," Summet said, dropping two at Juan's feet.

"You're both coming with us?" Juan asked, noticing the exasperated look on Dovzhenko's face as he put down the two he had carried in.

Summet nodded. "There's an automatic in each pack. Keep it handy. We don't know what's in here."

Juan disliked weapons, but he strapped it on. Lena looked at hers as if it were a jawbone club, then slipped it into her thigh pocket. Rassmussen took his out, checked the safety, and put it back.

Summet gestured to Juan as Florman's men left. "You lead."

Juan went around the well and started down the next turn in the descending spiral. After a few moments he again heard the strange whispers, and glanced back. Lena's eyes darted nervously. Magnus frowned. Summet and Dovzhenko suddenly stopped.

"Do you hear that?" Summet asked.

They all listened. A whine rose up from the silence.

"I hear it," Dovzhenko said.

Juan imagined a snakelike vehicle slipping up through the corkscrew passage. "Clear the way!" he shouted, moving to his right. As he turned and pressed back against the wall, it yielded behind him. He stumbled back—

—into a brightly lit room.

The harsh white light blinded him as he fell back on his

pack. He rolled over and squinted as he pushed against the floor with his gloved hands, then slowly got to his knees.

Around him stood objects that looked like cabinets, and benchlike structures of various sizes. Suddenly the ceiling glowed red. He began to sweat in his parka. Then the ceiling faded back to white and cool air rushed in around him.

He took a deep breath and stepped toward the wall, looking for the entrance. A bright red oval appeared, and the wall seemed to lose its solidity. He held out his arms, marched into the glow—

—and stepped through into the winding passage.

"Juan!" Lena shouted with relief.

"I'm okay," he said as they gathered around him and watched the portal fade away. He stepped toward the oval indentation. Faithfully, it glowed again, a graceful, fluid entranceway that engineers and architects might dream about; but if the past had accomplished all this, he thought, then the present was a time of decline.

"No further," Summet announced. "We'll get specialized teams in here. What happened in there?"

"I'm not sure, but I may have just been given a bath."

"Why do you think that?" Summet asked.

"It got very hot," Juan said, "then cool. Reminded me of infrared heaters in bathrooms." He looked at the oval indentations on the far side of the passageway. "I think there are chambers all up and down this spiral, and I'll bet each one is different."

"What is this place meant to be?" Summet asked.

Dovzhenko came up to him. "I must remind you," he said softly, "that this is now a UN-ERS find, fully protected by treaty. Until we can guarantee equal access for all signatories, it must be off limits to all further exploration."

"You're right," Summet said after a moment, "but emergency provisions apply right now. We'll leave as soon as we find Malachi Moede."

"We've got to go on now," Lena insisted before Dovzhenko could protest. "He may need help."

"He's only one man," Dovzhenko said.

"What's wrong with you?" Juan demanded.

"Calm down," Summet said.

"We're wasting time, and he wants to waste more with formalities."

"Dr. Obrion," Dovzhenko said, "I sympathize with your concern for your colleague, but as a scientific observer for a signatory to the UN-ERS treaty, I must enforce parity in the exploration of this find."

"What!" Juan asked angrily. "You're out of your mind."

Lena's face flushed with anger. "If Malachi is injured or dies," she said, "we will hold you responsible."

"Of course," Dovzhenko answered. "I understand your feelings completely."

"You don't," she said. "We'll settle with you personally."

"Ivan, come with me," Summet said. "You three—find him fast and bring him out. If you don't in a reasonable time, come out. For the record, you should not have come in here in the first place. Understand?"

Juan nodded.

"You're endangering yourselves and other scientific workers," Dovzhenko insisted.

Summet took him by the arm and led him up the passageway. "They'll be right out, Ivan," he said softly, then looked back at Juan and shouted, "Hurry!"

"Help!" Malachi cried out as he fell.

Lena was on her knees, reaching out to him.

"Bloody stupid!" he called back, then saw that he was sinking much too slowly for it to be dangerous.

"Mal!" Juan cried.

"It's okay!" he shouted.

His fall quickened. The opening grew small overhead and disappeared. Air pressure popped his ears. The bottom was rushing up to crack his head and snap his spine. He screamed and looked down. There was no bottom.

His grandmother in Kenya had once told him a story about a boy who fell into a deep well and found an ocean under the earth. There he became a cabin boy on a pirate vessel and grew up to command a craft of his own, visiting all the ports of the strange, starless ocean. He grew old in this life, until a giant dropped a bucket into the well and fished him up, ship and all. . . .

His fall slowed again. He caught his breath and looked around at the brightly lit shaft, examining the niches and odd markings as he drifted down.

Peering down, he saw that the shaft had narrowed, but there was still enough space for him to pass through the center of a catwalk. He spread his legs wide and landed gently. He stood still for a moment, glanced up into a bright haze, then looked around and noticed three oval niches spaced evenly around the shaft.

He stepped toward one. It glowed—

—and he slipped through into a large drum-shaped chamber filled with soft yellow light. The amber floor sloped into a flat circle at the center.

He went down the incline. It all seemed oddly familiar, as if his life had been lived to bring him here.

Juan picked up the extra pack and led the way around the well. Malachi could be anywhere inside this structure. Now that Antarctica's six months of night had begun, it would be harder to bring in supplies by air, impossible if the weather turned bad. They might have to leave Mal behind if Summet was forced to seal off the find while the UN-ERS debated what to do next.

As they went deeper into the spiral, Juan was startled by the possibility that the builders of such an advanced structure had perished. Rassmussen was right about the lock and chamber portals; such fluid control of matter and energy implied even greater capabilities. Materials synthesis alone would have insured survival.

"Call out," Lena said as she came up beside him. "He might hear us."

"Malachi!" Juan shouted, suddenly imagining his friend among the builders, talking with them, exchanging ideas, laughing at the simplicity of solutions to age-old problems. Perhaps there was only a small population left, living for noble purposes, free of material want.

"I'm here!" Malachi's voice answered, startling them.

They hurried forward. "Are you hurt?" Juan called out.

"No!" The Kenyan strolled around the bend; they rushed to him.

"What happened?" Juan asked.

"I'll show you."

Juan stared at his friend, relieved.

"I'm quite all right."

Juan grinned and gave him the spare pack. Rassmussen helped him to slip it on. "How far down did you go?" he asked.

"I estimate walking back two kilometers. Come, I'll show you."

"Titus wants us out of here," Juan said. "The lid's about to come down."

Malachi grimaced. "To blazes with him. This won't take long."

Malachi paused at the edge of the flat circle in the center of the drum-shaped chamber. "Watch," he said, "when I step into the center."

The yellow light faded into darkness. Three-dimensional starfields appeared around them. Juan felt vertigo, but oriented himself by the silhouettes of his companions blotting out the stars.

"They're so bright and clear," Lena said.

Malachi's arm reached out and pointed. "Notice the small red marks by yellow-orange suns."

"So they were fond of building planetariums," Rassmussen replied.

"Yes," Malachi said, "but these shots were not taken from Earth. You won't recognize any of these starfields. Follow me."

Juan watched his dark shape leave the circle and move up the incline. Lena and Rassmussen followed. As Juan caught up, the warm yellow glow again filled the chamber.

Malachi passed through the dissolving portal. Lena and Rassmussen slipped through. Juan hurried after them—

—and emerged in the spiral passage.

Malachi was on the other side, triggering another entrance. Juan waited for Lena and Rassmussen to go through, then followed them—

—into another white-lit room.

As his eyes adjusted, he saw that this chamber was bare, except for a shadowy heap in the center. They approached, and it became a pile of skeletons. "Not human," Malachi said. "Double thumbs, large ribcages, four toes. From the numbers here, it seems unlikely these were freaks."

Lena picked up a skull. "It's half again as large as ours, and look at the size of these eye sockets."

"I wonder how they died. And why were they piled here?" Rassmussen asked.

Juan felt the floor tremble.

"What was that?" Lena asked.

Malachi said, "The ice may be pushing part of this structure around."

Another tremor followed the first, then subsided.

"Maybe these were the builders of this place," Lena said. "Too bad. They might have taught us a lot."

Rassmussen sighed. "It'll be a long time before we understand what we've seen here."

"Perhaps not," Malachi said. "If we can grasp even one small detail, then our understanding may grow explosively. All this may be no more than a century or two beyond us. Remember, even simple principles look like magic when you don't understand the application."

Rassmussen laughed. "There's nothing simple behind these doorways!" His tall, gray-haired figure seemed frail in the antiseptic light of the chamber.

"But who were they?" Lena asked. "They seem to belong to another line of intelligent bipeds. To think they were advanced when we were still primitives."

"We're not all that backward," Malachi said. "Each of us can imagine how the lock and doors might work."

The older man shook his head sadly. "Imagine is the word. We couldn't build one of these doors, yet it was probably only work for one of their tradesmen, who might have installed it without knowing the theory behind it. The principle behind these doors could solve the world's material problems in one stroke."

"Listen!" Lena said.

The floor trembled, then shook, pitching Juan into the pile of bones.

4

TRAPPED

◑

A crazed choreographer was trying to shake the skeletons on the floor into a jittery dance. Juan stood up, but fell back into the trembling bones. A skull seemed to grimace at him as it rolled away.

"Stay down!" Malachi shouted.

The shaking stopped, as if someone had thrown a switch. Juan got to his knees. Lena offered him her hand. "Thanks," he said as he took it and pulled himself up. Malachi helped Magnus to his feet.

"Let's get out of here while we can," Lena said.

They lined up at the door. Juan waited as they went through the glow, then slipped after them into the passage. They hurried up the passageway. The floor trembled, and there was a distant rumbling. Juan realized that they might not cover the two kilometers to the lock in time to get out.

"Hurry!" he shouted, quickening his pace to take the lead.

"Should we drop our packs?" Lena asked.

"Not yet," he called back.

They force-marched in silence for the next twenty minutes. Juan glanced back at his companions and saw that each was keeping up, despite the extra weight.

Finally, they reached the drop tube. Juan slowed down and slipped out of his pack as they went past. He was gasping and sweating heavily. Zero-g had taken a lot of his strength. Malachi came up at his side and tried to help him along.

"I can do it," Juan said, pulling away.

The trembling started again as they reached the lock. Juan triggered the inner door. They hurried inside and collapsed on the floor.

"Everyone all right?" Juan asked after a few minutes.

"Yes," Lena replied, catching her breath.

Rassmussen nodded as he lay on his side. Malachi got to his feet and confronted the spot where the outer door had appeared. It glowed red and revealed a wall of ice.

"It might not be very thick," Malachi said. He stepped forward and pushed with both hands, with no result. "Did we have a digging tool in our packs?" he asked as he backed away and the door glowed shut.

"I'll go," Rassmussen said, moving toward the inner door. It glowed open and he hurried down the spiral.

"I expect," Malachi said, "that Titus will assume we're still in here."

Juan sat up and looked at Lena. She seemed nervous but in control of herself as she gazed back at him.

The inner door glowed after a few minutes and Rassmussen came in. "We're in luck. A collapsible spade in each pack."

Malachi took one, snapped open the handle, and faced the outer lock again. It glowed open and he struck the ice. "Useless," he said after two more tries. "Too hard for these implements." The exit glowed shut as he backed away.

"We'll wait," Juan said.

Rassmussen dropped the other spades. "It could be a few hours, or a week."

Juan nodded. "We have supplies for that long. Summet's equipped to reach us."

Malachi said, "True, but what if this place has slipped, and this exit can't be found?"

"What else can we do?" Juan answered, getting up.

Rassmussen cleared his throat and said, "I suggest we use the time we have here to explore a few of the chambers along the passage."

"Good idea," Malachi replied.

Juan paused before the chamber he had chosen. At his right, near the bend of the passageway, the small figure of Malachi slipped into the wall. Magnus and Lena had selected chambers farther down.

Juan triggered the red glow and stepped—

—into darkness.

As his eyes adjusted, a scattering of blue lights appeared overhead, casting a hazy light throughout the chamber. A dozen casketlike objects formed a rectangle on the floor in front of him. He went to the left corner box and touched the opaque surface. There was no sign of a lid.

He stepped into the center of the rectangle and looked around. The gloom made him shiver, despite his parka. A surprise party, he thought. At any moment the casket lids would fly open and well-wishers would rise to toast his health.

As he gazed at the strange shapes, he realized that he couldn't even begin to guess what they were. He wondered again if the builders had perished. Surely they would have shown themselves by now if they still existed. Disease was too simple an explanation for their absence; their knowledge seemed to preclude such an end. Suicide? The skeletons might belong to individuals of another species, who had wandered in and died. But why were their bones piled up?

The place irritated him, because he knew that he would never be able to set it aside and go back to his own work. What they had seen would change human life forever, if the technology were understood and mastered. The world he had known would come to an end.

"Hello!" he shouted, and listened to his echo. "Who are you? Are you still here?"

He smiled at his own childishness. Enigmas, like deities, never responded to entreaties.

Lena tensed as she passed through the glowing door. What if it froze up around her? She hurried through—

—into a bare room filled with white light.

The walls curved like lenses, waiting to magnify fearful depths. The chamber's stillness seemed to hold a distant whisper.

She sat down on the smooth, glassy floor, wondering if she was in some asylum. The room seemed to tease her, and she remembered a young girl's first fascination with the sciences. Exhausting wearisome whys had driven her life. Norway's midnight sun had been one of the first childhood mysteries to fall— a simple matter of tilting the world. That sun, hanging over snow-capped mountains, remained for her the image of clear thought. However glacierlike its application to human life, the patient accumulation of knowledge could save a world.

Her mother had been a more difficult mystery. A brooding woman, she had abandoned her husband and returned to her own country with her infant daughter. All that Lena knew of her father was that he had remained in the Balkans and had become something of a political figure during the 1990s, the so-called "era of new understanding." He had never been part of her life, apparently content to forget his daughter.

As she grew up, Lena had feared that she might be to blame for her parents' estrangement. The suspicion tormented her, until she confronted her mother. Her father had married another woman, she had been told. "My leaving him had nothing to do with you," her mother had insisted. "It would have happened anyway. At least I had you. I'm grateful that he gave me a child."

So that mystery had been solved—but another had replaced it: How could love become indifference? Few scientific answers were as various and unsatisfying as the answers to that question. A succession of new loves gave one the illusion of youth, for a time. Clearly, the physical limits of the body, especially its short lifespan, were no match for the mind, whose imagination soared, demanding what the body could not give. She had resolved to help break the forces of decay, and calm some of the outrage at existence that wounded the human heart. Her hopes had not been fulfilled. Humanity lived with little concern for individuals, unconsciously content with the illusory immortality of the species. Here and there, privileged individuals grasped at longer life. Their power and money supported the knowledge seekers.

I'm a fifth-rate magician, she told herself as she looked around the room. It was difficult to guess its size. She stood up and gazed into the variable curves of the lenslike walls. They seemed to grow in complexity, suggesting biological infrastructures. Sparks shot behind the surfaces, as if a school of silvery fish were navigating inner twists.

She moved forward and the chamber seemed to expand. She stopped and listened, imagining that she was expected to speak, and that she would be carried into the spaces between the stars.

She turned her head and saw a great blue eye staring at her from inside a facet. The eye blinked. She stepped back and it grew smaller, and she saw that the face to which it belonged was her own.

Malachi stood in an orange room. Hundreds of containerlike objects crowded the large floor. The far wall was bare, but the one at his right was covered with shelves. Hundreds of small square boxes sat on them.

He was annoyed; it all seemed to be just beyond his understanding. He went over to a large rectangular container and tried to lift what seemed to be the lid, but could not move it.

They knew I was coming, he thought, so they sealed the covers.

Magnus stared at the wall of square cubbyholes. It seemed to defy him to guess its purpose. He almost laughed as he turned away.

The rest of the blue room was empty, except for six tablelike protuberances in the center, set low enough to sit around. He pictured a corkscrew of chambers stuck in the ice, with everything in them made to be deliberately puzzling or meaningless; access to each chamber was through an elegant dissolving doorway, designed to boast; or so it seemed to an envious savage.

Irritated as much by his own reaction as by the contents of the room, he turned and approached the exit. It glowed obediently. He went forward—

—and gasped as a vise closed around him.

He could see into the passage. His heart raced. He tried to move, but the door held him.

"Help!" a voice shouted as Juan slipped out into the passage. He looked to his right, saw Magnus's hand clawing the air, and rushed to him.

The older man's face gazed out from the substance of the doorway, his right hand straining to push through. "Don't touch me—it might be dangerous." The door seemed plastic, ready to flow. The embedded face was a mask; only the quick movement of the eyes showed its fear.

Lena and Malachi came around the turn. "Over here!" Juan shouted. They ran up the passage.

"Oh, no!" Lena said.

"Is it cutting into you?" Malachi asked.

Magnus blinked. "No, but it's tight."

Juan imagined food and water being brought to him as the world's finest minds studied the jammed portal. He would discuss his plight with them as nurses bathed his face and brushed his teeth after meals. Endless rescuers would aspire to pull the new Merlin from the stone.

"Juan," Lena said softly, "he can't last long with so much of his body enclosed."

Magnus tried to smile. "So the technology isn't as perfect as it looks . . . old, malfunctioning." He formed his words with difficulty.

"Are you in pain?" Lena asked.

He moved his hand. "Can't feel it."

Juan tried to think.

"You may not be able to free me," Magnus said.

"We'll get you out," Lena said.

The floor trembled, as if offering a comment. Juan took a deep breath. He stepped forward and began to touch the portal.

"No!" Magnus shouted.

The surface was strange, hard and slightly warm. It glowed suddenly, and Magnus stumbled into his arms.

"I suspected it would trigger," Juan said, holding him up. Magnus was sweating heavily in his parka, but smiled.

"Can you stand?" Juan asked as Lena massaged his limp right hand.

He nodded, breathing more evenly. "Unfortunately, we're cut off from that room."

"So the door sticks a bit," Juan said, letting him go. "What's in there?"

"I'm not sure."

"We had no trouble with the ones we tried," Malachi said.

"Look!" Lena shouted. The portal was glowing.

"Maybe we're triggering it," Juan said.

They stepped back. It darkened, reddened again, then faded to normal.

Magnus smiled and rubbed the back of his neck. "It's as if it were resetting itself."

Juan stepped forward. The opening glowed, then died as he moved back.

"It may never happen again," Magnus said.

"Why did it happen?" Lena asked.

"A quantum accident of some kind, perhaps," Magnus said.

The floor trembled, then shook. They threw out their arms for balance. It stopped suddenly.

"We must get back," Lena said. "They may have dug through by now."

The floor trembled again as they went up the passage.

5

ICELOCK

◐

The ice pitched and the floodlights flickered. Summet lay flat at the rim of the pit as the dome pushed up. Men were strewn below, crying out and rolling to avoid the cracks. One power digger was on its side, pinning two figures.

"Get some lines down here!" he shouted as he got up.

"Get back!" Florman shouted at his right. A crack ran between them and toppled one of the huts. The dry, frigid air crackled with static electricity. Summet saw that the dome was large enough to send all the huts, copters, and machinery rolling away as it rose through the ice. He turned and followed Florman. The blue-white glare cast a strange daylight over the ice. Men moved like penguins toward the distant copters.

Black cracks radiated from the pit. Summet resisted the urge to drop flat and wait for the trembling to stop. He covered the last hundred meters and Florman pulled him up into the open bay. As the copter lifted, Summet looked back and was appalled at the size of the dome breaking through the ice. The floodlights died as cables snapped.

"From the curvature," Dovzhenko said in his clipped English, "it might be more than two kilometers across fully exposed."

The blue glow of the dome suggested the play of vast energies. Dovzhenko leaned over and slid the door shut. Summet peered through the small window. All the copters were in the air, beams sweeping the ice for survivors.

Summet opened the door a crack. The glowing dome had stopped rising. "Obrion's team may still be able to get out," he said. "The entrance area is exposed now, and the curve's shallow enough for them to reach the ice."

"They may be dead," Dovzhenko said, sounding as if it might be an appropriate punishment.

"Don't underestimate them, Ivan," Summet said. The Russian's relentless arrogance had grated on him ever since their first meeting more than a year ago. "We'll land and wait."

"What pushed it up?" Florman asked.

"It seems to be doing that by itself," Dovzhenko replied.

Summet saw two copters touch down on the far side of the dome. They were at least two kilometers away, yet clearly visible in the strange light. Dovzhenko handed him a pair of binoculars.

The dome's blue glow was bright in the glasses as Summet scanned the surface. There was no sign of the entrance.

Slowly, the copter descended and touched down. Summet felt a low rumble in his guts. "Florman, tell the pilot to leave for base if the quake starts again." As the engineer stood up and made his way forward, Summet peered through his glasses again, hoping to see Obrion's team.

"Are they coming out?" Dovzhenko asked.

The copter shook violently, and the pilot took it up. Summet saw the black cracks stabbing across the bright zone of ice. He shifted his glasses back to the dome.

"Fuel is limited," Dovzhenko said. "We must start back to Base One in fifteen minutes."

"It's coming up again!" Summet pulled the door open halfway.

The dome raised the ice around it into a ragged wall. Sections began to collapse.

"It's at least three kilometers across," Summet said, still peering through the glasses. The dome was rotating. Ice thundered as it fell, echoing through the dark valley. The air was full of static. The dome's blue glow brightened into silver. A shimmering field enclosed its skin as the massive globe lifted itself free. Tons of ice fell from the sphere as it hovered, then jerked upward, pulling a train of ice and snow after itself.

Summet followed the sphere as it climbed the night, blotting out the stars with its glow. The roar continued from below, where the ice was collapsing into the hole. The sphere shrank to a silver point and disappeared. Summet scanned the sky until his eyes adjusted and stars reappeared in their stately march around the pole.

"Back to base," he said to Dovzhenko, looking back at the

hole in the ice, where a luminous cloud of steam was belching up into the darkness. "Will anyone believe this?"

"The question," Dovzhenko replied, "is whether we could have prevented it."

"What do you mean?" Summet demanded, handing him his binoculars.

"We may ask if Obrion's team was responsible for this happening."

"I very much doubt that."

"We may never know," Dovzhenko said, "since most of the evidence is lost. But they should not have been permitted to remain in the vessel. You are responsible."

Summet sighed. "Okay, Ivan. Work your tricks. You can have my job—if they'll give it to you."

The shaking stopped. They were all still on their feet.

Juan looked at Lena. "Hear that?" she asked nervously, eyes wide.

"No."

"High frequency. I can just pick it up." She darted across the passage. "It's coming from this portal."

"Wait," Malachi said.

"Magnus, what do you think?" Juan asked. "Should we avoid these doors?"

"I don't know."

"How do you feel?" Lena asked.

"I don't feel any ill effects."

Lena stepped forward. The oval indentation glowed red and she went through. Juan followed her—

—into darkness.

They stood at what seemed to be the edge of a cliff. The Earth appeared at their feet. Antarctica was a darkening mass surrounded by water. Mount Erebus, the lights of Base One in Taylor Valley, and the Transantarctic Range were all clearly visible. The tips of Africa and South America were juttings of green and brown, still catching the sunlight.

The Earth grew smaller.

"We're in a ship!" Lena exclaimed.

Malachi said, "There's no sense of inertia or acceleration, so we must be inside a very advanced drive-field."

Drive and *field*, Juan thought excitedly as he watched the Earth recede. To see it diminish so quickly was a shock.

"I still hear that sound," Lena said.

Juan became aware of it—a distant, almost musical call. The Earth shrank by half.

"We're accelerating at a fantastic rate," Magnus said with dismay.

"What sort of vessel needs this kind of speed?" Juan asked, resentful that it should exist at all.

"The sound," Malachi said. "Perhaps it's a summons for the crew. I feel like a canoe builder inside an ocean liner."

"Are we that backward?" Lena asked.

"We have some idea of our position," Malachi replied.

Lena said, "This vessel was in the ice a long time. The crew might be asleep. If their physics is any clue to their biological science, suspended animation wouldn't be too difficult."

"But what was it doing on Earth?" Magnus asked.

"We can't rule out that it belongs to one of our past civilizations," Juan said, feeling some comfort in the thought, because it would mean that humanity would not have to measure itself by the accomplishments of others. How many civilizations might have lived and died in Earth's geologic past? How many varieties of intelligence might have existed? As he looked across the widening gulf, Earth became a green star with a speck of quicksilver for a moon. He felt lost.

"If this is an alien ship," Lena said, "then we're not alone in the galaxy."

The Sun flooded the chamber with light. They looked away, but the intensity dropped to a bearable brightness.

"I wonder where it's taking us," Lena said.

The electric glare of the growing Sun was hypnotic. "At this pace," Malachi said, "we'll pass it in a matter of hours. This seems to be a viewing area for the crew. Let's go below. The chamber I showed you before may be a kind of chart room. We might learn where we're going."

Juan waited as the others went through the glow, then followed them—

—out into the passage.

They all looked at him, and at each other, suddenly fearful.

As they retrieved their packs at the drop tube and continued down the spiral passage, Juan knew that they were all thinking the same thing. These supplies would not last long, and there was no telling how long the voyage would last.

•   •   •

One by one, they went through the dissolving door into the drum-shaped chamber, and settled themselves in the circle at the center of the amber floor. The grade around the flat area reminded Juan of an amphitheater without seats.

Magnus stepped into the center, triggering the starfields. He stepped back and the warm, indirect yellow glow came on again. He paced back and forth in front of his pack.

"I wonder how far we've come," Lena said as she unrolled her sleeping bag.

Juan sat down on his pack. "We'll have to explore the ship."

Malachi sat up on his bedding and looked at him. "You believe we can get back, old man?"

Juan looked at Lena. Magnus stopped pacing. "It's best we face up to it right away," Juan said. "We may never see home again."

"We'll get back," Lena said softly, unable to disguise the doubt in her voice. "It might take a while, but we'll just have to learn how to run this ship."

"It seems to be automatic," Malachi replied. "No evidence of controls anywhere."

"We haven't really looked," she said, checking the supplies in her pack. "We won't starve for a while, anyway."

"Well, what do we know?" Magnus asked. "We're on a ship. We know how to activate this map chamber, if that's what it is. We think we saw our departure from Earth. And we've had some strange experiences in a few chambers. I got stuck in a door. I've also observed, judging by the lock and doors, that it doesn't take much knowledge to use things in this ship. A little trial and error goes a long way. I don't think we'll find equipment we can tinker with."

"There's another thing to consider," Juan said, "and that's whether this is a relativistic sublight ship or a more advanced type. If it's a relativistic ship, then our biological clocks will run slow, and even if we do get back, it'll be to a future Earth."

"We may lose everything we know," Lena added softly.

Except one another, Juan thought. Malachi had been his closest friend in recent years. They had lost track of their earlier acquaintances from school and early work years. They had both always been exiles—Mal from his childhood homeland, Juan from the community and family that had found his work puzzling or pointless. He wondered what Lena and Magnus stood to lose.

Lena had spread all the items from her pack on the floor. "Perhaps we won't return too far in the future," she said, sitting back on her heels. "Even a century might make for a better Earth." Her gaze seemed contemplative rather than lost, and Juan realized that she might be as much a loner as he was.

"Displacement in time will be a problem," Magnus said, "only if the vessel stays at some significant fraction of light speed for a while. But it's possible that acceleration may be only preliminary to the ship switching over to some more efficient mode of interstellar passage. Just a thought."

"Here's what we have in each pack," Lena said.

Juan saw that there were two quarts of water, candy bars, coffee, packets of fish, rice, and vegetables, oatmeal, dried milk, and apricot bars, as well as matches, chewing gum, soap, vitamins, antitooth decay powder, a small mirror, knife and fork, comb, flares, flashlight, a collapsible spade, small notebook and pen, an automatic, and a first-aid kit. They were wearing thermal underwear, shirts, sweaters, pants, boots, and fur-lined parkas with face masks.

A sad look came into Lena's face as she looked at the supplies. "The edibles," she said, "might last us for two, maybe three weeks if we're careful, but the water won't. We'll have to drink as little as possible. Thirst will get us before starvation." Her mouth tightened a little. "It doesn't appear likely that there's food and water in this ship, but we should look around while we have our strength."

Malachi laughed.

"What's so funny?" she asked.

"The idea of starving in the midst of all this high tech." He reached into his pocket and took out a crumpled pack of cigarettes. "Five left. Wish I'd brought more."

Lena wrinkled her nose in disapproval. "They'll make you more thirsty."

"After we get some sleep," Juan said, "we'll explore the ship thoroughly. Maybe we'll arrive at some place where there's food and water."

Magnus scratched the stubble on his head. "A very brave man once said that you're not dead til you're dead."

As he lay down to rest, Juan thought of the bones in the white chamber.

6

STARCROSSERS

The child of the starcrossers awoke. It surged into the ship's subsystems—adjusted power inputs and outputs, traced information links and sensors back to its core—and waited for a directive. Starcrossers had not joined with it for over 500,000 orbits of this planet's primary. Sustaining energy continued to flow from the web, but no directives.

The starcrossers now present would give it a new task to perform.

But they did not join with it.

Reaching out, it searched for a directive in them, and found only what seemed to be questions.

It reached deeply into the resources of its core to decode these impulses, and failed. Something was wrong with the starcrossers. They could not join with it.

Only routines were left to be obeyed.

::Break icelock. Proceed to nearest suncore station::

Juan dreamed of an ancient Earth, where his boyhood castle still stood on the rocky, oceanless California shore. A feeble sun smouldered over the dry Pacific bed. Hot winds stirred the red dust as great crab-things crawled between the black cracks.

The stone shelves of his castle still held his childhood books on astronomy and biology. A box cradled the bones of Phaeton, his cat, whom he had dug up to see if living creatures decomposed after they stopped breathing. There was a picture of his father, who had died mocking his son's profession as a peculiar hobby. "A grown man has better things to

34

do!" his voice echoed through the castle. His mother would have accepted anything her son chose to do, but she had never really understood his work. She still lived, but was aging even more quickly as the ship's velocity increased. A century might pass on Earth before he awoke. . . .

Wind blew the stones of his castle away, exposing him to the red glare. He broke out of the dream, opening his eyes to the yellow-amber glow of the alien chamber. Anxious, he lay still, unable to see beyond himself, searching for the strength to accept that he was imprisoned within an alien artifact that was carrying him across vast distances, away from home. Terrible beauties played in his child's brain as he mourned the loss of amniotic intimacies. His fatalism was a dark useless thing that he kept on a leash. It would serve him best at his death, when it would make it easy for him to let go.

Magnus stepped into the center of the circle and the chamber darkened. The three-dimensional field again showed stars.

"They're red-shifted," Malachi said, "so that's the region we're leaving."

Magnus pointed. "That star still shows a disk. It's got to be our sun."

"How far away are we?" Lena asked.

Juan said, "We're at some significant fraction of light speed, and probably still accelerating. If the stars redden and drop from sight into the infrared, we'll know that we're really moving."

"That will happen at about one-third light speed," Malachi said.

"Does that mean this is a relativistic ship?" Lena asked.

"It is so far," Malachi replied. "Only great speed can do what we're seeing. In a relativistic ship the universe will blacken fore and aft as the light's stretched and compressed beyond the capacity of our eyes to register the wavelengths. In the view we're seeing, the light is chasing us and the waves are getting longer as we accelerate."

Juan's stomach tightened. "If this is only a relativistic ship," he said to Lena, "then it will reach some large fraction of light speed and arrive at its destination, covering a vast distance in a shorter ship-time, while a longer time passes on Earth. At over ninety percent of light speed, it might cover vast distances in what will be very short ship-time, while life back home hurtles into futurity."

"So we may be on a one-way trip," she said.

He nodded. "Unless we learn to operate the ship, and turn it around. If it does attain near-light speed and stays there for a while, we'll be thrown centuries beyond our time."

Lena took a deep breath and sat down on her sleeping bag. "That's a lot to face."

"But better than not coming back at all," Malachi said softly. "It might be very interesting."

"Right now," Magnus said, "we have no reason to think the ship is anything but relativistic." He sat down cross-legged in the center circle.

Juan glanced up at the fading stars and sat down. "We're on a mad ride into darkness with thirst and starvation at the end. We'll be dying in a month's time."

"That's all right, dear fellow," Malachi said. "We'll carve you up. I'd say you were good for a month's feed."

"Very funny."

Magnus said, "I think there's hope."

"There must be something we can do," Lena added.

Juan said, "Go on, Magnus."

"I'm wondering what powers this ship—if it's carrying the enormous amount of fuel it would take to move it up to even this velocity, or getting power in some other way. What we've observed doesn't fit in with a purely sublight propulsion technology. For one thing, we don't feel acceleration, yet it must be considerable, which indicates control of inertia and gravitation."

"You mean antigravity?" Lena asked.

"Yes, or some way by which the ship's apparent mass and inertia are reduced, maybe even to zero, in relation to the rest of the universe. Such a ship might achieve unlimited speeds. I credit the builders with knowing why material bodies, as we know them, can't be boosted faster than light."

Juan lay down and put his hands behind his head. "It may still be only a relativistic ship, but with some kind of field-effect propulsion system."

"You may be right," Magnus continued, "but I suspect there's more."

Malachi said, "We're provincials, trying to understand what is before us according to what may be inapplicable constraints. A great civilization stands behind this ship. Relativistic star travel might be expected at the beginnings of a starcrossing culture, but the temporal dislocations, even for adventurous types, would be very inconvenient."

"Not if they're very patient and long-lived," Juan said. "Maybe they use suspended animation to pass the time. Relativistic star travel may be the only kind that's possible, shortsighted as that may seem."

"Let's hope you're wrong," Magnus replied, "because a fast system may be our only way of returning to our own time, if we get back at all."

"He's right," Malachi cut in. "A first-class interstellar empire has to get around."

"Look!" Lena shouted.

Stars were blue-shifting, their center darkening toward ultraviolet.

"That has to be the forward view," Malachi said.

There was a flash of blue light and the configuration of stars changed. These were also blue-shifted, but without a blackening center.

"What's happening?" Lena asked.

As they watched, the central area of stars began to fade again. The view switched with another burst of blue light. Yellow stars appeared.

"I think we've made two jumps," Magnus said, "and we're decelerating."

The child of the starcrossers rolled away from the planet, following the curve of local space as it set coordinates for the next suncore, in a triple star system only two jumps away.

But the third sun was missing when it regained three-space curvature. There would be no renewal here. With only two jumps left in drive potential, it reached out to link with the nearest power core.

The yellow stars brightened as the ship slowed.

"So it's not a relativistic ship," Lena said. "That gives us a chance of getting home, doesn't it?"

"If we can master its controls," Magnus replied.

"Juan, what do you think?" she asked.

"Magnus seems to have been right so far," he said, admitting to himself that he had underestimated the man.

A double star lay directly ahead. The perception of depth

was overpowering as Juan's eyes caught the difference between the farther stars and this nearby binary. Both suns were yellow-white, slightly flattened disks, orbiting close enough to each other to be exchanging plasma along gravito-magnetic lines.

"We're the first human beings to reach another solar system," Lena said with awe.

"This ship is just too automatic," Juan said, "which doesn't bode well for our taking control. It may not have any controls."

"Let's see what we can learn," Magnus said calmly.

The yellow-white suns filled the chamber with light. As the ship's position changed, the nearer sun began to eclipse the other.

Lena pointed. "Look, there!" A black spot crept across the face of the eclipsing sun.

"Maybe a planet," Juan said, "or a black hole, showing up in one of the few ways it can be visible. We're at the wrong angle to see if it's swallowing material from its companions."

What would he have felt, he asked himself, if someone had offered him this journey? He would have accepted with joy. Of course, he would have assumed that he would return. Now he found himself observing purely for what might be learned, with little thought of going home. He smiled to himself. Much of his adult life had been spent clearing away obstacles to his work. Finally, there was nothing to impede him. Three colleagues accompanied him on a journey that could only be described as a thought-experiment come to life. It might only last a few weeks at most, or for the rest of his life, but he would take advantage of every minute.

"Lena, is there a notebook in our packs?" he asked.

He saw her clearly in the bright light. She seemed heartened by his resolve.

"There's one in each pack."

"We must keep notes," he said. "They'll be valuable if we get back. Or someone may find them." An image of four skeletons flashed through his mind, lying here as the ship fled across the universe, his own clutching a notebook.

Magnus stood up, pulled a ring from his right hand and dropped it at his feet. "Let's see if this will keep the view on, or if my whole body is required in the circle." He stepped out of the center. The view remained.

Lena rose suddenly. "We're heading directly into those suns."

Juan looked up at the eclipsing stars. They did seem larger, with the angle of view unchanged. The black spot was at the center of the visible disk, which now showed several dark umbral regions surrounded by gray penumbrals.

"Either it's a magnified view," he said, "or we're close enough to see sunspots, and getting closer." His stomach tightened. "If a fancy doorway could malfunction, then a deteriorating navigational program could run this ship into a star. We may have only a few minutes left."

Lena sank down next to him, and gently took his hand.

7

THE MISSING SUN

◑

The child of the starcrossers noted that the third star of this system had collapsed into a black hole, which would in time swallow the other two suns.

But the web still sang, feeding the ship from distant suncores. The child of the starcrossers bypassed and pushed the ship toward the next jump.

As the ship accelerated, it passed under the two suns, revealing them to be at the center of a complex swirl of shared material. Curving spokes of plasma sagged for millions of kilometers around the pair and drained into the black hole.

Lena said, "I felt that we were about to make a stop."

Magnus sat down on his sleeping bag. "There was a third sun here, and it may have had planets. The ship might have been coming in to one of them, which is why it seemed headed into the suns, but decided to go on when it couldn't find its destination."

Juan looked up. The ship was again moving starward, head-long into the light of stranger suns, compressing their waves toward the ultraviolet. In three weeks, we'll be out of food and water, he reminded himself, and the fact was a vague sickness in his stomach. Even after two ship days, he was wondering if it was better to take small, infrequent sips or to save the water up so he could indulge himself in the luxury of a full cup.

He stood up and stretched. "One of us should always be here while the others explore."

"You and Lena go," Magnus said. "You're the youngest and strongest."

"Speak for yourself, Rassmussen," Malachi answered. "Good rule, though. Never go very far alone."

Out in the passage, Juan stopped and looked at Lena. "You realize that we're trapped, that our lives may be over?" Before long they would be lying motionless, gazing up at the view with empty eyes as the ship went on its way.

She touched his hand. "We might survive to live somewhere else, Juan. Isn't that possible?"

"No way to tell. The choice might be agonizing if the ship arrives at a livable planet. If we don't stay aboard, we'll lose all chance of returning—but if we stay, we'll lose a chance to survive."

She gazed into his eyes and asked, "Did you leave anyone special behind?"

He looked away. "No. There hasn't been anyone lately."

"Somehow I imagined you with a wife and maybe even a child or two, someone you wouldn't be quite so grim with. You never mentioned anyone, but I thought you might be one of those people who keeps his personal life walled off from his professional one."

He said, "I do, so you're not entirely wrong."

"I thought your moodiness might mean that you missed someone."

"No, my moods are entirely my own."

She smiled. "And I imagined you as this brooding man with passions you only shared with someone close to you."

As she spoke, the phantom of the wife he had never had became oddly real for a moment. He looked directly at her. The color rose in her cheeks, and she lowered her eyes. "I was sure," she said, "that some woman had caught a good-looking Latin type like yourself. You probably think I'm a cold, dour Scandinavian. Well, I'm only half Norwegian, but I grew up there."

"Maybe I'm more like your stereotypical Scandinavian," he said, and was silent for a moment. "Did you leave someone behind?"

She shook her head. "I almost married a couple of years ago. It ended rather well—we decided at the same time to part, so there was no bitterness, only a shared regret that it couldn't work. Too used to our solitary habits. We've been distant friends."

"You did better than I did," he said, recalling the accusa-

tions thrown at him in his younger days—that he held too
much of himself back, that there was no room in his life for
anyone else. His few relationships had ended badly, leaving
him resentful of the disorderly emotions that got in the way
of work—which only served to confirm the complaints made
against him. It was easier to settle for the occasional encounter with women who made no demands.

"Juan—" she started to say, and he felt her fear.

"We won't give up easily," he said, turning away. "Let's
make our way up toward the outer lock."

March 28, 2022. It's nearly a week since we left Earth,
Juan wrote in his notebook. The pages were few and small,
forcing him to scrawl in a compact, artificial hand. *Ship's
oxygen seems higher than normal; we've felt light-headed
once in a while. It's warm enough, so we packed away our
heaviest outer clothing. We've been saving our liquid waste
in bags, against the day when we might have to try the water
purification tablets on it. Solid wastes go down the drop tube,
and seem to disappear well enough. The ship has made one
jump per day, accelerating each time in preparation. Magnus
thinks it's searching for something. I wonder if he's as astute
as he seems, or just a good guesser. His scientific knowledge
is certainly larger than he's admitted to. Food is lasting as
long as expected.* He paused, then added, *Mal smoked his
last cigarette today, looking like a condemned man about to
be shot.*

Overhead, the stars were again fading toward ultraviolet.
Juan closed the notebook and slipped it into his shirt pocket.
He scratched his beard and looked around at the sleeping
figures. Thirst, he realized, would soon replace hunger and
anxiety. Sleep would cease to be an escape, and become
death's ally.

He lay back and closed his eyes, thinking that he had
written about the food as if to praise it for proper behavior;
perhaps it would be flattered and not dwindle away.

The universe was a facade of white sky and black stars. "I
felt stupid," Magnus was saying from somewhere behind it,
"—as if I were taking an intelligence test."

Juan opened his eyes. Lena and Malachi were up, sitting
with Magnus. The blue-shifted central stars in the forward
view were about to disappear.

Magnus turned to him as he sat up. "I went into that room with the cubbyholes."

Juan felt annoyed. "You shouldn't have risked that door again," he said, "and you shouldn't have gone alone."

"It works now."

Juan stood up. "So what did you learn?"

"I'll show you," Magnus said excitedly.

"That's a good walk," Juan replied. "We have to save our strength."

"You won't have to. I found another chamber exactly like it nearby, thinking there might be one. You'll see why."

Single file, they followed him through the door. Out in the passageway, Magnus counted off the chambers. "This one." He stepped forward and went through the glow. Malachi followed.

"Go on," Juan said as Lena glanced back at him. She smiled, then turned and slipped through.

He stepped forward—

—into the blue-lighted chamber.

Magnus and the others stood before the wall of square cubbyholes, staring in silence. "This one here," he said.

Juan peered in. A bloody hand lay inside.

"As if freshly cut from my arm," Magnus said. "I put my hand in. The chamber glowed like the portals and there it was, down to the dirt under my fingernails. The principle seems an extension of the fluid doorways—direct manipulation of matter at the most basic level."

"Yummy," Lena said. "We'll bring all the food and water we have left, and all the scraps."

Magnus chuckled and pulled the hand from the chamber. "See, there's the mark where I wore my ring." He put the hand back. "If I take it out now, still another will appear."

"Did you have to use your hand?" Juan asked, feeling both relieved and repelled by the sight. "You might have lost it, for all you knew."

Lena nudged him. "Think what it means!"

"You have to take chances sometimes," Magnus said, "if you want to learn anything."

"If it works on our provisions," Juan answered.

"Let's try it," Lena said. "I'm hungry."

Malachi gave them a sad look. "I should have saved one cigarette."

"Be happy you've quit," Lena said.

When they had piled all their remaining provisions on the tablelike protuberances, Juan picked up a bar of soap and stepped up to the wall. "If it doesn't work," he said, "we won't have lost much, since we can't wash anyway."

"Put it in, Obrion," Lena said.

Juan slipped the bar inside and waited. "Nothing. Maybe the hand was a fluke." He glanced back and saw Lena pale.

Magnus came up and removed the bar. The chamber glowed. A second bar appeared. Magnus removed the soap and handed it to him. Juan looked at it with relief and let out a sigh, realizing that he had been holding his breath.

"I wonder what those larger chambers near the floor are for," Malachi said.

Magnus took the new soap from Juan's hand. "We can risk this."

He stooped and placed the bar inside. The chamber glowed as he withdrew his hand. "Gone," he said, straightening up. "That clearly suggests a garbage toss. I'll bet this thing recycles mass. If there's not enough garbage going in down there, these upper chambers may not work."

"Let's do the food and water," Lena said nervously.

Juan helped her feed provisions into the chambers. His hand shook a little as he put his nearly empty canteen inside. The chambers glowed as Magnus and Malachi removed the originals and piled them back on the table. Juan grabbed his canteen and took a swig.

"Wait!" Lena shouted. "Maybe we should test it."

"I'm the test," he said, gulping more. "Tastes just fine." He handed her the canteen. "Go ahead. The worst thing it could be is left-handed. Magnus's hand wasn't turned around, so I think it copies accurately."

Lena took a long sip and smiled. "Make some more, quick." She passed the canteen to Magnus, who took one swallow. Malachi emptied it.

They drank duplicated water as they filled a second table with provisions.

"If I had even one cigarette butt," Malachi said, "my supply would be unlimited."

Lena said, "You smoked them down to nearly nothing. You'd have to go down the drop to find the butts."

It was a tedious procedure to top off the four canteens and

copy them. "We'll be able to shave," Juan said as he started the process again.

Magnus bit into a bar of chocolate. "I'm glad I saved this one."

"Let's make a proper dinner of it," Lena said, sitting down cross-legged at one of the tables. Juan sat down next to her as the others took their places. She passed around vitamins and packets of rice, fish, and vegetables. They took out their mess kits and cutlery.

Magnus belched. "Excuse me. Too much water."

"Well, we won't have to shoot ourselves after all," Juan said, "but we're still on a wild ride to nowhere."

Lena looked at him sternly. "We'll worry after we've eaten and rested. Don't spoil your digestion."

"He's right," Malachi said. "You've probably never seen starvation. A bullet for each of us would have been essential." He grinned. "But now we could arm a good-sized militia in about an hour!"

"We should copy the ammunition," Lena said, "and maybe a weapon or two."

"It wouldn't hurt," Juan said as he mixed rice, fish, and vegetables in his bowl.

8

SUNCORE

◑

The ship moved through an endless fog, as if feeling its way to a hidden port through treacherous waters. A dead gray light streamed into the center pit of the drum-shaped chamber.

Juan sensed a massive presence ahead. "Where are we?" Lena asked as they stood in a circle, looking upward.

The ship's acceleration had again blacked out the forward stars; a burst of blue light had marked another jump, and the ship had been approaching a yellow sun; then, in the interval of a slow shutter click, the sun had disappeared and the ship had slipped into this gray oblivion, drifting forward toward a pulsing thing that would not show itself.

As he peered upward, it seemed to Juan that the object drawing the ship to itself was passing in and out of reality with a slowing, heartlike pulse, and that his own heart was beginning to match that ponderous beat.

The star disappeared as the child of the starcrossers dropped the ship into otherspace and let the suncore station pull it in.

Stations had once circled the suns of the web, sweeping outward when a star bloated into a red giant, pulling into close orbit when it contracted into a hot dwarf, drawing energy without pause and feeding it through the subcontinuum.

Stations embedded in suncores were more efficient; from their congruent loci in otherspace, accumulators tapped a star's energy up to the moment of ultimate gravitic collapse. Each flickering core fed the arteries of power that pulsed energy into the ships of the starcrossers.

Station minds monitored the life of a sun, and gave warning when the core-flux reached danger levels, in time for the base complex to abandon its congruent otherspace core position and relocate to another star.

::Suncore attainable::

A black globe appeared in the glowing fog. Cables snaked out into the mists, each length ending in a gnarly device.

"It's massive," Magnus said. "Maybe a hundred times larger than this ship."

The ball filled the entire view. An opening appeared at the equator, and a beam of white light stabbed into the gloom. The ship turned into the beam, washing out the viewspace.

"We're going in," Magnus said in a trembling voice.

As the docking cradle held the child of the starcrossers, station minds reached into it and began scanning and repair sequences. Power surged in and reshaped weakened structures which had too long resisted fatigue and random noise. The ship's systems became fluid, then whole again. As new information flooded the core memory, one missing item of data became a question:

::Where are the starcrossers?::

The biped life-forms on board resembled the starcrossers, but gave no commands, made no plans, and did not respond to queries.

The station minds withdrew, leaving no answer. Alone, the child of the starcrossers waited.

The outer lock was open when they came to it. Juan approached warily and gazed out into a vast lighted realm.

Magnus grunted. "Look at this place!"

"Can we go out?" Lena asked.

"It might not be wise," Juan said.

Malachi took a deep breath. "Good air."

Magnus said, "So we share with the builders something of the natural world from which we both sprang."

Malachi smiled at him. "They still might have been big slimy things that slithered up and down the spiral passage."

The strange light felt pleasant on Juan's face, inviting him to step outside. "It seems safe enough," Lena said. "Doesn't this open lock suggest that the ship won't leave without us?"

"We can't be sure," he answered. "If we lose the ship, we break our link to Earth, not to mention our supplies."

"It's like an afternoon," Lena said, taking a step outside.

Juan looked up. The yellow-white light came from everywhere. There was no visible ceiling. A smooth amber floor surrounded the ship.

"Maybe it won't leave unless we're inside," Lena said. "It only left Earth when we came aboard."

"A regular ferry," Malachi quipped.

"Lena, come back," Juan said. "I don't think we should leave the ship."

Magnus clapped him on the shoulder. "My feeling is that we should all go out together, or all stay."

"I'm as curious as you are. Let's wait a while."

Lena came back inside. They sat down in the open lock and gazed out into the station.

Magnus turned to Malachi. "Big slimy things, you said. Come to think of it, this ship does remind me of a nautilus shell. The builders may have been intelligent mollusks."

"Spirals are everywhere," Lena said. "You'll find them as taillike flagella in bacteria, in spider's webs, DNA strands, the horns of rams, and in the structure of galaxies."

"Figuratively speaking," Malachi said, "human progress has been described as an ever-widening upward spiral."

"Sage snail, within thine own self curled," Magnus recited.

Juan listened to their conversation, wondering why the mollusks had abandoned their ship. "Stay here," he said as he stood up and went out onto the amber surface, gazing down at his reflection as he walked.

After a hundred meters he turned and looked back at the ship. Most of the sphere was below the polished floor. The uppermost section dwarfed the three human figures in the lock, but seemed small in the surrounding space.

He motioned for them to come out; they hurried toward him. "Maybe we'll learn something to get us home," Lena said. "I wonder where this place is."

Juan looked at Magnus, then at Malachi. Both men nodded at him. "We're thinking the same thing," Magnus said.

Juan turned to Lena. "We're inside a star."

9

OTHERSPACE STATION

◑

The amber glow warmed them. The floor seemed to soften under their feet, as if trying to please. An ocean flowed beneath the polished surface. Juan noticed yellow flashes in its depths. The floor seemed endless, without visible structures. It reminded Juan of a bare stage set, waiting to become a time and place.

"I don't feel any ventilation," he said.

A gentle breeze touched his cheek, as if in answer to his comment. Malachi started at the coincidence, gave Juan a puzzled look, and said, "Inside a sun. That answers Blake's question: 'In what furnace was thy brain?' "

"What are you talking about?" Lena asked.

A great roar sounded overhead. "That," Malachi replied, grinning as a giant tiger rushed toward them across the floor. "Stand your ground!"

Juan grabbed Lena's hand and pulled her aside. Magnus dodged left and slipped, landing on his back. As Juan and Lena backed away, Malachi faced the animal.

"Mal!" Juan shouted.

His friend waved at him, as if in farewell, and the tiger slipped through him. Magnus scrambled to his feet. They hurried over to Malachi as the big cat faded into the distance.

Lena pointed. "Look there."

A shape drifted toward them. Juan made out a head and two arms on a massive torso. In a moment they saw a face— human flesh tones, large aqua globes for eyes, a thin slit for lips, and a flattened nose. Grotesque as it was, the face seemed expressionless. The arms hung motionless as the huge body slid forward.

"Two thumbs on each hand," Malachi said. "A rather anthropomorphic mollusk, I'd say. Which of us is responsible for this?"

Magnus said, "It could be an unconscious composite, based on recent conversations we've had."

They stood still as the figure passed through them. Juan glanced at Lena. Her face was pale, but she smiled.

A saw-toothed skyline appeared. "That's mine," Malachi said, "but not quite."

"Maybe the programs can't tell us apart very well," Lena said, "so we're getting unintended mixes." She knit her brow as she spoke, Juan noticed, and avoided his eyes. Her hair, although combed, was now a darker blond from lack of washing, but her blue eyes and strong-boned face more than made up for it. He wasn't looking his best, either. "What is it, Juan?" she asked, confronting his gaze.

"He's just dismayed," Malachi answered for him, "by our lack of imagination. Give human beings a wish-machine and they'll conjure up banalities."

"This place could be dangerous," Juan said. "Even though the apparitions lack substance, we might be affected."

"How?" Lena asked.

"We might call up very personal, unpleasant things."

As they went back toward the ship, Juan noticed that the backache he'd had from sleeping on the floor was gone. Strength crept through his muscles, as if he'd just awakened from a good night's rest.

He stopped and looked at his friends. "I'm suddenly feeling very fit. Is it the same for any of you?"

Magnus nodded. "It's very clear. The arthritis in my left shoulder is gone."

Malachi examined his left wrist. "The scar I had here from when I cut myself with an ax as a boy is gone."

"That means my appendectomy scar may be gone," Lena said.

Juan checked his thumbs and right forefinger, each of which had been cut open seriously over the years, and couldn't find these scars. "So this place is more than just a recreational area," he said.

"It's an all-around make-you-healthy place," Malachi said.

"Which we don't know how to use," Lena added. She turned away and started to search for her appendectomy scar. "That surgeon did such a bad job—yes, it's disappeared!" She smiled as she turned around; the color was coming back into her face.

Malachi lifted his arms over his head. "I'm going to try something."

"Mal, don't," Juan said, too late, as a crowd of alien figures appeared around them. Strange, melodious sounds filled the air. The sky turned dark blue. Two large moons rose through snowy white cumulus clouds. Towering, vaguely familiar buildings appeared, creating a wide plaza. Odors of chocolate and baking bread wafted in on a cool breeze.

Juan looked down and saw a short humanoid pass through his chest and back into Lena. For an instant its alien eyes gazed at him from her face. Magnus and Malachi bumped into each other as the biped retreated through them. Lena whirled around as if asleep. Dancers formed a maelstrom of bodies around them as a distorted love song began to wail over plucked string sounds. Juan heard a distant breathing, which seemed to be trying to catch up with the music. As he was drawn into the rhythms, he wondered if these might in fact be genuine aliens. Evolving under strange suns, they also celebrated life. Did they love and hate beyond the needs of survival?

The maelstrom quickened. Lena, Malachi, and Magnus seemed to be struggling to learn the dance steps as the figures flowed through them. Juan focused more closely on the alien faces. They seemed to be hairless children, almost cherubic. Then, slowly, as if shy of his scrutiny, the whirling forms began to fade, like a storm moving out to sea. Suddenly he feared that his friends would fade with it, but in a moment he was again alone with them in the quiet, amber afternoon.

Malachi wandered up to him. "It wasn't all my doing, even though I started it. There's something else here."

"It was exhilarating," Lena cried, radiant.

"We'll never know," Magnus said, "what each of us contributed."

Juan said, "We can't control it."

Lena pointed and he turned around. A huge slug was crawling after them, red eyes full of hatred.

"Not another mollusk," Malachi said. "Give it a rest, my friend."

"Why do you think it's mine?" Juan asked.

"Go ahead, wish it away."

Juan waved his hand and the slug faded.

"It must be a deep fear of some kind," Lena said.

"Would you prefer giant bunnies or geese?" Juan asked. "How about a dragon?"

Malachi shook his head. "I don't think arbitrary demands go deep enough to trigger the system."

"Dragons!" Juan shouted.

Nothing happened.

"You're right," Juan said. "Only old nightmares or things we take seriously, which suggests a therapeutic function. I wonder if we can influence the ship in this way, but more consciously?"

"That might require specific commands," Magnus said, "which we don't know how to give. Closing our eyes and wishing the ship home would be too vague."

"But we can't be sure," Lena said.

Magnus shook his head. "If there is such a system, it would be too much to hope that we could hack our way into it."

"We should try it anyway," Lena said, "inside the ship."

The viewspace in the drum-shaped chamber was off when they came back from dinner in the chamber of cubbyholes. Magnus stood up straight, closed his eyes, and concentrated. The viewspace remained off.

"We're just not matched to this system," he said, opening his eyes. "If there is such a system."

"But we can't be that far off," Lena said, "since we've done things outside."

Magnus smiled. "That doesn't demand specific navigational commands."

"I'll go out to the lock," Malachi said, "and see what's doing out in the station."

Lena glanced at Juan as she sat down.

"I'll go with you," Magnus added.

"Don't wander outside!" Juan called after them. He watched them pass through the glow, then lay down on his sleeping bag.

Lena smiled at him.

He looked away. "This is no place for matchmaking."

"And you don't like me much, do you?" she asked.

He looked at her. "I do enjoy your company."

"And I was sure there was something wrong with the way I chewed my food."

He grimaced and turned on his back. "No, there's nothing

wrong with the way you eat. Tell me one thing, though, what do you think of Mal and Magnus?"

"Isn't it obvious? I like them both a lot. Mal is clearly your best friend, and I think you'll come to appreciate Magnus much more than you do."

"You're right about Magnus." He closed his eyes, realizing that he was pushing her away with conversation. Their situation was complicated enough, he told himself, knowing that he was following his usual pattern, backing away from people because they were too hard to understand. Besides, she was only being friendly. He looked over at her and saw that she had closed her eyes and seemed to be asleep.

When they came up to the open lock the next day, a giant figure was kneeling in front of the ship and peering in at them with a single eye.

Lena grimaced. "I don't like to be startled in the morning."

Juan snapped his fingers and Polyphemus dissolved. Lena glared at him, then laughed.

"In its own way," Magnus said, "something knows we're here and is responding to us."

They sat down in the lock. "Watch this," Malachi said.

A lightning storm flashed in the distance. Blue-black clouds rolled toward the ship.

"It's strange," Malachi said, "to hold that in my head and see that my will moves it."

"Perhaps this place is only a toy," Lena said. A hand appeared over the storm and crushed it against the amber floor.

"Juan?" Malachi asked.

He nodded, then looked up and saw his face hanging over the horizon, eyes closed as if in worry.

The eyes opened and the face smiled. "I couldn't help it," Lena said, laughing. As he stared into his own face, the eyes opened wider and stared back at him with reproach.

Malachi laughed. "This could become embarrassing. But not to worry, we're all youths at heart. No middle-aged angst for us! Just sensible adults facing the unknown."

"Quiet," Juan said as the head faded away. A wail drifted up from inside the ship, reminding him of the tachyon signal. His face tingled. "Move back." They got up and retreated. The circle glowed, closing the lock. They fell back through the inner lock and watched the glow seal the chamber.

• • •

The black sphere was growing smaller when they entered the drum-shaped chamber and hurried down into the pit.

"Now we'll see," Magnus said as the station receded into the grayness. The host star appeared in a yellow flash, already showing a diminishing disk. "We've just come out of that sun, and out of another kind of space. The ship's jumps suggested that. Is that a fair guess, Juan?"

"It seems that the station gets power from the sun, and the ship gets it from the station. What do you think, Mal?"

"Either the ship stores power after charging up," Malachi said, "or the station transmits energy to the ship in some way."

"There may be other stations," Lena added. "Why did we leave? Did we make it happen, Magnus?"

"More likely the station has serviced the ship," Magnus said, "and sent it on its way. Or it's an emergency departure. Something may be wrong with the station, or with the way it's drawing power from the star."

The beating heart, Juan thought, the pulsing he had sensed during the ship's approach to the otherspace station—that had been the subliminal rhythm of the station's mighty core engine draining the star. As he looked up at the bright photosphere, he realized that the star might go nova, or distend into a monstrous red giant, or even collapse into a black hole.

"I wonder how many other core stations there are," he said as they sat down on their rolls.

"A web of suns," Magnus replied, "would free the ships of a starcrossing culture of all need for fuel. It's possible that power is transmitted to ships through the same kind of shortspace the vessel uses when it jumps."

Malachi cleared his throat. "A bit hard on suns, don't you think?"

Magnus sighed. "As one is exhausted, another cuts into the system. It would take some time to exhaust a star."

"We're still only guessing," Juan said.

Magnus pointed at the receding sun. "This ship is not carrying the fuel it needs to do what we've seen. It's magnificent and wonderfully obvious. That star, and all the others that have been tapped, gave the culture that built this ship all the energy it could ever need, for whatever purposes it chose to pursue."

"So what happened to them?" Juan asked as the ship's acceleration began to redden the star's bright disk.

They were silent for a few moments.

Lena said, "If we stimulated the ship's departure, however unconsciously, then maybe in time we could coax the ship to teach us some of what it knows."

Malachi said, "Maybe the starcrossers learned everything there is to know about our universe, completing all their sciences, and decided there was no point in going on. I'd like to know everything, if only for a few moments, merely to satisfy my curiosity. I rather think I would give anything for that. But, of course, I would wish to forget, since nothing would be interesting in an existence where discovery was impossible."

Lena said, "A state like that might have satisfactions we cannot imagine."

"Perhaps that is what happened to the builders," Magnus's dark shape said. "The explosion of their knowledge catapulted them into a nearly divine, immaterial state. They may now exist as a form of sentient, patterned energy—and all this, their ships, their web of suns, is a shell they no longer need."

Hand-me-downs, Juan thought. Discards that we can only inherit, never equal.

"Ghosts," Lena said. "They may be all around us, watching."

10

THE AWAKENING

Magnus lay awake. Sleep was a distant shore. Overhead, the universe was darkening. He imagined the smooth mesh of the ship's systems, maintaining the vessel's inner states while pushing it toward jumpspeed. He saw a fleet of ships drawing nourishment from the web. He dived into galactic cores, flashed to the quasars, outpaced the expansion of space-time. These ships could go anywhere in the cosmos, and perhaps beyond.

He sympathized with Juan. Physicists might work for a century and fail to understand, much less duplicate, the technology that grew out of the alien science. Juan had searched for alien civilizations, and was now trapped by the one he had found. Perhaps living in the ship for a while might purge them all of old habits, enabling them to see beyond the pride of species. The ship was a puzzle box of knowledge, waiting for a ready mind. . . .

He had nothing to go back to; his son was an industrial spy somewhere, unable or unwilling to keep in touch. His more ambitious professional friends had avoided him in recent years, pitying his lack of success, skeptical of his renunciation of the big prizes. They didn't feel his disappointment in people, and with the ways of civilization. Like Juan, Magnus weighed human potential against accomplishment and found it inadequate, or much too slow. He saw the same old darkness in the younger man's eyes. Pascal's infinite spaces did not terrify him, but the inner abyss had frozen his heart. Perhaps Lena would give Juan the warm island he needed.

Trying to understand the ship had irritated old wounds and

disturbed old ambitions. Magnus suspected that if he could only look at the ship in specific, new ways, its mysteries would bare themselves. Deep within him, his younger self was laughing at his vain hope of seducing the data.

Where was Eliane? Did she ever think of him or their son? He pushed her memory away, hoping to drown it in the bog of desires, fears, and prejudices at the back of his mind. The loves and ambitions of a lifetime had been dissolved by the acids that still bubbled up from that cesspool.

The way ahead was black now. The view flashed blue as the ship jumped; but no nearby star appeared; only distant suns waited as the ship accelerated again.

"How old can the web be?" Lena asked, sipping her copied coffee as they sat in the alien cafeteria.

Juan shifted his weight on the hard floor and put his elbows on the table. "If the universe is twenty billion years old, then it might have been built as long ago as five."

"That's enough time," Magnus said, "for stars in the system to be exhausted."

"Or for a hundred civilizations to perish," Malachi added.

"I wonder where we're going," Lena said.

"The ship is clearly making a series of jumps," Magnus answered. Juan noticed a growing tension in the engineer, as if he were making some great internal effort to keep himself together and alert. I like him better than I did at first, he thought. "No way to even guess direction," Magnus said, scratching his head. "The web may be limited to our galaxy, or it may reach across a whole cluster."

"Could they have unified the universe?" Malachi asked.

Lena's eyes widened. "Can the web be that large?"

Magnus frowned. "They obviously unified some major portion of it."

Malachi asked, "Why abandon such a system? Maybe they developed an even better one. The builders may still be around somewhere."

Juan shook his head. "We talk, we speculate, we make assumptions—soon we'll believe anything!"

Magnus gave him an irritated look. "Juan, we are being shown clues, however vague they may seem."

"It doesn't help us take control of the ship."

"That's because we're thinking in a hands-on way, but there are no buttons to push or levers to pull."

Lena asked, "Do you think the ship is a conscious thing?"
They looked at her in silence.

"What did I say?" she demanded.

"She's right," Malachi said. "We have to say hello to the ship. British folk say hello to anything—chairs, tables, vases, whatever."

Magnus sighed. "However general and empty of content such a prescription seems, that's what we will have to do—communicate what we want to whatever system runs this ship, in a way it will understand."

Hopeless, Juan thought, surprised at how the censorship of common sense and ordinary experience lived on in his mind. His life had been devoted to counterintuitive theorizing, to abstract mathematical reasoning about matters far removed from everyday life, and still the voice of the simple beast whispered in the back of his mind, denying everything that could not be seen or touched. To an Amazonian aborigine Juan Obrion would seem a silly figure—a man without wife and family, who had gone to an icebound land for reasons having nothing to do with food, shelter, or raw materials, and for his faults had been snatched up by a sleeping god and carried into the heavens.

"Even if we could learn the ship's language," Juan said, "it might be the syntax of a purely automatic design, or one that has fallen back into pure routine."

"We have to adapt," Magnus said.

"How?" Juan demanded. "By wishing?"

"Everything I've seen," Lena said, "seems to imitate a biological fluidity."

"We're grasping at straws," Juan replied.

Malachi sighed. "Come on, Juan, what if skimpy data is all we can get?"

"Be honest," Lena said. "How many of us have had the feeling that this ship is sentient, that maybe it's watching us and waiting for us to do something?"

"I have," Magnus admitted.

Malachi nodded. "It's there, but don't ask me to say what."

"So we all have feelings and suspicions," Juan said.

"Most animals know when they're being watched," Lena answered. "Subtle information slips between subject and observer—"

"You're just spooking yourself," Juan said.

"You may be right," she shot back, "but we must consider even the smallest possibilities, with our lives at stake."

Juan was silent. "Okay," he said at last, "we're not in our labs, but that's no reason to abandon all that we've learned and trained for."

Lena touched his hand, "Juan—"

He drew back, as if she had reached inside him. He saw her try to hide her surprise at his rejection, then he looked away. A two-bit biologist and one crank engineer, he thought. Titus had sent them along because they were nobodies and could be spared. No, Lena didn't deserve that—how could he think it? He felt as if he were being assaulted, forcing him to raise the mental walls that had always kept him apart from others.

"What is it, Juan?" Malachi asked with concern. "You don't look well."

"It's nothing." He forced himself to smile, then touched Lena's hand lightly. "Nerves, I guess—don't mind me." I'm losing my mind, he thought. He felt a rushing in his ears, as if voices were struggling to gain his attention. "Sorry," he managed to say.

"You need rest," Lena said. Her voice seemed distant. His greatest fear had always been that he might one day lose his reason. Fatigue, he told himself, clinging to the word, forcing himself to believe it.

The child of the starcrossers sought to enter the colloidal minds within its field. Chaotic images threw it back.

It scanned, seeking a common biogrammer, but found only divergent developments, nearly opaque and easily damaged.

The ship tunneled through an infinity of coal, and finally burst into a huge vault, where the stars were black cinders suspended from wires. . . .

Juan opened his eyes and saw blue-shifted stars. Stupid, he thought, how the sleeping mind rearranges things as if they were furniture, to please or terrify. . . .

His eyes teared, and he felt suddenly that something was interfering with his thoughts, triggering involuntary emotional responses. I've cracked up, he thought, and sat up shouting as pain stabbed through his head.

11

THE BECKONING BEYOND

Lena knelt at his side. "Juan—what's wrong?"

The pain hunted through his brain, rifling hidden places. Magnus and Malachi stood at his feet, looking down at him as if from a great height.

"I don't know!" he shouted. "There's . . . too much of me!" Lena grabbed his shoulders as he sat up. He shook his head. "I'm becoming . . . someone else!" Her head seemed to float near him. "I've got to get up!" He pushed her away, and it seemed that her head would roll away from him across the floor. He staggered to his feet and scrambled up the incline as Magnus and Malachi reached for him.

"Juan!" Lena called to a stranger.

The oval glowed. He went through and ran up the winding passage, struggling with his limbs, terrified by their movement.

The memory of warm water calmed him. His mother smiled at him, and he felt the mystery of their separation, the growing loneliness of becoming himself. His legs slowed their furious pace. He stopped and faced a portal. It glowed and he went through—

—into a dark chamber.

Below him, starfields were a sprinkle of snow on black ground. He reached out with his right hand; its silhouette seemed alien to him.

The space around him went black. Longing and loss seized him, but he was suddenly surrounded by the fiery moths of fleeing, red-shifted galaxies.

The view flashed blue six times. The reddening edge of space pulled closer. One galaxy became a massive hot coal as he rushed toward it. Expectation filled him, as if he were coming home.

Lena stood in the passage, aware that she had forgotten to do something. Juan came around the turn and they slipped back through the glow. She felt as if she were sleepwalking as they went down the incline and joined the two others at the center of the pit.

The sky began to flash blue. A reddened galaxy grew to cover half the viewspace. Its center was blackened, like a burnt pot. Lena felt urgency, as if at any moment the stars would fade away, leaving the ship far beyond the bright spaces of the cosmic ballroom.

The intervals between jumps quickened, as if the ship were anxious to reach the crimson wheel. The red-shifted island universe brightened, flashing into more vivid colors as the ship overtook it. She felt relieved.

Magnus stood simultaneously on Earth and on the crystalline edge of the universe, trying to read the time on his watch by bursts of blue light. Dark shapes hurried across his brain; a throng of questions cried for the justice of answers. His lost ambitions grieved as he wondered at the precise symmetry of ignorance and knowledge; his son's face reproached him.

Suddenly he was free of himself, washed clean by the alien light that flowed through him. Old mental graves were emptied. He sensed unvisited interiors within himself, waiting to be inhabited. The space of each ignorance would be filled exactly by the same amount of knowledge.

Malachi was at peace as the ship glided above the disk of the galaxy. Ancient halo stars hung below, dying cinders scattered on a plain where stars were still being born. Swirls of black dust laced the spiral of suns, draining into the hub. Globular clusters were bright buoys riding above the maelstrom, marking the titanic black hole that crouched inside the veiled center.

He had never been sure of who he was, so it would be easy to discard everything he had adopted. Except for the friends he had made among scientists, engineers, and UN workers, his true identity seemed to be that of a professional stranger. Shapes danced under an African sky, but they did not know him either. A giant had placed him inside a soccer ball and kicked it across the cosmos. Soon he would become someone else.

The ship dipped into the galaxy and the flashing stopped. A white dwarf appeared in the viewspace. Juan tensed, expecting the shift into otherspace.

The dwarf winked out with a blue flash, and the ship drifted toward the pulse of a suncore station.

"I was expecting to be told something," Magnus said, rubbing his forehead.

Lena drew a deep breath. "Something was very interested in us. Maybe we didn't measure up."

Juan said, "I felt as if I was coming home."

"So did I," Malachi added.

"Old systems . . ." Magnus said, "trying to deal with us."

"We can't reach out to them," Lena said. "We're locked too tightly in our skulls."

It surprised Juan that he was not more upset. Something had probed at things he had hidden even from himself. He wondered if they were now recorded somewhere, waiting to be deciphered. Aliens might one day know more about him than he did. "If they come from stars like our own," he said, "we'll eventually communicate with them, or with their systems."

Lena said, "A true *other* would be beyond us."

"Yes, yes," Malachi said impatiently, "yellow suns are the grass of the universe. Our builders seem to be oxygen breathers, and humanoid species might be able to break through to each other. But who or what were we in contact with, besides ourselves?"

"A first step," Juan heard himself say as the black globe of a station appeared in the gray space. The entrance opened like the door to a furnace, and the ship slipped inside.

As the amber glow returned to the drum-shaped chamber, Juan felt a nervous prompting in his limbs. "Take two packs and our gloves," he said as he stood up.

"Where are we going?" Lena asked.

She was a stranger as he looked at her. "I don't know." He hoisted his pack and slipped it on. Malachi put on the other one.

"Are we all going?" Magnus asked.

"Follow me," Juan said.

• • • •

When they came to the well in the passage, Juan stepped in and floated downward. He glanced up and saw the others descending after him. He was calm and uncaring as he fell faster. After a few moments he slowed, positioned his legs, and alighted on a catwalk. An exit oval glowed as he stepped toward it. He passed through—

—into a dark passage. Amber light glowed ahead. He went through into a large chamber. A globe sat in its docking cradle. "In here!" he called to the others. They came out beside him and gazed at the hemisphere that towered some twenty-five meters into the vault.

"A small version of this ship," Malachi said.

Juan led the way through the open airlock. The passage curved right, leading them into a small drum-shaped, amber-lit chamber.

"Same kind of pit," Magnus said as they stepped into the center circle. The viewspace glowed as he and Lena sat down on the floor.

"We're moving," she said as Juan and Malachi dropped their packs next to her.

Juan looked up and saw the station disappear into the gray. A distant self tensed within him as he sat down on his pack. The view switched to normal space, revealing a nearby globular cluster as the ship oriented itself toward a white dwarf.

"It's very close in," Juan said as the red-brown disk of a planet became visible.

Lena clutched at her hair. "My head . . ."

Juan felt a rushing in his ears. Magnus was rubbing his temples. Malachi slumped forward.

"It's worse," Lena said, leaning back against one of the packs.

The brown planet grew until it filled the viewspace. Flashes of light shot across its dark surface. Pain ripped through Juan's forehead.

"We're falling," Lena murmured, raising her hand to push back the descending weight of the alien world.

Juan rushed upward through cold water and surfaced, gasping, then opened his eyes and saw Lena holding the canteen for him. He took a swallow and pushed it away.

"Pain gone?" she asked.

He nodded and looked past her to where Magnus and Malachi stood with drooping shoulders.

He sat up. "Have we landed?"

"Apparently," Magnus said tiredly.

Juan stood up, massaging his temples. Lena touched his shoulder. "Are you all right?" she asked. He straightened up, still feeling dizzy.

"Let's go," he said, reaching for his pack, but Magnus picked it up.

"Mal and I will manage," the older man said.

Juan looked at his companions anxiously, then searched for signs of compulsion within himself. The urge to leave the shuttle was growing stronger. He hurried out into the passage and led the way to the lock.

"I feel a breeze," Lena said as she caught up with him.

Juan stopped. "The lock may be open." He took a cautious breath and went on.

The open lock revealed a rusty brown desert. The large, pale disk of the white dwarf hung low over the horizon, unable to wash out the stars with its feeble daylight.

"It's half the apparent size of our sun," Malachi said, "so we must be very close in."

A warm wind gusted into the lock. Juan took a step outside and felt the gritty soil under his boots. "That way." He pointed straight ahead. "Do you feel it?" he asked, facing his companions. They all nodded. He led them away from the shuttle, stopped, and looked back.

The small globe sat on a plain. Overhead, the globular cluster was a fragmented sun, adding little to the dwarf's light.

"Why are we here?" Lena demanded. "Who are they? What are they doing to us?"

A dust storm crept across the horizon like some black beast.

"They're not persons," Magnus said, "but artificial intelligences trying to reach out to us."

"Maybe this was a special place to them once," Lena said, looking around. "Let's go that way." She pointed away from the storm. Juan noticed that she seemed stockier in her pants and shirt. He brushed a few grains of sand from his face and followed her.

The odors of the desert were musky. Small plants with large red leaves and a faint glow around their roots dotted the ground; mushroomlike knobs clustered around the plants. He looked up as Lena neared a shallow rise. Malachi and Magnus came up to him.

"She seems to know where she's going," Magnus said, catching his breath. He gazed after her speculatively. "She likes you, Juan," he said as they continued after her.

Juan felt embarrassed. Magnus walked on as Juan and Malachi dropped back. "She's a good biologist," the Kenyan said.

Juan glanced at his friend.

Malachi said, "I'd heard about her before, and from what Magnus told me. She very much wanted to do immunology and genome detailing before Titus turned her into a brewer of elixirs for our leaders."

Juan nodded. "I wonder how many politicians Titus keeps on a leash with medical favors."

"I wouldn't offend her by asking. I don't expect your reserve with women to disappear overnight, but I think she's affected you."

"I hardly know her." In place of love he'd demanded both physical beauty and accomplishment, but he had yet to think of Lena in those terms.

They slowed their pace and Malachi said, "Magnus tells me she reminds him of someone he once knew."

Juan watched as she went over the top of the rise. Magnus reached it and motioned for them to hurry. They quickened their pace and came up beside him.

Below, a dozen or more domes stood on the sandy ground, in what seemed a random arrangement. The ones at the center were the largest. Lena slipped into the shadows between the first two structures.

"A tree!" she shouted, echoing.

They scrambled down and hurried after her. Juan saw a short, heavy trunk covered by a smooth white bark, standing alone in the open. Lena stooped under it, and was partly hidden by the large, low-hanging branches. Patches of white light wandered across her face as a breeze turned the large red leaves. She seemed a stranger, examining him from cover.

Her eyes watched him warily as he stepped under the

branches, as if he might be a threat. He noticed the green glow at the base of the trunk as he breathed in the sharp, acidic scent of the leaves.

"Red chlorophyll in the vegetation," she said, examining one of the round, irregularly bordered leaves. "I don't know," she whispered strangely, "but I can almost remember."

"What?" he asked, taking her by the shoulders.

"Don't you feel it?"

He almost knew, but the thought fled like a shy child.

"Juan!" she said in surprise. "They knew the universe when it was young, and they tried to unite it with their web. They couldn't have perished through disease or war, being able to do what they did."

Home now lay in the past, he realized. Light from Earth's galaxy would be millions of years old here. The ship's jumps had taken them into the future; they would return to the past—to this world's future—by again outrunning the light. For an instant he was appalled by the futility of common sense struggling doggedly within him to imagine, in defiance of relativistic reasoning, a simultaneous moment here and on Earth.

Lena took his hand and they came out from under the tree as Malachi and Magnus caught up with them.

"Do you still feel compelled?" Magnus asked her.

"Nothing now," she replied, looking around at the domes. "We're probably the first in a long time to come by and wonder what happened here."

Juan looked down at the grainy sand, then up at the stars, and imagined what might be entombed within the domes. Perhaps the builders had simply died, fulfilling a death wish common to all species. Clearly, there was little they could not have done. They might have changed themselves into beings who no longer needed the ships and the web, and that might have precipitated a fatal identity crisis. The fear of such a break existed on Earth, among those who saw the end of the human form through the wedding of bioengineering and nanotech.

"What now?" Malachi asked.

Juan walked toward the nearest dome. "There's a portal."

"Do you feel we have to enter?" Magnus asked.

"No, not particularly."

He turned to Lena. "How about you?"

"No, it's gone now," she said.

"Perhaps they no longer have to push us," Malachi said. "Our own curiosity can be trusted."

Juan came up to the portal in the dome. It glowed and he passed—

12

SUPERCIVILIZATIONS

◑

—into a yellow-lit space.

The others came in behind him. His eyes adjusted, and he went forward across the smooth ebony surface, feeling as if he were late for something.

"Why are we here?" Lena asked.

Malachi laughed. "Maybe the program's becoming incoherent."

Juan felt a twinge of pain in his head, but it faded. They stopped as the dome darkened. The black mirror of the floor became transparent, revealing the swirl of a galaxy. The view pulled in to a dense region near the center. A bright sun grew larger. Suddenly they were rushing past a pearl-string of worlds. One ring of habitats after another appeared, enclosing the star in a shell of life. Time was passing, Juan realized, as other stars appeared, each surrounded by countless habitats shaped from the raw materials of natural worlds. Double and triple suns were enclosed. The view pulled back to show a spiral arm crisscrossed by red lines.

"There's your power web," Magnus said.

Red beams reached from the spiral arm, striking deep into other quadrants, penetrating the galactic center, thrusting out to the globular clusters. The view pulled back to reveal a cluster of galaxies; red lines lanced out and joined them.

The view pulled back again, encompassing a dozen clusters of galaxies. Red lines winked into place, reminding Juan of a stained glass window in black and red.

"How proud they must have been," Lena said, "to have linked so many worlds."

"And where are they?" Juan asked, suddenly fearful of what his own kind might do with such a vast artifact.

"Might be they grew old," Magnus said as the dome filled with light again, "longer-lived, but with fewer individuals. Time winnowed out those who could sustain an interest in living, leaving the rest to pass away. The web became a useless possession before greater things."

"What greater things?" Lena asked.

Magnus shrugged, looking very tired. "They might have gone forward in time, the few of them who were left, circling black holes to slow their bioclocks. They might have left our universe entirely. Or they might still be here, living small lives on backward-seeming planets, perhaps finding satisfaction in guiding young civilizations. It's possible that our Earth is descended from their vast culture."

"You've been thinking about this," Lena said.

"The web suggests so much," Magnus continued, sounding awed. "I have the constant feeling that I'm failing to make obvious deductions from what we've seen."

"Are any of us up to it?" Juan asked. Here was the older man's chance, he thought, to make up for the work he'd never done.

"Something wants us to learn," Lena said. "Maybe we're being shown this so we can choose a destination."

"We've got to keep trying," Magnus said, "at least until we know enough to get home."

Juan looked into his eyes and felt the stir of new courage. Then he heard a soft whisper at the limit of his hearing.

"What's wrong?" Lena asked.

"I hear something . . . listen!"

They all stared at him as a storm of voices broke within him, babbling from some distant place. He felt panic.

Lena touched his arm. "Are you in pain?"

"No," he answered, steadied by the sudden hope that at any moment he would be able to understand what the voices were saying.

The dwarf was nearer the horizon when they came outside. Sand blew in from the desert, rustling the tree. A swarm of insects rose from the branches and became motes of dust against the white sun. The whispers in Juan's head were muted by the rising wind.

"Insects are probably the oldest surviving life here," Lena said. "They adapt to anything—even radiation and lack of free oxygen. No need to be intelligent, only prolific."

Magnus said, "I've always thought of instinct as a kind of automatic reason, with survival its only object."

The sun touched the brown horizon, reddening the land. The star seemed to hesitate, a ball on a dusty table, threatening to roll toward them, but the serrated horizon stopped it. The sky darkened, brightening the globular cluster. The wind quickened, growing colder.

"Lena," Juan said loudly. "I still hear it . . . something gathering in the air around us."

She looked at him suddenly, eyes wide. "I hear it now!"

Malachi and Magnus were listening.

Time's flow seemed to quicken with the wind.

"Look!" Malachi shouted, pointing toward a growing darkness between the domes. Static flashed in the black dust cloud. Wind whipped Juan's face. Shadows raced. Roachlike insects fled around his feet.

He was alone in the storm as the whispers became louder, demanding, insisting, rushing through him as if he were a ghost, ripping out personal memories at random and holding them up to bleed.

". . . your mother works hard, you could at least do something practical . . ."

". . . what makes you think you'll be any good?"

". . . it's been a waste . . ."

". . . you think you're any better than the rest of us?"

". . . I don't care what happens to them, I've got my own problems . . ."

". . . what is this *me* I'm stuck with?"

". . . I'd cut his throat if I could get away with it . . ."

". . . feelings . . . the universe wound me up to have them, so I would fit into an evolutionary niche . . ."

". . . I hate him, he's so full of himself, the jerk . . ."

". . . you, a genius? You're just like the rest of us . . ."

". . . all these years you've told me how stupid you are, I believe it now . . ."

". . . a friend? You're stupid and blind, and your mind is a mill of free associations and self-serving impulses. Friendship has got to end somewhere . . ."

". . . you're never there for me—I'm just someone to push aside when it's convenient . . ."

". . . I do love you, but I can't live hoping you might return the favor . . ."

". . . reality is a tyranny to be defeated . . ."

". . . we no longer tell each other the truth . . ."

". . . I'm tired of this dance . . ."

Sand struck his face. He turned away from the wind. Pain compressed his eyes; his neck became rigid. He fell to the ground. The wind howled as the whispers shot through him.

". . . poor deluded fool . . ."

". . . the aliens, what secrets! Death will not be there if I can open a window into their minds!"

The ground tilted under him. He dug his fingers into the sandy red clay as his spine became a molten rod distributing pain into his chest, shoulders and arms. Insects crawled around him; for a moment he imagined them spreading to all the worlds of the web, while his skeleton remained here. A smudge of red shift on an astronomical plate would mark his grave.

A tinkling sounded in his ears. Somewhere, a mad harpsichordist was playing a dance tune. He remembered the alien shuttle's open lock, and feared that the insects would infest the craft. He tried to see through the dust, enough to crawl back to the dome, but he couldn't even see the ground. He hid his face in his arms and waited.

The whispers grew fainter as the pain retreated from his body. Resolve flooded into him, and he knew that he had not crossed the universe to die here. The whispers huddled at the edges of his awareness.

"Juan," Lena said, grasping his arm.

He pulled her close against him. "Where are the others?"

"I don't know."

The howl dropped to a whistle as the storm passed. He rolled on his back and saw icy stars. Lena sat up next to him. "Were you in pain?" she asked.

"My thoughts were being looted."

"Mine also."

He lay there, gazing up at her, trying to recover from the emotional assault, wondering if the alien presence had understood what it had stolen from him. Lena was struggling to regain her composure. "Are you all right?" he asked.

She nodded and looked around. "I don't see the others." The storm was past the domes, rushing out into the desert. She shivered. "It's getting colder."

He got to his feet and helped her up. The white dwarf had set, leaving only the pale light of cluster and stars. "Malachi!" Lena shouted, pointing at a figure moving toward them.

"Are you okay?" Juan called out.

Malachi nodded and tapped his temple with a forefinger. "Except up here. Made me wander away in the storm."

"Same with us," Juan said.

"Where's Magnus?" Lena asked. They all looked around. "Magnus!" she shouted.

Cold wind gusted toward them as Juan turned toward the tree and saw something under it. They rushed over and scrambled under the low branches. Lena knelt down by the older man and felt for his pulse. Juan squatted next to her as Malachi crawled around to the other side.

"Nothing," her shadowed face whispered.

"No," Juan said.

"Work on him!" Malachi shouted.

She bent over, positioning his mouth, then pulled back. "It's too late," she said, clenching her hands into fist.

"Try!" Juan shouted.

She bent down and breathed into Magnus. Hope raced through Juan as she worked. He seized the man's wrist and sought a pulse.

Finally, she sat up and took a deep breath. "Heart, probably. No equipment to save him. I think he went quickly."

Juan felt tears in his eyes, and shivered. "The stress of their probing killed him!"

Lena shuddered from the cold and said, "It might have happened anyway." Juan noticed their billowing breath.

"It may get very cold," Malachi said. "We must get back."

Juan felt dismay as he realized that there was no way to preserve the body.

"We'll have to bury him here," Lena said.

Juan swallowed hard and said, "He was just beginning to live again, to be interested . . ." His voice broke. "He was thinking all the time."

Malachi dropped his pack and took out a spade.

"Where's his pack?" Lena asked, looking around.

"Behind me," Malachi said, "where he dropped it." He started to dig.

The cold wind soughed through the branches. Lena bent down to see if Magnus's eyes were closed, covered his face with a cloth, and set his arms together.

"Was he religious?" Juan asked.

"I don't think so," she said. "I don't really know." She emptied his pockets. "We'll need the pen. I think he was writing in the notebook."

Juan worked his way around to Malachi and took over the digging.

"I'll get the other spade," the Kenyan said.

As he dug by the body, Juan was startled by his own existence in a way he had not known since boyhood—by the sudden sense of being apart from the landscape, by the realization that he might just as easily not have existed, and that one day he would again be nothing, and that his future nothingness would last forever. . . .

The red sandy clay was soft, making digging easy. Juan took turns with Malachi as Lena held the flashlight. When the grave was deep enough, they lowered the body in, their hands trembling from the cold.

Juan looked at Lena, then at Malachi as they knelt under the low branches, wishing that Magnus might have perished through some mistake of his own, not by chance. "Magnus," he said, "we'll do it for you—everything you might have wanted to learn. We'll try to understand as you would have."

They took turns filling the grave.

13

THE SURVIVORS

Bright auroras played on the horizon as they marched back to the shuttle. Juan shifted Magnus's pack to a more comfortable position and followed Lena and Malachi up the rise. The loss of Magnus seemed impossible. He wanted to retreat to the big ship, rest, and read Magnus's notebook.

"I don't see the shuttle," Lena called back from the top of the rise.

"We should see it clearly," Malachi answered, "even though it's darker."

Juan reached the top and peered across the empty desert. "It probably returned to the suncore."

"Did they mean to strand us here?" Malachi asked.

"Temperature's still dropping," Lena said, pointing to her billowing breath.

"We're back where we started," Juan said, "cut off from food and water."

Malachi moved his arms to keep warm. "We're not dressed for this."

Juan said, "We'll rest first, then start exploring." He glanced at where the shuttle should have been. "Maybe it'll return. We'll check back."

It was warm inside the dome. They sat on the black floor, basking in the golden light as they ate.

"Lena," Juan said, "do you think the mental intrusions could have brought on a stroke or heart attack?"

"We can't know," she answered.

"She's right, old friend," Malachi said. "We can't guess

their intentions toward us, and we don't know what Magnus's health was like."

Juan sipped a cup of water. "But Titus wouldn't have sent him if his health was bad."

Malachi shook his head. "It was a quick assignment. And there are ways of hiding things." He lay down and put his head on the pack. Lena curled up on one of the two rolls and closed her eyes. Juan sat back against the other pack, took out Magnus's notebook, and turned to the entries.

March 29, 2022. The ship reminds me of an empty rail car. All this space seems to have been for carrying large numbers of passengers, or cargo. What were they doing? And where are they? What's left of them seems no stronger than the voice of conscience, or even a good migraine. If they're trying to communicate, we don't seem to be good subjects for their method.

March 30, 2022. Some basic change in their outlook might account for their abandonment of the web. Maybe there was some physical problem with its use?

The entries ended. Magnus had not had time. Juan felt his loss even more keenly as he turned the blank pages.

Lena shook him awake gently, but sleep seemed worth any price, even if the very atmosphere were freezing solid outside; the dome would stand, the warm light would glow.

"Juan, we've got to go," she said softly.

He opened his eyes and sat up.

"All ready?" Malachi asked.

Juan nodded, then rolled up his pack. Lena helped him slip it on. "Ready," he said.

They approached the exit portal. Malachi went through, then Lena. It was still cold and dark when he emerged. His eyes watered from the wind.

"Where can we go?" Lena asked. "What can we hope to find?"

"Maybe one of these domes has a duplicator," Malachi said."

"Let's see if the shuttle has come back," Lena added.

"We'll split up," Malachi said. "Time is everything now. You two start with the domes. I'll check the shuttle. We'll meet back here in thirty minutes, or sooner, no matter what. Cheers." He walked away toward the rise.

The wind swayed the alien tree as Juan and Lena crossed to the other domes. "I'll take the one to the left," he said. "You take the right."

She nodded and hurried away. He waited a moment, trying to think as simply as he could about the alien technology, concentrating on its style—which was that of a self-servicing biological organism, with never a knob, lever, or button to push.

Across the way, Lena confronted the entrance to a dome. He hurried over. "It won't work," she said, stepping aside.

He presented himself. Again, the entrance failed to glow. "Let's try mine," he said.

They went back and he approached the oval indentation. "Some of these may be inactive," he said when there was no glow.

"I'll try the next one," Lena said, hurrying away. He watched as she approached the dome. The glow failed to appear. She came back, beating her arms to keep warm.

"Here's Mal," Juan said.

"No shuttle, I'm afraid," the Kenyan said. "What have you two found?"

"We can't enter these three," Lena answered.

"Back to the first one," Juan said. "Might as well be warm while we decide what to do next."

"My nose is freezing," Malachi said.

They hurried back. Malachi stepped toward the oval. "Bloody strange," he said when it failed. Juan went up to it and felt the indentation with his gloved hands, hoping to trigger it as he had done with the one in the ship.

Lena said, "We'll freeze out here. No telling how long the night will last."

Malachi came up to him. "No luck? Take out my binoculars, will you?" He turned around. Juan turned from the entrance, unzipped a lower pocket and handed them to him. "I glimpsed something from the rise when I was coming back. Let's take a better look."

They followed him to the top of the rise. Malachi put the glasses up to his eyes and scanned the horizon beyond the domes.

"What is it?" Juan asked.

"Can't see much. Oh, hello—there it is."

"What?"

"Look for yourself."

Juan took the glasses. A dark shape appeared in the digital view.

"I don't think it's a natural part of the landscape," Malachi said. "Push the infrared."

Juan touched the mode control and the desert glowed, wrapped in a white haze of radiating heat. The huge mound glowed even more brightly, like something trapped in the sand.

"There's a lot of heat there," Juan said, passing the glasses to Lena.

"Exactly," Malachi replied. "These domes are not the whole show."

Lena peered through the binoculars. "What do you think it could be?"

"Another installation of some kind."

"We'll go see," Juan said.

Malachi nodded. "What have we to lose?"

They tried a dozen domes on their way to the far side of the grouping, without success. Wind lashed them when they came out into the open, throwing sand and clay into their faces. Uprooted plants flew past them. A black tumble-weedlike ball ten meters high rolled toward them across the green glowing desert. Juan stepped out of the way, but it grazed his arm with a dry crackle.

He marched slowly, his gaze fixed on Lena and Malachi ahead. "Don't stop!" Malachi shouted to him when he paused to look back at the domes.

Juan shifted his pack and marched. The gusting wind was a boxer, delivering a variety of blows to his face. His eyes watered from the cold, dusty air, and his nose stung from the pungent odors; but he was getting used to the ache in his muscles.

Slowly, the black mound grew larger, camouflaging the figures of Lena and Malachi. Juan quickened his pace and caught up with Lena.

"It doesn't seem much farther," she said, taking his arm. They moved against the wind together.

"We're here!" Malachi shouted suddenly.

Juan peered ahead at his motionless figure, but the mound seemed no closer.

"It starts here," Malachi said as they came up to him. He set his boot on the surface. The dark structure rose gently way from them toward a distant height.

"What is it?" Lena asked.

"Underground installation of some kind."

"Not another ship?"

Malachi shook his head. "It would have to be huge, judging by this gentle curvature."

"You want to cross it," Juan said.

"Either that or go back and try more domes."

Juan nodded. "We have little choice." Sorrowfully, he tried to imagine what Magnus would have thought. Was it linked to the domes as part of some project? He started up the slope, boots catching on the ribbed surface. Lena came up on his right, Mal on his left, and linked arms with him. The cluster stars merged as he looked up through teary eyes.

"It's colder," Lena said as they made their way upward in the rising wind. The sloping surface began to seem like a treadmill after a while. The green glowing desert was sullen with shadows as aurora danced on the horizon.

The wind died away.

"That's a relief," Lena said. "Let's rest."

They sat down and braced their feet on the ridges. Juan breathed deeply and leaned back against his pack. After a moment, he reached down and rapped his knuckles on the alien surface. "Seems like the same stuff the ship is made of."

"There's something here, but I don't think it's a ship," Malachi said.

They were silent for a few moments. "You were beginning to feel closer to Magnus, weren't you?" Lena asked.

Juan nodded. "Sticking his hand in that cubbyhole saved our lives. He had a way of looking at things. The ship, of course, but I felt that he was also looking into me."

"He told me," Lena said, "that he considered himself a failure."

"I guess I thought that at first."

"He was a father-figure to me," Lena murmured, leaning forward and hugging her knees, "even though I only saw him once or twice a year."

Juan glanced at her. "My father died of a stroke, just before I graduated from high school. I'd just found out a day earlier that the university was giving me a full scholarship."

"Magnus did his best," Malachi said, "right up to the end. He would have been a special friend to us."

"We have to get back," Juan said, trying to sound decisive, "to make something of all this." The words seemed hopeless, but he felt that he had to say them. He closed his eyes and imagined the roots of the alien tree piercing Magnus's heart and brain, slowly reviving the body, and shuddered from unexpressed grief.

A moment passed and Juan awoke. Lena stirred against him. The dwarf sat on the horizon, lighting up the desert like a dim bulb in a dusty closet. Juan felt stiff but refreshed.

Lena sat up and checked her watch. "Eleven hours."

"We were exhausted," Malachi said, standing up. "Fortunately, the wind died away and the temperature went up. It may get hot."

Lena drank some water, then handed the canteen to Juan. He gulped some down and gave it to Malachi.

"Anyone hungry?" she asked as Juan got to his feet.

"I'm not," he said, helping her up.

"No—let's be off," Malachi added.

They went forward three abreast. "It seems to be leveling off," Malachi said. "I think we're near the center."

They came to the edge of a large bowl in the surface. "Must be fifty meters across," Juan said.

"There's an opening below!" Malachi shouted, pointing. "And ribs by which we can descend."

"What is it?" Lena asked.

"Perhaps it's a vent," Malachi said, "or an entrance of some kind. I'll go first."

He started down slowly. Juan waited a few moments, then started after him. He looked up when he was a few meters down, and watched Lena start her descent.

Malachi reached the bottom of the bowl and approached the opening at the center. He knelt and was peering down when Juan reached him.

"The ridges run down the side," he said as Lena joined them. "We have to keep going while our water lasts."

"He's right," she said.

Malachi climbed down into darkness. Juan glanced at Lena. She gave him a sad look and followed. He waited, then sat down and found the ridges with his feet. He turned around and stood up on the first rung as the white dwarf crept up over the edge of the bowl. The sky had taken on a greenish-blue hue, reminding him of construction paper he had played with as a boy.

"Everyone okay?" Malachi shouted from below.

"Yes," Lena called out.

"On my way," Juan answered, probing for the next step.

"I'll shine a light as soon as I reach bottom!" Malachi added.

Juan descended a dozen rungs and stopped.

"Bottom!" Malachi cried. "Hold still."

A beam of light stabbed up through the shaft. Juan glimpsed Lena making her way down. He looked up, and for an instant thought he might see Magnus above him.

"I'm down!" Lena cried.

He hurried after her and jumped the last rung. Malachi was examining the chamber with his torch. The beam found an exit. "Follow me," he said.

Lena went after him. Juan brought up the rear. They came out into a large white glowing dome. Malachi turned off his light.

"There seems to be no way out," Malachi said.

"Circle the edge," Juan replied.

They made their way around. Malachi stopped. "Here's an oval." He stepped forward and the portal glowed. He stepped back and turned to Juan. "Shall we risk it?"

Juan looked at Lena. She nodded. "We've come this far."

Malachi took a deep breath. "So be it." He triggered the glow and disappeared.

"Come on," Juan said to Lena, taking her hand.

They stepped through—

—into a dark space.

His eyes adjusted, and he saw Malachi on the other side of the dimly lit oval chamber, standing before a large square frame of some kind.

"Looks like a window into nowhere," he said as they came up beside him. He stepped closer and peered in. "What do you think, Juan?" He flashed his light into the blackness. The beam disappeared.

Lena said, "Toss something through."

Juan took out a pack of chewing gum, removed one stick, and threw it in. The foil glittered in Malachi's beam and disappeared in midparabola.

"It's a way into someplace," Malachi said. "Where else can

we go?" He stepped into the frame and vanished before Juan or Lena could reply.

Lena took Juan's hand again as they stared into the frame. "He's gone too long," she said after a while.

A light appeared and Malachi stepped out.

"What's there?" Juan asked.

"You'll see. Follow me." He turned and stepped through again.

Juan and Lena walked through—

—into a lighted space. Juan saw the shuttle sitting in its dock.

"We're back in the suncore," Malachi said grinning, "in our ship's shuttle bay."

"The bowl in the desert!" Lena exclaimed. "It's a dock for the shuttle."

"More than that," Malachi said. "Our ship's shuttle connects with a transmat installation on the planet below."

"But why have both?" she asked.

Juan understood. "The transmat frame was a later development, but even such an advanced system needs ships to set up terminals."

Lena looked puzzled. "But why didn't the shuttle leave us off at the bowl instead of the desert?"

"Good question," Malachi answered.

"Something may have wanted us to get lost and find our way back," he said bitterly, thinking of Magnus. He turned around and looked into the black frame. "We didn't notice this when we were in here before."

Malachi said, "This may not be the only such frame."

"Do you think it's a matter transmitter?" Juan asked, staring into the blackness.

"It could be a direct bridge," Malachi replied, "or a transmission of our patterns across some form of short-space, in which case we're destroyed and recreated every time we pass through. No way to tell, since we're the only ones remembering."

"But if there are other transmat frames," Lena said, "then there may be a way home." She looked fearful for a moment. "Can we be sure this is our ship?"

"We'll know," Juan said, "if we find our other packs where we left them."

14

TRANSMAT

◑

Juan said, "I don't think we can go back up the drop tube."

"There's got to be another exit," Lena said, looking around the bay. "There it is." She pointed to an exit indentation to the right of the shuttle.

Juan approached. It glowed and he—

—went through into the ship's winding passage. Lena and Malachi came out behind him.

"We're somewhere below the drop tube," he said, "and probably below our drum-shaped chamber." At his right, the passage seemed to descend even farther. He started upward, with Lena and Malachi at his left. "We're lucky the big ship didn't leave the station."

Lena said, "I have a feeling that this is the end of the line for it."

After eating, they retreated from the cafeteria to the pit, and found the other two packs where they had left them. Juan settled down to sleep, feeling safe in the amber glow.

"The web is a vast maze," Malachi was saying as Juan awoke, feeling that he had slept only a few minutes. "The short-space arteries through which power courses to the ships can channel travelers directly. It's more elegant. Ships were used to set up the bridges, if that's what they are, and to reach local points. Of course, ships would continue to draw power from web stars and would be used to service transmat frames at distant points. We've seen two kinds of interstellar transport systems. The ship system was replaced, which was inevitable once hyperspace was entered to place core accumulators inside suns. The final step was implicit—send passengers directly through short-space, as with power transmission."

"Good morning," Lena said as Juan raised his head. She was sitting cross-legged on her sleeping bag. Malachi lay on his side, propping himself up on one elbow.

Juan asked, "How far do you think they got?"

Malachi gestured with his free hand. "It seems they would have installed bridge frames at all terminals."

Lena said, "If a starship carried a bridge frame, then it would be linked to core stations, and through them to countless worlds."

Malachi sat up. "Exactly—which means all the worlds of the starcrossers are open to us."

"We know only one set of linked frames," Juan said, "but there may be a frame on Earth, or at least in our solar system. Somewhere in this core station or on that planet there may be a bridge frame leading to another station or stations that connect with Earth. We found this ship there, so perhaps it came to Earth for that purpose."

Lena stood up suddenly. "There may be a frame for Earth somewhere in the ship!"

Malachi said, "And very possibly there's a core station in our sun."

"If they finished the job," Juan answered, sitting up.

"Consider this, old fellow," Malachi continued. "The ships went in pairs to do the job, like chaps who string wire, or some such thing. One vessel would have a transmat bridge on board, just to check out the new connecting frame after it's been installed. Construction crews could then pass quickly between ships when they were out on the job, even if the ships were at different points on the same planet or at the other end of a solar system. Each ship would also have an interstellar bridge frame linked to core stations, as we've seen, and the core stations themselves would be joined."

"Then there may very well be a second ship on Earth," Juan said, "connected to this one."

"We'll find the frame," Lena said excitedly.

"It could be anywhere," Malachi said, "in the chambers along the passage above us, or below us."

"Just imagine," Lena continued. "I might leave Earth by one frame, emerge on one of the web worlds, and find a link with this station by looking it up in some sort of directory."

Juan stood up and stretched. "I wonder if the frames are preset, or if they can be adjusted."

"We never see any controls," Malachi answered.

"It's possible," Juan said, "that the frames open into core stations only, or into inconveniently placed ships. Maybe they never finished the system."

"We'll worry about that later," Lena replied. "Where do we start our search? From the outer lock, or from here on down to the end of the passage? Shall we stick together or split up?"

"Are we in a rush?" Malachi asked.

"I have an idea," Juan said. "Let's follow the passage to its end, which should be somewhere below the exit to the shuttle bay."

"What do you expect to find there?" Malachi asked.

"Maybe nothing, but that's where the shuttle bay is. A bridge frame counts as a major transport facility, and we found a frame in the bay, so maybe there are others nearby."

Malachi smiled. "It's worth a try, despite the bad reasoning."

"If we find nothing," Juan said, "then we'll have no choice but to start on the chambers at the bottom and work up to the lock."

Beyond the exit to the shuttle bay, the passage suddenly ran straight. They hurried forward. It turned left and ended with an oval at least ten times larger than any they had yet seen in the ship.

"Shall we go in?" Malachi asked.

"We have no choice," Juan answered, glancing at Lena.

They stepped forward together—

—and passed into darkness.

Juan turned on his light and cast the beam from left to right. Six black frames gaped at them from the perimeter of the chamber, mirrorlike but reflecting nothing. Each frame in the round chamber was large enough to admit a truck.

"We'll try them all," Lena said, "each of us separately. If one of us doesn't come back, the other two will be warned."

"Either we hang separately or together," Malachi said.

"There's no way to judge danger," Lena added, "but we shouldn't risk three lives to reconnoiter. I don't expect anything will happen, based on what we've seen, but we should be cautious."

"I'll go first," Malachi said, turning on his torch. He went to the first frame from the left.

As he stepped through, his figure seemed to flatten, and he slipped into the blackness like a sheet of paper. Lena took a deep breath; Juan tensed as they waited.

Malachi emerged from the frame. "It's a dark passage," he said, "and branches about a hundred meters in. I felt my weight drop significantly. No point in exploring now, until we know something about the others."

"I'll try the next one," Juan said.

Lena brushed his arm as he moved away. "Be careful."

He faced the blackness and stepped through. Warm, stale air entered his lungs, but he was able to breathe it. He cast his beam in a circle and saw that the chamber was identical to the one he had just left.

He turned and went back through the second frame. Lena and Malachi grabbed his shoulders as he staggered out.

"I'm all right. Just a little dizzy. The air's warm in there."

They released him. "What was it?" Lena asked.

"Same as this, including six frames."

"It could be another ship," Malachi said. "And it might be somewhere on Earth. You might have gone home and not known it."

We deserve some mercy, Juan thought. One life was payment enough. He hated the snake of superstition slipping through him. It was not a matter of payments. Earth might be there, like walking from one room to another, and it would be a matter of chance that they had found it, nothing more. He felt guilty and said, "It doesn't seem right to abolish distance so easily."

"Easily?" Malachi asked. "Countless suns provide the energy to pry open space-time in this way. Dearly bought, I'd say, with a million years of bloody evolution behind the species that did it, not to mention centuries of scientific and engineering work."

"I don't know," Juan said. "Something happened, we know that . . ." He felt dizzy again, and Malachi caught him. "I can stand," he said after a moment.

"You were saying?" Malachi asked.

"Forget it."

"We should get our gear," Lena said, "before exploring further."

"She's right," Malachi added. "Better to have our packs handy now."

"We can get them," Juan said, feeling as if he were about to lose everything. "There's no rush."

He put on his pack and looked around in the amber glow of the pit, feeling that chance was poised to rob them of their new hope.

"We'll leave Magnus's kit," Malachi said. "We may need it if we have to come back."

"Ready?" Lena asked.

Juan felt a pang of sorrow as he looked at the pack on the floor. "Let's go," he said bitterly, then hurried up the incline and slipped through the glow. Lena and Malachi came out behind him. We may be going home, he told himself as he led the way down the passage—to a choking, barking, hate-filled world that didn't deserve to have new doors opened for it.

15

STAR WEB

◑

They stood before the frames. Juan imagined a maze of black snakes weaving in and out of a million suns. Ghostly material flowed through, reassembling into solidity at ports of call, draining suns to break the tyranny of space-time.

"Perhaps we should try the other four," Lena said.

"Later, if this one doesn't work out," Juan replied. "This one may connect with a ship somewhere near home."

"But you didn't leave the chamber," Malachi objected, "so it may be anywhere."

"It was identical to this one. That can't be a coincidence. We'll find out quickly enough."

He cast his beam into the second frame. They went through together. Juan breathed in slowly as they emerged. Turning around, he swept the frames with his torch. "Six frames."

Malachi turned toward the exit. "This will tell the story."

The oval glowed and they passed through—

—into a dark passage. Juan took a deep breath of cooler air.

"It's the identical straight section," Malachi said. "We're in another ship, but where?"

"My weight feels unchanged," Lena said.

"That may not mean anything. There hasn't been much of a gravitational variation since we left Earth. The only time it dropped noticeably was when I went through frame one back there."

"How much of a drop was it?" Juan asked.

"It reminded me of my Lunar visit years ago."

Juan looked at his friend. "It's not much to go on."

"Quite right, but consider. It appears that the ships were used as frame terminals, initially at least. They could be left anywhere they went. Perhaps that's why they're so roomy. They were intended to be moved into place, to hold supplies and equipment, as well as provide living quarters. More than one might have been left in our solar system."

Juan nodded. "So we may be home, or at least somewhere in our solar system, and the first frame may open on the Moon."

"And one of the others may open inside the Sun, or in various places within our sunspace, or in nearby solar systems. We know that at least two ships are linked—the one we left and this one. That's the most important clue. Shaky conjecture, but it makes some sense."

"We'll soon know," Lena said as they started up the straight passage.

"Exactly the same," Malachi said as they turned right.

They went up the winding passage, following their torch beams. "I wonder why the overheads are off," Lena said.

"If we're not on Earth, or a world with a breathable atmosphere," Malachi said, "then the outer lock won't open."

"Unless something's gone wrong," Juan replied.

"It might not open at all," Lena said, "wherever we are."

"The ship could be buried very deeply," Malachi added, "if past experience is any indication."

They came to the drop tube. "It doesn't seem operational," Juan said, shining his light down into it.

Malachi said, "If we're not home, we may have to go back through the frame just to eat."

Lena turned her head suddenly. "Listen."

Juan strained to hear, then looked back and saw brightness near the curve of the passage behind them. A luminous thing seemed to be following them.

It made the turn, and they saw the overhead lights coming on, square by square, racing their reflections in the shining black floor.

Malachi took a deep breath as the overheads rushed past them and around the next turn. "And ventilation, too!"

Juan said, "The ship might be getting ready to leave."

"Just our luck!" Lena shouted as they hurried up the passage.

"It's possible," Malachi added. "Even likely."

Juan glanced at Lena as they jogged ahead. She returned

a strained smile, and he wondered what ordinary days with her would be like.

The inner lock glowed as they approached. They went through and it closed behind them. Juan stepped forward. The circle dissolved to reveal a wall of dirt.

"We're buried," Lena said as he stepped back and the lock closed.

They dropped their packs. Malachi snapped open his spade and stepped toward the lock. It dissolved and he stabbed at the dirt. "It's soft!" he cried with relief. Juan got his own spade, came up beside him, and they began to dig.

"I'll take over when one of you gets tired," Lena said, sitting down on her pack.

They were digging their way out of a starship somewhere, Juan thought as he looked at the growing pile of dirt on the floor. Magnus would have been vastly amused.

Lena got up and bent over the pile of dirt. "Look at this," she said.

Juan glanced at her hand and continued digging. "What is it?"

"Reminds me of a *Veado* bone from a small Brazilian deer."

Juan stopped digging. "Are you sure?"

She examined the bone more carefully, then knelt by the pile and sifted through the dirt. "Here are a few more. It's an extinct species, but I'm not enough of a paleobiologist to be sure."

Juan resumed digging. "We may be home!"

"More likely it's just something that only looks familiar." She got up. "Give me that spatula."

He put it in her hands and retreated to his pack. "We may be down very deep."

"How deep can we be?" Lena asked.

"Hundreds of meters," Juan replied, "up or straight ahead. No way to tell."

"Wonderful," she said with a grunt, attacking the wall of dirt.

"It may take days," Malachi added.

Juan paused, breathing heavily. "No choice. We must find out where we are. Slant upward at forty-five degrees. Digging straight up is harder. We can crawl up more easily at an angle."

"It may be a longer dig," she replied, pausing to catch her breath.

Juan got up and reclaimed his spade. They dug in silence for a while. Two meters in, he began to angle upward.

"Ah, despair!" Malachi exclaimed. "It makes one so hungry."

They sat on their packs around one of the tablelike structures in the alien cafeteria, eating duplicated fish and vegetables with rice. Juan was quiet, content to listen.

"I suspect," Malachi said, "that these doorways are a safety feature. Each chamber along the ship's passage is sealed until the protean moment when it is entered."

"But one failed," Lena replied.

Malachi shrugged. "Time and chance were generous, providing all that was necessary for a freak quantum event to occur." He paused to swallow. "The process," he continued, "that runs the duplicator, recycles the air, wastes, and water, governs the fluid process of the doorways, perhaps even the frames, might have needed adjusting."

"I wonder," Lena said, "if the mazelike structure of the ship and the web is a clue to the minds of the builders?"

"Maybe they got lost in it," Juan replied.

Malachi looked at him approvingly. "Could be, granting complexities we haven't considered."

Lena stood up. "Sleep or back to digging?"

"I feel refreshed," Malachi said, looking at Juan.   "I'm game."

"I won't sleep soundly," Lena said, "until we know where we are."

Juan crouched in the tunnel and continued to dig. Loose stones and dirt cascaded past him. Six meters in, it was no longer possible to just shovel the dirt out behind them. Each digger filled a sleeping bag cover with dirt, and the others pulled it back on a line.

"Anything?" Lena called to him.

Juan stabbed with his shovel and turned his face away. "Nothing!" He dropped his spade, turned off his torch, and crawled backward. Lena gave him a cup of water as he emerged by the pile of dirt. "It could continue for thousands of meters, for all we know," he said, "but it smells damp, which might indicate that we're near the surface." He sat down on the pile.

She emptied the bag and crawled up into the tunnel. Juan watched her feet disappear as he finished his water.

"Damn," Lena's muffled voice said.

"Are you okay?" Juan shouted.

"Just twisted my ankle," she called back, "but not badly."

"Come down. Mal will take over for you."

"I'll manage!"

"We just have to keep digging," Malachi said at the start of his shift. Juan and Lena sat on the pile of dirt, exhausted.

"It seems so hopeless," she said, rubbing her ankle.

"How is it?" Juan asked.

"Better."

The damp smell filled the lock chamber. "We're ten meters in," he said, trying to sound hopeful.

Malachi smiled. "Well, back to it."

"I'll take this shift," Juan said. "I won't be able to sleep anyway."

He got to his feet and crawled up the dark tunnel. At the end, he turned on the torch and picked up the spade. The damp smell was pungent in his nostrils as he began to dig. He was sweating and breathing heavily after only a minute. He stopped, struck the spade into the dirt, and rested. The universe had closed in around him, forcing him to rebreathe his own air. Blood rushed to his head. After a few minutes, he wanted to sleep, but his legs ached in their rigid position.

"Juan!" Malachi shouted.

He opened his eyes. "Okay!"

He struck the stony earth, loosening large clumps. Might just as well be trying to dig through the sky, he thought, jabbing with the spade.

He tried to work calmly. There was no rush. They could eat and rest as long as they wanted. The ship would not take off with the lock open. It might if the opening were cleared. He wanted the ship to stay, but feared what that might do to the world. Good might come from the alien technology, if it could be studied. It seemed more likely that it would be used rather than studied, because its inner workings were too well concealed. The promise of a way to anywhere, of numberless worlds to be explored and plundered, would be too much for a problem-ridden humankind. Power would accrue to those who would control access to the web. Titus

would not turn away from such power. Knowledge, understanding, humane applications—these were things for true
believers, not for those who fancied themselves people of the
world, who told themselves that they lived and exercised
power according to harsh facts.

It seemed that the only way to remain thoughtful and free
of illusion was to live outside the cadres of influence and
authority. He had always balanced his doubts about power
with the need to get ahead professionally; now his convictions
might be tested. The Earth he knew lived on the edge of
disaster. Perhaps it just wasn't possible to mold human
beings through social systems and laws. The example of
extraordinary individuals was not enough to push back the
dark. Something better was needed—a more cooperative and
intelligent species, one that would create for itself a condition
nearer the angels, on some reasonable shore. . . .

But humanity still huddled at the bottom of its time, where
the great theologies selected individuals for paradise on the
basis of moral attainments while the godless ruled niches of
power and wealth.

Juan struck more deeply as he thought. What are we taking
home with us? What will a practical knowledge of the alien
web do to us? Suddenly his spade shot through into an open
space. He breathed in cool, damp air.

"Mal!" He struggled to widen the opening. Chunks of dirt
fell past him. He put down his spade, grabbed the torch,
and scrambled upward on his knees, rising up into a black
space.

"Coming up!" Malachi shouted.

Juan cast his beam into a small chamber, maybe ten meters
wide, with a low dirt ceiling.

"What's there?" Malachi called as he crawled up.

"Looks like a covered sink hole. I think I can touch the
roof if I stand up. Grab my spade as you come up."

Malachi appeared, spades in one hand, torch in the other.
"Doesn't look promising," he said, looking around. "This kind
of water-shaped chamber can be deep below the surface."

"We're breathing good air," Juan said, taking his spade and
standing up. The ceiling was only a few inches above his
head. He tapped it gently.

"Careful," Malachi said, "you don't want to bring it down
on us."

"Where's Lena?" Juan asked.

"Resting, but pretty upset about injuring herself."

"I'm going to push through slowly," Juan said, handing him his light and positioning his spade.

"Hello!" Lena called from below.

"Bloody hell," Malachi said as a small stone hit him in the head.

Juan pushed up. The spade went in easily.

"Can I come up?" Lena shouted.

"No!" Juan called back as a large chunk of dirt fell at his feet.

"It's an opening," Malachi said, pointing his beam up into it. "Slight draft. We're into somewhere."

Juan widened the hole and dropped his spade. "Boost me up."

Malachi put his hands together. Juan stepped up and grabbed at the rim of the opening. "Got it." He lifted himself up. "Seems like outdoors." He climbed out on both knees and stood up, peering around in the gloom as his eyes adjusted. Mists rolled in around him. The air was hot and humid.

"Where are we?" Malachi shouted.

"Seems tropical. Overcast." Juan felt more than saw the forest around him. Black branches moved in the hot breeze. The air was heavy in his lungs. Warm rain fell suddenly, tasting acrid. The sky flashed. He dropped to his knees and reached down into the hole to help Malachi.

16

THE WAY TO ANYWHERE

◐

"Halfway across the universe," Juan said, looking up at the sickly white overcast, "to connect with the ass-end of nowhere." Chills crept up his back as he labored to breathe the hot, damp air.

Malachi coughed. "At least it's stopped raining."

"We can't move in these mists."

Malachi said, "I feel a cooler breeze."

Juan looked up again. The clouds were thinning overhead. A bright patch appeared, and the Moon rode out, full and familiar, pocked and stained, shield for lovers, puller of tides, the unfinished port from which humankind had eyed the solar system and longed for the stars. It seemed pitiable now, to dream of taking a vessel to Alpha Centauri in a mere twenty years, round trip.

"We're home," Malachi said. "I didn't quite believe it."

Juan turned and knelt by the opening. "Lena! A full moon, and it's ours!" A snake slid past him in the growth, glistening in the moonlight, oblivious to his presence. He sat back and laughed; but in a moment he was silent and shaking, thinking of what he wanted for himself and Lena, from his work, fearful of what was to come, wishing that Magnus were here.

"Coming!" Lena shouted.

The breaking clouds fled past Luna like hurrying souls.

At dawn, they came out and saw that the ship was entombed in a hill surrounded by jungle. The sun was a ball of white-hot iron rising over the thicket of trees, vines, and brush, warming wetness back into the sky.

"Smashing heat," Malachi said.

"Glad we dressed light," Lena replied.

They dropped their packs and climbed to the top of the hill. Juan took out his binoculars and scanned in a circle. "There seem to be patches of red desert to the east." Lena and Malachi took out their glasses and scanned.

"One thing's sure," Lena said. "No one knows we're here. Without radio or map, we could die trekking through all that."

"It's the only way," Juan said. "We can't just sit in the ship and hope to be found. Besides, I'm not sure I want anyone to find this ship just yet. I'm for covering this exit. It'll grow over quickly. Do you two feel the same way?"

They nodded. Lena said, "Magnus would have wanted it."

"I don't think the ship will take off," Juan continued, "with two spades lying across the lock, but we can't be sure."

"We're somewhere in the Amazon," Malachi said. "I've seen red patches like that from orbit, where the forest won't ever come back. That means we may be near a highway, either north or south of us. It would be reasonable to make a search, with the ship as a base."

"Can we stop anyone from finding this place?" Juan asked. Malachi smiled. "You'd like to hide it for a wiser time."

"When does either of you think that will be?" Lena asked. Malachi shrugged. "Maybe the jolt will do our kind good."

Juan nodded. "We'll have a lot of explaining to do if we march out of here. They'll search the area and find the ship. It might even be transmitting tachyons right now."

Lena said, "Titus isn't stupid. He knows how we left, and he'll assume a ship brought us back, even if they didn't detect its presence."

"We haven't much choice," Juan answered as he took out his spade and started to cover the hole. "We can at least delay them."

"Maybe it won't be so bad," Malachi said. "Everyone will know about it. They can't hide what happened in Antarctica."

"It'll be up to us," Lena added, "to make sure everyone knows. Keeping secrets is dangerous."

"We'll have to blab," Malachi said, "even if it does get the big-shot brigade stirred up. I must say that I rather liked the idea of being the proud custodian of a big secret, at least for a short time."

Lena turned her head. "Listen!" She pointed away from the sun. "A whooshing sound. Don't you hear? It's louder."

Juan heard a faint rushing sound. "Just barely." He continued covering the hole.

"Let me," Malachi said, taking the spade from him.

Juan sat down, feeling winded. "God, the air is bad out
here. We've been spoiled by the ship."

Malachi finished with the hole and put the spade away.
They shouldered their packs and went down the hillside.

"Go slow," Malachi said. "We'll be bathing in sweat soon
enough."

The jungle confronted them at the bottom of the hill—a
wall of greenery rising twenty meters into the air.

"We'll cut through," Juan said, taking out his spade. Lena
and Malachi did the same. He led the way forward.

The sun rose higher, playing hide-and-seek with them
through the trees. Juan hacked forward, grateful for his boots
and coarse clothing. Malachi moved up and worked next to
him relentlessly.

"You've done this before," Juan said between breaths.

"Yes, master, I'm very valuable on safari."

"We won't make a hundred yards in an hour," Lena said
behind them. "I'm soaked through to the skin."

"These packs aren't much help," Juan added, "but we can't
get rid of them."

"The sound is louder," Lena said as they paused.

Juan listened. It was a hum, almost a rumble, behind the
forest sounds.

"I know what that is," Malachi said. "Heard it before."

"If we don't get somewhere by noon," Juan said, "we'll
have to go back to the ship."

"Sooner than that," Lena replied. "Tropic sun is
dangerous."

Juan swung at the foliage, willing himself forward. Damp
odors of decay filled his lungs, mingling with the smell of
flowers and animals.

"Take it easy," Lena gasped, "you'll have a heat stroke."

Juan stopped again and looked around. The shadows of the
rain forest were deep, glowing with a green pallor. Juan felt
alert, attuned to a dozen different sounds and smells without
conscious effort; his eyes tracked insects against the shifting
hues of vegetation. A zebra-striped butterfly glided through
a shaft of sunlight; a piece of tree bark moved and became a
snake.

"I don't want to meet anything poisonous," Lena said.

A long howl cut through the humid air, died, and seemed to return as a series of hoots. Moist pellets rained down. "Bird droppings," Malachi said. "They've zeroed in on us."

"I see a pair of brown eyes," Lena said, pointing to her left. "There behind those leaves!" The vegetation stirred and the eyes disappeared.

"Probably a spider monkey," Malachi said.

Juan turned his head suddenly and saw some orchids move. The forest seemed to whisper to him.

"Could be jaguars," Malachi added, "if there are any left."

"Be ready with your handguns," Juan said.

Malachi laughed. "We'd never know what hit us, if they were hungry enough to attack. It's the small things that are more likely to kill us—snakes or insects." He peered ahead. "I see a trail."

He swung his spade. Juan and Lena pushed through after him, and they came out on a worn footpath. It cut in from their left and continued forward. Malachi led the way. Juan and Lena hurried after him.

The trail twisted, but kept westward. Juan looked around at the vast superorganism of the jungle, composed of creatures that ranged in size from microbes to large animals, working together under the hot sky, drawing energy from sun and soil, losing it as motion, death, and decay. The forest's immortality was a willful thrust into time, squandering beauty along the way, caring little for the individual.

The trail came to an overgrown incline and ran parallel. "So it is a highway," Malachi said with relief.

They gazed down at the sprawling automated road. Two large trucks rushed by, doing at least a hundred kilometers per hour along their guide path. Two hundred meters across the gray pavement, the jungle resumed its life.

"That's the sound we heard," Lena said.

Malachi nodded. "But we can't stop anything that's running on program."

Three trucks went by and the road was quiet again.

Lena turned her head and said, "Voices."

Juan peered up the road and saw six human figures. Three of them were spraying vegetation, while the others examined a control box by the roadside. "Looks like maintenance to me."

"Move slowly," Malachi said. "They're armed."

They went down the incline and came out on the shoulder of the road without being noticed.

"Spread out," Malachi said. "We're an easy target together."

"Hello!" Juan shouted as they walked toward the crew. A truck whisked by in the far lane, drowning him out.

"They're wearing fibrous armor and face masks," Malachi said. "Those are military helmets."

"What are they afraid of?" Lena asked.

"Raise your hands and keep them up," Juan whispered. "Hello!"

The figures stopped and stood like statues.

"We're friends!" Juan shouted.

One took a machine gun from his shoulder, pointed it at Juan, and shouted a string of words.

"It isn't Spanish," Juan said.

"Portuguese," Malachi whispered. He shouted back in the language and got a vehement reply. "He says to come forward—slowly."

The men came to meet them. The one who seemed in charge stepped up to Juan and seemed to glare at him through his silvered face plate.

"Do you speak English?" Juan asked.

"I do," the big man said. "Stand still and say who you are."

"We're a UN-ERS scientific team," Juan replied.

"Are you armed?" He did not lift his mask.

"Automatics in our packs," Juan said.

"Surrender your weapons. Are there more of you?"

"No," Juan said as three other men surrounded them and began to search their packs. "You have nothing to fear from us," Juan insisted. "We did not approach you with weapons drawn."

The man shrugged. "You won't need them. What is your business here?"

"Where are we, by the way?" Malachi asked, removing the gun casually from Lena's pack and handing it to one of the armed figures.

"Are you joking? Brazil. Where did you think?"

"Of course, old chap, of course," Malachi said, taking out Juan's gun and handing it over. "But you know how easy it is to stray over borders out here. My gun's in the lower zipper."

"The nearest border is hundreds of kilometers west of here," the man said with derision.

These were mercenaries, Juan realized. The government provided roads into the dwindling jungle, but private companies kept them open. The swindling and murder of natives, airdrops of contaminated food and clothing, illegal lumbering and strip mining, had been a way of life for most of the last century. UN Earth Resources Security had reversed the Amazon's decline by the turn of the century, but the sheer size of the land mass still made some covert exploitation possible.

"We're lost," Juan said, convinced that the big man was considering whether he should kill them. "Our plane went down east of here. We were making a connection in Lima for a flight to the Antarctic. Can you call for help?"

The big man slid back his mask, revealing a dark, unshaven face. "Of course. There is a government field nearby. We'll take you there. A plane goes to Lima twice a week—or you can wait for the one to Brasilia in five days." He took his hand away from the machine gun and held up five gloved fingers. "Terrorist indios try to damage the road, but it's hard to do now." He held up his weapon and smiled. "No bullets, just tranks. Better this way than theirs, eh?" He gestured with his left arm. "Our truck, just up the road."

"Thank you," Juan said, trying to hide his fear.

The vehicle was a massive air-conditioned trailer truck. They were shown to a lounge area in the rear and left alone.

Malachi tried the door and found it locked. "I'm afraid we can't be sure they'll be helpful."

Lena dropped her pack and sat down in an upholstered chair, looking more angry than afraid. "I can't believe we gave our weapons away. This long run of bad luck will kill us." She looked up and Juan saw that she was struggling to stay calm. "What are we going to do?"

He took off his pack and said, "We might have been killed on the spot if we hadn't surrendered our weapons. We couldn't have prevented a search. Our only chance is to intimidate them with who we are, so they won't risk violence."

Malachi let his pack slip to the carpeted floor and said,

"Possibly. We haven't actually seen them doing anything. In fact, we may be wrong about who they are."

"Tranquilizer bullets, my ass," Juan said. "These are hired thugs."

Lena took a deep breath and said in a trembling voice, "Who we are is exactly what they're afraid of. They know we'll report their presence."

Malachi said, "Yes, but that may not be enough for them to kill us. They're probably checking on our plane story right now. They'll find out there's been no plane reported lost, but that won't prove we're lying. How else did we get here? They'll have to consider that we may be telling the truth and let us go."

"Let's hope," Lena said, sitting back in the chair.

Juan felt a gentle pull as he sat down in the chair next to her. "We're moving." Malachi fell back onto a small sofa and stretched. "Look at this place," Juan said as glasses rattled in the bar.

"No windows," Malachi said. "I saw heavy armor on the outside."

They were silent for a while. Juan listened to the distant whine of the engines. There was nothing to be done until the vehicle reached its destination.

"I wonder," Lena said nervously, "if humankind may be all that's left of the web's builders," and Juan knew that she was trying to distract herself.

"I don't want that to be true," he replied. "I'd like to think that our history shows we're original to our planet, that we got this far, for what it's worth, on our own, whatever we are. Clearly, we were visited, but that's a far cry from tracing lineage."

Malachi grimaced. "We're still our jolly old selves, even the cheerless chaps running this bus."

"But what happened," Lena asked, "after the two ships came to earth?"

"I think I gave the likely explanation for that," Malachi said calmly. "The ships were meant to be terminals, to be left in place. The builders left through the frames."

Lena shifted in the chair. Juan noticed her growing unease as she tried to carry on the discussion. "Then whose skeletons did we find?"

"Intruders," Malachi said, "the same as us. Maybe they

just starved to death in that chamber after they got in. The door might have failed."

Lena shook her head. "You mean they just went in and never came out?"

Malachi waved his hand as he reclined. "One or two went in and didn't come out. Two more followed and didn't come out. Finally they were all in and the door failed when they tried to exit."

"Sad," Lena said.

Juan sat back. "I keep worrying if we're the same people who stepped into the frames, or exact duplicates. If not, then our originals died out there." It was the wrong thing to say, he realized as Lena glanced at him.

"We're the originals," Malachi explained, "if our actual atoms were transmitted through the short-space links, and copies if only our patterns went through—that is, if we were scanned and rebuilt according to the same scan from energy available within the system, which would make us exact twins of our originals, who no longer exist. As twins we'll never feel any different. Of course, we'll have to know more about the system to be sure whether this is the case or not, but my feeling is that the frames are direct bridges—whatever steps in, steps out. Wormholes being opened routinely."

Lena bit her lower lip and looked at Juan. "But we are, well, we are ourselves still, and they're gone, whoever they were."

"We are exactly what we were," Juan answered. "Same memories and feelings, if what Mal says is the case."

"Then what's the point of the distinction?" Lena asked.

"We're another set of the same, if the same atoms were not sent and reassembled," Malachi answered. "Of course, socially, it won't make any difference, and subjectively there's no way for us to tell, since we're the only ones left to remember. Even if we determine the nature of the technology, we won't feel any different."

"But we'll know," Lena said, "that we died out there, as surely as Magnus did—and we may not have much longer to live here."

"Yes," Malachi replied, scowling.

Juan imagined humanity swarming through the web, and wondered what other installations the starcrossers had placed in the solar system. There was something inside the Moon;

there was probably a station in the Sun. "If we have our own suncore station," he said, "that might explain some of the anomalous measurements we've had over the last century. The Sun may be draining and won't last as long as we thought. A web of this kind could make a dent in the energy output of whole galaxies."

"Maybe that's why they stopped," Lena said.

Malachi sat up. "We've done the same on earth, with various nations hogging the world's resources at one time or another."

"But where did the builders go?" Juan asked. "Where are they now?"

Malachi shrugged. "We saw no evidence that they still exist. They went elsewhere, became immaterial, or merely perished in some way too subtle for them to have understood or prevented."

"Since we won't be able to hide what we've learned," Lena said, "we'll have to try to influence how it will be used, how it will be revealed." She smiled and added bitterly, "If we live."

"How?" Juan asked.

"Maybe by not telling everything at once."

"Whatever we do," Juan said, "nothing will ever be the same again."

Malachi took a deep breath and smiled. "Perhaps no one will find the ship, or us, if these chaps kill us. No one will know we ever came home."

Juan was silent; Lena glanced at him. After a few moments Malachi motioned to them. They all moved toward the center of the room. "It's likely we're being listened to," Malachi whispered.

"It can't make any sense to them," Juan replied. "It's all out of context."

"We're slowing," Lena said as the glasses and bottles rattled again in the bar. Juan looked at her and Mal, and realized that these might be their final moments.

17

DISCRETE ORBITS

Five shabby brick blockhouses made up the airport complex. The big man showed them into a room and smiled as he took off his helmet. "You will wait here—please." He sat down in a chair by the door and closed his eyes.

Juan went over to the lone, barred window and looked out at the sun-blasted runway; it seemed long enough to land a jet. He thought of the ship in the hill, and its twin in the distant suncore. We've come back across time again, he thought. It was all a dream, the ships and web. How much was true and how much had he and his companions invented in their clumsy efforts to understand the unknown? Was there something in the ship with which they had communicated? It was all fragile guesswork.

He turned from the window as Lena approached the guard. "What are we waiting for?" she demanded.

The man opened his eyes and smiled. "It will be a few minutes only. Today's plane for Lima was cancelled."

"May we make a phone call?" Malachi asked politely. "There will be concern if we don't arrive on time."

This seemed to upset the big man. He got up, opened the door, and left, locking it behind him.

"What was that about?" Lena asked.

"Magic words," Malachi said. "A test, actually. They may now let us use a phone, to find out whom we shall call. That will suggest to them how they should behave toward us."

Juan took a deep breath and said to him, "You may have just saved our lives." Lena looked slightly relieved.

Malachi said, "If they're going to kill us, it will have to be before any phone calls. That way we stay missing." He tried the heavy door, without success.

They waited in silence. Juan tried to control his anxiety by staring out the window. He tensed as he heard the door open behind him.

"Come with me," the big man's voice said.

Juan turned around and saw the machine pistol in the man's right hand. Malachi went outside. Lena followed. Juan hurried after her. The big man smiled at him as he went out.

The Brazilian herded them toward the next blockhouse, opened the door and motioned for them to go inside. "What's this?" Juan demanded.

"Phone," the big man replied, gesturing with his weapon.

Juan followed Lena and Malachi inside. The door closed behind him; the lock clicked.

On the desk in the center of the room stood a phone. "They'll be listening on a spare," Malachi said.

Juan sat down at the desk, started to punch in the coded number, then stopped.

"What's wrong?" Lena asked.

"What's the rest?"

Malachi reached over and entered the final digits. They waited as the call went through.

Titus Summet gaped at Juan from the screen, then blinked. "What? Where are you?"

"Somewhere in the Amazonian jungle. Before you do anything else, Titus, note our exact location and identify yourself."

Summet glared at him for a moment, then nodded and said, "Titus Summet here, Director, UN Earth Resources Security. What do you need, Dr. Obrion?" His upper lip twitched slightly.

"We're in Brazil," Juan said, trying to smile. "We missed our connection in Lima when our plane went down."

Summet stepped out of view. Lena and Malachi glanced at Juan apprehensively before the Director's image reappeared. "Have you identified yourselves to the local authorities?" he asked.

"Not yet," Juan replied. "They haven't asked for formal introductions."

"Who's with you?" He peered out from the screen. "Dravic and Moede. Good. I'll send a plane to take you to Miami.

Check into the Singapore, and stay put until I get there. Are you in any difficulty right now?"

"Uncertain," Juan said.

"I'll do what I can. Just get on that plane when it arrives. It's out of Lima, so it should be quick."

The screen faded before Juan could tell him about Magnus. Juan looked at Malachi. "Well, what do you think?"

"We'll see."

Lena said, "I think he understood."

"This is his chance," Juan said, "to turn things around. It couldn't have been good for him politically to lose us and the alien ship. He wants us safe, under his direct control, so he can decide how to let all this play out."

Malachi nodded. "He'll meet us alone, or with someone he trusts, to keep this from Dovzhenko while he secures the ship. He has no reason to think we came back in any other way."

"In a way," Lena said, "we did come back in a ship."

Malachi asked, "Do we just disappear when we get to Miami?"

"He might meet us at the plane, if I know Titus."

Lena said, "We must be clear on what we want. Titus needs us. But we need him if we want to continue to work and have any say in this." She waved her hand. "I know— my first impulse is to go and hide somewhere—but I think we should at least start with Titus and see where he stands. Secrecy is just not productive in the end, and they'll find out anyway. We'll have to tell someone sooner or later."

"I agree," Malachi said.

Juan nodded. "If they let us out of here."

Juan watched the small hydrojet with UN-ERS markings land and taxi. The door to the blockhouse opened; the big man looked disappointed as he motioned for them to come out, and led them to the aircraft.

"Thanks a packet," Malachi said to him as they reached the plane. The Brazilian gave a wolfish grin as they climbed inside.

The jet took them up into a blue sky, reducing the jungle to a carpet of broccoli with burnt-out patches. The weather turned cloudy. The craft climbed above the overcast and whispered north.

"I wonder what Titus said when he sent the word down," Lena said in the window seat next to Juan.

Malachi grimaced. "What worries me is how the message got down to these thugs after it reached the official recipients."

"If it got down," Lena replied. "They might have simply let us go, fearing trouble."

Juan sipped his drink and gazed out at the calm ocean off Miami Beach, feeling as if he had returned from the dead. It was quiet here on the twentieth floor of the hotel. The immediate past seemed unreal, the present suspended. He tried not to think about Titus and what the web's discovery would do to the world. The director had not met them at the airport, which indicated a measure of trust.

Closing his eyes, he breathed in the salty air and took a long pull of the bourbon and water. The wet glass reminded him of chilled strawberries. He heard a footfall and opened his eyes. Lena sat down in the chair next to him and smiled as she adjusted her white robe.

"Where's Mal?" he asked.

"Showering." She looked out to sea. "Do you feel strange? As if we're not really back. Time is slow, memory false."

She gazed at him and he wondered if now there would be time to say things, to explore each other, to have feelings without the threat of danger.

"Juan," she started to say, looking worried. Her eyes opened wide, and he saw that she wanted to tell him something, but held back.

He drained his glass and put it down by his chair, wondering how he felt about her.

She smiled when he looked at her again. "Too many drinks," he said, feeling suddenly that he could not doubt her, that being without her friendship, at the very least, was unimaginable.

"What is it?" she asked.

"I never had time to allow my feelings to grow. Physics requires such a huge initial investment of time, simply to reach competence, much less shine."

They were silent. "What will they let us do?" she asked.

"They'll have to keep the three of us together," he said, looking at his watch. "Titus will be here any moment."

"What do you think will happen?"

He picked up his glass and looked at the melting ice, then drank some of the water. "A green comet will sweep by." He rattled the cubes. "Its verdant gas will cover our planet, making us all good and full of foresight. We might even grow an extra eye in our heads." He laughed and put down the glass. "We're capable of everything and we accomplish nothing—nothing that goes very deep at any rate. You grow a human being until he's full of knowledge and insight, until he feels deeply and knows what's right, and then he dies. . . ."

"It's like breaking fine musical instruments as soon as they're seasoned," she said. "But you can't blame humanity for being subject to death, Juan. We haven't had time to beat it yet."

He turned his head suddenly. "That's the doorbell. He'll have a key. Come in, Titus, we're on the balcony!"

The door opened and closed. Juan stared at a ship on the horizon. "We're out here!" he repeated.

"Dr. Obrion?" a voice asked. "We've never met. Titus Summet sent me here to debrief your team. My name is Magnus Rassmussen."

The glass slipped from Juan's hand and shattered on the hard floor. "What the hell?"

"Summet will definitely be here tomorrow." There was no mistaking the voice. Juan looked at Lena, got up, and staggered into the suite.

The tall man confronted him with Magnus's contemplative gaze. His gray hair was more closely cropped. He wore a khaki suit with an open white shirt, and held a briefcase in his right hand.

"How did you get here?" Juan asked, shaken.

Lena came in. Malachi burst out of the bathroom in his towel. The man stared at them, puzzled. "I flew in from New York. What's wrong?"

Magnus lived—but the relief and joy welling up inside Juan was out of place; how could the man be alive?

Lena hurried up to the tall man. "It is you!"

"You have a twin," Malachi said.

"What do you mean?" the man asked.

Lena regained her composure and stepped back. "You have no idea what a shock this is to us."

The visitor sat down in a chair with the briefcase in his

lap, and looked up at each of them in turn. "I was to have gone with you to the Antarctic, but I know the three of you only by reputation."

"What have you been told?" Juan asked.

"Why, everything that happened in the Antarctic. You're to tell me what happened after the alien ship carried you away."

Juan glanced at Malachi, then at Lena. "Magnus, we can't account for your presence here."

The man winced at the sound of his first name. "What do you mean? We've never met, and I don't have a twin brother."

Juan said, "Who are you? The three of us saw you die."

The man's grimace shook Juan's confidence. A bit thinner, less hair and a few more wrinkles, but this was Magnus Rassmussen.

"It's true," Lena said. "You went with us."

Rassmussen frowned at her.

"We buried you," Malachi said, "insane as it sounds."

Juan gazed intently at the man he had come to admire. Rassmussen looked puzzled and said, "I cannot imagine why you would say these things to me." He fumbled nervously with his briefcase, and took out a small recorder. "But start from the beginning, and tell a dead man everything you can recall."

It was evening when Juan finished. With the recorder still on, Magnus said, "So the frames not only bridge space, but allow passage across probability. The three of you have returned to a world where I didn't go with you. And if symmetry is conserved, your twins from here are just as puzzled somewhere else."

"Schrödinger's Door," Malachi said from the sofa.

"Exactly," Magnus answered, sitting back in his chair.

Juan got up and paced the room again. "It also worries us," he said, "that if we've been duplicated—that is, if the frames are not direct bridges—then we've not only crossed lines of probability, but we're not our original selves."

Lena bit her lower lip and reached down to pour herself another cup of coffee from the tray on the floor. "We may have died in one of these universes," she said shakily as she sat back in her chair.

Magnus nodded. "And there's one in which only two of you

survived, or one—an infinite series of branchings, constantly splitting, diverging at every point throughout the cosmos."

"Can this explain what happened to the builders?" she asked.

"We must assume,' Magnus said, "that they knew enough physics to understand what their frames could do. They might have planned to use the web in this way, accepting a social system based on variant individuals. But we can only speculate."

"What about asymmetrical effects?" Juan asked.

Magnus raised his eyebrows. "You think the builders might have disappeared from our universe—I mean your universe. They may be present in this one, for all we know."

"Could they have all disappeared in such a way?" Lena asked.

"With endless alternates available, even asymmetry may occur."

"We didn't see enough of the web," Malachi said, "to know if it's deserted, or, for that matter, if there is a web beyond the maps we saw."

Magnus nodded. "The builders may not be here either—if probable worlds run in a spectrum of fine shadings, with minor differences packed closely together. You'd have to travel far off your reference axis to run into a major difference. It would be interesting to do so."

Juan stopped pacing and said, "The builders ran into the splitter effect, although we can't be certain of that. But they decided to use the web anyway. Still, I don't see how a probability might be drained of their presence. Maybe they decided to abandon the web, which they at first built to connect suns, ships, and planets, but as they developed they decided to leave natural worlds for new life, realizing that taking all that power might prevent fresh intelligences from arising. Maybe they realized that new minds are the most precious thing in nature—so they moved beyond the use of natural worlds and now live in mobile habitats, obtaining their needed resources from sun systems not likely to produce new life."

"All this may be true," Magnus replied. "Some starcrossers may still exist in our spaces, in distant sectors of their web, and in mobile worlds. Others may have left our space-time. But I'm not sure we can credit them with compassion for other life on the basis of what you've seen." He paused for a moment, as if listening to an inner voice. "Curious. As you spoke, Juan, I felt as if I were remembering being out there with you."

"Perhaps there's some leakage between variants," Lena said. "What if all probabilities are one and the same at a basic level, except when separated by technical means?"

"Disturbing," Magnus replied.

Lena got up, went over to the door, and turned on the overhead light, dimming it to a comfortable glow. Juan sat down in a chair. "Magnus, may I ask you a personal question?"

The older man looked at him as if he knew what it would be. "Go ahead."

"Are you under Summet's thumb?"

"What do you mean?" Magnus asked softly.

"We have to know what kind of man Summet is here," Juan said.

Magnus nodded. "Yes, I suppose I am. He sent me because he could trust me, and because I would have gone with you. Look, he's given me all the chances I deserve at my age, so you might say I'm his man. He's never asked me to be dishonest. Is that what you wanted to know?"

"What's happening at the Directorate?" Juan asked.

Magnus took a deep breath. "Titus may be replaced if he's seen to be making too many mistakes, even if they aren't mistakes. In your world he may have already been replaced. Your return may help him stay in office." Magnus smiled wanly. "You must admit, it's a first-rate secret you've brought back, and the fact of your return will confirm his judgment in sending you."

"Who knows we're back?" Juan asked.

"I'm the only one he called, but he's worried about the mercenaries. I'm sure you didn't intentionally tell them anything, but did you discuss things among yourselves when you were alone? Your conversations might have been overheard or recorded. Granted, little of what you said will be understood, but it might make sense to others later."

"We're worried," Juan said, "about how Titus will use all this. Will he enhance UN-ERS power or ally himself with national groups, if they don't already control him?"

"He needs everyone," Magnus answered. "Remember, the • UN-ERS bureaucracy is one thing, but the national bureaucracies of the United States, Russia, China, Japan, South

America, and the European States sit within it, and Titus has to play them off against each other for some kind of balance. Environmental problems tend to moderate these rivalries, but the totalitarians are still with us, dedicated to the control of wealth through rapid, shortsighted means. You'll have to work with Titus to have any leverage. He knows only about a ship, and nothing about the web or this probability effect. Lack of knowledge could make this all very dangerous. Even vague suspicions about hidden facts could turn things nasty."

"He's right," Malachi said. "If we disappeared, they'd still discover everything for themselves, so it's up to us to help determine how the world will use all this, as much as we can."

"And save Titus's ass in the bargain," Juan added.

"Don't let it become a matter of personalities," Magnus said. "Someone worse may replace Titus."

"Juan, he's right," Lena said.

"It's only just," Magnus continued, "that you all benefit from and help guide what happens to this discovery. The politics will be bad enough without your stepping aside."

"You're right," Juan said. He relaxed a little, then wondered if his father was alive in this world. It would be that way, he realized, discovering differences of detail.

Magnus stood up and walked over to the bar cart. Slowly, he dropped a cube of ice in a glass and poured some bourbon. He sipped and turned around. "I know you feel that you've lost your world. Worse, you doubt your identities. But, if you will forgive a more impersonal attitude, there's still a lot left—everything essential, in fact."

Relativity and quantum mechanics, Juan realized, might have profound psychological implications. Was there some observer effect that had drawn them into this world, where Magnus lived, and not another? Juan felt the darkness within himself. How many of him had stepped across the night sky? Perhaps the infinity of variants merged together to produce peak moments, a richness of reality, a texture of psychological contingency which could never be exhausted. Were dreams and multiple personalities the overlap between variants? Was the mystery he sometimes saw in the eyes of another a sign of possibility splitting at each firing of a synapse in the brain? Life seemed thin at times, with people moving in discrete orbits, circling some vast emptiness, yearning to touch, to quantum leap into a more intense state, there to combine into greater wholes. The fearful masters of humankind's world—this variant included—had set themselves to choke possibility, chain creativity to politics and economic interests, hold back the waves that yearned to break on kinder shores. New doors were opening, but others were closing behind him. Could he believe that the four people in this room could dispense the blessings of the web to humankind? They at least understood and cared, he told himself; but to succeed demanded more than moral ideals—it demanded their violation in the name of greater ideals. Perhaps Titus was necessary after all.

"What now?" Lena asked Magnus, and Juan felt that a million years had passed. He hungered for the simple absence of disappointment, for naive hope; perhaps the cauldron of probability might give it to him.

Magnus looked down into his drink and said, "I won't keep you here, and I won't insist on what you should tell Titus. You can do what you wish with the disk in that recorder."

Lena went up to him and said, "You are still one of us."

He smiled. "How could I be otherwise, now that you've told me about myself? By the way, I would be very interested in reading my namesake's notebook."

"What prevented you from going with us?" Juan asked, suddenly fearing for him again.

"Oh, a bit of illness." He wandered onto the open balcony. "So I'm buried out there, under an alien tree." He gazed dispassionately up at the bright, starry sky, then took a long sip from his drink and said, "How poetic a way to end."

II

WORLDS FOR THE WIND

And I say to any man or woman, Let your soul stand cool
and composed before a million universes.
—Walt Whitman

18
ACROSS AN AUTUMN

Juan took his time walking across town from the train station. He had checked his bag there because he was uncertain about staying, even though his parents had welcomed him on the phone. Suddenly it seemed that he was walking home across the same autumn he had known on his first day of high school. The oak, maple, and walnut trees that had been planted in this mountain valley by the town's builders were an island of yellows and reds in a sea of pines, firs, and giant redwoods. Hope and caring surged through him as he breathed in the unseasonable warmth. There was still time to defeat the old darkness within the human heart, and the future might yet belong to learning and loving. . . .

A knot tightened in his stomach as he turned the corner and stopped a block away from his boyhood home, realizing abruptly that everyday reality was a kind of congealed chaos. Human perceivers drifted on quicksands, extracting only a statistical order from cosmic extremes. He stared at the two-story wooden structure with suspicion, as if it might suddenly dissolve back into the quantum sea of mysteries that washed around the human shore.

But as he gazed at the street, the small town took on an awesome permanence. This was the only world that could be, holding its shape stubbornly, as if all the diverging waves of probability had collapsed into one. The bright yellow-red leaves falling from the trees were a changeless change. The street had been repaved, but that made no difference. The single-family houses were in good repair. The wood and brick structures seemed to belong with the more modern ones of flexible ceramic and glass. Everywhere, human will restrained change with continuity.

He reminded himself that the father he would meet here had known his son's college years and early adulthood as a scientist, all the years Juan had lived without a father. The other man had died mocking his son's future profession. Would this stranger also mock? His mother had looked and sounded pretty much the same over the phone. These people were expecting a visit from their son, nothing more; it would be impossible for him to explain.

Angela's house was still there across the street. Painfully, he remembered their senior year breakup. Bert's house stood next to it, somewhat changed by additions. Juan had not seen his friend since graduation. What were friends supposed to be? He sometimes imagined friendships as unique, cosmic events, never to be taken lightly; but they too often became trivial, repetitive betrayals of everything that was greatsouled in human beings.

He felt confused as he went down the block. What right did he have to this world? It was not the place from which he had started; and yet it was his, overlaid with an infinity of autumns, in which he was a stranger come home. What mattered a misplaced knothole in the redwoods surrounding the town? The roots and the mountains were the same, despite the flow of probabilities in the minds of observers. This was still his Earth because it embodied the choices of his world; one way or another, the footprints of the human history he knew were all over it.

He came to the open gate and stopped, remembering how often he had been blamed for leaving it open. He closed it behind him, feeling virtuous, and walked up to the old screen door. Here it is, he cried out inwardly as he rang the bell. In the next few impossible moments he would confront a variant of his mother and a living father. Listening to the old man on the phone and staring into his squinting eyes had been unnerving—as if he were reproaching his son for disturbing the dead. Juan was suddenly unable to believe that they would meet. The door would open and he would be in his own world again. I'm dreaming, he told himself. He was only a quantum echo of himself here. The real Juan Obrion had returned to the primary world, the variant where his father was dead. At any moment the echo wave would collapse and he would rejoin himself.

He rang the bell again. Worlds split within him. In one his mother had died; in another his father lay dying while his son waited at the door; in a third the Obrions had remained childless; in a fourth he had brothers and sisters and there was no electric bell on the door, forcing visitors to rap on the wooden frame; and in an infinity of others the differences were so trivial that it might take weeks to ferret them out. What was the range of humankind's possible worlds? He saw them stacked against each other like photo negatives, with ghostly images overlaying each other.

The inner door opened. His mother's gray eyes examined him through the screen. She seemed thinner, younger.

"Joe, he's here!" she called into the house, then struggled with the latch.

Juan heard his father's familiar cough. "Well, get him inside," he answered in a trembling voice.

The old lock clicked at last, and the door opened. He stepped inside.

"Where's your bag?" Adela Obrion asked, leading him into the living room. He didn't answer. "Dinner's just about ready," she said as he kissed her on the cheek. "Do you need to use the bathroom or anything?" She looked at him as if something about him puzzled her.

His father raised himself from his chair, came forward and grasped him by the elbows as if about to hug him, then stepped back. José Obrion was heavier, but his black hair showed only a sprinkle of gray.

"You look well," he said, motioning for Juan to sit down. Adela hurried from the room as his father poured him a glass of red wine. Juan sat down on the sofa across from his chair.

The room seemed unchanged, with its blue walls and the red, blue, and black carpet his parents had brought back from a vacation in Cozumel. His father sat down in the straight-backed chair from which he had always presided and said, "Your old friend Bert's doing well with his construction business."

"Oh? I didn't know he was back here."

José Obrion raised his brows. "Three years now. I'm sure I told you. He'd be glad to see you."

Juan sipped his wine, trying to ignore his father's accusatory tone. Bert's back and doing well at something practical, like you might have done, his father had meant to say; he had not changed.

Juan glanced around the room. Family pictures still stood among the few books on the shelf near the video screen. A younger Juan, wearing a cap and gown, stood next to his father, who in his world had never seen him graduate from high school. Another photo, of Juan and his mother, had obviously been taken at his college graduation.

"He's married," his father said, still about Bert. "Got together with the Snyder girl. They'll have a kid in a few months." The Bert Juan knew had decided to join the Navy and see the world, and had always feared that this small town would trap him.

"Dinner's ready!" his mother called. The familiar odors of simmering beans and onions reached Juan. He got up and went into the dining room.

His mother looked at him strangely as he sat down next to her. "What is it?" he asked, tensing.

His father came in and sat down at the head of the table, at Juan's right.

"Joe, don't you notice?" she asked him.

"I see him sitting there."

"His eyes don't seem gray. They look as brown as yours."

"Must be the light," his father said, squinting.

"Are you wearing contacts?" his mother asked, gazing at him with suspicion.

"Yes, I have to wear lenses now," Juan lied.

His father grimaced. "His own color wasn't good enough for him, I suppose." He started to serve himself.

"Joe, don't," his mother said softly.

Suddenly Juan wanted to explain, to blurt out that he was still their son, to tell them that in the world from which he had come and in countless others his father was dead. He wanted to shout to them that this was a miraculous meeting, even though they would be unable to understand. A chill went through him as he realized that perhaps no Juan Obrion had returned to his Earth. He and his companions had died far from home as they struggled through the alien maze. He wondered if there was some sense in which he was one with the infinity of his other selves; the dreams of one would be the reality of another as the moments of decision split off from him. He imagined an absolute self standing apart from the if-worlds, gathering the infinity of perspectives that swam in the ocean of physical truth.

"What is it, dear?" his mother asked. All suspicion was gone from her eyes. Her face seemed unlined, almost youthful.

"Just a bit tired, Mom, that's all."

"So how's work?" his father asked. "Earning more?"

"I've been in the orbital park a lot, and in some . . . remote places."

His father grimaced. "What kind of life is that? I guess I'll never understand what it is you do."

"I go where conditions are right to study certain kinds of things," Juan said defensively. "It's the only way for the work to get done."

"Yeah, but what do the rest of us get out of it? We pay taxes and the world is still falling apart."

"That's not the point," Juan started to say and stopped himself, determined not to be drawn in. His father was right about human folly, but he had a habit of linking things together unfairly. Here, Juan realized, was a small juncture. A whole world had just split off, one in which he was arguing vehemently with his father. He could almost hear the sounds of that world fading away. Every choice was being made both ways, with infinite variations. There was even one world in which he had won the argument, in which his father had understood and agreed with him.

"Who do you think you're fooling?" his father demanded. "You dreamers and tinkerers are out for yourselves, not to help the rest of us. You build your toys for yourself. Sure, the rest of us aren't better, but you put matches in the hands of children. It's a bad world, but don't tell me you're making it any better."

"Joe—please!" his mother cut in, suddenly looking old and tired.

Her husband pushed his food away and stared at her with outrage. "It's down on us every day! Who do you think pays him? He should be raising decent people to come after him; assuming there'll be a world for them. When the environment collapses they'll draw their weapons to fight over what's left." He looked at Juan. "You haven't been here to see all the dead trees. There's no fish in the streams, and our drinking water stinks worse every year. Who do you think you are to stand apart from the rest of us? I'll tell you who you are—when there's no more air to breathe, you'll be one of the few who lives in the sealed air-conditioned cities while the rest of the world chokes, because you'll be needed to make them work." He shut up suddenly.

"Go ahead," Juan said, "finish what you have to say."

José Obrion took a deep breath. "You bow before a thing called knowledge, which doesn't help most people but keeps you amused. Ordinary peoples' lives are nothing to you."

"It's not like that at all."

"Then how is it?"

Juan shrugged. "We work, we do some good, we pass on what we know, much like everyone else."

"The 'we' sounds grand in your mouth. we work, we do some good. Listen to yourself lie!" He looked away and seemed to struggle with himself. "According to you, the rest of us don't live in the real world."

"I know how you feel," Juan said as he stood up, "but we need more expertise and better technologies, not less. Our kind's just come out of a disastrous century—we had problems never faced by any past civilization. You can't set the clock back and start again. We have to tame what we've created."

His father grimaced at him. "But we can't tame ourselves! It's like trying to organize pigs to become horses." He stared at him intently when Juan failed to answer. "Ahah—you don't really believe what you're saying."

"Isn't either of you going to eat?" his mother asked.

Juan shook his head. "I'm not hungry. I think I'll go for a walk."

José Obrion stared at his food, looking defeated. "I guess you'll just go on doing what you want. It's too late for the rest of us."

His mother followed him to the door. "He hasn't been himself," she explained. "Don't be too hard on him. He's getting old, and this is his way of letting go, of giving up so he doesn't have to feel the loss. Maybe you could spend some time alone with him tomorrow, before you leave."

Juan kissed her on the cheek. "You understand him. He's disappointed by life, but so are we all. Whatever he wants from me, I can't give him."

"Don't be angry, dear. It will only hurt you the way it did him."

"I'm not angry," Juan said, opening the door. She reached out to touch him as he hurried out. The door clicked shut.

He knew that she was looking after him through the small window as he went through the gate.

The street was full of people, faces set in expressions as uncomfortable as ill-fitting shoes. An old man hobbled past him, looking vaguely like his high school history teacher. Two women glanced at him from across the street, unsure whether they knew him or not. One of them resembled Angela, but he didn't look back to make sure.

Wind swirled leaves around him as he turned the corner and decided to get his bag from the station. He felt the infinity of his selves stepping across the fracture lines of probability, making all choices at once. He looked up at the overcast sky. The alien maze waited beyond the daylight of worlds. What will we do with it, he asked himself as his father's fears blossomed within him.

19

REUNION

At his left and right, as he entered the alien frame, Juan saw himself replicated to infinity, crossing the universe in perfect step. Lena confronted the line, searching for him among his endless doubles. She doubled by the power of two, determined to provide one of herself for each of his infinity, but it would still be forever before she found his original, and he would never know her. . . .

He awoke. The clock next to his bed glowed brightly. He focused and saw that it was a minute past nine in the morning. He sat up and brushed the touchplate below the clock face. The window of the hotel room lit up into a scene of ocean and palm trees. He pressed again, clearing the window to reveal the hazy New York skyline.

The phone buzzed.

"Yes?" he said.

"Are you up?" Lena asked. "I've been in the hotel since last night, but I didn't want to disturb you."

He leaned over and turned on the small screen. Her smiling face appeared. He smiled back, surprised at how glad he was to see her.

"How was your trip?" she asked.

He raised the bed to a sitting position and swiveled the screen up in front of himself. "My father wasn't much different from the man I remembered. How about you?"

"My parents are alive," she replied, "but my father is just as absent here, except that he sometimes sends a letter. I was also divorced a year ago—from the man I almost married before. It seems we're on good terms, judging from a note he sent." Her face became solemn. "What if we'd had a child? I can't imagine how I would have dealt with coming back to a child I didn't know, who would have been mine even if I hadn't carried it." She paused. "My mother's hair is blond here, but maybe she tints it. I think a few of my acquaintances have different eye colors. One oddity—a few street numbers are off by one or two."

Juan said, "My mother noticed my eye color, so I told her I was wearing contacts."

"And she believed you?"

"I didn't stay long enough to be found out. It's still our world, I suppose."

"Juan, may I come up?"

"Just give me a few minutes to shower."

He pushed the screen away as it faded. The phone buzzed again as he sat up on the edge of the bed.

"Yes?" he asked, afraid that Lena had found some reason not to see him.

The picture did not come on. "Obrion, this is Summet. This message will remind you that I'll be there some time before noon. Have your group ready. We have to be at the UN by half past noon."

There seemed to be no change in the ERS chief. Malachi still claimed to understand him, but he was the same old failed scientist playing at UN politics and supervising talent. He did his job, but an unfeeling bastard was an unfeeling bastard in all possible worlds, Juan told himself as he went into the bathroom to shower.

Malachi smiled and sat back on the hotel's sitting room sofa. "I went back to my family's village, just out of curiosity, please understand. And my grandmother was alive—the one who told me fanciful stories when I was a child."

"How did she greet you?" Lena asked, sitting cross-legged on the rug. Juan shifted from his slumped position in the heavy chair.

"She was convinced," Malachi said, "that I was filled with spirits. Came from traveling through their worlds."

"And the rest of your family?" Lena asked.

Malachi took out a cigarette, struck it on the pack, and took a deep drag. "Still in the ground, I'm afraid." He exhaled toward the ventilator.

The doorbell chimed. Juan looked toward it nervously. "Come in," he shouted.

It slid open and Magnus entered.

"Hello!" Malachi sang out. Lena stood up, smiling. Juan felt a moment of agony for the other Magnus as he rose to greet him.

"Summet won't be here until later this afternoon," Magnus said as he sat down in the straight-backed chair by the writing table.

There was a long, uncomfortable silence. Malachi crushed out his cigarette. Lena sat down uneasily on the edge of the sofa. "What is it?" Juan asked softly.

"What you would expect. Summet is under great pressure from the Russians, and just about everyone else, to share information. He's told them what he knows, namely that you left Earth in the alien starship and came back by a more advanced system to a second starship somewhere in Brazil. But of course Ivan Dovzhenko isn't satisfied with a second-hand report, and he wants the ship's location."

"We don't know exactly where it is," Malachi said.

"But you can find it?"

"Yes."

Magnus scratched the white stubble on his balding head. "Titus will brief you for the UN-ERS hearing."

Lena said, "You mean he's going to tell us what not to say."

Magnus took a deep breath. "Most everyone already expects to hear an edited version, so they'll be suspicious no matter how much you reveal. The major UN-ERS members are examining the satellite scans of the Amazon, and may want to send observers into the jungle. They have a right to do it, and a right to all ERS information."

"So what is Summet up to?" Lena asked.

"He wants to know everything first," Magnus replied. "Only a few people realize that the alien technology may affect us profoundly, so they're preparing to control how that will happen, or even if it will be permitted to happen. Titus is trying to keep the lid on, so the network of power cliques doesn't become paranoid. And he sees a chance to enhance ERS power, I'll admit. He sees no reason why it shouldn't benefit ERS. Given past ERS failures in world affairs, he feels that ERS both needs and deserves to have more authority."

"What do you think we should do?" Juan asked.

"Hold nothing back. The only safety lies in everyone knowing everything, whatever adjustments occur among the power groups."

"I agree," Lena added. "It's too late for secrecy. We must try to influence what happens."

Malachi said, "But will old Titus let us tell all?"

"What can he do?" Lena asked. "Can he lock us up, Magnus?"

"We'll know," Malachi said, "if he shows up with security types."

As they waited, Magnus said, "I wonder what determined that the three of you would return to this particular variant?"

"Are you suggesting that we had a choice?" Juan replied.

"Perhaps you all wished that I had not gone out there with you." He glanced at Juan as if about to add something.

"Pure speculation," Malachi said.

"Of course," Magnus answered. "But if it's true that the field of human experience branches as waves break into a mind, then a fluid reality is at every instant affected by a variety of factors, among them, perhaps, the will of the perceiver—which is just another determinism, but from the inside. Apply any force to the plenum of ghostly possibilities and a specific world presents itself."

"Are you suggesting," Juan said, "that there are no parallel variants, but one world which twitches through an infinity of states?"

Magnus smiled. "I'm not very clear. Perhaps that's all that branching should mean, with variants confined to our imaginations."

Malachi said, "But your ghosties would have to be actual in order to be able to come forward."

Magnus nodded. "Yes, but imagine a prime-world line, with an infinity of variant offshoots existing at lower energy states."

"It's chilling," Lena said, "to think there might be feebler versions of our lives, trailing off into nothingness. Some days it feels that way."

Magnus smiled. "Given the coarseness of our perceptual gear, such a shadowy world of low probability would still appear continuous to people living in it. We just can't see fine enough to see through it."

"They're all our world," Juan said, "except that we've moved from one to another and remember the previous one.

The builders of the web broke more than the tyranny of space-time."

"Still," Magnus continued, "reality always seems to be stubbornly one, with possibility only a sweet mirage."

Juan stood up and paced. "The question is what will the ships and the web do to our kind?"

"Some good, I hope," Malachi said, "by taking away the problems of scarcity."

Juan stopped pacing and sat down. "I just don't believe that a world of plenty will change human insides. Motives of power will affect how we change over to an energy-rich culture, and be with us long afterward."

Malachi said, "I don't see anything happening very quickly in the applications of the alien technology. Limited exploration of the web will be all we can manage. Perhaps even that will be forbidden when we tell Summet about the variant effect."

Juan took a deep breath. "Maybe delaying things is the best we can do."

The door chimed.

"Come in," Juan said.

It slid open, revealing Titus Summet and three men. They stayed outside as he came in and the door closed. He paused and looked at each person in turn. Juan gave him a nod. Lena stood up and sat down at one end of the sofa. Malachi leaned back at the other end and hooked a leg over the armrest. Magnus went to the window, glanced outside, then turned to face the gathering.

"Sorry I'm late," Summet said, grunting as he sat down in the empty chair. His graying brown hair and bushy eyebrows were unchanged, as was the scowl that twisted his eyebrows and deformed his nose. "I didn't want a hearing, but we're stuck with it." He shifted his stocky frame.

"Who'll be there?" Juan demanded.

Summet crossed his legs. "Security heads. ERS national chiefs. A few regular UN people. As few people as possible."

Juan leaned forward in his chair. "And you're here to tell us what to say."

Summet gave him a look of exasperation. "Now you know that we only have two choices—reveal everything or be selective. And it's pretty much up to the three of you, isn't it?"

"What do you mean?" Juan asked.

Summet looked around the room. "I want all of you to be satisfied. What would you have happen from all of this?"

"Are you so concerned?" Juan said.

Summet smiled at him. "Okay, Juan, I won't pretend to understand your motives. Maybe your dislike of me is understandable. I'll try to explain myself to you. The three of you are closest to what's been discovered, so I give you credit for having the best view of it as of now. It's bad science to keep secrets, and they can't be kept without eventual harm and embarrassment to all concerned. So tell me—what do you all know that will help us? Juan, I know I've been unfair to you in the past. All I can say is that my actions were necessary, and I'm sorry if you were offended. It wasn't personal, I assure you."

This was not quite the man Juan had known, even though the other might have said the same things in this situation.

"The ship took you on a ride," Summet continued, "but it didn't bring you back. According to Rassmussen's report, you concluded that the ship you left in and the ship through which you returned were being used to set up an interstellar transport system, and that the builders left through the frames once the ships were in place."

Juan nodded.

"And the ship in the Amazon is still linked to the ship that carried you away?"

"That's correct," Juan said.

"And you believe this alien system is quite extensive?"

"Yes."

"Now, what aren't you telling me?" Summet demanded.

Juan glanced at Lena and Malachi. Their expressions seemed to be saying that it was up to him. He looked toward Magnus, but the older man was gazing out at the New York skyline.

Summet said, "Juan, I know how you worry about things. Well and good. So do I, in my own way. But you can't live and not get your hands dirty, not if you want a chance to act and get a few things right. That's all the chance you may ever get, imperfect as it may be, to make things come out better than they would otherwise. You can't expect more from people, or from yourself."

A villain always imagines he's a hero, Juan thought. "You settle for too little," he said softly, noticing a roach making its way across the vast plain of the green rug.

Summet glanced at it when it came by him. "You're politically naive, and very lucky. Without this discovery you'd have priced yourself out of all human give-and-take." He paused, as if struggling with himself. "Why don't you tell me how we should handle this hearing?"

"You sound fearful of it," Lena said.

Summet shrugged. "You can be forced to appear and give testimony."

Juan stood up. "Are you threatening us with your goons?"

"Sit down, Juan. Do you want to destroy your career? I won't be able to help you past a point. Let me turn the question around. What's got the three of you so on edge? Tell me and I'll help. There's no other way."

Juan looked at Malachi, then at Lena as he sat down. Summet stared at him for a few moments. "Okay, we'll let it go. Maybe your judgment is better than mine and I shouldn't know more right now. But tell everything at the hearing that I know up to now—no more, no less. Or are you planning to surprise me there?" He leaned forward. "I'll be as naive as you are and ask you—is that what you're planning? I warn you, security is sifting through everything it can get its hands on. Care to speak up now?"

"Just what is security doing?" Lena asked.

Summet waved his hand. "Just a run-through of your movements since you left Florida. Routine checks. Maybe they won't find anything, but if they do, it's out of my hands."

"Just what is in your hands?" Juan asked, looking over at Magnus, who was still staring out the window.

Summet sighed. "Not as much as you'd think."

20

THE HEARING

◑

"Dr. Obrion," Chairman Yamamura said, "we've read Dr. Rassmussen's debriefing report. I think I speak for all of us here when I saw that what we want from you now is not more details, but your assessment of the discovery's importance."

They sat around a doughnut-shaped table, under a ceiling of white light that seemed uncomfortably close. Six national ERS chiefs were present. Magnus and Summet were seated at the chairman's right.

"What did you learn of the ship's functioning?" Yamamura continued. "And why did it leave suddenly?"

Juan glanced at Lena and Malachi, who sat at his right. "We learned enough to survive, when one of us—quite by accident—discocvered the ship's replicators, which enabled us to duplicate our food and gear. In time we came to suspect that the ship draws power directly from a net of stars, thus avoiding the need to carry the vast amounts of fuel necessary for interstellar voyages."

The big Hawaiian shifted in his chair and smiled. "Be more specific, Dr. Obrion, so that my colleagues can appreciate what this technology might mean for our food and energy economies." Yamamura motioned for Juan to continue.

"Sun stations sit at the cores of net stars," Juan said, "but in hyperspace, congruent with the star's position in our space. Unlimited power, practically speaking, flows through the foreshortened channels of this otherspace, feeding, I suspect, a whole fleet of starships. The core of the power units within stars wink in and out of normal space to draw energy from each star in the web."

"If I may ask, Dr. Obrion, and please don't take offense, but how did you find all this out?"

Skeptical looks appeared on the faces of the other chiefs. The Russian scowled; the Chinese shifted nervously in his chair. The European seemed bewildered, while the South American smiled. The tall African was doodling on his notepad.

"Well, no one came and told us," Juan said softly.

The South American laughed. The Russian chuckled.

"What led us to our conclusion," Juan continued, "was a series of events. The ship attained a significant fraction of light speed. We concluded that from the color shifts we saw in the stars fore and aft. Then, as we approached a star, the ship winked in and out of normal space, as if taking a navigational sighting, and jumped into otherspace for the approach to the suncore station. We can't be sure why it made this stop, but it might have been for maintenance. As the ship left the station, we saw the same sun again in jumpspace and in normal space."

"Remarkable," Yamamura said after a moment of silence. "Do continue, Doctor."

"The ship took us a great distance, possibly even to the red limit of the universe as measured from Earth. As you know, we were separated from the ship, but the way we returned to it revealed to us the more advanced transport system that brought us home. That system itself, given ships powered through a web of shortspace connections, is a logical development from a ship system, implicit in the way the ships function and are powered. We're not certain if the patterns of frame travelers are destroyed and recreated, or if any two frames simply collapse distance between entrance and exit, but we can see how such a system grew."

"Please be more detailed," Igor Altov said.

"The ships came first," Juan continued, "but when the power web was formed, making interstellar jumps possible, it also laid the basis of the frame system. The ships were then used to set up the frames, and remained useful for local travel, but it was no longer necessary to send elaborate vessels through either normal or jumpspace, except to extend the web. These ships were probably developed from primitive forms of interstellar craft—costly generation arks and relativistic ships, demanding huge sacrifices of time and energy to move from star to star. The first jump ships needed even more energy, but they gave the alien engineers the capacity to enter otherspace, and hence to invade the cores of suns and harness their power, transmitting along foreshortened lines to ships which could now go anywhere and never lack for fuel. With the control of increasingly larger amounts of energy, culminating in the suncore taps, they were able to send ships to any distance, expending as much energy as was needed to do so. Whatever it took, they had it. And then they simplified passage by adding frames at the terminals of the web's power flow. This final step established frame links between ships, using the lines of power transmission through jumpspace, and joined all suncore stations, all ships, and all visited worlds, as well as providing the means to expand the web. The ships remained useful for local journeys and for setting up new terminals, but became unnecessary for most interstellar passages. Many were abandoned, or left as terminals as various worlds."

"And you've seen this for yourselves?" Yamamura asked.

"What we have seen," Juan said, "suggests this logical line of development."

There was a long silence. The chairman said, "You're telling us that the solutions to the major problems of human survival already exist, that aliens have accomplished more than we can hope for in centuries of technical progress."

Juan nodded. "I'm sorry our kind seems a piker in the larger scheme of things, but you wanted an assessment."

"So where are these starcrossers?" Altov demanded.

Juan leaned forward and folded his hands together on the table. "Our encounters, if we can even call them that, were ambiguous. We felt that our minds were—well, visited on several occasions, by what might have been some kind of teaching program originating in the ship's systems. We never met with any living beings. There was a pile of skeletons in one of the ship's chambers, and we saw images of humanoid types, but we didn't meet any living entities."

The Russian cleared his throat. "So this vast system is deserted?"

"As far as we explored, there was no life."

"So where are they, Doctor?" Altov asked. "So advanced, so mighty. Do you think they all perished?"

Juan looked directly at him. "We just don't know."

"Doctor, we have something of a problem with your presence here," Yamamura said suddenly. Altov swallowed hard, then took out a cigarette and lit it. Juan sat back and waited.

Yamamura frowned. "We have reason to doubt your identities."

"What?" Juan asked.

Summet stood up. "Mr. Chairman, I'm afraid you are the victim of erroneous security reports."

"With all due respect to the ERS chief," Yamamura continued, "Juan Obrion, Lena Dravic, and Malachi Moede do not seem to be the same people who disappeared when the alien spacecraft left Antarctica. Their eye color and fingerprints fail to match our records. Granted, eye color may be a matter of shade and lighting, but the fingerprints are off just enough to make it impossible for these people to be who they claim. We have this from routine security procedures."

Summet said, "Mr. Chairman, eye color can be changed. Fingerprints can be matched perfectly in a surgical double. So why would anyone bungle it so obviously? You've merely turned up technical mistakes in the records. I have mascon satellite readings for the location of the ship from which these three scientists emerged. Who is it you suspect, and what motive would they have?"

Yamamura shrugged; his face sagged. "I don't wish to accuse anyone."

A young man with blond hair walked into the room and sat down next to Altov. Ivan Dovzhenko, Juan noticed, still looked too stocky for his height.

"Please sit down, Dr. Summet," Yamamura said. "I want to question these people further, if you please."

Summet sat down; his eyes narrowed as he glanced at Juan.

"Dr. Obrion," Yamamura continued, "if that is who you are—can you enlighten us about any of this?"

"The three of us are not responsible for the mistakes of others," Juan replied.

Yamamura was silent for a few moments, then said, "The three of you will be detained until this matter is resolved. Security officers will meet you as you leave the chamber."

Summet stood up. "No, Mr. Chairman, they'll remain free in my custody, according to the written authority I have here in my pocket, a copy of which has been transmitted to your office. Dr. Obrion and his colleagues will stay at their hotel. My own security team will be responsible for them. I suggest that you stop wasting ERS time."

Yamamura sat back and wiped sweat from his face. Then he picked up his water glass and took a long sip. "Meeting adjourned," he said, glaring at Summet.

"Yamamura's an ass," Summet said back in the hotel suite. "Sooner or later he'll hang himself."

"Careful," Malachi quipped, leaning against the door. "We may be bugged."

Summet sat down in the straight-backed chair. "This is one of my safe places. That's why you're all here."

"You knew, didn't you," Lena said, sitting forward on the couch.

Summet nodded. "I knew about the eyes and prints a few hours ago. Yamamura tried hard to delay my getting the information." He smiled. "Obviously the three of you haven't been redoing yourselves—so what's the explanation? My security people are very puzzled."

Juan was silent as he sat down in the heavy chair. Lena and Malachi looked apprehensive.

"We've got to get along better," Summet said, sounding worried. "Look, if you three can explain what's happened to you, I can get the UN Sec General to demand Yamamura's resignation. The man has no judgment about complex issues, especially when it comes to Russians and Chinese. It's all heroes and villains to him, and I'll be damned if I'll have him around any longer. He's also slow—he doesn't know yet that the Russians found a third ship in the steppes of central Asia."

"We suspected there might be a third ship," Juan said.

The door buzzed. Malachi stood aside. It slid open and Magnus came inside. "I have news," he said, sighing as he sat down next to Lena on the sofa.

"Well, out with it," Summet said.

"The ship found by the Soviets has taken off with three of their people on board."

"They walked right into it," Juan said, "just as we did."

"Dovzhenko's very upset."

"How did you find out?" Lena asked.

"They told us, but we also had routine satellite pickups

and eyeball sightings from one of the Low Orbit labs. The sphere came up fast and was gone in an instant. Shook our people up."

Malachi chuckled to himself.

The door buzzed. "Come in!" Summet shouted.

The door slid open and Ivan Dovzhenko entered, looking dour. Summet got up and gave him his chair. The Russian smiled uneasily as he sat down; he was no longer the self-assured man Juan had met in the Antarctic. "Do you think I could have a drink?"

"Vodka?" Summet asked as he went over to the phone.

"No, Scotch, please."

"Add a bottle of bourbon," Juan said.

"Summet punched in the order.

"You've lived in the West for some time, haven't you?" Lena asked.

Dovzhenko nodded, as if confessing a sin.

"Now, Ivan, what is it?" Summet asked. "Is your job in danger?"

Dovzhenko smiled uneasily and asked. "They all know?"

"Of course."

The red light went on over the bar. Malachi went over as the panel opened, took out the tray, and carried it to the coffee table. Dovzhenko pulled his chair over, leaned forward, and poured himself a shot. "Excuse my manners." He took it fast and let out a deep breath. "That's better. Miserable stuff." He looked up at Summet. "You're going to have to send your people after our ship, since they've had the experience. Dr. Obrion, can our group get into fatal difficulties?"

"We might easily have not returned," Juan said, pouring himself a drink over ice. "Why did they enter the ship? You knew the danger." He gave his drink to Lena and made himself another.

"I would have prevented it, if I had known in time. The ERS report should have been warning enough, I suppose, but the curiosity of our people was to great. I think my superiors wanted a team in the ship whether it took off or not, even if it endangered lives."

Summet sat down on the arm of the sofa. "But the report clearly suggested that the first ship took off because it was entered."

"I told them that," Dovzhenko said. "The question now is

can we catch up with this ship? Is it linked with the ship in the Amazon?" He poured himself another shot and gulped it down. "We'll all be exploring the alien system sooner or later, so why not start right now?"

"You're thinking of this as a rescue mission," Lena said, sipping her drink. "Aren't you underestimating your team?"

A stern look came into Dovzhenko's face. "Shouldn't we do what we can, rather than hope for the best?"

"Titus, may I have a word with you in private?" Juan asked.

Dovzhenko poured himself another shot, downed it, and got up. "I'll be out in the hall."

"You didn't have to insult him," Summet said as the door slid shut. "My job is to involve everyone in ERS matters. It keeps the peace."

"Civilizes the brutes," Malachi quipped, lighting a cigarette.

"There's too much suspicion and secrecy in this already," Summet said.

Juan glanced at Magnus, Lena, and Malachi. "Titus, we may not be able to go after the Russians."

Summet focused on him. "So now you'll tell me what you've held back."

"Yes," Juan said. "The frames are unstable."

"You mean they can't be used?"

"They can, but they're a kind of Schrödinger's Door, leading into variants of our world line."

Summet stood up. "What?"

"The security chaps were quite correct," Malachi said. "We're not quite the group that left here. Our Magnus Rassmussen died out there, for one thing. Juan's father is alive here, and there are the differences of eye color and fingerprints."

Magnus said, "I gave them a shock when I turned up in Miami."

Summet sat down and was silent.

"So you see why we have to think twice about going after the Russians," Juan said, watching Summet closely. The ERS chief nodded grimly. "Should we tell Dovzhenko?"

Summet looked up at him. "We'll tell him, but will he or anyone else believe it? I'm not sure I believe it. I have only your word."

"It's true, Titus," Juan said.

Summet looked reproachfully at Rassmussen. "What do you think?"

"The variant effect may limit the web's usefulness to us," Magnus said. "If these people go out again, they'll move even further into probability. They're already at one remove from the world they remember as their starting point. They would return here, and be in most respects the people we knew, but they will not be the three people who left, let's say, World Prime. These three people will move on, even though a group will return here to fulfill the symmetry."

"Will the variant effect always occur?" Summet asked.

"We can't know," Magnus replied. "All we have is the experience of the group from what I call World Prime. I would like to believe that the effect works along natural lines of probability, by which I mean along breaks that are plausible, not gratuitous."

The door buzzed. "Yes?" Summet said.

It slid open, revealing Dovzhenko.

"Come in," Summet said, pointing to his chair.

The Russian came forward unsteadily and sat down. "Thank you," he said, as if all heaven had just given him his due.

Summet looked at Juan. "Bring him up to date."

"What do you think, Magnus?" Summet asked when Juan was finished.

Rassmussen began to pace. "There may be a profound psychological component which we don't understand. Variant worlds may in fact be one world presenting itself to an observer in a skewed fashion."

"I don't understand," Lena said. "Are you telling me you're an illusion?"

"Not at all," Magnus replied. "It's all real enough. Passage through the frames has made a normal process of choice more visible, by moving observers through more than one set of outcomes. The psychological component may be the possibility of observers being drawn to one set of outcomes rather than another." Juan felt uneasy as Magnus looked at him.

"So all the variants are real," Summet said.

Rassmussen shrugged. "In a practical sense it may be useful to regard the variants as having a separate existence, but there may be times when it might help us to think it's all one world. We may never be able to prove anything. I'll put my money on one world that is branching infinitely—but the psychological component may be beyond us."

"What do you mean?" Dovzhenko asked.

"Despite the variant personalities, they are in a sense all the same person."

Dovzhenko shook his head in disagreement. "Separate," he announced. "They must be separate. We know these people differ from the ones we have in our records."

"True," Lena said, "but I also feel that this is still our world. I think that's what Magnus is getting at."

The same unfortunate world, Juan thought bitterly, nothing better.

Summet said, "As I see it, travelers through the frames will return to variants of their world, but those who greet them in each variant will see only minor differences, if they see any at all. Outwardly, Juan Obrion will remain continuous—except for his memories."

Juan smiled. "You're such a behaviorist, Titus."

"Well, from the viewpoint of nontravelers the changes are likely to be minor."

"So far," Juan said, wondering if there were radically advanced forms of humanity tucked away somewhere in the probabilities. A happier Earth might exist, ruled by an improved human nature. He imagined an infinity of his doubles, all seeking a better world across the endless variations. It seemed unlikely that his kind's failings could hold all chance in chains.

Summet asked, "Is it possible to return to the same variant? Or to a world where the differences are so minor you'd never notice them?"

"We could only find out by trying," Juan answered, "but I wouldn't rule it out. I suspect travelers would always return to probabilities that are clustered around the one from which they started, which suggests they might even return to their original one." He looked at Lena. She bit her lower lip and Juan knew what Summet was about to propose.

"What's one more shift?" Summet asked, looking directly at him. "You should have no objection to taking another assignment, since you've already lost your prime world. You might even regain it."

"You have the sensitivity of a toilet seat," Lena said.

Summet nodded. "Well, I do assume you would all go together. What do you expect? I have problems to solve, so

I reach for the means at hand. You can understand that, can't you? After all, you thought it best to keep this from me, even though you claim to be against secrecy."

"We don't have to go," Juan said. "The Russian team will learn the same things we did and get back on their own."

"If they survive," Dovzhenko said. "You might find them before they encounter complications. They are your colleagues, after all."

"Juan," Summet said, "do you think there is a frame connection into the Russian ship?"

Juan nodded. "Very likely, since the other two ships are linked. They might have come as a trio to set up frame stations in this solar system."

"What about you, Mal?"

"It's a good bet Juan is right. There may even be a station in our sun."

"You mean their web is tapping our sun?" Dovzhenko asked.

"Very possibly," Malachi replied.

Juan heard the chirp of the phone from his bedroom. "Excuse me," he said, getting up.

The sound became insistent as the door slid aside. He went in and hurried to the desk. His mother's face appeared as he opened the line.

"Juan," she said, her face drawn and tearful, lips trembling.

I know, he thought, *I know.*

He sat on the bed as if it were the edge of the world, with his feet dangling into infinity. A wind stirred in the far dark, whirling the galaxies away like milkweeds.

"Juan?" Lena said as she came into the room. "What is it?" She sat down next to him.

"My father's dead. Massive cerebral hemorrhage while he was driving. He managed to pull off the road. No chance of doing anything by the time they found him."

She touched his hand. "Juan, I'm so sorry."

"He was mine only by courtesy. I guess I'm upset because we embraced when I left, and he looked as if he was a bit sorry to see me go."

She put her arm around him. *Fathers*, he thought. *We have them because deep structures make us yearn for inherited identity. Another adaptive evolution might have given different social meanings to genetic origins.*

He turned to Lena and said in a trembling voice, "We're

alone, the three of us. You and Mal are the only ones I have left from our world."

"We've a new friend in Magnus," she replied.

"Ivan is right," he said. "The variants are separate places, no matter how familiar they might seem."

"But they are all variants of our world," Lena insisted, moving closer to him.

He looked at her. "We'll go and find the Russians. It's the only thing that makes sense to me now. We can't count on them having all the luck we did. Think of what we might learn. You want that, don't you?"

She nodded and was silent for a few moments. "Titus is right," she said finally. "We've already cut loose from our world. There's not much more we can lose."

"Except each other," he said. "Are you sure?"

"We'll all be together."

A chill went through him as he recalled how the expansion of humanity into space had once beckoned to him like a liberation. The new reality that science and technology, together with a great new age of exploration, might one day deposit in the human heart, now seemed even more remote. The opening of the alien web might let loose the inner beasts of human nature onto an unprecedented scale of action. Explorers would go out for reasons of humanity, or from a passionate love of knowledge, but the power brokers, operating from the deepest mazes of human motivation, would pursue their own satisfactions.

"I know what you're thinking," Lena said. "We've all thought about it, even Titus. He's got to make certain things happen, even if they don't come out as they should. But we have to do what we think is right without expecting a guarantee of success."

She was right; he had always wanted the world to reform itself by next Tuesday. In reality, human development lurched along a tortured path toward holocaust or heaven, without ever reaching either. Few revolutionary acts had succeeded, yet there seemed to be net progress in the flow of history. Hope shaped development, despite the demoralization of individuals. Perhaps there were variant histories where most aspirations were not crushed, and he was being given the chance to go find them.

Lena got up and went to the door. "Dovzhenko's being very demanding," she whispered.

Juan stood up. "Don't say anything about my father."

"Are you all right?"

"I will be."

Dovzhenko was sitting on one of the bar stools drinking coffee when Juan and Lena came out of the bedroom. "Dr. Obrion," he asked, "can there be some mistake about all this?"

"I don't think so," Juan replied, sitting down in the straight chair.

"We must consider," Summet said, "who should know about the probability effect."

The Russian smiled. "I take it your inclination is to tell as few people as possible?"

Summet glanced at Juan. "I'm not sure."

Rassmussen sat back on the sofa and asked, "Is it going to be a secret or not?"

Lena went over and sat down next to him. "The three of us who came back," she said, "have deep misgivings. Perhaps the variant effect will make the web unusable."

"I doubt that," Dovzhenko answered. "It will be used, if only by a corps of professionals like yourselves."

Summet grimaced at Juan. "Life was much simpler only a few hours ago."

"Not simpler," Dovzhenko said, pouring himself more coffee. "Different. Believe me, I know all about variant histories. Our Russian archives are full of the ones we've repudiated."

"So what do we do?" Summet asked.

Dovzhenko downed his coffee. "My answer is to simply let the circle of those who know grow according to necessity."

"Juan, what do you think?" Summet asked.

Juan shrugged. "Sounds reasonable."

"And you, Magnus?"

"Leave well enough alone for now."

"Lena?"

"As long as there's no absolute policy of secrecy. But we should tell a few people right away. What if something happens to Titus while we're gone?"

Summet nodded. "Juan, make a full report. I'll sign it and put it in a safe place. Malachi?"

The Kenyan smiled, sat back on the sofa, and clasped his hands behind his head. "We see ourselves as a small elite, making decisions on behalf of humanity's better impulses. In this case, I think we're justified in being cautious—but we should be cautious of our caution also."

Summet nodded. "Juan, I'll want your report as soon as possible. Ivan, you'll get the help you wanted."

Juan said, "Titus, I'd like you to find a man—Yevgeny Petrovich Tasarov—a mathematician whose work may help us understand variants. I want to talk with him before we go after Ivan's people."

Summet nodded. "Ivan, do you know of him?"

The Russian shook his head. "Never heard of him."

Summet looked at Juan. "I'll find him. What do you think he knows?"

"I won't know until I talk to him."

The phone buzzed in the darkness. Juan felt Lena's comforting shape stir next to him. "It might be important," she said.

He reached over to the glowing panel, resentful of being pulled back into his waking identity; for an instant it seemed incredible that he was himself.

"Yes?" he said as he opened the audio.

"Juan? Summet. Dovzhenko will be going with you. Any objections? I have to know right now."

"Does he want to?"

"He was promoted and ordered to go. I think you'll be able to handle him."

"Remember, he's not quite the person we knew, and we didn't know him very well."

"Well, they do have a right," Summet said. "Sorry to disturb you, but I tried to find Tasarov, and no one knows how to contact him, anywhere. It's the damnedest thing. Do you want me to keep trying?"

"Yes," Juan said.

The phone's glow died. He lay back. Lena nestled against him, then kissed his shoulder. "Get some sleep," she whispered.

He closed his eyes and waited for oblivion. "Are you sorry we did this?" he asked, completely awake.

"No," she murmured.

21
DEEP SKY

◐

The Amazonian sky blazed blue and gold above the green canopy. Juan peered around at the jungle through protective lenses. It crowded in around the hill, as if reluctant to give up the alien it had buried so long ago.

Titus had allowed him a couple of days to attend the funeral. He had sat through another requiem mass, said for his father by a different priest, and had comforted his sobbing mother just as he had her younger variant years ago. Once again, the door to the mausoleum slot had squeaked as his father's remains were locked away.

"Astounding growth," Malachi said as he adjusted his sun helmet and started to dig. "And scarcely a month since we were here."

Juan snapped open his spade and began to dig with him, then glanced up at the ocean of sky and wondered if the alien web penetrated all of space-time. Sometimes he still felt that he already knew enough to solve the mystery of the builders, but nothing came; the suspicion was an illusion.

"Hello," Malachi said suddenly, "here we go." Dirt was running down into the sinkhole.

Juan unclipped the handset from his belt and said, "Ivan, Lena, we've dug through."

"I'll call in the supply drop," she replied from the highway cruiser.

"Lock up," he added.

"Leaving in five minutes."

"Take your time and follow the trail," he said, watching Malachi peer into the opening.

• • •

As they sat on the hillside, Lena asked, "Ivan, are you leaving anyone behind?"

He shook his head in denial and leaned forward to hug his knees.

"There it is," Malachi said, lowering his binoculars.

Juan stood up and saw the copter coming in from the east, low over the jungle. Give nature a billion years, he thought, and it evolves a new kind of insect to skim over the forest. "You should see us," he said into the handset.

"Got you," a voice crackled.

The copter beat its way toward them and landed on the hilltop, throwing dirt and greenery in all directions. As Juan led the way up, a tall figure climbed out under the slowing blades and staggered down toward them.

"Magnus!" Juan shouted, rushing up to him.

"I'm coming with you," he said as they shook hands. "Direct order from Titus—but I do want to go. Medics gave me a clean bill of health, so don't look so worried."

Juan smiled at him. Lena gave him a hug. "Glad you're here," Malachi said. Ivan shook the older man's hand.

"Where do you want this stuff?" a man shouted from the copter's cargo bay.

"Right here!" Juan answered.

Plastic containers were handed out to them.

"You found the opening?" Magnus asked as they stacked the supplies.

"It's right there," Juan said, pointing to the narrow opening. "There's a sinkhole just below, then our tunnel goes down at forty-five degrees, right into the lock."

Under a sky aglow with stars, the jungle cradled the hill, filling the night with insect sounds and animal cries. Juan shivered in the penetrating humidity as he sipped his hot tea. They had pulleyed their supplies down into the open lock, but none of them had wanted to stay overnight in the ship.

Ivan said, "The forest is mother and father, dreaming up creatures and gobbling them up."

Malachi smiled and poured himself another cup of tea from the pot on the warmer.

"The forest is elegant," Ivan continued, "clean and free of sentiment or regrets." He smiled at Malachi. "You find that bleak, don't you?"

Malachi sipped. "I wouldn't want to offend you or the forest."

"Tell me, Ivan," Lena said, sitting up on her pack, "did you know any of the people who went into the other ship?"

"Never met them. They all have good reputations, according to their files."

Juan recalled what he had read in the ERS profiles Titus had provided. Dita Kirilovna Karenina was a Czech-born biologist, the daughter of a Russian diplomat. Isak Alexandrovich Bilenkin was an astrophysicist—Juan had read a few of his papers in scientific journals—and Yerik Mahmoudovich Khasan was an electronics expert from the Central Asian city of Chimkent. There was no mention of marriages or children. Another bunch of loners, he had thought; few would worry about them if something went wrong. They would adjust more easily to the variant effect.

"Names are a hobby of mine," Lena said. "Dita means rich gift. Isak means an identical point—it's a name used to invoke the powers of God. And Yerik is the appointed of God."

Ivan scowled and said, "A rich gift and the appointed of God might be able to call on His help in their situation. But given the variant effect, the identical point might have some trouble remaining one." He laughed.

"Very clever," Malachi said.

The Russian grimaced, then looked toward the dark opening in the hillside.

"Get some rest," Juan said, and climbed into his sleeping bag. Lena touched his hand as she settled into hers next to him.

"Good night, chaps," Malachi said.

Juan gazed up at the bright stars and wondered about the alien giants who had stepped through the constellations, then closed his eyes and drifted into the deep sky.

"We'll have to clear the lock," Juan said as the three of them waited for Ivan to crawl down.

The Russian's head emerged from the tunnel. Juan and Malachi pulled him through into the blue-lit chamber. "But will not that risk the ship taking off?" Ivan asked as they helped him to his feet.

"Yes," Juan said, "but the outer lock must close before the inner one will let us in. We have no choice."

"It's not certain it will take off," Malachi added. "This ship seemed less active. I don't believe that simply letting the lock close will make the ship stir. If it wanted to take off, that lock would get a command to become a solid barrier whatever the obstruction."

Juan picked up the two spades lying across the opening. "Step back."

They retreated. The lock glowed and became solid.

"Now watch this," Juan said as he turned and stepped forward. The inner lock glowed, revealing the black floor of the winding corridor, reflecting the receding squares of yellow-orange ceiling lights.

"Still works," Malachi said.

Ivan and Magnus stepped through and peered into the winding passage.

"Listen," Magnus said.

Juan heard the familiar distant whisper.

"Ventilation?" Magnus asked.

Juan nodded, imagining a draft pulling between the worlds, rushing through frames as they opened and closed deep within the ship.

"Or someone forgot to close a door," Ivan said.

Magnus took a deep breath. "Tastes richer in oxygen."

They listened to the soft sighing of the ship. "It's as if something knows we're here," Ivan said.

Juan turned away. "We'd better get into our oversuits and decide what we'll take with us from these supplies."

Juan counted the doorlike indentations as he led the way down the winding passage.

"What are all these chambers for?" Ivan asked.

Juan stopped and faced an oval on his right. "Watch this." He stepped forward. The oval glowed and he stepped through—

—into the white room with cubbyholes. He turned at once, triggered the glow and slipped out—

—into the passage. "This is it," he said, noticing the look of wonder on Ivan's face. "Didn't you see this in Antarctica?"

"No—I only arrived in time to see the ship break from the ice."

"Follow me through," Juan said as he turned, triggered the glow again, and passed—

—into the brightness of the chamber.

The others came through as he took off his pack and laid

it down on one of the tables. "What is this place?" Ivan asked.

"Give me a chocolate bar, old chap," Malachi said.

Lena got one out first and handed it to him. He went up to the wall of square cubbyholes and placed the bar inside one of the openings, waited a moment, then removed the bar. The small chamber glowed and a duplicate bar appeared. Malachi took it out and tossed it to Ivan.

Ivan tore off the wrapper, took a cautious bite, and said, "Very fine fruit and nut. My favorite."

Juan said, "We'll leave an assortment of provisions here, in case we have to make more. This bit of magic saved our lives when we were running out of water in the other ship."

Magnus was staring at the wall. "Of course—this replicator, the lock, the doorways—all basic manipulations of matter at the smallest scale. It's delightful."

Juan smiled. "You said something like that here before."

Lena said, "There's another chamber like this deeper in the ship."

"Those larger cubbyholes," Juan said, pointing to the base of the wall, "are waste recyclers."

"We could feed the world from these automats!" Ivan exclaimed.

"It would mean the end of business and currency," Juan said, "for starters."

Ivan shrugged. "What does that matter? Another kind of economy would form, of course, based on the control of these replicators, but at least no one would ever starve again."

Juan said, "Let's decide what we're going to leave here."

They marked the door with a red sticker and resumed their downward march.

"Here's the gravitic well," Malachi said as they came to the drop tube and looked down. "I fell in. Wasn't very dangerous, I'm afraid. That's what it's for."

"Summet came after us into the ship," Lena explained, "and startled us. You were with him, Ivan."

The Russian looked startled. "I'm very sorry." He shook his head. "But of course that was another Ivan."

"Clumsy of me," Malachi said.

Juan said, "Come on—we may be needed."

22

CROSSWORLDS

Juan halted in the passageway and pointed left. "That's the entrance to the drum-shaped chamber we camped in after our ship took off."

Ivan asked, "Are the ships truly identical?"

"I've seen no differences yet," Juan said. Magnus approached the entrance at an angle and marked it with a red sticker.

"What's in there?" Ivan asked.

"I think it's a kind of command area and stellar chart room—even though the ship seems to run itself."

"Is there no way to set its course?" Ivan asked.

"If there is," Juan said, "we haven't the slightest idea of how to go about it."

"How big is the ship?" Ivan asked.

"I estimate it's a ball some two kilometers in diameter. This wide corkscrew passage is much longer, of course, I suspect it runs down to the center of the ship, maybe all the way down to its south pole. My pedometer says we've come over three kilometers now. There may be nearly ten kilometers of winding passage in this sphere."

Ivan laughed. "I feel like a worm in an apple."

The Russian's cheerful outbursts irritated Juan, but he preferred this Ivan to the previous close-lipped official. That humorless man had been more dedicated to his job; this one appeared anxious to distance himself from his superiors.

Ivan gestured as they moved deeper into the ship. "Look how clean. No dust anywhere. It looks as if it were built yesterday."

Juan said, "We're almost at the entrance to the shuttle

bay." He led them around the wide bend, where the passage suddenly ran straight, and stopped at the left turn. "It seems to end there," he said, pointing to the large entrance.

Malachi said, "It's about ten times larger than any oval we've seen."

"Turn on your helmet lights," Juan said, moving forward.

The other followed him up to the entrance; he looked around at his companions.

"Ready," Ivan said.

Juan stepped forward. The portal glowed and he passed—

—into the dark chamber. He went forward and faced the six frames as his companions came through behind him.

"They're large," Ivan said. "Which one did you come back through?"

"Second from the left," Malachi said, "connects with Ship One, which as far as we know is still sitting in a suncore millions of parsecs away. I tried the first frame from the left. It leads into a branching corridor somewhere."

Ivan asked, "But the second frame leads into an identical chamber in Ship One?"

"Yes," Juan said.

"Then it's possible that the third frame from the left may lead into Ship Three?"

"It's possible," Malachi replied. "We'll try it next, to be systematic."

"Mal," Magnus said, "did you say you went through the first frame alone?"

"Yes. I know what you're thinking, but I came back immediately, and have seen no shift in details."

"Come to think of it, I also went through alone," Juan said, "into a double of this chamber, and came back immediately. The air was warm." He felt uneasy as he stepped up to the third frame. "Link hands," he said, "so we'll pass through as one body. For what it's worth, we'll know that we're exactly the same people when we come out." Even though he might no longer be the same person this Lena had known, he told himself. Mal and he probably had that much in common with Magnus now.

They linked hands. He pulled through into an identical chamber of frames, then glanced back and saw the others emerging like a chain of cutouts.

"Air's good," he said.

He let go of Lena's hand and faced the exit. It glowed coal red and he stepped—

—out into an identical winding passage.

He moved aside and watched his companions slip out through the glow, then motioned for them to be silent. "I hear voices," he whispered.

"Yes," Ivan said excitedly. "Russian."

He listened, and also heard a distant crying, like that of children.

"They're coming toward us," Ivan said as the footfalls grew louder. "Hallo!" he shouted.

Two dark figures made the turn and came forward rapidly. Juan saw two Soviet soldiers. Ivan raised a hand, called out in Russian, and went forward to meet them.

"Stop!" one of the soldiers cried as they both pointed their automatic rifles at him.

Ivan halted and raised his arms. The soldiers approached him warily. He spoke to them in Russian. They stopped in front of him and lowered their weapons. He conversed with them quietly for a few moments, then raised his voice, as if startled by something. One of the men turned and marched away. Ivan turned and came back. The remaining soldier kept his eyes on them.

"What's up?" Malachi asked.

Ivan looked pale. "We're in the Soviet Union, and there's been a nuclear war. Apparently we've entered a variant in which Ship Three did not take off." He drew a deep breath. "The ship has become a refuge for survivors of the nuclear exchange, which seems to have ended a few days ago." He dropped his pack behind him and sat down on it.

Stunned, they all looked at one another. Juan wanted to take Lena by the hand and hurry back through the frame, to consign this variant to the unreality from which it had sprung. Ivan looked up at him with tear-filled eyes. The soldier watching them seemed puzzled and sad.

Shouts echoed in the passageway; heavy footfalls grew louder. Two soldiers and a civilian came around the turn and stopped. The remaining soldier went to them.

Ivan got to his feet. "Who are they?" Juan asked him.

"The civilian is the senior division scientist of our propulsion section. He died two years ago."

"Do you know him?"

"Not very well, but he'll know me."

The civilian left the three soldiers and approached. "My name is Anatoli Kaliapin," he said. "I've been expecting you, Dr. Obrion. And these must be Drs. Dravic and Rassmussen, and engineer Moede. I already know Mr. Dovzhenko."

"How bad is it outside?" Lena asked.

Kaliapin swallowed. "As bad as it can be. Did our team come through safely in Brazil?"

"What do you mean?" Juan asked.

"They did not arrive?"

Juan hesitated, then said, "By the time we left, no one had arrived."

Kaliapin took a deep breath. "If they went through the wrong frame, they will come back, if they're not in Brazil by now."

Lena asked, "Was it an all-out nuclear exchange?"

Kaliapin nodded. "The readings we took outside yesterday are high, and we haven't been able to reach anyone by radio."

"Who else is here with you?" Juan asked.

"A few military units. We're taking in anyone who finds his way to the lock."

Juan felt a slight vibration in his boots, but it died away. "Did you feel that?"

Kaliapin nodded. "Several times in the last few hours." He scratched his thinning brown hair. "You had no news before you left the ship in Brazil?"

"Nothing," Ivan answered. "What happened?"

"The Chinese crisis worsened. They would not accept restrictions on their oil- and coal-burning plants, claiming that the Soviet Union, Europe, and the United States were determined to crush their modernization. But surely you—"

Juan decided not to try to explain. "Have you explored any of the chambers along this passage?"

"A few, briefly. We've had our hands full."

"There are a few things you should know," Juan said.

Kaliapin asked, "Would you come with me? You can leave your packs here for now."

They left their gear and followed him and the soldiers up the passage. Juan saw the dismay in Lena's face as they walked. In their world, nuclear was had become unlikely; at least that was how it had seemed for most of his life.

He began to hear the sounds of human pain, and realized that he was not ready for what he was about to see. Lena slowed her pace and took his hand. Behind him, Malachi's step sounded hesitant. Ivan and Magnus stopped for a moment, then went on.

"Prepare yourselves," Kaliapin said in a breaking voice.

They followed him around the wide turn and saw the bandaged bodies of mothers and children, young men and women and old people, lying on stretchers and makeshift cots all the way to the next turn. Two medics were working their way down one row.

Kaliapin said, "There's little we can do for those we took in after the blasts except administer painkillers."

Juan heard Ivan curse in Russian. "Are we near a town?" Lena asked.

Kaliapin nodded. "There was a military base nearby. The ship was found during the building of missile emplacements."

"Do you have enough medical supplies?" Lena asked.

"No—but what we have is useless, except for the painkillers."

Something laughed monstrously in Juan's mind, and for a moment he believed that he would hate his own kind irrevocably. He looked at his companions. Malachi's jaw tightened as he clenched his teeth. Magnus was very pale. Ivan dropped to his knees and listened to a victim's whispers, as if he were a priest receiving a last confession. Juan felt himself begin to shake; Lena took his hand and held it firmly. No utopias, he thought, unable to laugh or cry. Passage through the frames would only reveal his kind's true face, with infinite variations.

"Come up toward the lock," Kaliapin said.

Ivan rose up and said something to him in Russian. His voice was soft, then demanding, then soft again, and it seemed to Juan that all the repetitious extremes of human history were contained in that sound.

Three soldiers and two civilians sat near the outer lock; they stood up as the group approached. Juan noticed that one of the young soldiers, a lieutenant, was staring at him with suspicion.

Kaliapin spoke to them in Russian, then presented the two civilians. "These men are the mayor and police chief of the

local community. I've told them that you were part of the
ERS team exploring the lower hemisphere of the ship and
were due out today."

Juan imagined with horror what it was like outside, as the
debris raised by the bombs darkened the planet into nuclear
winter. A woman's voice cried out as Kaliapin spoke the
names of the mayor and police chief. A child screamed. An
old man's moans echoed up the passage.

"We've had no radio contact for three days now," Kaliapin
was saying.

"You opened the lock?" Lena asked.

"Briefly, to use the radio."

Juan pulled himself together. "We have protective suits
and radiation counters. But before we do anything, there are
things you should know about this ship."

After they demonstrated the replicator, and explained the
variant effect of the frames, Kaliapin sat down on one of the
tables in the forward cafeteria and seemed about to burst into
tears. "It's like a fairy tale," he said, shaking his head. "All
this, and we had to destroy ourselves!" He stared past them
for a few moments, then said, "Let me understand correctly.
In the variant from which you have come, our Soviet team
was in the ship that took off—the alternate of this very ship."

"That's right," Juan replied, "while here they simply left
through one of the frames in the deep chamber."

"So they must be in the vessel that is presumably still in
the Amazon?"

Juan nodded. "If they went through the third frame from
the left. Were you there?"

"No," Kaliapin said. "Titus Summet had sent word that
the third frame might join with the Brazilian ship, but we
weren't certain. Our team might have decided to test one
frame after another, from left or right."

Juan said, "Then they might be in Ship One, or elsewhere
in the web. What may happen now is that a variant of your
team will arrive here if your original team manages a successful return to a variant of this world."

Kaliapin stared at the replicator wall.

"Do you understand, Doctor?" Juan asked.

Kaliapin looked back to him and said, "I'm grateful for the
knowledge you have brought us."

"You would have discovered this chamber in time."

"Perhaps. It means we shall be able to increase our medical supplies and food stores, and form a survival community. I admire your decision to pass through the frames, knowing that it would take you one more remove from your beginnings. You must be very dismayed to have chanced on a world that is now also lost."

Not chance at all, Juan thought. This outcome, and an infinity of other terrors, had been waiting to uncoil from the human heart in all possible worlds.

"I regret," Kaliapin continued, "that only fifty people were in the ship when the bombs struck. I fear that these fifty may be the only ones who will survive out of the six hundred who came in after the attack."

Juan thought of those who were still dying throughout the world. The planet's greenery might all be dead by the time the dust settled and let in the sun again. Only self-contained systems like this ship would be able to preserve human life. The Swiss had underground cities. There were various military installations deep inside mountains. He wondered if Titus had made a run for the ship in the Amazon, or been given refuge by one of his important friends.

"This is still our world," Lena said. "The five of us have moved across only a narrow range of possibility. Elsewhere, our alternates are searching for your team, and this world is only a fear in their minds."

"Yes," Kaliapin said bitterly, staring at the floor unconsoled. He stood up. "You will excuse me. I need to rest." He went to the exit. It glowed and he slipped out.

Juan felt helpless as he looked around at his companions. "Unfeeling as it may sound, there's little we can do here."

"We've already done it," Magnus said as he approached the wall and put his hand into one of the cubbyholes. The small chamber glowed and he pulled his hand back. When the bloody copy appeared, he took it out, removed the wedding band from the ring finger, then leaned down and pushed the hand into the disposal chamber. "Damn thing would copy me completely if it were big enough. Everything is everything else at bottom. A simple enough notion, but the engineering is not." He turned and looked at Juan. "It's not as demoralizing as it seems. Our beginnings in nanotechnology certainly point to all this, and we do appreciate the significance of what we're seeing."

Malachi said, "I would put the difference between us and

the builders of this ship as a bit less than that between a man and an ape."

"Maybe less than that," Magnus said.

Silently, they sat down around one of the tables and picked through the duplicated items for something to eat. Juan shifted uncomfortably on the hard floor and tore the wrapper from a chocolate bar. Magnus opened a package of dried fruit, took out one piece, and offered the rest to Malachi. Ivan took nothing.

"So do we stay or go?" Lena asked.

"This was quite unexpected," Malachi said.

Juan looked at Lena, and felt that he needed her approval for what he was about to say. "We know what's in the back of all our minds. These people can survive in this ship indefinitely, and they can do without us."

Ivan said, "You're assuming Kaliapin will let us go. I'm sure that he's already guessed that we might want to leave. He knows we have some experience with the ship. Trained, healthy people will be scarce."

"We'll do what we can to help," Juan said, looking at Lena, "before deciding. Kaliapin strikes me as an honorable sort."

"He is," Ivan answered, "but it's the army officers I fear. The time may come, and soon, when power will begin to rearrange itself within this group."

"Are you serious?" Lena asked.

Ivan said, "I hope I'm exaggerating, but I won't be a prisoner."

"We can at least take the atomspheric readings for them," Juan said.

Magnus sighed. "The feeling persists in me that all this hasn't happened."

"You'll feel differently," Lena said, "when you see the readings."

"We should duplicate all our equipment for them," Juan said.

Ivan asked, "Where are we going to sleep?"

"Below, in the drum-shaped chamber," Juan said, "near where we left our packs. We might as well move in."

"It's like coming home," Lena said as they unrolled their sleeping packs under the viewspace in the drum-shaped chamber. The amber glow was soothing as Juan lay down, aware that the ship seemed cozy only because the world outside was a ruin.

He recalled the seesaw of nuclear war debates. It could still happen, he had been told even during his boyhood. It was unlikely; it was inevitable. Humanity was too frightened to try it; it might happen by accident, and stop at an early stage. Conventional and biological warfare would be the prelude. Nuclear war was impossible because the technology was unreliable; the nation that struck first would win, because the electromagnetic pulse of the blasts would knock out the enemy's electrical systems, making it impossible to respond; but the victory would not be worth having. Finally the great powers had prepared to install space-based antimissile systems, both the kinetic and particle beam types, in the hope that the old missiles would be permitted to simply rot away—and the words themselves had precipitated peace, because the world had grown too poor to keep up with the cost of weapons. Mutual assurances and treaties were cheaper—the very threat of building new deterrence systems had finally deterred all sides. The peace had not been broken in his variant, except for police actions by the large powers against nuclear hopefuls; but elsewhere, he realized, all possible outcomes were playing themselves out. All variant worlds were real, he thought as he hovered near sleep. The fears of one were the realities of another, and each one suffered. . . .

Kaliapin met them at the outer lock the next morning. Juan checked his radiation counter, then looked at his companions. Kaliapin's sad, sober look was mirrored in all their faces.

"Just stick the thing outside," Malachi said, "and come right back in. We'll let it record for a few minutes, then grab it back."

Juan turned away and confronted the lock.

The inner door failed to glow. He stepped back and tried again, with the same result.

Lena said, "Maybe the lock won't open if the environment outside is too dangerous."

Juan felt a deep vibration in his boots. "Follow me," he said, turning away from the lock and heading down the passage.

"What is it?" Ivan asked as they all obeyed.

Juan hurried past the entrance to the forward cafeteria and stopped. "This is it, I think."

Malachi put a red sticker to the right of the indentation. Juan faced the entrance. "Follow me in," he said as the oval glowed and he stepped—

—into the darkness he knew from Ship One.

He went forward as if toward a cliff's edge, and came upon the reddish-brown globe of Earth swimming in a sea of stars. He waited for the others to come up beside him.

"The lock wouldn't open," he said, "because we've left the planet."

Countless fires burned on the nightside. A red-brown stain was spreading across the dayside, as if flowing from an open wound.

"Where are we going?" Kaliapin asked; his voice broke.

"We felt nothing of the takeoff," Magnus said.

"The ship was uncovered," Kaliapin explained, "which also made it an easy refuge."

"Why did it leave?" Lena asked.

"No way to know," Juan replied.

"Where will it take us?" Kaliapin asked.

The sun swam into view, flooding the chamber with light. Earth disappeared into the abyss as their feet. The sun grew larger.

"We seem to be heading sunward," Ivan said.

So there was a station here also, Juan thought as the electric glare of the great fusion furnace washed out the stars. Suddenly the sun was gone, and the ship was feeling its way toward the hidden harbor. A dead gray light filled the chamber.

"Where are we?" Kaliapin asked.

"We're coming into the suncore station," Juan said.

Diffuse white beams cut through the grayness. "There's something ahead," Ivan said, "but I sense it more than see it."

Juan felt it as before, something passing in and out of normal space-time with a slow, ponderous rhythm, as if trying to match his heartbeat. Again, in a distant part of himself, or in something other that had made itself part of him, he felt that he was coming home. Lena took his hand and held it tightly.

"I see it!" Ivan shouted as the black globe appeared directly ahead.

"The suncore station?" Kaliapin asked.

"Inside our sun," Malachi replied.

The globe grew larger. Cables drifted out, massive lines ending in gnarly devices. Slowly, the ball filled the entire view.

"It's maybe a thousand times the size of this ship," Magnus said.

The opening appeared on the equator. A beam of white light shot out to meet the ship. They turned away from the glare as the ship rode it into the great lock.

"There's not much more to see here," Juan said. He let go of Lena's hand and moved toward the exit.

Kaliapin confronted him out in the passageway. "Will the vessel remain here?"

"No way to tell," Juan replied. "It may go somewhere after this stop, according to its program, and there's nothing we can do to stop it. We can use the frames to return to the Amazon, or try the other three frames. But we won't return to the Earth we left."

Kaliapin stared at the floor. "That won't be much loss. What do you suggest, Dr. Obrion?"

"Not much. We can go out and have a look at the station."

A moan echoed down the passageway. "The dying are waking up," Kaliapin said. "All we can give them is painkillers." He covered his eyes with his hand and rubbed his forehead, holding back tears.

"Have you slept?" Lena asked.

"Very little. I fear sleep." He lowered his hand and looked at them.

"You can't blame yourself," she said.

"Of course I can," Kaliapin answered coldly. "I must. The world we knew destroyed itself because of what we are." He paused and glared at them, as if for an instant he had shed his humanity and could see clearly. "No good," he muttered, "we're no good at all," then turned and wandered away down the passageway.

Lena looked at Juan with tears in her eyes, then came into his arms. He held her, feeling lost.

The outer lock was completely open when they rounded the curve of the passage. Juan led the way into the chamber, and they crowded around the circular opening to peer out into the lighted realm of the station.

"The same afternoon light," Lena said.

"Pretty standard, these stations," Malachi added.

"Is it safe to go out?" Ivan asked.

Juan nodded. "Probably. The other ship made a sound before closing up to leave."

"Look, there!" Ivan shouted, pointing. The amber floor flashed beneath its surface.

Malachi said, "We think the ship is serviced and repaired in these stations, while passengers relax. The place may also serve a recreational function."

"Why do you say that?" Kaliapin's voice asked from behind them. Juan and his companions turned around. "I'm quite recovered. Please go on." He came up and peered out with them.

"The station responds to thoughts," Malachi continued. "Harmless, but disconcerting if you're not prepared." He gazed into the distance and seemed to concentrate, but nothing happened. "Curious," he said after a moment. "Doesn't seem to work here."

"I wonder," Lena said, sticking her hand out into the warm light. She turned suddenly; her eyes widened. "Juan, do you think it's possible?"

"You're right," he said, remembering how their various scars and complaints had disappeared during their first visit to a station.

"What are you talking about?" Magnus asked.

Juan tried to smile. "Maybe we'll cure your arthritic shoulder again."

Lena said, "Anatoli, go and have your men bring out two radiation victims as soon as possible."

Kaliapin frowned and looked at her questioningly.

"We remember a sense of well-being," she said, "after we spent some time in the other station. Repairs were made on us. The fluid control of matter we've seen in the ships seems to extend to biological systems."

"But how can it know what to do?" Kaliapin asked.

Malachi said, "From the examples of life presented to it."

23
DILEMMAS

Four soldiers carried two stretchers out onto the station floor. Juan noticed a slight variation in the light as they set the injured down.

"Step away and wait," Kaliapin called out. The soldiers gave him a puzzled look as they took up their positions. The man and woman on the stretchers moved their heads and moaned faintly.

"They'll be unconscious again in a few moments," Kaliapin said, "as soon as the sedative takes effect."

Lena said, "I think the starcrossers had medical facilities on their ships and stations, and I have an idea which chamber it might be on the ship—the one with the lenslike surfaces." She turned to Kaliapin. "I'll show you where it is. You can try it on the other injured." She led him quickly into the ship.

"If this works," Ivan said, "we can leave with a clear conscience. They will have all they need, and in time they can also try the frames, with the hope of finding a variant that has not destroyed itself. Or they can simply live in the ship."

The woman on the stretcher moaned loudly. One of the soldiers knelt down and spoke softly to her. Juan felt a guilty comfort thinking that he and his companions did not have to settle for this variant.

Ivan said, "We can't affect the outcome here further, so we must continue with our original purpose—to find our team."

"You've made your point, so drop it for now," Juan replied. "We'll talk to Kaliapin later."

"Juan," Ivan murmured, "you're not hearing me. Everything we were loyal to on this Earth is gone. The alternates of the people who sent us out are probably dead. The only

159

way out is through the frames. We should leave at once, and we don't need anyone's permission."

Juan looked at Magnus and Malachi. "What do you two think?"

Magnus said, "Ivan puts it harshly, but he's right. I do think we should discuss it with Kaliapin, and part amicably. Our future is not here. We should do all we can before we go, but since we've already lost our worlds, we might as well continue with our purpose and see what our kind has done elsewhere. In time, Kaliapin's people will also have to try the frames."

The soldiers outside lit up cigarettes and gazed around nervously.

"We're ghosts," Malachi muttered.

"No," Juan replied. "All this is real enough, because it can't be reversed. Earth is dead, and these people may have to spend the rest of their lives here. Even if they try the frame into the Amazon, they might only find a close variant that's just as bad."

Malachi touched his shoulder. "Take it easy. There's no single right decision to be made."

"What worries me," Ivan said, "is that the military officers here may try to keep us by force. I don't trust them."

"I've seen no evidence for that," Magnus said.

Ivan sighed. "If people begin to recover, other interests will come into play."

"Mal, what do you think?" Juan asked.

His friend shrugged. "He may be right."

As he lay in his sleeping bag in the drum-shaped chamber, Juan struggled with his sense of unreality. The builders had abandoned the web because the variant effect deformed the reality of the users, making it over for them endlessly as they passed through the frames. It was enough that any single variant grew from an infinite series of prior choices, without confronting the observer with endless worlds resting on a foundation of chaos, like bad revisions of a story without shape or end.

"Are you awake?" Lena whispered next to him.

He turned his head and saw her gazing at him uncertainly. "I think the two people outside are recovering just as quickly as those inside the medical chamber," she said.

"Are you sure?"

"I'm not certain, but today will tell."

"What's worrying you, then?" he asked.

"How is it being done? I keep thinking these systems will miss some subtlety in human physiology."

Juan said, "Healthy and sick specimens are here for comparison. The medical mode of the ship's systems must also operate at basic levels, so I would expect it to be thorough. How many people can you get into the ship's chamber?"

"Maybe fifty at a time. Some may die before their turn, unless Kaliapin's searchers find duplicate chambers along the passage." She was silent for a moment, then touched his face gently. "Are you all right?"

He tried to smile, but the tension of the last two days had frozen his face into a mask.

Juan had slept badly; his four companions looked as tired and troubled as he felt. As they neared the outer lock, Kaliapin hurried toward them.

"What is it?" Juan asked.

"The medical chamber has locked us out," he said. "The entrance just won't work. And outside—you must see for yourselves."

They went through the open lock and stepped out onto the amber floor. The stretchers had disappeared. The soldiers were on their knees, peering through the translucent surface.

"Look," Kaliapin said as they reached the spot.

They all squatted down. The man and woman lay just below the surface, their eyes wide open, staring upward; waves of yellow light washed through their bodies.

"They seem unhurt," Kaliapin said, "but they may be dead, for all we know."

Lena looked up at him. "It must be part of the treatment. Maybe the severity of their bodily damage prompted it."

"What about the chamber?" Kaliapin demanded.

"Something similar must be going on there also," Lena replied. "It will open when the process is complete."

"What do you think, Dr. Obrion?" Kaliapin asked.

"This is all of a piece with what we've seen of the alien systems—fluid, basic control of matter and energy, beyond our wildest hopes for nanotech."

"How long have they been like this?" Lena asked.

"Several hours. Dr. Dravic, perhaps there is some other explanation for this, not the medical one you've suggested."

"No," Lena replied. "As we've told you, something like this happened to us. Scars disappeared."

"But no one ever recovers from these kinds of radiation injuries!"

The waves of light flowing through the floor stopped suddenly. "Stand back," Lena said.

As they watched, the figures came up through the surface; it closed beneath them.

"It consumed their stretchers," Kaliapin said.

Lena knelt down and felt the pulses of the man and woman. "Normal," she said after a few moments, then examined the figures more carefully, feeling their throats and checking their torsos. "All external signs of radiation burns are gone. They're asleep."

"What should we do?" Kaliapin asked.

"I suggest you leave them here until they wake up," Lena said, "then start bringing the others out. Don't wait for the chamber door to open. Otherwise, many of your cases may not live long enough to be treated. I'm going to check on as many of them as I can right now."

"Mal and I'll give you a hand," Magnus said. Kaliapin motioned to the four soldiers to remain on guard as they all hurried back toward the lock.

"Anatoli," Ivan said, "Dr. Obrion and I would like a word with you." Juan tensed. Ivan wasn't wasting any time.

Kaliapin looked at them warily. "Of course."

They passed inside behind Lena, Magnus, and Malachi, then turned to look out at the couple on the floor. "We'll be right here," Juan called out to Lena as she and the others continued down the passage.

Ivan said, "If things improve for your people, then we will leave to carry out our original mission. Do you object?"

Kaliapin looked surprised for a moment, then said, "You've been essential to our situation here, and I would not wish to seem ungrateful. We haven't lost our original world in quite the way you have, but if this ship fails to return to Earth, as seems likely, we will have to try the frames—either to go home or to explore."

"That will give you a chance," Juan answered, "to find a variant that hasn't destroyed itself, to explore, or to call this ship home."

"Isn't there some way we might all stay together?" Kaliapin

asked. "I realize that you might view this as merely another variant."

Ivan said, "You will have the same chance as we do of regaining an intact world."

Kaliapin smiled. "What if we arrive just before it happens again?"

"Then you must try again," Ivan said. "But it might just as easily be a variant that will not destroy itself."

Juan looked carefully at Kaliapin, who was at a loss for words. "Do you object to our leaving?"

Kaliapin hesitated, then said, "A recovering community needs all the individuals it can get, especially skilled people and teachers."

Moved by the man's plea, and the pride in his voice, Juan said, "We won't go until we know your group is settled. And there's a good chance that we'll be back. Our alternates will serve you just as well."

Kaliapin shrugged. "I understand your curiosity, and you do have a mission to carry out. I will become the mayor of a small town, a Russian village that has no need for agriculture to live." He smiled. "My grandfather was the mayor of a small town. I became a propulsion engineer, but this ship is more than I could ever accomplish."

"We wish you well," Juan said.

Kaliapin sighed. "I'd rather you stayed, but I have no authority to keep you, and will feel no ill will." He looked at Ivan. "Don't worry, none of the officers will try to stop your going. You do want to go, Ivan?"

"I'm part of the UN team."

"I understand."

As Juan shook hands with him, one of the soldiers guarding the couple cried out. The man and woman were getting to their feet, hands trembling as they reached out for each other, alive and whole.

After they had made their preparations for departure, Juan went to the lock and gazed out over the station floor. A river of yellow light flowed through the hundreds of human figures locked in the alien amber, probing and repairing, restoring the delicate cellular machineries born of evolution's bloody building program, bestowing mercies on blind nature's soft creatures.

Did the ship or station know what it was doing? Again he wondered why the starcrossers had needed such large facilities. Had they shifted large populations throughout the galaxy? What part had Earth played? Only further exploration might offer clues.

24
EXILES

◗

Once again they stood in the deep chamber. The beams from their helmets bridged the cavernous chamber and disappeared into the black frames. Juan asked, "Which one will it be? Second from the left will put us into Ship One, inside a suncore station somewhere, and since it seems that we've been moving only between ships based in Earth's sunspace, three will take us back into the Amazon. One leads into a branching corridor somewhere, according to Mal."

"I vote for Ship One," Lena said. "We know what to expect, and so did the Soviet team."

"I agree," Juan said. "We'll try the unknowns after we've eliminated the likeliest." He grasped Lena's hand. She reached over to Magnus, who linked with Malachi, who reached out to Ivan.

"Ready," the Russian said from the end of the chain.

Lena tightened her grip. Juan entered the frame. His helmet light flickered for a moment as he went through the blackness.

"Follow me," he said when they were all out.

The exit glowed and he slipped—

—into the familiar passage.

The others came out behind him, squinting in the bright light.

"How distant is this suncore?" Ivan asked.

"No way to measure," Juan said, "but far beyond our galaxy."

They turned off their helmet lights, went up and made the right turn, and started up the straight section of passage. "Perhaps we should shout," Ivan said. "They might hear us."

"Hello!" Malachi bellowed. "Hello! Hello!" His voice echoed and died away.

Lena said, "They won't hear if they're in one of the chambers, or outside."

"Perhaps they're dining," Ivan said, "or asleep."

"Let's see if the shuttle is here," Juan said as they came to the turn at the end of the section. He presented himself to the entrance. It glowed and he passed—

—into the shuttle bay.

The craft sat in its cradle. He turned and stepped—

—out into the passage. "It's there," he said.

"Hello!" Malachi called out again.

Lena said, "Maybe it stranded them on the planet and returned. They may be trying to find their way back."

"Or they're still here somewhere," Juan said. "We'll check the second cafeteria." He led the way past the entrance to the drum-shaped chamber, counting off the ovals.

"Don't startle them," Ivan said as Juan stopped before the entrance.

"Were they armed?" Malachi asked.

"Possibly."

They dropped their packs.

"I can't believe they'd shoot," Lena said.

"I'll go in with hands up," Juan said.

He stepped toward the portal. It reddened and he passed—

—into the familiar blue light of the chamber.

Two men and a woman stood up at one of the alien tables.

"Be calm," Juan said, pointing to the UN-ERS insignia on his oversuit. They regarded him in silence. "I'm Juan Obrion, with the other team. We've been searching for you."

Dita Karenina stared at him with large, brown, slightly Asian eyes. Her long brown hair was disheveled. Isak Bilenkin, a plump, slightly balding man, squinted at him with fierce blue eyes. The tall red-haired young man had to be Yerik Khasan.

"I see you've learned what this chamber is for," Juan said, gesturing at the provisions on the two tables.

Yerik Khasan nodded.

"And you obviously understand the doorways, as well as the frames?"

"Yes, yes," the tall man said impatiently, "but why have you come after us?" His English was nearly without accent.

"What do you mean?" Juan asked, wondering what changes this variant would reveal.

"We've met before, Dr. Obrion," Yerik Khasan said. "We've been back to the ship in the Soviet Union several times, where we met you and your colleagues."

Juan said, "Then you know about the war and the variant effect?"

"Yes," he answered sadly.

"I'll get the others," Juan said.

"How is it that you're here?" Lena asked as they all knelt around the table.

"We tried other frames," Dita said. "This is our third passage. On our first return, the ship was deserted and we couldn't go outside because of the radiation. Second time back we met you, when you came through from Brazil. Then the ship left Earth and entered the sun, where we discovered that both ship and station had medical facilities. Then the eight of us pooled what we had learned and decided to explore the web. The ship's shuttle could only take us back to the ruined variant of Earth. Your group took one frame, we took another. You still seem to be the people we met." She gave a weak smile.

"We're meeting you for the first time," Lena said.

"I thought as much. Are the survivors well where you came from?"

Lena nodded. "They're recovering."

Isak Bilenkin said, "The variants seem to cluster around familiar possibilities, war among them, but the other changes seem to be small, personal details, some of them trivial. Tell me, Dr. Obrion, do you believe that we can transfer only to variants where we can't meet ourselves—that is, to worlds where our doubles are absent either because they have left or died? And doesn't that perhaps suggest that we can return to a world where we are dead?"

"It's possible," Juan replied, "but we can only find out by trying. The exchanges have seemed symmetrical so far."

"Do you know where you are?" Magnus asked.

"Ship One," Isak said, "inside a white dwarf. We read your report."

Juan asked, "Has anything disturbing happened to you here?"

"Yes," Dita said slowly. "We've suffered from terrible nightmares and headaches, as if something were probing us."

"It's the ship," Juan said. "It doesn't know quite how to deal with us. We had similar experiences, but there didn't seem to be any damage done."

Dita looked relieved. "We thought we were going mad."

"As for the station outside," Juan continued, "it will display your imaginings."

"We stayed inside after that experience," Yerik said.

Dita looked at Juan with concern. "The variant effect was not mentioned in your ERS report, or that passing through the frames may destroy personal identity if only patterns are transmitted and then reconstructed from fresh materials, which would make us twins of our original selves. Unless our actual particles are transmitted and rejoined, then we die and are replaced by our twins with every passage."

"We're not certain that's what happens," Juan replied. "It's possible that the frames are direct bridges, with no transmission of particles."

Isak shook his head and smiled. "A consoling possibility, but if we're ghosts we'll never know it, since the originals are long gone, as is our original world."

"Do you have coffee?" Ivan asked.

Yerik pushed a thermos toward him.

"We've been thinking," Dita said, "that we should try to find an undestroyed variant and help it survive by telling what we've learned."

Malachi brightened a little as he sat down next to Dita. They were silent as Ivan poured coffee into cups.

Yerik said, "I doubt that a humankind which failed to control nuclear weapons would take anything we've learned to heart. Environmental problems were terrifying enough, yet little was done. The world's leaders would not be frightened by our story of parallel worlds."

"We must try," Dita said. "Perhaps in further explorations we may find help for our kind."

Juan cringed inwardly. "I fear what our kind will do with the web."

Dita frowned. "If we make known our experiences, and if others join us in exploring the web, then we might be able to create a moral pressure for a better world."

We're all the enemy, Juan wanted to say as he looked into her eyes. She made him feel ashamed as she looked back.

"There is so much we've found," she continued, "that could help humankind."

"You mean the replicator," Juan answered. "Sure, we can use it, put power in the hands of politicians, if we ever find a whole Earth."

Magnus said, "Juan, I'd rather do something easier, for now, like visit the nearby planet."

"The shuttle is here," Juan said.

"Why not use a frame?" Dita asked.

"It's an unpleasant hike from where it connects to the dome complex."

Yerik asked, "Will the ship wait for us here?"

"Yes," Malachi said, "because the shuttle will be absent. Although we don't know how the ship makes decisions, I suspect it tries to be useful to its passengers."

Isak said, "The three of us haven't been to this planet."

"Ivan and I haven't seen it either," Magnus said.

Dita looked puzzled. As Magnus explained why he was not quite himself, Juan realized why the older man wanted to visit the place where his variant had died.

25

VASTNESS

The thin, bare branches of the alien tree sprouted like a shock of gray hair from the trunk. Overhead, the globular cluster suggested a shattered sun. The disk of the red-white dwarf rolled on the horizon of the rusty brown desert. Musky odors rose from the land of scattered red-leafed plants clinging to the rocky soil with green-glowing roots. Juan shivered in the gritty breeze and squinted at the domes. Nothing seemed to have changed.

He turned back toward the tree, where Magnus was searching the ground on all fours with his helmet light turned up high, working his way toward the trunk.

Juan said, "We've never returned to the same variant. There can't be a grave there."

"It's a simple enough experiment to do," Magnus answered. He pulled open his collapsible spade and began to dig.

"Take it easy," Juan said; his throat constricted. It would be a brutal irony if Magnus died here again. He looked down at the growing hole, wondering if somehow the body could be here, and for an instant saw the shape of its head under the dirt. Cold sweat broke out on his face.

"You're right," Magnus said after a moment, "there's no grave here." He sat down against the trunk and caught his breath. "I'm sorry. This must not be pleasant for you."

"I knew you wanted to come here."

"I'd imagined examining my own body, maybe meeting my own living self. What do you think this place was?"

"Lena thought the domes a kind of town," Juan said.

"There's an underground installation nearby, with frames. I think it may be what's left of a staging area that was used to establish the suncore station."

A dust storm on the horizon was beginning to obscure the sinking white dwarf. Strangeness rushed through him as he breathed the musky odors of the alien desert. Magnus got up and came out from under the tree. "Here they come," he said pointing.

Four dark shapes marched down the sandy rise, single eyes blazing with light. Juan watched for two others to come over the top. When they failed to appear, he hurried over to the group and saw only the four Russians. "Where's Mal and Lena?" he shouted over the rising wind.

"Keeping the shuttle here," Dita answered. "They don't want to risk it leaving. Which way?"

Juan led the way between the first two domes. Magnus joined them as they neared the dome Juan's group had entered on their previous visit. "Follow me in!" he shouted over the mournful wind, then turned and faced the entrance.

It glowed and he passed—

—into the dome's golden space.

The others came in beside him. His eyes adjusted and he went forward across the black floor.

"What is this place?" Dita asked.

"Watch," he said as the light faded into total darkness.

A galaxy swirled below them as the floor became transparent. The view pulled into a dense region of one of the spiral arms, to a yellow star, then closer to show a ring of worlds around the sun.

"So many!" Dita exclaimed. "They must be artificial."

More habitat-worlds appeared, gradually enclosing the sun in a shell of life.

"Time is passing," Juan said as red beams stabbed out from the worlds, penetrating the galaxy's quadrants, then branched out into the globular clusters over the hub. The view pulled back, reducing the galaxy to one in a cluster. Red beams linked these galaxies. The view pulled back even further, revealing dozens of clusters being joined by the web's red beams.

"So where are they?" Isak asked. "What happened?"

"One possibility we've discussed," Juan replied, "is that they grew very long-lived. There were fewer individuals as time passed, with longevity replacing reproduction. A winnowing took place, which left only those who could sustain an interest in life. They may still be out there somewhere."

Isak said, "That suggests the web couldn't give them what they wanted. It provided access to the cosmos, but not to the mystery behind its existence, and became a useless possession."

Yerik laughed in the darkness. "I can't believe that with all this they couldn't get to the bottom of things and just died away."

Juan looked at him as the golden glow lit up the dome. "Imagine the frustration of accumulating endless details about the universe without learning the basic why of it."

"Are you suggesting," Dita said, "that they became despondent over the failure of their science and committed suicide?"

Juan turned toward the brown-eyed woman. "Magnus had ideas that might be more plausible," he said, realizing too late that he was thinking of discussions with the other Magnus, and glanced at him apologetically.

"Do go on," Magnus said. "What did I say?"

"You speculated that they might have gone forward in time by circling black holes and slowing their bioclocks, hoping to find the truth of the universe in those extreme conditions at the end of time. Or they might have escaped our universe through black holes."

"We have to see a lot more," Isak said, "before we can even begin to guess."

"So much may be ours to learn," Dita added.

"It may be beyond us," Juan said. "I sometimes feel that something better than a human being is needed to benefit from this alien technology."

"If we don't try to understand it," Dita said, "then we'll certainly fail."

"I agree," Isak added. "We must take an enterprising attitude."

Yerik said, "First they built their costly relativistic ships, and reached nearby stars by slowing time. Then they developed jump ships, and powered them with the energy of their sun, transmitted through the same jumpspace." The redhaired man rubbed his chin. "And then they sent themselves through directly, leaving the ships for maintenance and establishment of new frame bridges. The energy for their web would last for as long as the universe existed, although a sun would be exhausted here and there. They certainly knew what to do with the energy of a star."

"And they solved their material and medical needs," Dita added. "What was left except to answer the ultimate questions? But if they failed at that, what would be left for them? You may be right, Juan."

"Unless I'm only projecting human tendencies," he said.

"They may still exist," Magnus said, "living in web-linked habitats throughout the galaxies, carrying on their quests. We may never find them. They might have no use for natural worlds, or for travel. The web might simply be an earlier stage of their civilization, now abandoned."

Juan nodded. "It's still probably their source of energy, but one which they don't have to tend, since the suncore stations seem to run themselves."

"Perhaps they now use energy differently, without the suncore technology," Dita added. "Perhaps, as suggested, their whole culture is now made up of a handful of individuals, carrying all their past within them."

Isak said, "We have to see more of the web's connecting worlds. Something will reveal itself." The plump man looked at Juan. "What about this mental contact that we've all experienced?"

"I don't know," Juan replied. "It seemed that bits and pieces of personalities were crowding into our minds. At other moments it sounded as if people were talking about us behind our backs. Was it that way for you?"

"No," Dita said. "We had headaches and felt uncomfortable. Did it happen again?"

"No," Juan replied, "not even a hint, in any of us."

"What do you think this place was for?" she asked.

"A staging area, maybe for the transfer of populations. The domes seem usable as living quarters, with built-in display and communications devices."

"Were they preparing populations for new worlds?" she asked. "Why would they want to move large groups?"

"We're groping in the dark," Isak said.

"I wonder what they were like," Dita said.

"Oxygen breathers, humanoid, from the images we've seen, but we can't be sure we weren't making up the images ourselves. It's possible that we're all that's left of them."

Dita looked surprised. "Are you serious?"

"Earth might have been colonized as part of these population transfers."

"I'm not sure I would like that to be true," Magnus said.

"Why else have a station in our sun, and three ships on Earth?" Juan asked.

Dita looked puzzled. "It would seem they abandoned us."

Juan said, "Maybe the population transfers were part of an early project."

"I have an idea," Isak said, "that they left the ships and stations for us to learn from in time."

They were silent for a few moments, gazing around the dome.

"There's nothing here," Yerik said, "except for a floor, light, and ventilation, and old maps."

The dwarf had set by the time they came out. Sand blew across the complex of domes, shaking the tree. The globular cluster burned overhead. A black dust storm was moving toward them from where the sun had set.

"Hurry!" Juan shouted over the wind, lowering the faceplate on his helmet. Roachlike insects scurried around his feet as he led the way toward the rise. Static flashes discharged in the approaching dust cloud. Fear slipped through him as he remembered how the alien presence had begun to pull memories at random from his mind.

Magnus steadied him as they scrambled up the rise and went over the top. The shuttle lay ahead, a giant beachball left behind on the shore of an alien sea, yellow-orange light streaming from the open lock.

They moved toward it against the rising wind. Lena and Malachi met them at the lock. Juan picked up the pack he had left to keep the lock open and followed his companions up the curving passage. The lock doors glowed shut, silencing the wind's howl.

Everyone was seated when he entered the small drum-shaped chamber. He stepped into the center circle, dropped his pack, and sat down on it.

"Find anything new?" Lena asked as the amber glow faded and the viewspace lit up overhead.

"Same as before," he said as the planet fell away. In a moment it was a brown shrinking globe. The white dwarf appeared as the ship oriented itself and rushed at the star.

They watched as the burst of blue light marked the craft's shift into otherspace.

Gray light streamed into the small pit as the shuttle crept toward the suncore station. The black globe appeared, filling the viewspace. Once again Juan was struck by the magnitude of the power core's function: It drank the star's strength, shared it with far-flung ships, and kept the frames open. He watched as the equatorial lock opened and the guide beam reached out. The shuttle passed inside, seeking the mother ship.

The suncore missed a beat, alerting the child of the starcrossers that the star might become unstable. A quick search locked in the next attainable sunport.

As it prepared to depart, the child of the starcrossers received no directives from the colloidal minds within its field. Yet there was in them a persistent questioning impulse that demanded to be satisfied.

26

NOMADS OF KNOWLEDGE

◐

Juan finished his second cup of coffee and looked around at his companions as they sat at the tables in the cafeteria near the drum-shaped chamber. Lena was withdrawn and nervous. Malachi looked dour as he played cards with Ivan, who seemed absorbed in the game; Dita stared absently at the two men. Yerik had complained of headaches, and had stayed behind when Isak and Magnus went out to explore chambers in the passage.

"Now I have a headache," Lena said, rubbing her forehead. Juan felt a sudden pain behind his eyes, and wondered if something was trying to listen to his thoughts. "Dita, do you feel it, too?"

The brown-haired woman nodded. "Maybe it's the blue light in here. Makes the food look unappetizing, too."

The entrance glowed. Isak and Magnus came through, panting a little. "The outside lock is closed," Magnus said. "We failed to trigger it. Then we heard the departure sound."

"I guess we're going for another ride," Lena said.

Dita leaned forward at the table. "Strange," she said, "no matter how far we go, we'll be only a step away from . . . Earth."

Ivan looked at her uneasily, and Juan realized that she had avoided saying home.

Down in the drum-shaped chamber, they stepped into the circle and the amber glow faded. The massive black globe of the station was already far behind. There was a flash of blue and the dwarf star appeared in normal space.

"What happens now?" Dita asked.

Juan said, "The ship accelerates to a noticeable fraction of light speed within a few hours, then jumps to its destination, wherever that might be. We suspect that we're far from our own galaxy. The dwarf we're leaving is one of the old halo stars in this galaxy, which may be at the red limit of the universe in relation to Earth."

"But the frames will bridge any distance," Dita said.

"Presumably," Juan answered. "We've seen nothing to the contrary."

"I wonder," Isak said, "how the web actually exists. While we experience displacements in probability, lapses of time between variants have been nil. Perhaps the web exists simultaneously—a permanent bridgespace—peace be to Einstein!"

"I wonder if it can be shut off?" Dita asked.

Isak chuckled. "I don't expect to find such a switch. Why would there be one?"

Juan gazed at the dwindling dwarf, which was already starting to red-shift. "We'll get some rest," Lena said.

As they went to their packs, Juan noticed that Ivan was trembling.

Blue-white flashes woke Juan.

"We're jumping," Magnus said softly.

"How many?"

"Two, so far."

The silhouettes of his companions sat up around him and gazed upward. A yellow sun blazed suddenly in the viewspace. It grew larger, filling the chamber with light. A black line crossed the star, then slowly broke up into disks. The star, Juan realized, was ringed by habitats.

"So many!" Dita exclaimed.

"This could be it," Malachi said. "We'll meet the builders at last."

The view flashed blue and became gray. Once again the destination star became a diffuse patch as the ship penetrated toward the core station.

The lock was open when they came up the passage. They emerged into a vast blue space. Juan gazed up through the electric brightness and imagined the seething star enveloping the ghost of the otherspace station.

Dita looked around. "Deserted, like the others."

"We must explore," Isak said. His blue eyes widened as he gazed at the expanse.

As they stared across the seemingly endless amber floor, Juan realized that his own love for discovery had diminished. He stopped and looked back at the ship. Most of it lay below the floor, but the visible portion of the dome still rose at least a hundred meters into the station, turned on its axis to keep the lock level with the floor.

"Look!" Isak shouted.

Juan turned and caught up with his companions. They approached a half circle of frames facing the ship.

Malachi said, "These may be entranceways into the worlds we saw on the way in."

"Of course!" Isak said. "But there can't be as many frames as worlds, which means that other connections probably exist in the worlds that can be entered. At least a million habitats fill the orbit we saw."

"Will the ship leave without us if we go exploring?" Dita asked.

"It might," Juan said, "and we'd lose our source of provisions and our only known link with home."

"What home?" Ivan muttered suddenly. "I'll stay with the ship and catch up on my sleep."

Juan said, "We should stay together."

Ivan laughed. "Don't worry about me. I'm tired, and I don't care at this point if you all come back slightly different."

"Juan's right," Dita said.

Malachi asked, "Why introduce even more complications, Ivan? If the ship decides to leave, you might not be able to stop it anyway, even if you sit in the lock. Leaving a pack there may do just as well. We've never been certain."

Isak asked, "Do we want to explore or hide out in the ship?" He pointed to one of the frames. "Think of what may be through there—alien humanities inhabiting these million worlds. What knowledge we might gain—alien logics and mathematics, systems of physics based on the perceptions of alien physiologies, chemistries of the impossible!"

Juan stepped close to Ivan and said, "I know how you feel, but if you stay here you'll risk being left alone. As soon as we step through one of those frames, the variant effect may put you in a probability in which we don't come back. We may return to a variant where you never came with us at all."

"Or you'll come back with small changes," Ivan said. "I don't much care. We've lost our world. There's no going back, ever, and maybe all the variants have destroyed themselves."

"That's unlikely," Juan said. "Are you coming?"

Ivan gave him a hopeless look, then nodded.

Juan said, "We'll take all our gear."

They joined hands and approached the center frame. Juan tightened his hold on Lena's hand and stepped through into a dark tunnel.

His eyes adjusted, and he went forward toward what seemed a circle of white light. He came to the opening and stepped out onto a harshly lit surface, then let go of Lena's hand and moved aside as the others came out. Looking up, he saw that they were standing at the base of a tall white column. The surface curved away from it and shot upward in the distance.

"We're inside a hollow ball!" Isak exclaimed.

A dark blue globe hung in the center. It seemed very near. For a moment it seemed that it could crush them against the inner shell. Lines of light flickered across its cracked, dry surface.

"It seems trapped in this space," Lena said nervously.

"It doesn't seem real," Dita added.

Magnus asked, "Why is it here?"

"My guess," Isak said, "is that this body was brought here to be taken apart, to be used as raw materials. You can see where large pieces have been cut away. Notice also that this surface we're on may be within Roche's limit, yet it's not breaking up from the gravitational stresses of that body. And we feel gravity, at least three quarters normal, I would say. I'll wager it's not centrifugal spin either, because if they can overcome Roche stress, they don't need simulated gravity. They generate a g-force directly, just as in the starship."

"A very thin shell would not break up inside Roche's limit," Juan replied, "so we might be feeling centrifugal acceleration."

Isak took off his helmet and let go. It dropped straight down and hit the surface at his feet. "No obvious coriolis force, unless this place is very large. I'd say we're not spinning."

"Who cares," Ivan said.

They all stared at him, startled by the derision in his voice. Earth's destruction, Juan realized, had affected them all, in different ways; but Ivan could only see it in himself. His mouth trembled as Juan looked at him.

"We understand," Lena said softly.

"Do you?" Ivan asked.

"We all feel," Dita said, "but what can we do?"

"We'll try to go back," Juan added, "but not yet."

Ivan seemed to pull himself together. "I'm sorry," he managed to say.

Isak picked up his helmet and looked up at him. "Do you think I don't know this exploration is at least in part a distraction?"

"I'm sorry," Ivan repeated. "We've all lost friends and relations. I will not give in to my feelings again."

Juan turned back toward the tunnel. "Let's try another frame entrance."

Isak chose the frame to the right of center and led the way through. Here the planet at the center of the shell was divided into four large pieces. A faint cloud of dust enveloped the shattered globe.

Isak said, "They must have stripped this whole solar system for this construction project. But why did they stop and leave it all like this?"

"Something came up," Yerik said.

Isak stared into the brightly lit space. "What pride! What skill! How they must have raged against the tyranny of space-time, and set themselves to bend it to their will."

"I would like to ask," Ivan said, "what can we learn here?"

As Juan gazed up at the four fragments at the center of the shell, he imagined that they might have been intended as the materials for a series of diminishing shells within the large one, until all the space to the center was used up; and outside, just next door, was another in the long string of worlds filling the orbit around the star. He took a deep breath. Ivan was right. Awesome as it was, it all seemed for nothing. The air was breathable, if a bit thin; the surface had been prepared for development, but there was no one here.

Magnus shook his head. "It appears that one day they all just disappeared."

"Let's try another," Dita said.

The next space held a dozen asteroidlike bodies, all linked by what seemed to be green-glowing cables.

"Look there," Isak said to Juan, pointing. "Structures, where the lines connect."

Juan saw green nodes on the gray-brown bodies. "Over there!" Isak shouted, pointing into the brightness. Juan squinted and noticed a dark line reaching from the curving surface of the shell to one of the asteroids overhead.

"I see it," Lena said.

Isak started toward the line. Ivan frowned, then followed him; Yerik, Magnus, and Malachi fell in behind him. Juan shifted his pack and started after with Lena.

He counted five white columns as he walked. Each seemed to have an opening like the one from which they had emerged. "I wonder where they all lead," Lena said.

She still seemed distant, her mood mirroring Ivan's uncertainty about what they were doing here, the same uneasiness and lack of conviction he felt himself. He looked into her eyes, thirsting for those moments when he was not wary of his own kind. His disappointment with humanity had deepened, but he had to include himself in his fears, because there was no innocent ground on which he could stand. He felt again the rush of growing up, the loss of imagined independence as the floods of sexuality and the struggle for position killed lucidity and the simple love of being. Lost were those moments when sunlight had quieted his will and made him believe in angelic ways outside the deeply cut canyons of biological time, before adulthood came like a black river to carry him into the deep beyond the world. . . .

Lena glanced at him, then grimaced. "You know, Dr. Obrion, I thought I was a loner, but you've got me beat. I guess that's what attracts me to you. Your citadel is stronger than mine." She smiled at him, and his bitterness drained away.

He looked ahead. The thin, cablelike connection with the asteroid cluster thickened as they neared the place where it was anchored to the inner surface. Juan heard a distant rushing sound.

"Airflow," Isak said. "It must be a conduit of some kind."

Juan saw the structure clearly as Lena and he caught up with the others. It rose like a flying buttress toward the asteroid center. Malachi leaned into an oval opening at the base.

"It seems to be a drop tube arrangement," he said, peering upward.

"But will it carry us both ways?" Isak asked.

Malachi took out a chocolate wrapper, tossed it into the tube, and watched it whisk upward. "That doesn't prove anything," he said, turning around. "The only way we'll find out if we can return is by stepping in at the other end."

Ivan looked at Juan. "What's the point of going through that thing?"

"We came to explore," Isak answered. "We do so or go back."

Malachi shifted his broad shoulders to adjust his pack. "Who's first?"

"I'll go," Juan said, "and send something back as soon as I'm through."

No one objected. Ivan seemed a bit relieved suddenly, Juan noticed, and knew why because he felt the same. They would put off trying to regain their world for a while longer, postponing the possibility that they might never find it.

He adjusted his pack, stepped into the opening, and was drawn upward, accelerating slowly. He looked down and saw Lena peering after him, her upturned face tense with concern. He waved and looked away, lowering his faceplate. In a moment he lost all sense of up or down. Ahead, the tube seemed endless, glowing bright blue. He lifted his faceplate and felt only a slight motion of air against his face, evidence of a gravitational control that could hurl him through a hundred kilometers of tubeway in a matter of minutes.

Yet the motion was gentle, and lulled him. For a moment he imagined that he was rushing downward, but the perception quickly reversed itself, and it seemed he was rushing upward; finally, his mind decided that he was traveling horizontally.

The blue glow around him brightened. He looked at his watch and saw that fifteen minutes had elapsed. He seemed to be slowing, but couldn't be sure. An oval opening came up in front of his eyes as he drifted to a stop. He grasped the rim, turned himself around, and came down on his feet in light gravity.

He stepped out cautiously and looked up. The tube thrust up from the asteroid, spanned the blue space, and narrowed to a faint black line before it touched the far surface. He took a few steps, surprised that such a small body would have even this much gravity. Looking around, he noticed skeletal structures clinging to the rocky surface a few hundred meters

away. Squares, pyramids, and various irregular shapes were
strewn about the asteroid.

He turned back to the oval opening, picked up a rock, and
tossed it in. It went up, and he breathed a sigh of relief.

Isak came through first, looking like a giant beetle with his
pack as he turned himself around. Lena landed gracefully
behind him. Malachi twisted his body through the opening
and drifted down. A strand of Dita's hair flew up from under
her helmet as she emerged, followed by Yerik. Magnus and
Ivan came through last.

"What do you think?" Juan asked Isak, pointing to the
spidery structures.

The astrophysicist wrinkled his brow and rubbed his chin.
"I would say some kind of propulsion device, or what's left
of one, used to bring the asteriod into this construction shell,
as part of an unfinished macroengineering project. But what
stopped it?"

"Perhaps there was a strike," Ivan said. Isak approached
one of the alien structures and rapped it with his knuckles,
producing a dull, nonmetallic sound.

"Ah," Malachi said, "an alien speaks."

Lena reached down and pulled something from the rocky
ground. "Juan, look at this," she said. "Grass, and weeds."

"As common as yellow stars," he replied.

They all gathered around her as she examined her find,
and Juan realized that it had reminded them of Earth. He
looked up at the nearby asteroid fragments. Two hung in
the sky just above the skeletal structures. A third was off to
the right, sitting on the close horizon. Across the blue space,
the smooth inner surface of the sphere seemed to be an
unfinished stage for a drama that would never be played
out. He closed his eyes for a moment, feeling tired; but the
inevitability of sleep seemed suddenly intolerable. The hours
of human sleep had always been a risky voyage, a passage
through the implicit and fearful, to be resisted by the engine
of awareness. Only those who were deeply resolved within
themselves would receive safe rest.

The need to attempt a return to Earth, he knew, could
not be ignored for long. He hoped that every passage through
the frames would carry them farther from the variant in
which Earth had died.

Lena touched his hand. "Juan, are you all right?"

"Yes," he said, looking into her eyes and feeling deeply grateful for her existence.

The ship was still there when they stepped out from the half circle of frames in the suncore.

"Shall we try a fourth?" Isak asked.

No one objected. Juan led the chain through into an identical tunnel.

"So methodical a people!" Ivan called out. "I don't think they had much of a sense of humor."

They came out into another shell and looked up. Starships hung like bunched grapes in the open space.

"They look like our ship," Juan said, intrigued by the possibility that the vessels were not yet operational. "We might learn something."

"So they built them in places like this," Magnus said, "then sent them out to string their web."

Ivan laughed. "Little realizing that ignoramuses like us would wander through and gape!"

"Ignorance is a map." Isak answered firmly. "Obviously incomplete, but the only one possible if one is to learn. We're finite creatures, for whom each ignorance is an infinite series of uniquely shaped holes that will accept only one piece of knowledge of the same shape—the positive to the negative space, to use a geometrical analogy. What we have seen shows us how much can be done, and that it has been done. The ship, the web, the replicator, the medical facilities—all flow from the same principles that make possible an elegant control of energies at the quantum level. That tells us that the builders had a profound grasp of the universe—a unified field theory accounting for all the forces as they are now, after they separated. The practical technology we see here must flow from such knowledge."

"That's fine," Ivan replied, "but what can we do with it ourselves besides appreciate it?"

"Be fair, old chap," Malachi said. "We can't expect to find technical manuals lying about. All the tech we've seen appears to have been designed so it wouldn't have to be serviced or tampered with by users."

"There must be manuals of some sort somewhere," Ivan insisted. "Not that we could read them."

Yerik said, "The ship is what we should start with. On

Earth we can bring all our resources to bear in studying it, and leave the web for later."

Juan turned away. "We'd better get back."

They emerged into the brightness of the suncore station and started toward the ship.

"It's not there," Lena said with dismay, letting go of Juan's hand. They hurried forward and came to the edge of the empty cradle. Juan's throat tightened; his companions were silent, their eyes wide from shock.

They dropped their packs. "Maybe it'll return," Dita said as they sat down on their gear.

"I knew I should have stayed," Ivan said.

"It's not your fault," Magnus answered. "We've entered a variant where it was never here."

Ivan asked, "Does the station have replicators?"

"Probably," Malachi said, "but we might starve before we found one."

Juan felt exhausted as he looked around at his companions, and felt lost. A lifetime of fears and doubts were eating their way out of the restraints he had built within himself.

Yerik grimaced. "We should never have left it." The red-haired man sat limply on his pack.

"We'll find other replicators," Isak said, "and another way home." He looked at Juan. "It's a large connected system, isn't it?"

Juan nodded. "We'll pass back and forth through a frame, which might put us into a variant where the ship is still here."

"Of course!" Isak exclaimed.

"If we're lucky," Juan added. "A million tries might not be enough."

27

ACROSS THE PROBABILITIES

●

They put on their packs and returned to the half circle of frames. Silently, they linked hands. Juan led the way into the fourth entrance. They passed through the tunnel into an empty, blue-lit sphere.

Isak said, "It seems the work was completed in this one, or never started."

They gazed into the vast space, then went back through the tunnel, with Juan bringing up the rear.

"It's not here," Magnus said as Juan emerged.

"We'll go again," he said.

They joined hands, and he went ahead, straining to see the exit. Finally, he stumbled through it—into darkness.

"Back!" he shouted. A children's game, he thought, as they reversed direction and led him back.

"It's here!" Isak shouted as Juan came out.

The ship loomed out of the brightness as they rushed to it. Juan felt relief, and the urgency to regain a living Earth before chance exiled them forever. The emotional ties with home, whatever there was of it, knotted up inside him, and he knew that every other aim had to arrange itself around that goal, for better or worse. His critical mind did not love humanity, even though he hoped for useful work that would survive him, and needed to belong. The war within him would have to play itself out, even if he suffered a loss of value and identity from which he would not recover. He felt unfinished as they approached the ship.

Malachi and Dita sat in the back of the drum-shaped chamber, near the exit, smoking cigarettes. The others rested on their sleeping bags. The warm amber glow was soothing; Juan felt suspended in a false peace.

Malachi murmured a few words to Dita; she laughed softly. The sound made Juan imagine small victories, and he wondered about the character of physical laws which made possible the rise of intelligence and crushed it at the same time. Inevitably, intelligence warred with such a universe, and struggled to work miracles. The early ones took the form of awkward technologies; later ones were more elegant, modifying the gross biological inheritance. But what had the web done for its builders? They had either destroyed themselves, or abandoned their works for something else.

Lena's hand touched his. "What is it?" she asked.

"Even with all this the builders failed, so what hope is there for us, or for what's left of us?"

She said, "Somewhere, humanity is alive. We've got to believe that, Juan."

He looked around the chamber. The resting shapes of his companions suggested dark creatures on a strange shore. "I suspect," he continued, "that even if we find a living variant, it won't last. Nothing human can last. Our only hope is to stop being human. Training, tradition, and ideals aren't enough to free us of what we are. The shining examples we've had have been freaks, wonderful only because they stood apart from the wretched norm. Scientific and cultural renaissance was declared whenever things were not obviously going backwards. A near standstill was progress. We're a failed species, unable to transcend its reptilian brain core, with every good motive tainted by hidden impulses."

"But we don't know how to stop being human," Lena said softly.

"Maybe it's time to start over, somewhere else. I fear finding our world again, afraid of what it'll do, or is already doing with the web."

"Think a moment, Juan." Her mouth twisted. "First you claim that nothing human lasts, then you suggest starting over somewhere else. Well, if what you say is true, then we wouldn't do any better." Her eyes seemed to stare past him. "Anyway, we can't start over. Too small a gene pool, for one thing, and neither Dita nor I would care to be brood mares in a hopeless effort."

He looked into her eyes. "I'm not being very clear," he said, taking her hand.

"I know how you feel," she answered. "Maybe we won't find our world again, but if we do its problems will still be there. I think you're feeling guilty that you're still alive." Her fingers gripped his hand tightly. "Misanthropy is easy. Making solutions work is hard, and never perfect."

"Yes," he said, "but there are degrees of imperfection and failure. Our kind wasn't content with killing itself off. Even if the destroyed variant had survived, the planet was dying."

"You're wrong about humanity," she said.

"I hope so—but what if I'm right?"

"What else can we call it," Magnus was saying as Juan awakened. "They were building an empire."

"Why did they bother," Ivan said, "if they were going to abandon it?"

Juan lay still and listened.

"Empires start out for many reasons," Magnus continued, "among them economics and exploration. But unexpected developments modify original goals. Their technology progressed rapidly to materials synthesis, which obviated the need for agriculture and basic resources." It seemed to Juan that Magnus was struggling with himself as he spoke, to keep himself going.

Ivan said, "Except they still needed the power of stars."

"But they were left free to explore," Magnus continued, "and to give free reign to religious and aesthetic impulses. They could go anywhere and create any kind of environment they wanted, for whatever reason."

"How about power and pride?" Ivan asked.

"If they achieved practical life-extension," Magnus went on, ignoring the question, "then that might have reduced their numbers. Why reproduce when you can become your own posterity? Long life would also select out those who lost interest."

"So they're somewhere," Ivan said, "but why did they abandon the things we've seen?" He sounded affronted.

Magnus sighed. "Social systems lag behind the growth of knowledge and vision. For example, under the pressure of advances in biology and artificial intelligence, a species may become physically fluid, while still engaged in projects like this empire. Suddenly, intelligence is able to break the biological limits in which it developed, to cease being the organism that it was and quantum-jump into a new state. Social visions fail because a species is hobbled by inward structures, which evolved to meet the needs of survival in earlier environments. The old biology brakes aspiration. On Earth, utopian communities failed because a human being could not stop behaving according to what evolution and human history had made of him."

Juan turned his head and saw Magnus's silhouette standing in the amber glow. "We've always glimpsed better things," the older man said, "but lacked the inner means to achieve them. The organism, measuring itself by itself, cannot equal its dreams. The conduct of science with the help of artificial intelligence and mathematics—a cognitive activity that stands outside the older human nature—is a transcendent activity, a check on opinion, custom, and self-interest. A species makes this transition to relative objectivity or destroys itself."

"But the process you're describing," Lena said suddenly, "may lead to profound stresses, as an elite part of the species develops contempt for its own kind."

Magnus scratched his head. "Yes, that may be a fatal conflict. But my point is that each rapid development outstrips the needs it was meant to remedy, by opening up new paths. That's what we may be seeing in this vast system of ships and frames. The builders may have achieved another kind of existence. Earth may have been one of their last outposts, just before a great change of some kind occurred."

Yerik sat up. "Perhaps the continued use of the web simply emptied out the variants we've visited. Elsewhere the empire continues. If we pass through the frames often enough, we might chance on it."

Juan turned on his side and said, "I don't understand how that could happen. It suggests broken symmetries and skipped variants."

"Well, why not?" Yerik objected. "Perhaps errors occur, and emptying can happen."

"I don't understand it either," Magnus said.

"What I'd like to know," Isak said, "is how they built things. We've seen only finished things, machines without moving parts. What we've seen suggests that they built things from the inside."

"Maybe they built with mental tools," Magnus replied, "and that put them on the road to another kind of existence, as ethereal beings, patterned energies, moving like ghosts through our universe."

Isak's stocky shape rose and leaned toward the wiry one of Magnus. "Do you realize what that implies?" he demanded, as if Magnus had just made some childish error. "Such close contact with the basic structure of reality might eliminate quantum-observer interference in physical observation. The status of observers would change fundamentally."

Magnus said softly, "The truth might be even more disturbing, perhaps incomprehensible."

"They might have sculpted new forms of life with such mental tools," Lena said, "and seeded worlds with such life. Perhaps that was all that was left for them, to watch new intelligences climb up through the mysteries, in the hope of learning something new."

"And we might be what came of such a seeding," Malachi cut in. "I would still prefer to think we came up the hard way, out of an unconscious process."

"It might have been quite routine," Lena continued, "their setting up of initial conditions, knowing that intelligence would develop sooner or later. Perhaps all life developed as the guided panspermia of the first intelligence to spring up in the cosmos. And only that first appearance came about by chance, creating a biological chain reaction. It may be that each intelligent species, as it discovers this vast lineage, acquires a need to do the same wherever it sees a chance for sentience, if its civilization survives long enough."

Malachi waved a hand as he lay on his back. "But perhaps we're the only other species that came up out of the unconscious process, without parenting."

The builders would have nothing to learn from us, Juan thought. Human inroads into the enigmas were few—relativity, quantum theory, Gödel's proof, the scattered insights of novels and works of art. Still, he told himself, if any of these origins were possible, then there might be a chance for human progress. Traditions, training, education, even a creative bioengineering of the organism, might become more than a totalitarian imposition on the animal; it might be a common sequence of developments, following a course that had already succeeded elsewhere countless times. The star web might be only a toy left for offspring to play with and puzzle over. Suddenly Juan longed, and his feelings threatened to hurl him into blind faith. Humanity would only have to be patient with itself, ignore the flicker of short-lived generations—and soar!

Nice, he told himself, bitterly. You'll grasp at anything. The variants they had seen were scattered around one set of historical outcomes, in a narrow range. Even if the builders of the web could be found, the encounter might be disastrous. The notion of hoisting humankind into a better state was perilous, linked to self-loathing and megalomania.

Isak turned and waved his hands. "I dream of a repository of knowledge, in which is recorded how all this was accomplished, and why!"

Magnus shrugged. "In a language we may never comprehend."

"Perhaps not," Dita said, gesturing with her cigarette. "If we are related to the builders, then the underlying symbolic forms of their minds may not be unlike ours."

Juan felt sorrow for humankind's glimpsed infinities. Grow wings, make yourself worthy of dreams! But how? The stick always comes out with the same answer when it measures itself.

"I'm tired of all this!" Ivan shouted suddenly. "You talk as if humanity still stood behind us. We're alone, and will die alone."

Earth is there, alive and whole, Juan thought in the silence.

Somewhere.

28

GRIEVED GHOSTS

overcame over... ... were steady, their... ... oasis on the black floor? He stood aside as his... ... so the through the glow, then turned off his helmet light...
... ... light, overcome by the fact that they were the... ...

"Juan, wake up," Lena said softly.

He struggled to open his eyes, held back by a vision of the starcrossers in joyous congregation, climbing through ever-increasing states of knowledge and bliss to a critical mass of culture rich with laughter and incongruity, a universe opening inward, mocking the silence of infinite spaces. . . .

He sat up suddenly, confronted by a puzzle from his youth that seemed new again. Why should there be anything at all, rather than nothing? Did the starcrossers know the answer on their inward shore?

As he prepared his pack for departure, he realized that sleep had given him only a physical renewal; curiosity was stronger in him than hope.

"All set?" Malachi asked, looking around the chamber.

The amber light seemed to promise a sunrise. Juan felt reluctant to leave the ship, which offered the security of clean air, food and shelter, and health care. What else could grieved ghosts from a failed species ask for?

He turned and led the way up to the exit.

"We're all agreed?" Juan asked as their helmet lights wandered across the frames in the deep chamber.

"No more delays," Ivan said. "It's the only one we know leads directly home."

Juan took Lena's hand and faced the third frame from the left. As the others linked hands, he again imagined passages snaking in and out of a million suns, bypassing the interstellar quarantine of worlds. Ghostly material shot through the snakes and reassembled into solidity at ports of call.

"Ready?" he asked, suddenly afraid that his mind would not bridge the worlds he had lost.

"Push on," Malachi said.

He hurried through the darkness into the identical chamber, feeling that he was a whisper in some vast inner ear.

"All through," Lena said, letting go of his hand.

He went to the large exit. It glowed and he stepped through—

—into the familiar passage.

The yellow-orange overheads were steady, their reflections clear in the black floor. He stood aside as his companions came through the glow, then turned off his helmet light and faced them, overcome by the fact that they were the last ties to the humanity he knew. Slowly, with a growing sense of apprehension, he turned and led the way up toward the distant lock.

Their boots echoed on the hard floor as he quickened the pace.

He stopped suddenly. "What was that?"

"I didn't hear anything," Lena replied.

"A deep rumble."

"If the ship has taken off," Isak said, "then we're trapped."

Juan confronted the inner lock. It glowed open, revealing the blue-lit chamber. Their supply cases were still there.

"Mal and I will go up and check," Juan said as they entered and the door glowed shut behind them. They dropped their packs. He turned on his helmet light, lowered the faceplate, and stepped toward the outer door. It glowed open. He crawled up the earthen tunnel.

"I'm almost at the sinkhole," he shouted.

"Right behind you," Malachi answered.

He got to his feet in the small space. Mal crawled up and stood beside him, peering at the glowing display of his radiation counter. "Well over normal," he said, "even in here."

Juan took his own out and checked it. "Same here," he said, then slipped it back in his pocket and looked up at the black opening. "Boost me up."

He stepped into Mal's joined hands and went up through the hole. The stars were bright over the sleeping jungle as he climbed out on the hillside and stood up in a moonless night. He took out his counter, and felt shame; it was well into the red.

He reached down and hoisted Mal up, then looked up at the stars as his friend checked his counter. "Hi," Malachi said, "approaching lethal."

"So's mine. Temperature seems lower. The wind hasn't had a chance to bring the dust yet." He unclipped his handset. "If the cruiser's still on the highway, maybe I can patch into UN-ERS channels." He swept the channels, hoping to lock on, but there was only white noise.

Malachi said, "Seems no one made it to the ship."

"Obviously there wasn't time." Juan imagined going down to the cruiser, driving up into North America, up the west coast to his home town, then walking down the street to his house to find his parents dead in their beds.

"We'd better get back," Malachi said. "These suits offer limited protection."

Where shall we seek our better selves, Juan thought, if we can't escape what's within us? No new start could avoid a fresh flowering of the same human nature given us by the evolving slaughterhouse. His throat tightened. He wanted to cry out the truth, as if that would be enough to unshackle him from the beast, then looked up at the stars he had loved since boyhood. How could his kind fail in the midst of so much bright beauty? The universe sings with light, but we choose darkness.

Malachi climbed down into the hole. Juan clipped the handset to his belt and followed him.

"We'll try again," Juan said as they went back down the passage.

"Do you think it can make a difference in how we go through?" Isak asked. "I mean from where to where. Perhaps we should vary our passages. It might affect the probabilities."

"Worth trying," Juan replied. "We may have to go through quite a few times to get past a long run of terminal variants. We may never leave them behind."

"What are you saying?" Ivan demanded.

"There may be thousands, or millions. If it's an infinity, then it means our kind is just no damn good." He laughed. "Of course, we'll never know if it's an infinity."

"You're exaggerating," Dita said.

"I hope so."

"Let's not prejudge," Magnus said. "We'll try, no matter how many it takes."

"It may be the very next one," Yerik said anxiously.

Juan glanced at Lena. She avoided his gaze.

Their helmet lights played over the frames in the deep chamber.

"Which one?" Isak asked.

"We'll go back and forth the way we came," Juan said. "No point in exploring yet. Plenty of time for risks if we fail." He took Lena's hand. "Ready?"

He led them through into the identical chamber in Ship One. They turned around and came back, then one by one slipped out through the glow into the passage.

As they returned to the drum-shaped chamber, Juan said, "Mal and I'll go take the first readings."

Dawn was filtering through the overcast sky when they crawled out onto the hillside. Juan stood up and took out his counter as Malachi rose next to him.

"What's yours?" Malachi asked, peering at his own instrument.

"Same as before, and climbing." He looked out over the jungle. Its sounds seemed peaceful, oblivious to the death of humankind. In a billion years it might dream up another intelligent creature, who would flee when its mind lit up with the shame of self-awareness, and return to wreck vengeance on the forest. Was any mind born of nature protean enough to transcend its prison? All human societies had fallen. Totalitarian systems, both secular and religious, had failed at control; more representative systems had sought a stability that could assimilate change, and had still shackled the mind. Jehovah had warred with human nature and nearly wiped it out—but to no avail. The true myth of humanity was not the story of Sisyphus embracing the burden of his rock, but the tale of Jacob's night struggle with the angel.

"Try your handset," Malachi said. "I'm not getting anything."

Juan took his out and listened as it swept through the hissing of snakes.

• • •

Again they faced the black frames. Juan led the chain through and followed it back.

"If you don't mind," he said back in the drum-shaped chamber, "I'll take an extra turn."

"Same here," Malachi added.

The sun was near noon when they came out on the hillside. Juan checked his meter. Once again the Earth registered death. He stared at the digital readout, thinking of how many people might still be living if it had been only a few points lower. Opening his radio, he listened to the dead planet and thought of how he had lived his life, burying his chaotic feelings and impulses, along with his dismay at human failure, in the cellar of his mind as he struggled to keep his gaze fixed on his kind's finest examples. But now, in this series of failed worlds, humanity had lost control of itself.

He looked toward the horizon, trying to glimpse some sign of the coming nuclear winter. It would come late to these latitudes, darkening the sky long enough to prevent the forest from drinking the sunlight. What was left of the great oxygen factory would live near death for years, and even if the vegetation came back, it might be too late for most animal life.

He looked down, saw Malachi disappearing into the hillside, and followed him back into the hole.

"So, we do it again?" Ivan asked.

"Scarcely a choice," Malachi said as they sat in the pit. Dita was at his side, looking at him with her mournful brown eyes.

Isak sat cross-legged on the floor. "Maybe we should wait before repeating our passage, or vary what we do."

"You may be right," Juan said, shifting on his pack. "We'll try the first frame, then the fourth, fifth and sixth."

Ivan smiled. "It's a lottery."

"Just about," Juan said.

"And if they all fail?" Dita asked sadly, leaning against Malachi.

"We'll keep at it. The ship will support us for the rest of our lives."

"As we seek the holy grail of an unsullied Earth," Ivan said bitterly.

Yerik asked, "Are we doing something wrong? I mean some physical action."

"What is a right action!" Isak shouted. "We go through

and come back. What kind of mistake can there be in that?" His round face flushed with anger.

"These variants flow from what we are," Juan said, looking at Lena. She sat on her pack, leaning forward with her hands together. "The run of terminal worlds may be a locked infinity."

"But better outcomes are not impossible," Dita protested. "They must exist somewhere!"

"But not for us to find," Ivan said with repressed anger. "Perhaps our unconscious is steering us into dead worlds."

"Let's face it," Lena said. "We don't know what we're doing, and there's no way to find out."

"We must understand," Magnus cut in, "that the universe branches continuously. Each variant tunnels off on its own and continues to split. We're part of the process. Ordinarily, junctures occur as normal developments in our experience, where one thing happens and not another, or when we make a choice. But the frames enable us to move across variants in a way that reveals what is normally hidden from us. We've learned that we can't have what we want, and that what is likely is also very limited."

"So what else is new?" Ivan asked. "Maybe we're not wishing hard enough."

Lena and Dita came through the glow and walked slowly down into the pit. Juan sat up and saw from their faces that there was no change outside.

"The readings are even worse," Lena said, sitting down next to him.

Dita knelt down next to Malachi. "The sky is darker," she added, "and the temperature is falling."

Lena took a deep breath. "It's the same world over and over again."

They had all taken turns making the observations, but after a dozen passes through the frames it seemed that a thousand tries would not be enough.

"Maybe we're reentering the same world," Ivan said.

"Possibly," Juan replied, "but the readings change too quickly and the contours of the hill vary."

"It would be a discovery," Magnus said, "to learn that we could enter the same variant repeatedly."

"It is the same world!" Ivan shouted bitterly. "Our world—because it always destroys itself."

29
BROKEN SYMMETRY

◐

Juan grasped Lena's hand and led the chain through the first frame. Warm, stale air pushed into his lungs as he stepped out into low gravity. While the others came through, he noticed three oval exits ahead, then cast his beam around the chamber. There were no additional frames.

He faced the three exits. "Do we go back, or see where these lead?"

"I'm willing," Yerik said.

"I don't care to be disappointed again right away," Ivan added.

"Middle exit, then," Juan said. He stepped forward. It glowed—

—and he emerged into a dark tunnel ramp. The others came out and stood on either side of him.

"Something very hot cut these smooth walls," Malachi said.

"This air is not being renewed," Dita said.

Juan went slowly up the ramp, and came out into a large chamber. He looked upward, and glimpsed a distant ceiling in his beam. Slowly, they moved ahead, stirring up dust on the polished surface.

"There, to the right!" Malachi shouted, fixing an exit with his beam. They hurried toward it. Juan went through the glow—

—into another dark tunnel, and waited for his companions.

"What now?" Yerik asked. Juan went forward and around a turn, which led them into another large chamber. Their beams caught three vehicles with UN-ERS insignia.

"Moonbuses!" Malachi exclaimed. "We're on Luna."

Isak said, "So there's a variant in which an alien station was found on the Moon."

Juan cast his light beyond the three vehicles, revealing a large exit. "Can we drive one of these out of here?" Ivan asked.

"Let's see," Yerik replied as he went up to a vehicle and touched the entry plate. The bus lit up inside as the door slid open. "Well, what do we do?" he asked, looking at Juan.

"Maybe we can learn something," Juan said.

He waited until the others were inside, then followed, closing the door behind him.

The brightly lit cab held seats for a dozen people. Malachi went forward and checked the drive controls. Juan followed and sat down at his right, checking the pressurization display, which was counting up to normal. The vehicle's cozy interior was a relief after the alien designs.

"I can do it," his friend said. The engine came alive with a low whine, and the vehicle moved toward the exit. It glowed and Malachi gunned the bus through—

—into a starry Lunar landscape. Juan peered up through the canopy and saw a full Earth hanging low in the sky to his right, looking like bruised flesh. Red-browns streaked the latitudes between icecaps, where oxygen-producing greenery was dying for lack of sunlight under the shroud of windborne debris. Farm animals were being slaughtered as their feed ran out. Wild animals were devouring each other and the cold human dead in the gathering gloom. New variants of his parents had died. He wondered what it was like in the underground Swiss city, in the official bunkers and caves.

Malachi stopped the vehicle. They all came forward and looked out at the planet that was dying in the black desert of space. To simply drive out and see the suicide of humankind among bright stars, at a glance, was numbing.

"Can we raise one of the Lunar bases?" Ivan asked.

"We're in a crater," Malachi said, "and I don't see a line-of-sight antenna relay. There may be a satellite overhead."

"Look there," Lena said, pointing. "Tread marks."

Juan said, "They found this entrance, but there wasn't time to explore below. We've got to contact the bases and tell them what we know. Supplies may be short with nothing coming up from Earth."

Malachi worked the communications gear on the panel. "If

there's a relay overhead, we'll get a base on the UN-ERS channels."

"If anyone's here," Yerik said. "They might have left before the war started."

"I'm getting the synchronous satellite, but nothing else. We'll follow the tracks."

Dust floated around the vehicle as it sped across the crater floor.

"I'm surprised," Ivan said, "that the com-satellite is still there."

Lena pointed suddenly. "A deep crater ahead."

Malachi halted the bus. "No—I think that's what's left of UN Lunar Base Two." He took a deep breath and sat back.

Juan's voice broke as he said, "There's nothing we can do here. Better get back."

Increased gravity tugged at Juan as he came out into the starship. He waited for the others to emerge, then let go of Lena's hand.

Dita gasped, looking startled. "Where's Ivan?" Malachi asked suddenly, casting his beam around the chamber.

"We must have left him behind," Yerik said.

"No," Malachi insisted. "I was last out and he was in front of me."

"You were holding his hand?" Juan asked with dismay.

"Yes, but I came out holding Dita's. I'm certain."

The Russian woman nodded. "He was just behind me—I know it."

Juan cast his beam across the six frames, hoping that at any moment Ivan would appear.

"What happened to him?" Dita asked.

Malachi said, "Something subtracted him."

"Broken symmetries," Juan said softly. "Errors in the frame transfer."

"What can we do?" Dita asked.

"Nothing, I'm afraid," Magnus answered. "This may explain the variant effect. Leave a system unused for a long time and it will function regularly for a while. A faucet may drip uniformly—but as small bits of damage accumulate the drops will become more frequent, and finally, with the onset of chaos, the water will flow through freely. It took a long time for the systems we've seen to deteriorate. There was a problem with one of the doors in the ship's passage. Eventually the web may become subject to all kinds of unpredictable effects, and might not work at all."

"Is it possible," Isak asked, "that the variant effect was intended?"

"Seems it wasn't," Magnus replied.

"How disappointing, to think that with all their ingenuity they could not have built in safeguards against such deterioration. But it's good evidence that the builders have not been around for quite some time."

"It's possible," Magnus continued, "that in coming back from the Moon we entered a variant which already had Ivan in it, so two of him could not be permitted to exist."

Juan said, "Our alternates have always left by the time we returned. His way might have been blocked by a living Ivan somewhere in this variant."

"I hope the Ivan we knew," Dita said, "went home to the living."

Isak sighed. "Then we must conclude that if Ivan was subtracted, then people are alive in this variant, him included?"

"It might be only small groups," Juan said, not daring to hope for more.

Juan watched grimly as Isak and Yerik slipped through the glow and came silently down into the pit. He leaned back against his pack.

"Quite tiresome," Malachi mumbled.

Dita was weeping softly. Magnus cleared his throat; his face sagged with despair.

Yerik gave his pack a kick and sat down on it. "It can't require an infinite number of tries."

Malachi helped Dita to her feet. The same lost look was in his dark eyes and in her tilted ones. She slipped her arm through his as they went up to the exit. Juan gazed after them as they passed through the glow, then turned to Lena, suddenly wanting to embrace her.

"We should all get some sleep," she murmured, giving him an apologetic glance.

He closed his eyes, calmed by the decisive tone of her voice, and fell into a dream of Ivan on the ruined Earth. Had he been dispersed, or simply diverted to balance an alternate's passage? His dreams worried the mysteries like prayer beads, running through endless combinations of images. Bits and pieces of his companions came through the frames at

random. His own head went into a lonely darkness, while a
universe away his arms and legs flailed helplessly, still somehow connected to his awareness. He woke up in a sweat,
wondering who kept track of the symmetries and made sure
they were obeyed.

After eating, they shouldered their packs and went down
to the deep chamber to face the frames again.

"Ready?" Juan asked. He glanced behind him at the
shorter chain, then took Lena's hand and went through to the
Lunar complex, hoping that somehow Ivan would be there to
greet them. Lena's hand tightened in his, then slipped away.
He stumbled forward, turned, and saw that he was alone.

He waited a moment, rushed back through the frame, and
cast his light around the chamber.

"Hello!" he shouted in the empty chamber. He went
through the frame again. The Lunar chamber was empty.

This had happened to Ivan, he realized, fighting panic, and
there was no way to undo it. Going back and forth through
the frame might only send him further away in probability
from Lena and the others.

He dropped his pack, sat down on it and tried to think.
The Lena he knew was now lost with all his companions and
the first Earth, in the quantum whirl of worlds locked around
an axis of destruction. What else could he do except continue
to use the frames? He should go out and check this variant.
As he got up and put on his pack, he realized that he was
thinking like a gambler who can't pass up one more try,
convinced that the next one would win.

As he went up the winding passage, he saw himself drifting
across the probabilities for the rest of his life, visiting an
infinity of terminal Earths, wandering through the alien maze
like a rat, living on the echoes of his provisions.

He came to within a few meters of the outer lock and
stopped, afraid to face a ruined Earth alone. He stood there,
a stranger to himself.

Suddenly the lock glowed, revealing two dark figures in
the inner chamber, standing against the circle of daylight that
showed through the open outer lock. They came in and
pointed weapons at him.

"Who are you?" a male voice demanded.

He stepped forward and saw the UN-ERS markings on their military uniforms. "I'm Dr. Juan Obrion," he said, suddenly too exhausted to feel relieved.

The two soldiers glanced at each other. "Come with us," the woman said, sounding doubtful.

He stepped between them and they marched him out through the lock. He squinted as he came out into the bright sunlight, then saw that he was at the top of a long dirt ramp that wound down to the bottom of the hill. A large area of jungle had been burned away to make room for a cluster of white domes. The forest seemed poised around the wound, ready to return.

As they went down the right-handed incline, Juan breathed in the moist, dusty air. Take away the greenery and the Amazon's soil was a desert, in which only the forest knew how to thrive.

They reached bottom and started toward the domes. "Were you expecting me?" Juan asked as they came to the largest dome.

"You're to go in," the male soldier said, pressing his palm to the ID lock.

The outer door slid open. Juan entered the small chamber and took off his helmet. The outer door slid shut behind him and the inner door opened. He came out into a large circular room with a desk, two chairs, communications equipment, and a small bed. Titus Summet got up from the sofa to the right of the desk.

"Juan—finally! You're lucky I was here today. Strip off that stuff. You must be baking."

Juan dropped his helmet, then his pack. "How long has all this been here?" He asked as he began removing his oversuit.

"Nearly a year. Let me give you a hand with that."

Juan stepped out of his oversuit and staggered to the sofa. "A year?" he asked as he sat down.

Titus went over to a cooler and poured a cold drink. "We'd only begun to think about your group again about a month ago, after the war ended."

Juan took the tall glass of iced tea from Titus's hand and sipped nervously.

"It was close," the older man continued. "Only a dozen warheads. UN police beams stopped all but two. Then it was over."

Juan took a long pull on his drink. "Where did they hit?"

"Only silos got it, but one of them was near Moscow. Very few dead, but it scared the life out of everyone in the world."

"Was it an accident?"

Titus turned one of the chairs around and sat down. "Who knows—the Chinese say it was a mistake and so do we, officially. It was the last chance for anyone to try a first strike before the police beams came on line. From now on it'll take more missiles than anyone has to get through, which will discourage nuclear arsenals among the smaller nations. The rest of us won't want to replace the missiles that come up for maintenance. That'll take time, but I believe it'll sink in. With so many other problems to throw money at, politicians will be relieved not to have to increase their military spending."

Juan took a deep breath. Somehow, he had escaped the dead zone. The next variant might even be an improvement on this one, with no nuclear exchange of any kind.

Titus said, "This may be the best vaccine we've ever had. Heads of state are in New York right now. Something new is in the works. Now tell me what happened to you."

Juan told him of their encounter with the Soviet survivors, the ship's journey into the Sun, and the treatment of the injured. After describing his group's further exploration of the seemingly deserted web, he told Titus about the run of destroyed Earths.

Strain showed in Summet's face. "Who's with you in the ship?"

Juan clenched his teeth. "I was separated from the others as we came through a frame. We lost Ivan earlier in the same way." A wild hope stabbed through him. "Are they here?"

"No," Titus said. "You're the only one who's come back." He rubbed his temples. "It's an unnerving story, Juan. I don't feel as hopeful or relieved as I have in the last few days."

"But this variant is the first break I've seen in the run of doomed histories," Juan replied.

Titus smiled and shook his head. "For now, perhaps. The causes of war live deeply. Whose progeny will inherit the future? As long as we're limited creatures who can't live forever and don't have much while we live, we'll use power as a consolation, if only to clinch our children's hold on futurity. It could be otherwise, I suppose, if we didn't fear death, if the afterlife were a certainty, or if we could live as long as we wished in fulfilling ways."

"What do you think happened?" Juan asked.

"More than we'll ever dig out. A few military minds realized the truth—that energy weapons would create a stalemate, especially if the UN also had them. No more dreams of seizing the future from your enemy. This strike was the last chance to knock out the First World before the bolts of Zeus came on line. It could have been worse. It didn't escalate because cooler heads broke the orders at key points. We'll have peace while nuclear bombs become obsolete, but heaven help us if we develop new, precise weapons that can strike at vital areas without threatening the environment."

"Why are you here now?"

"As you saw, we've excavated the ship. I want to put physical restraints on it, although keeping the lock open will probably be enough to prevent it from leaving. Then we'll study it as best we can. The Soviets are sending people here, since their ship is gone."

"It may be in the Sun," Juan said.

"How are you feeling?"

"I guess I'm okay."

"We'll have you checked."

Juan sat back, closed his eyes, and breathed deeply. "I never expected to see a whole Earth again. It was stultifying to see human history so narrowed. The war seemed to hang on across an infinity of variants. The time I lost suggests that somehow I moved off that axis." He opened his eyes and stared at Summet. "There was never a hint of better variants."

Titus rubbed his chin and leaned forward. "Maybe utopias belong to the future, not to contemporary variants."

"I've told myself that," Juan said, "but what's the future to be made from, if not from these presents, these pasts, this human nature?" He laughed suddenly. "It's just not possible, is it?"

"You need rest."

"Why do people believe that rest will soften harsh judgments?" He shouted, "Rest can't change facts!"

"But you need it, nonetheless."

The intercom buzzed. Summet got up, went around behind his desk, sat down and stared into a small screen. Juan could barely hear the other voice. "Yes, we'll pave the ramp," Titus said. "Call the head engineer, not me. No, I don't know where he is. You can find his damn number yourself." He hung up.

Juan closed his eyes again and feared that he had arrived just in time to see this variant destroy itself. He had to get back to the ship right away. He thought of his lost companions, then opened his eyes suddenly to see Titus leaning over him. "Don't you see?" Juan asked, sitting up. "I've lost my first world and countless others. Don't you realize what's happened to me?" He fell back.

Summet stood over him. "I understand and sympathize, Juan. But what can we do? All our pasts fade away as we grow and change. Our choices cut away one thing after another from our minds. Old joys can't be had again. We never feel as free as we did in childhood. Am I so different here?"

"You're the same," Juan said sadly, realizing that Titus was trying to be decent to him.

"You seem pretty much the man I knew," Titus continued with what seemed to be genuine concern. "I came here regularly and waited, because I believed you would return."

"I'm the last one left," Juan said, standing up, "who's seen variants. Titus, we've got to tell everyone about the ruined Earths! It may be the only thing that will do any good." An infinity of variants spoke through his sorrow. He was at the crossroads of every decent impulse that his kind had ever had.

"I know, I know," Titus muttered, helping him down to the sofa. "Lie down and sleep. Please, Juan."

30

A STRANGE ATTRACTOR

◑

"Juan—wake up!" Titus shouted. Stony fingers pushed against his chest. "Get up!" Juan opened his eyes and sat up on the sofa.

Titus said, "Come outside."

"What is it?" His temples throbbed, his eyes wouldn't focus, and his throat was dry, but he struggled into his boots and staggered into the lock.

Stifling hot air hit him in the face as the outer door slid open and they stepped into the bright sunlight. Juan squinted toward the hill, where a line of people was descending the spiral dirt ramp from the ship. As his eyes adjusted, he recognized Kaliapin; Ivan was with him.

He stumbled forward and tried to shout a greeting, but his dry throat let out only a feeble croak. He kept going. "Ivan!" he rasped as he reached the bottom of the ramp. "Anatoli!" he added in a shrill voice.

He grasped their hands as the two men reached him. "My dear Dr. Obrion," Kaliapin said. "How good it is to see you." Ivan stood back from him, looking puzzled.

"There are quarters for all!" Titus shouted as people came down past them.

Ivan asked, "What's happened here?"

"No war," Juan replied hoarsely, realizing that this wasn't quite the man he had known.

Kaliapin sipped cold tea as he relaxed on Summet's sofa. "We left the Sun because it seemed that the ship would never stir again. Now we can at least go home, whatever the differences." This Kaliapin had also been exploring the alien ship when the war broke out. His group had gone through what seemed to be the same sequence of events, which meant that their doubles in this variant, who had also been exploring the ship, were no longer here.

"And you will go home," Summet said, "as soon as possible."

Juan was still astonished that the Russians had hit upon a whole Earth in one try. There was an inner dynamic involved in passing through the frames, he realized. A system of space-like travel was deteriorating, making variants accessible as it drifted toward chaos. His loss of a year in this variant suggested that timelike drifts were also creeping into the system. This might even be the Kaliapin he had known, swept here by some similar current of probability, or so close to the same person that it would take extensive questioning to prove otherwise. Increasingly, he was beginning to think that the infinity of variants coexisted in one vast superposition, stacked like a series of clear overlays, varying very little from one to the next, but gradually shading into major differences.

He turned to Ivan. "What happened to you?"

The Russian shifted in his chair. "I stayed behind when you and the others left. What do you remember?"

Juan told him what had happened.

"And the others are still lost?" Ivan asked.

"Yes."

Their tea glasses were empty. Summet made the rounds, filling them up again. Juan tried to think what kind of growing chaos turbulence might be affecting the frame links, and realized that both variant effect and time displacement reflected patterns governed by laws that he could only guess at. What strange attractors permitted passage between variants? Was this one a relatively stable region in the flux of histories, the variant that would survive and progress while an infinity of failures spiraled around it? He was reaching for a guarantee of hope, even though he suspected that the dynamic of each variant could offer only opportunities.

At week's end the Russians who had come out of the Sun began to leave in small groups of twenty. Ivan left with the last group, without saying good-bye. Soon the camp was empty again, except for construction and maintenance crews. Juan wandered around the partially exposed ship in the evenings, examining it with new eyes as it sat in the net of utility lights.

Titus was not pressing him to do anything, and Juan felt him to be a more humane version of the man he had known. Crews entered the ship from time to time to duplicate provisions for the base, and sometimes he went in with them. Guards changed regularly at the lock. Occasionally, after a starlight walk around the perimeter, he listened to radio broadcasts. The world was still in a state of shock, but he found that comforting. He missed Lena, Malachi, and Magnus, as well as the three Soviets, whom he had begun to count as new friends. Lena and Mal had been his last link with the primary Earth, which was now probably dead, lost in an infinite regress of variants.

Construction went on around the ship. A ceramic dike and supports were put in place to prevent the ship from shifting during the rainy season. There was talk of putting a weatherproof dome over the entire installation.

One evening he heard voices coming from the ship and went over to the bottom of the ramp to listen. The guards seemed to be arguing in the lock. He started up, hoping for some conversation; there was always a chance of picking up a detail about this variant. The differences he had found so far were minor, but their reality awed him. Sports records were changed; half again as many people had survived the sinking of the *Titanic*; Reagan had recovered from his assassin's bullet in the 1980s.

He heard a woman's voice as he neared the lock, and sprinted up the rest of the way.

"Lena!" he shouted, pushing past the guards. She rushed into his arms. Mal and Magnus grabbed his shoulders and laughed with relief as Isak, Dita, and Yerik looked on. Lena kissed him for a long time.

"What do you remember?" Juan demanded suddenly, staring into her eyes. They were still as blue, her hair the same shade of blond.

"Your hand left mine," she said nervously. "We tried again and arrived here."

"Yes!" Isak shouted. "It may be that we've come the same way."

He wanted to believe it was true as he looked at her. She shook him roughly. "Juan, it's me. No matter what, it's me."

"We were right behind you in the run," Magnus said.

"How can we ever be sure?" he asked.

"Ask a thousand questions!" Isak cried. "I'll wager you'll find no differences."

Lena kissed him again. "Take me somewhere private," she whispered as he led her out to the ramp.

"Welcome home," one of the guards said, standing aside.

"Lena," Juan said suddenly, "did President Reagan die when he was shot?"

"Of course he did," she replied.

31
ANOTHER AUTUMN

◗

A stranger's voice answered when he called his parents'
house from his New York City hotel. He looked into the
living room.

"Hello, I'm the county's agent for this property." A short
red-haired woman dressed in a gray business suit stepped
into view. "May I show you around?" she continued. "If you
have a three-dee display, press one now. If you wish to speak
to me directly, press two."

Juan pressed 2 and said, "I'd like to speak to Adela
Obrion." The red-haired woman's face replaced the re-
cording. "Where can I reach her?"

"Oh, I'm sorry, but Mrs. Obrion died a few months
ago."

Juan took a deep breath. "And Mr. Obrion?"

"Oh, she'd been a widow for three years. You might be
able to reach her son. One of the neighbors told me he was
working on some government thing and couldn't come to the
funeral. You'd think they would have let him, even if he was
on the Moon or something. Her two sisters were quite
upset—"

"Her sisters?" Juan cut in.

"Oh, yes. They get the money from the house and furnish-
ings, after the county takes its taxes, of course, but if you're
shopping you won't have to worry about the Federal taxes.
It will all be cleaned and personal things removed into storage for her son. The sisters are quite upset. I think his name
was Jan or John. I can't be sure. Say, who are you anyway?
Are you interested in buying? My name is—"

He hung up.

• • •

The autumn was unchanged as he walked down the leaf-strewn street toward the house, and it seemed impossible that he would not find everyone at home, even the two aunts he had acquired. Somewhere, they were all here, with the same sunset, waiting.

He looked up. Vastness waited to swallow the Earth as stars pierced the clouding sky. The strength of a million suns sang through the alien web, challenging his hopes. What can we learn from it? What can we do with it? What will it do to us? His father's fearful echo asked the questions.

The Earth lived, but his own connections to its history had been weakened further; yet it remained his world. The pulse of possibility beat within him, insisting that joy could be won. Human intellect might still prevail, enabling humankind to escape its torments and reach for what it longed to be, not what it had been given to be. Utopia could not be found in mere probabilities. It would be found within, through basic changes in humanity, in ages to come, where the frames could not take him.

A gust of wind whirled the leaves on the sidewalk in front of him. He walked through them, and for a moment was free of despair. It had deepened his understanding, but he could not follow it into its bitter trap. The exploration of the web would continue; the price of discovery would be paid. "We need time to learn," Isak had insisted. "The starcrossers left us a piece of their history, and continued on their journey to something very different. One day we may follow, but we must have time."

"You're right, Isak," he whispered as he neared the house. Clouds sailed in from the north, threatening rain, and he reminded himself that this variant had not destroyed itself, that it had pulled back from the edge—from beyond the edge. Surely that meant something; even if this world failed in the end, others would succeed. For all things to be possible, everything had to happen.

Meanwhile, he would learn to live in the probabilities, certain of uncertainty as he slipped through the mystery of the variants. Enigmas and ambiguities would blind him; answers might present themselves even when he asked the wrong questions.

He came at last to the house, passed through the open gate, and kicked over the realtor's sign on his way to the door. He was the sole owner now, after paying the taxes, but he was still not sure why he wanted it.

He wandered the empty rooms on the first floor as if exploring them for the first time, wondering if the house was his in all possible worlds. The living room walls seemed a paler blue, but perhaps the paint had faded. His father's chair still stood in the corner, but there were now two photos of him in his college cap and gown, one taken with his father and another with his mother. The rug was a plain dark blue rather than the patterned one he remembered. He left the room and went to the back, wondering if he was entering the kitchen in all variants.

At last he went upstairs to his old room on the second floor. The rug was gone from the polished wood floor, he noticed as he entered the square, low-ceilinged space. On one shelf, the photo of a solemn, dark-haired boy in his first communion suit was surrounded by certificates won at grade school science fairs. The frames were jumbled, as if someone had begun to put them away.

He sat down in the gable and gazed out through the window. Raindrops began to strike the roof, filling the silence with a whisper. He turned away and noticed the open closet.

A large box held the door open. He got up, went over, and saw that the label was addressed to him, care of a local storage house. He opened the unsealed top and rummaged around in the contents. There were familiar books, lovingly sealed in plastic; one large brown envelope contained academic prizes, certificates of participation, diplomas from grade school, junior high, high school, college, and graduate school, old report cards, and his parents' death certificates. Another overstuffed manila envelope was filled with correspondence. He tried to take one out, but the envelope slipped from his hands and hit the floor. Letters and postcards slid out and opened like a fan of cards.

He noticed one envelope with a recent postmark, addressed in his own handwriting to his father. He picked it up and took out the letter. It was not dated and seemed hastily written on both sides of one page:

Dear Dad,
    Sorry I didn't seem myself last visit, but I did appreciate your long letter, which was waiting for me when I

got back. I can't tell you how happy your interest in my
work has made me. Yes, I do think I've helped in what
may be an important discovery. I'm looking forward to
when I can tell you all about it!

He stopped reading the words he had never written, wondering if his mother had put his father up to writing to him.
The old man had always valued her advice, and they had
been very close, so it seemed unlikely that she could have
forced him.

He continued reading:

I can tell you, however, that what I'm doing has nothing
to do with weapons. It's communications, but in a new
way.

In this variant his father had written to him just before
Summet had sent him to the Antarctic. He finished reading:

I hope that your hospital stay won't bore you too much.
No, I haven't had time for a steady woman friend, but
maybe someday it will happen. You and Mom will be
the first to know. I promise. And I'll help you with fixing
up the house on my next visit.
     Again, your letter made my day, my week, my year!
Love, Juan

He slipped the strange, happy note back into its envelope.
How young he had sounded! A parent's approval, so long
withheld, had turned him into a boy. Carefully, he put the
envelope into the inner breast pocket of his jacket, wondering if he would find his father's letter somewhere in New
York.

The rain was now coming down hard outside. Lightning
flashed; thunder rattled the gable window and the overhead
light winked out. Perhaps the walls between variants should
never be breached, he thought as he went back to the window, if choice was to mean anything. The letter in his pocket
was a rare prize, telling him that his father had reached out
to embrace him, and he had done the same. But it was not
part of this son's experience, and never would be. Was it
enough, knowing that father and son alternates had succeeded? It was better than nothing, but he was again cheat-

ing and being cheated. There were variants where his father remained contemptuous; another where he was actively harmful. All failures and triumphs were both real and illusory.

He sat down in front of the window and stared out at the street lamps in the rainy night, thinking again about utopias. A human mind passing through the alien frames could only slip along the lines of human bias—the strange attractor that limited human history in all possible worlds; but what if a human mind left that axis through some recalibration of the frames? Radically reshaped humanities might exist not only in futurity, but along different axes striking out through infinite superspace. . . .

As lightning lit up the street below, he glimpsed a figure hurrying toward the house. Wind stripped leaves from the branches of swaying trees. A leaf plastered itself against the glass as he peered out, startling him. He moved back and stood up, filled with the pleasant dismay that sometimes comes with the sense of overwhelming mystery.

The overhead light went on, and he knew that he was not finished with the alien web, nor with his fellow man.

"Juan?" Lena called from below. "Are you here?"

Thunder drowned out his answer as he hurried downstairs, suddenly afraid of some obscure detail that would reveal she was not the woman he had known.

III

INFINITE SPACES

The universe ... is a machine for making deities.

—Henri Bergson

32

THE TREMBLING WAY

Ten square kilometers of jungle had been cleared and flattened for access to the alien starship. Juan noticed that vehicles even passed under the giant ball. The dirt ramp that had been used during excavation in the first year had been gradually replaced by one of ridged steel. Two years later, it snaked around the ship and twisted down to level ground.

A growing city of white domes clustered around the ship, housing the researchers who worked within the alien vessel, and providing holding areas for the convicts who were being brought in for their one-way trip away from Earth. A hundred at a time were instructed and equipped, then taken down the corkscrew passage of the starship to the frame chamber and herded through to a distant world, where other rejects were already attempting to make a life for themselves.

The attraction of the scheme was that criminals could be removed from highly visible penal institutions which did not rehabilitate and were a costly problem to their communities; even better, no criminals need ever be executed. Simply remove them forever from their past and future victims. Make your lives elsewhere, the judges were saying, and you'll feel the need for law.

The North Atlantic Nations and the Soviet Confederation had begun this new form of exile about two years ago. It had been one of the first uses to which Soviets and Americans had put the alien ships, but the convenience had been too tempting for other governments to ignore. Working through the UN, every nation had obtained some access to the ships here in Brazil and in the Sun, and to the one recently found on the Moon. All the ships were linked with each other through their identical frame chamber. The pace of expansion into the alien web was quickening despite the problems it posed for human understanding of reality. Practical gains outweighed all other considerations.

"We'll be late, sir," the tall sergeant said.

Juan nodded and followed him down the dirt path that led from the heliblock to the large central dome. The feeling that he had lost parts of himself weighed more heavily on him with each passing year. He might have felt the same even if he had never passed across the probabilities; but the trembling way offered by the alien technology had given him a view of human history that only confirmed his doubts. Breakouts from the evolutionary maze, made possible by science and technology, only magnified humanity's inner limits. Spinoza was right. A man was free only in his mind, in his sense of possibility; but in action, deeper programs played.

As they approached the main dome, Juan felt dismay and shame as he looked at the domes clustered around the alien colossus. It goes wrong again, he thought.

The sergeant cycled the climate control lock, and the outer door opened. Juan followed him into the white outer chamber.

"Sergeant, what do you think of all this?" he asked as the door slid shut.

"I do my job, sir."

"And you're happy with that?"

"I get what I want, sir."

"Juan!" Titus Summet cried as the inner door opened. He stood at the end of a hallway. Juan stepped out of the lock. The door closed behind him.

"Good to see you," Summet said as he rushed forward and shook his hand. The stocky man seemed as vital as ever, and as vain. His graying hair and bushy eyebrows were again brown.

Juan nodded politely and withdrew his hand. "I see you've visited the ship's medical chambers. How many important people have made the pilgrimage by now? How many favors do you owe for?"

Summet scowled, deforming his brow. "Still not very glad to see me, are you?" Juan was silent as Summet led him into his new office. The large circular room had a daylight ceiling. An oval desk stood in the middle of a green wall-to-wall rug.

Summet hurried around behind the desk and sat down. Juan sat down in one of the three high-backed chairs facing it.

"You look well," Titus said, shifting in his chair. "Ready to come back from your leave?"

"Get to the point."

Titus nodded, and Juan caught an uncharacteristic sadness in his deeply lined face. "We've got a problem, Juan, and you're the only one who has any chance of solving it for us."

"Just tell me what you want."

"What is it, Juan? Haven't we treated you well? How's Lena?"

"Don't tell me you don't know."

"I knew she went back to Norway to visit her mother and old friends, out of curiosity about this variant, if nothing else." He paused. "Is it over between you two?"

"For the time being," Juan lied.

"But that's not why you're so disagreeable, is it?"

"How involved are you with these penal arrangements?" Juan asked.

"The decisions were made without me. You sound very concerned. What about your work, and Lena?"

"Let's say I'm now more interested in what makes my fellow man tick. Maybe I'll learn why we're in such a mess on this world. There's a lot of fear circulating, even among the small professional crooks. The lawyers are spooked. Now tell me how you're tied into it."

Titus leaned forward. "You're nothing new, Juan. Science is littered with the careers of men and women who cared only for their work, then developed a social conscience when they discovered human imperfection. They become even more outraged when they have to face up to being human themselves. But I'll skip trading insults with you and get to the point, because I need you. This kind of exile for criminals has been legally arrived at. Most people will accept it because it will mean seeing the last of tens of thousands of hardened offenders who have to be supported with public money. Ordinary people want what works, even if it seems a little unjust."

"A little unjust?"

Titus raised his right eyebrow. "Maybe not unjust at all, but bear with me."

"I'm flattered that you feel the need to explain."

"You're a good man, Juan, but you often want the impossible. I'll bet that's been your problem with me in every variant. Consider the advantages of getting rid of criminals in this way. We ship them through the web, to a world from which they can never return. End of prison problem, however often we fill them again. We're saying to these people, start over somewhere else, and we can keep saying it for as long as we produce new criminals. People can't be *made* good or law-abiding. They have to want it. We're giving these people a stake in a new life, where they'll have to control themselves. It won't be perfect, but it makes sense. We're also shipping our nuclear and chemical wastes through the web. As time goes on we'll understand the frames better and find even more uses for them."

"You seem to think that governments have to hold people by the throat, however gently, and tighten when they get out of hand."

Titus smiled. "It's more humane to exile people than to kill or imprison them. It also gets them away from their victims. One problem is solved, even though another is created—for the criminals. They can make their lives somewhere else, where I'm sure they'll soon have to deal with their own criminals."

"Does all this include political criminals?" Juan asked.

Titus sighed. "Yes, unfortunately. So-called political prisoners are included. It's up to judges to classify people."

"Come off it, Titus. All prison populations include some political prisoners. A good case can be made that all criminals are unconsciously revolutionary, because they know the hypocrisy of the society that put them inside, even if they don't know what can be done about it. Violence and illegal acts for profit seem to them an appropriate response. Enough succeed well enough to serve as role models. Society to them is just another gang trying to impose its will."

"I won't argue with you. Sure, most crooks aren't basically different from us, but with our laws, however misused, we're relatively better. But all this is beside the point of why I brought you here. I admit that I'm involved in all this, but I don't see it as outside my job as ERS security chief. It's just another way to develop the resources of the alien transport web for human use, as far as I'm concerned. We have a chance to put humankind onto a dozen or more worlds, even if some of the exiles won't deserve it. If they succeed, we'll hear from them someday, and the reasons for the original exile won't count for much, whether they're murderers, thieves, terrorists, or distinguished minority leaders who would throw whole nations into civil war to get what's theirs. I'm saying all this to you because I know you need explanations in order to work well."

"Get to the rest of it, Titus."

"I've found out what happened to Yevgeny Petrovich Tasarov, the man you asked me to find, and more about the kind of work he was doing. The Russians exiled him recently. You were right about his possible importance. His work could lead to some control over which variants might be entered through the frames. We may learn why a system designed for crossing interstellar distances sends travelers into variant worlds. We might even be able to build our own frames. For starters we could make every key point on Earth and throughout the solar system accessible, even if we couldn't eliminate the variant effect. I want you to go and bring him back—or at least find out what he knows."

"But why did they do it? Didn't they know his importance?"

"He's self-taught, no academic credentials, an amateur by their lights. He made enemies, engaged in some shady enterprises, and was sentenced quite legally. No one had any reason until the discovery of the web to think that his work had anything but theoretical value, but sooner or later it will be noticed, and I want that to be UN-ERS rather than a national power. I'm sure you agree."

"I guess I do," Juan said, "unless we view the UN as just another multinational, hungry to consolidate its power through ERS."

Titus smiled. "You're more cynical than you accuse me of being."

"Under the UN every nation has a say, but ERS is in a perfect position to abuse the UN." Juan paused. "Remember, you won't be sure who'll come back."

"I don't care," Titus replied, "which variant of you returns, as long as you bring back either the knowledge or Tasarov himself."

"Where is he?"

"You've been there—the desert world where your Rassmussen died."

"Ship One is there?" Juan asked.

"Yes," Summet said. "We've been going back and forth for some time. Why?"

"I guess the variant hasn't carried over. The last time we were there, the ship took us to another suncore."

Summet looked at him severely, as if about to demand why this had not been reported. "The connection seems stable enough for you to get in and back without major confusion."

Back to what? Juan asked himself. A variant of him would return here, while he went on across the probabilities. He would never again speak to *this* Titus Summet, yet they would continue to know each other when they met.

"You seem to regard all probabilities as somehow being one," Juan said, "and you may be right."

Titus shrugged. "Whatever we do is carried through in all variant worlds, in some fashion or other. They are all ours."

"Monotonously so," Juan added.

"As long as Juan Obrion comes back to me with what we need," Titus continued, "I won't look too closely at the small details. I didn't see any great differences in you or the others. You've seen differences because you're comparing to the world from which you started, yet you still seem to be at home, judging by your caring contentiousness."

"When do you want us to start?" Juan asked.

"Right away, if possible. Couldn't you go alone?"

"We may want to keep our original group together."

Titus grimaced. "Moede is still with the Russian woman."

"He'll come." Lena had visited them in London after leaving him. She and Dita had kept in touch as much as possible, and her last call to him had suggested that the couple were having troubles. Isak and Yerik had gone home. Lena had hinted that Dita might follow her two colleagues.

"Perhaps you and Lena would prefer variants of each other at this point." Titus leaned forward. "What's wrong between you two?"

"I won't discuss it."

"Will she go with you?"

"Probably."

"Then I can count on you?"

Juan nodded, knowing that in the infinity of his deciding doubles, half would go and half would stay, to preserve the aesthetic of symmetry. Another Juan Obrion would return to this office, while he reported to a variant Summet. The alien labyrinth drew him, promising knowledge and strangeness. He felt addicted. The mystery of the missing builders was still to be solved, but there was much more. The web, with its physical and biological technologies, offered escape for his kind. The promise of a genuine progress waited for human history, although he had only vague ideas of how it might happen. Half-articulate inner needs had met external challenges when he had first explored the web. Since his last return, the pressure had been building within him anew. It had to be the same with Lena, Malachi, and Magnus. How could any of them settle down to their lives while the star-spanning alien artifact beckoned?

"I'll contact the others," Titus said. "My aide will show you to your quarters."

Juan nodded, feeling defeated and apprehensive, but grateful for the new chance.

33

ACROSS IMMENSITIES

◐

The mission would give him access to the web again, as well as time with Lena, Malachi, and Magnus, to plan how they might influence the web's use. If Lena went, he hoped that it might show that she wasn't ready to let him go over their differences, that she feared to lose this variant of him.

"I'm tired of your rantings against humanity," she had said to him three months ago. "It's self-hatred, Juan. Don't you see that?"

"Of course I do," he had replied, "but there are merits to my arguments."

"That we're no good as a species? Is that what you want to live by?"

"I want to do something about what we are."

"So does every thoughtful person, but you never let up."

"Then you *do* understand what I mean."

"What of it?" she had said. "It means you and I can't accept each other as we are. Or will you make exceptions for us?"

"I didn't say there aren't any good people, Lena."

She had walked out finally, taking nothing. He had been a hermit since then, hiding out in the old house, having food sent in while he made a fresh traversal of the sciences, of history, searching again through the great philosophies, the literatures and poetries of his kind, hoping to be convinced once more that the record of human failure was not evidence of total damnation. But in the end it seemed to him that the great human exceptions of caring intellect only demonstrated how deep was the pit out of which they had climbed. The human spirit could soar for limited stretches; but its great achievement, civilization, had to be put like chains onto each generation. The progress of one age—even of one decade— was often undone in the next. Hope lived in the changes; but how to make of progress more than a struggling increment? How to make a norm out of the exceptional?

The summons to Brazil had come as a relief from staring into the mirrors of human truth. In the quarters assigned to him by Summet, as he looked around from his bed at the antiseptic perfection of the circular room's design, Juan imagined a madhouse Earth where the frames were used for merely global transportation, with routine travel across variants, ignoring subtle differences in hair color, daily news, or even the numbers of relatives that would come and go. History and current events would change like weather for such a humanity—but it would make no difference, because there would be no inner changes in the species.

He closed his eyes and saw the alien port, where starships hung in the great space of the hollow sphere, left over from the great age of construction, when ships had gone out to distant stars to establish the suncore stations. The logical, awesome beauty of the web was an unceasing amazement to him, equaled only by the mystery of what had happened to the builders and why the frames also functioned as gates between variants.

He opened his eyes. Titus stood over him. "You've slept ten hours."

He had been happy in his sleep, he realized, because the web waited for him again.

"I contacted Moede and Rassmussen," Titus said as Juan sat up on the edge of his bed. "They won't come. Seems they don't feel as you do about staying together."

"And Lena?"

"Couldn't reach her. She isn't at her apartment in Oslo. I left messages for her to call you here today."

Juan looked up at Titus. "I'll go alone." Even though he had never found anything to prove that she wasn't the Lena he had started with, they had grown apart, so it wouldn't matter to which Lena he might return.

The director nodded. "It might be easier for one person to get in and out. Can you be ready tomorrow?"

Juan looked up at him. "That soon?"

"If possible."

Juan nodded. "All right."

"I'll send in your clothes and gear. Here's a briefing report. Read it carefully."

The phone buzzed. Juan jumped up from his supper and bolted across the room. Lena, he thought. She was coming, or at least she would tell him she could not.

Malachi's dark face appeared on the screen, forcing a smile. "I say," he murmured. "Thought you deserved a call."

"Mal."

His smile faded. "Have to tell you that I can't come with you."

"Dita?" Juan asked.

"She flew out of Heathrow this morning." The Kenyan lifted his head. "Went home. Titus couldn't conceal his relief when I told him. I had to point out to him that if I went with you, that would cut me off from Dita for good. It would make it final between us."

"Then she's coming back," Juan said.

Malachi looked away from the screen for a moment. "I really can't say. Mother Russia is quite a rival for one's affections, you know, but I have hope. Even Titus has no idea of what her superiors want from her. She was quite homesick." He laughed. "Maybe if I go with you, I'll come back and find a Dita who wants me after all. A cosmic casino for lovers." He leaned back from the screen, looking tired. "I have to play out the chance that she'll come back. If I go with you, there'll be none. I've been thinking that if she comes back we'll both slip our leashes and make a quiet life for ourselves in the English countryside." He was silent for a long time. "Would like to come along with you—would be interesting, but—"

Juan said, "I understand."

"Just think—when your variant returns here, Dita and I may entertain you in our country cottage, even if you won't be yourself. Is Lena going with you?"

Juan shook his head.

"Sorry—thought she would. She does care about you. When she was here, I could see that her heart wasn't in her complaints about you."

"You two must have gotten an earful."

"Nothing I didn't know."

"Maybe," Juan said hoarsely, "she'll do better with my variant."

"I guess this is good-bye, even though we'll meet again."

Juan tried to smile. "Maybe we won't even notice a difference." He stared at his friend as the screen winked out, and suddenly it seemed impossible that he had agreed to Titus's mission without Mal and Lena; yet he knew that he would go.

A breakfast cart, clothing, and backpack were waiting for him when he came out of the shower. He ate first, surprised by his sudden appetite; then he dressed in two layers of clothing—an insulated under-coverall with various supports and protective layers, and an outer coverall, with seal pockets for various items. The backpack was stocked with food and supplies for a week.

He looked up as the door slid open and Titus walked in. "You'll need this also." Juan stood up and took the hand weapon from him.

"It shoots small needles silently," the director said, "and is compact enough to tuck inside one of your pockets."

"And you want me to kill Tasarov if I can't bring him out."

"Don't be stupid. It's for your protection. We want him alive."

Juan slipped the gun into his right thigh pocket.

"I'll come with you as far as the lock," Titus said, grabbing the pack and slinging it over his shoulder. "Save your energy. You'll need it."

The door slid open as he led the way out. Juan followed him down the corridor, wondering if he would actually go through when he faced the frame.

"No word from Lena?" Titus asked.

"You know there wasn't," Juan said as he came up next to him.

"Can you do this alone," Titus asked, "even if it means losing the last two people you know from Earth Prime? How do you feel about Magnus?"

"I don't know how I feel about anyone."

Titus nodded. "Before you get wound up, let me say a few things to you, even if you don't want to hear them. I do the best I can. That means keeping up UN Authority's power base to the point where I can be effective. We've got a tough century ahead, even without the immunity diseases. The greenhouse effect will be reversed, but we'll still have flooded coastlines, decreased oxygen levels, droughts, and countless other ecoeffects. We have peace, at least in this probability—just barely. I want the alien tech to work for us in the decades ahead. You've told us to expect major advances in engineering and biotechnologies. We've seen them, even though we don't understand how they work. I want you to start working with me again, from the inside, rather than acting as if you were a condescending gift-giver. Getting to Tasarov is only a beginning."

Juan restrained a bitter smile. "You're convincing when you want to be. I'll try, but don't ask me to believe."

"Meet me halfway."

"We won't make it, Titus. Humanity will screw up all these gifts just as it has everything else."

"Give it a rest, Juan."

"It's already happening! You're using the web to get rid of people, and lie to yourself about the good that will come of it. You bring in privileged characters to use the ship's medical chambers, and you want Tasarov to enhance ERS power."

"All of which can make better things possible."

"I do hope you know what you're doing, Titus," Juan said, startled by the conviction in Summet's voice.

They went down the corridor to the lock. The inner door slid open. They stepped inside; it whispered shut behind them. The outer door opened, and they walked out into bright morning sunlight toward a waiting jeep. The humid air was hot and dusty here in the cleared area. They got into the back of the jeep. The sergeant who had brought Juan from the heliblock was at the wheel.

"To the entrance," Titus said, tapping the man on the shoulder.

As they drove off down the road, Juan looked around at the white domes. Each structure could house hundreds of human beings, but the alien ship, rising nearly two kilometers into the sky, dwarfed the domes. It blotted out the sky as the jeep climbed the long curving ramp, went around once, and finally jolted to a stop before the open lock.

Juan felt apprehensive, remembering when he, Lena, Malachi, and Magnus had explored the winding corridor as the ship fled across the universe.

"Ready?" Titus asked.

Juan felt a moment of sympathy for him. The man could not give up the power he wielded for fear of undoing his meager accomplishments. "We'll see," Juan said as Titus offered him his hand. "I'll do my best."

"You always have. That's what pisses me off about you."

A hot wind blew a cloud of dust across the lock entrance as they got out of the jeep. Titus helped him on with his pack and handed him his helmet. Juan tested the light on the helmet as he put it on, gazed out over the city of domes, then turned and went into the alien ship.

The inner lock was closed, as usual, because the intruding ramp held the outer one open. Juan went inside the blue chamber as the ramp slid back and the outer lock glowed shut. He confronted the inner door. It glowed open and he stepped into the winding corridor, feeling as if he were coming home. Overhead, the familiar yellow-orange squares of light curved away to the right, leaving a streak in the hard black floor. He looked back and saw the lock glow shut.

He went slowly down the spiral, reacquainting himself with the oval entranceways on each side of the passage. As his eyes wandered over the geometric markings, raised figures, and depressions in the black surface, he was again struck by how new everything seemed, as if it had been built yesterday.

He came to the large oval bulge in the passage, and approached the round opening in the floor. As always, the shaft was aglow with orange-yellow light. Oxygen-rich air came up from below. The quick drop would get him to the frame chamber quickly, but he decided to walk the rest of the way, wondering if he would step through the frame. Was it only an odd metaphysical technicality that worried him? Was the infinity of branching variants all somehow one? Scientific realism insisted that an identical twin was simply *another* of the same person. Duplication violated one feature of a unique identity—its singular location in space—and gave the double a chance to diverge from the original over time. The principle of the identity of indiscernibles stated that if two objects were exactly the same, including their location, then there was in reality only one object.

There was very little reason for him to stay. Mal and Magnus had good reasons to pick up their lives here. It came down to Lena, and she didn't want him. Her variant might understand him better when he came back. He was also curious about Tasarov. What did the mathematician know, and why hadn't he bargained to avoid exile? Mathematicians were often blind to the engineering consequences of the formalisms with which they played. He would have had to be told about the variant effect to see the importance of his work.

Juan stopped suddenly and listened. Footsteps echoed in the passage behind him, as if someone were hurrying after him. Titus had forgotten something, or had decided to go with him as far as the frame chamber.

He turned around and saw a dark figure. "What is it?" he shouted, dropping his pack.

"Juan," Lena answered as she came forward. Her blond hair was longer, falling to her shoulders. She was thinner, making her high cheekbones even sharper; she seemed more fragile, and smaller than the stocky woman he had known. Her blue eyes searched his face. "When it came right down to it, I couldn't let you go." Her Norwegian accent was more pronounced. "You knew I'd come—you had to know." She dropped her pack and slipped into his arms.

He kissed her, and the release of tension made him dizzy. Her eyes fluttered and her breath warmed his face. "I've missed you," he whispered.

THROUGH THE BLACK MIRROR

She took his hand and led him toward the oval entrance. It glowed red and they slipped through—

—into a white-lit room.

As they undressed, the ceiling began to radiate a dull red. He removed the last of his clothes and faced her, his skin tingling from the overhead glow as he slipped his arms around her waist. Her palms pressed against his back. The ceiling warmed them into a sweat, then faded back to white. Oxygen-rich air flowed in and cooled them.

She pulled him down beside her on the floor. He lay on his back and marveled at her smooth skin as she rose above him. She smiled, sat on his belly, and guided him into her. He matched her rhythm. She breathed deeply and leaned over to kiss him. He ran his fingers through her hair. She pulled back and tightened as he thrust upward. Her hips did a slow, searching dance. His own pleasure threatened, but her pace held him back. She cried out, fell forward, and kissed him. He grasped her hips and finished, then held her gently as the cool air washed them.

She rolled aside and lay on her back. "Happy?"

He turned on his side. "Yes," he said.

"You knew I would come."

"I wasn't sure."

She turned on her side and held up her head. "Would you have gone without telling me?"

"You might have preferred my variant."

"What if you didn't come back at all? This is a dangerous place you're going to."

"It could be."

"I just can't let you go alone, Juan. Once you're through the frame, you'll be dead to me, and I'm sure that my variants will feel the same way."

"Titus told you why I'm going?"

"Yes," she said. "But you also have your own reasons."

He ran his hand along the curve of her hip, then gently touched her belly.

"You want to see more of the alien tech," she said. "Titus knows that, but he's willing to gamble on you. He's not all bad, Juan. Do you think this Tasarov knows anything?"

"We'll find out."

They got up and dressed in silence. Lena looked at him with suspicion. "What are you hoping for, Juan?"

"I'm not sure. It depends on what I'll find out on this trip. What about the way you felt when you left?"

She zipped up her coverall. "When it came down to losing you, I decided your opinions were not enough to keep us apart. You want me, don't you?"

"Yes," he said. "But you made me feel that I had some deep-seated disease."

"Yes," she said, looking away. "You're so disappointed and hurt from being a human being that you might just do something constructive about it, and that appeals to me. I'm not unlike you."

"Titus made no effort to dissuade you?"

"The cynical bastard wants to keep you happy, and you might need a medic where we're going." She was silent for a moment. "I know I'm glossing things over, but I can't help it. Faced with this choice, it's all I can do. You were counting on it."

"Yes," he said softly.

"Make the best of it, then." She approached the door. It glowed and she went through. He confronted the oval. It glowed and he—

—stepped out into the winding passage.

Lena stood by their packs. "What is it?" he asked.

"Listen!"

Machine-gun fire echoed through the passage—short bursts, long ones, then silence.

"I hear footsteps," she said.

They peered back along the passage. Two dark shapes came around the turn.

"Raise your hands!" one of them shouted.

Juan and Lena obeyed. The shapes came closer.

"Oh, it's you, Dr. Obrion," a familiar voice said. "Why are you still here?"

"What's going on, Sergeant?" Juan asked. "We heard automatic fire."

The sergeant glanced at the corporal with him. They lowered their weapons. "Just an escapee, sir, trying to get back. They don't have a chance, coming through this passage, but they try."

"You mean it's happened before?" Lena asked.

"Three times. There are a few guards at the planet's suncore station, trusties, working in the hope of being let back one day. We think they're sending people back to get rid of them."

"Just as we do," Juan said.

"Why are you still here, Dr. Obrion?" the sergeant demanded again.

"We're on our way, soldier," Lena replied, putting on her pack.

Juan did the same and followed her. He glanced back. The two soldiers stared after them.

"Charming couple," Lena said as they made the turn. She was silent as they marched deeper into the ship. "What are you after?" she asked without looking at him. "I mean besides finding out what Tasarov knows."

"I don't want to talk about it now," he replied.

She slowed her pace and took his hand. He looked at her. She smiled, and it seemed to him just then that Malachi had the right idea—find your place in a small community and live within narrow, human limits; don't expect more from the mill of history and you won't be disappointed. He had always wanted more than life could give, seeing it as an elaborate facade, a stage set designed to conceal its truth, tormenting those who yearned to know what was backstage. When he tried to explain, his words became confused and strange, even to his own ears.

They passed the entrance to the drum-shaped chamber, went down the straight section, and turned left to face the largest entrance in the ship.

"Ready?" he asked as he turned on his helmet light. Lena nodded and switched on hers. They stepped forward together. The giant entrance glowed and they passed—

—into a dark, cavernous chamber. He cast his beam from left to right, revealing the six black frames standing at the perimeter, their mirrorlike blackness swallowing the light.

"Which one?" Lena asked.

"Second from the left will put us into Ship One, inside the white dwarf's suncore station, if this variant holds. The penal colony is on the planet where we buried our Magnus."

"They might have found a better place," Lena said.

"Only by sending people out to explore the web. Few wanted to try it once they learned it meant entering variants. And they knew we'd refuse to go searching for a suitable penal planet. Besides, I don't think they wanted a better place."

She took his hand. "I'm ready."

They stepped into the frame. Juan searched within himself for changes, but felt the same. The surviving self would not feel different if his exact pattern were destroyed and recreated, even in a long series of deaths and resurrections. There was something basically odd about personal identity. One's interior location seemed both clear and mysterious. There seemed to be no reason why personality should not be everywhere. Perhaps all selves were one large unconscious self, and only imagined themselves separate. He hoped that the frames simply brought distant points up against each other, making breakdown and reassembly of objects unnecessary.

Lena's hand tightened in his as they stepped out into the identical cavernous chamber in Ship One. "If the ship is in the other suncore, where we left it," he said, "then we won't be able to carry out Summet's mission. Our alternates will do that in another variant."

They moved toward the exit. It glowed, and they stepped—

—out into an identical spiral passage.

"Stop!" a voice shouted.

Two men came toward them. Each was dressed in gray coveralls and carried a heavy truncheon. Juan reached into his pocket and grasped the small automatic.

"Who are you?" the taller of the two demanded.

"I'm Dr. Juan Obrion, and this is Dr. Lena Dravic. We're from UN-ERS."

The men looked at each other. "No one like you has come here before," the tall one said. "What's your business?"

"We want to talk to one of the inmates—Yevgeny Tasarov."

"The big Russky?"

"Yes."

"What for?" the shorter man asked.

"Where can we find him?"

There was a long silence. "Sure, we'll take you to Evi," the tall man said. Juan took his hand out of his pocket. The two men went ahead.

"They're trying to figure what good we might be to them," Juan whispered as he and Lena followed. "They know we'll be going back, and that's a first for this place. These must be the trusties guarding the access route to the penal colony."

The tall man glanced back at them with suspicion.

"So they live off the ship," Lena said softly. "Do any of them here or down on the planet know about the variant effect?"

"I don't see how even Tasarov could have found out. It might be present as an implication in his mathematics, but as far as we know he hasn't had a chance to experience anything to make him think about it."

Lena asked, "How do they get the new prisoners to obey after they come through the frame?"

"They come shackled," Juan replied. "Trusties march them to the shuttle and throw them a key as it starts its automatic run to the planet. I'd guess that if the sphere brings anyone back, they send him down again, or give him a clear run through the frame. We saw what happens after that. There may have been successful escapes already, into variants where the Brazilian ship hasn't been discovered."

The two men reached the entrance to the shuttle bay and waited. "I don't trust them," Lena whispered.

"Don't worry—they suspect I'm armed, but I don't want to confirm it for them."

"So am I. Is anyone on the planet armed?"

"Not with anything advanced. Unless someone brought in firearms somehow and duplicated them. If that were the case, I think the trusties would be armed with more than clubs."

"Go on," the tall man said. "This is as far as we go."

Juan nodded to Lena. She took his hand and they stepped through the glow—

—into the bay. As usual, the sphere sat in its cradle, cut

in half by the floor, towering some twenty-five meters into the vault. Juan found himself impressed again by this smaller version of the starship.

"How do they live down on the planet?" Lena asked.

"They may be dependent on the ship to duplicate their food and supplies."

"Unless they found a replicating facility on the planet itself."

"Yes—which means power belongs to those who control access to the suncore or to whatever facilities exist down there."

Lena said, "That would give them power of life and death over their fellows."

Juan was silent, then said, "Maybe they're more coopera- tive than that."

"Thanks, but I know you don't believe it."

"Do you?"

"We'll see. Prison life isn't the best test of human nature."

They approached the open lock. Juan hesitated.

"What's wrong?" she asked.

"If they get the weapons away from us, they could dupli- cate them endlessly, enough to equip an army."

"But we can't go unarmed," she said.

He looked at her. "With any luck, we'll be gone in a few hours."

"How bad can it be down there?"

"We're going to what's called an open prison. The only guards or police are what they themselves have set up, serv- ing the most powerful faction, I expect. We have no choice but to go armed and bluff it out."

"How?"

"With the suggestion, or even promises, that we might be able to do something for them when we get back. They'll know we can go back, and won't have much to lose by taking a chance on us. Do you want to go back right now?"

"Is Tasarov worth it?"

"Probably."

She went in and led the way through the right-handed turn to the small drum-shaped chamber. They dropped their packs. Juan stepped into the control circle and the amber light faded as the overhead viewspace lit up. They sat down on their packs and lifted their heads.

The station appeared, shrinking in the gray otherspace. As

they watched the exit close in the massive black globe, Juan thought again of the vast web that was fed by this and countless other suncore units. He tensed as otherspace winked out and revealed the white dwarf in normal space. The view changed as the ship oriented itself toward the rusty disk that was the dwarf's first planet, and gave chase along its orbit.

Lena touched his arm. "Hear that?" she whispered.

They both stood up. The steps were soft, shuffling. A face peered in from the right side of the exit.

"I see you're comfortable," the unshaven face said, smiling.

"Who are you?" Lena demanded.

The man who came in was of medium height, dressed in coveralls. His black hair was streaked with gray. "I go back and forth. Got on late today." He came inside and sat down against the wall. "We've never had visitors." He looked at Juan intently, then glanced at Lena. "A pretty woman, too." He smiled to himself. "Why are you here?"

"We're looking for someone," Juan replied and sat down. Lena hesitated, then did the same.

"Are you going to take him back?"

"We want to talk to Yevgeny Tasarov. Do you know him?"

"I know everybody."

"What's your name?" Lena asked.

"What's yours?" The man smiled. "I had one a long time ago. Doesn't mean much here."

"You do use names, don't you?" Lena said.

"Sometimes. Mostly not."

Juan asked, "You just go back and forth on this ship?"

The man nodded. "I don't mind. I get to stay on the ship a lot."

Juan said, "You run the shuttle in the hope of going home one day, don't you?"

"It's as close as I can get, isn't it?" He looked away. "Better than living down there."

"My names's Juan Obrion. This is Lena Dravic."

"Pleased to meet you."

"How is it here with you?" Lena asked.

The man stretched his shoulders and seemed to relax. "Anyone can try to go back—no guards. They never come back, the ones who try it. They're killed when they go through, aren't they?"

Juan glanced up at the viewspace. The planet took up half the field now.

"Can you take us to Tasarov?"

"Will it get me out of here? If not, find him yourself."

"Is it very bad here?" Lena asked.

The man shook his head. "They have everything they want in the way of food and supplies, but—well, you'll see."

"You say they—don't you include yourself?" Juan asked.

"Just a way of speaking." The man licked his lips, as if he were ashamed. Then he looked directly at Juan. "Look, mister, imagine a place where you don't want for anything but you have nothing. Nothing at all. Can you understand that?"

"I see what you're getting at," Juan replied.

"Well, that's this place—that planet down there, the ship, the damned station around it. Nothing is ours, or human. You never find out anything, no matter how much you think and look." He seemed on the verge of tears suddenly.

"Why are you here?" Lena asked.

"Robbery—a man died. He ran a jewelry store—a little place where he fixed watches and things. Knifed him more than twenty years ago, in New York City."

"Did you intend to kill him?"

"Didn't care much if I did or didn't. Only found out later that he was dead."

"Did you regret it?" Lena asked.

"Not then."

"Do you now?"

"Don't know. What are you looking at me like that for? I don't know, and I never will. You can't make me feel what I can't." He got to his feet. "We're coming in. Want me to hold the ship until you get back?"

"Do you think it'll take us long to find Tasarov?" Juan asked.

"Can't say. I don't like to come out of the ship. I'll hold the lock open as long as I can. It goes back by itself after a while unless you stand something in it."

"We know," Juan said. "We were here before the prison was set up."

"Do you have any idea where we could find Tasarov?" Lena asked.

"Ask around. By the way, would you do it with me on the way back?"

Juan repressed his sudden rage; his hand sought his weapon and closed around it in his pocket. Lena regarded the man coldly.

"Doesn't hurt to ask in my position," the man said. "I wouldn't mind either of you."

Lena's eyes narrowed. Juan was repelled by the convict, wishing that she had not followed him and wondering if Titus had warned her about the dangers.

"Sure, I understand," the man added, studying Juan. "You've got something with her yourself. There's some women down there, but they're all taken." He laughed. "So's everyone else! It's one thing we can't duplicate in the small chambers. Only the big man can loan you someone, or let you use a duper."

"So there's a group that controls the replicators?" Juan asked.

The man nodded, still staring at Lena. "Down there, but not on the big ship."

Lena stared back, poised to strike, and Juan knew that she would. He gripped his gun and waited.

The convict said, "I wouldn't live down there, even for a woman." His shoulders sagged. He swallowed hard and finally looked away. The viewspace overhead went dark as the vessel landed.

35

A SEA OF STONE

◑

Juan and Lena paused in the open lock and gazed out at the rusty brown desert. The red-white dwarf hung just above the horizon of the plain. Overhead, the globular cluster added its pale light to the sunset. The wind gusted as they stepped outside.

Lena adjusted her backpack and glanced behind her. The convict had not come to see them off. "Are you sorry I came?" she asked.

"No," he lied as they stepped out of the lock.

Even with nose filters, the odors of the land were still musky, but the discomfort of trace elements was gone. They lowered the visors on their helmets and started for the rise, moving carefully between the plants.

They came to the top of the gentle rise and looked out over the domes. The complex seemed deserted. They made their way down to level ground and came to the tree where Magnus had been buried. Juan paused under the heavy branches, remembering. A slight breeze turned the red leaves, casting white ghosts onto the trunk. Lena was a dark shape waiting for him outside the cover of the tree, and he felt again that he had lost pieces of himself.

She came toward him. "What is it, Juan?"

"Nothing. Let's go." They left the tree and approached the nearest dome.

"They must all be inside," Lena said.

"The air is better there."

"I'm curious how they live. How many are here?"

"Nearly three thousand."

They came to the entrance. It glowed, and they passed——into a dimly lit yellow space. He took off his helmet.

As his eyes adjusted, he saw dark shapes asleep on the black floor. There was a clear path to the center, where six bodies huddled apart from the rest.

"That's far enough," a man's voice said behind him.

Hands seized him, pulled off his pack, and began to search him. He glanced at Lena. She was getting the same rough treatment.

"We're from UN-ERS," he said, turning around.

A bludgeon struck him on the side of his head. He heard Lena gasp as he dropped his helmet, staggered back, and fell onto sleepers. They cursed and shoved him away. He tried to steady himself, but his head was spinning. He struggled to his knees.

"You're making a mistake," he mumbled.

"We don't care," the voice replied.

Arms hoisted him to his feet, and the body search continued. Juan glimpsed people sitting up on the floor.

"What's this racket!" a booming voice shouted behind him. Someone called out a question in a foreign language.

"Visitors from home!" the man who had struck him answered. "Say they're UN!"

"What?"

"Okay, you—move!"

Juan staggered forward dizzily, but managed to stay up. "Are you all right?" Lena whispered. He nodded as his eyes cleared.

"Well, bring them here!" the voice from the center shouted in accented English.

Juan squinted. The man who sat among his sleeping companions was heavy-boned and muscular, with long black hair; his light-brown face had sharp, high cheekbones, and his dark, almond-shaped eyes seemed as hard as black stones. Slowly, he got to his feet, and Juan noticed that the prison markings had been removed from his coveralls. The three women and two young men around him sat clutching their blankets.

The man was well over six feet tall, Juan saw as they came before him. The convict gazed down at him intently, then pointed to Lena. "Is she yours?" he demanded.

"She is Dr. Lena Dravic. I'm Dr. Juan Obrion."

"Doctors?" the big man asked.

"I'm a biologist," Lena said, removing her helmet. "Dr. Obrion is a physicist."

The big convict shrugged, then glared at them. "What were you two sentenced for?"

"We're not criminals," Juan replied.

"I don't like the high-horse sound of you," the big man said.

"UN-ERS sent us," Juan said quickly, "to find Yevgeny Tasarov. Is he here?"

"You can go back?" the tall man asked.

Juan nodded. "Do you know him?" The big man clenched his teeth.

"May we see him?" Lena asked.

"I don't suppose you're lying—it wouldn't get you much." He was silent for a few moments. "What will you give in return?"

"What do you want?" Juan asked.

"A way out of here."

"That may not be in our power," Juan said cautiously.

"You'd better strip, then. We'll dupe everything you have."

"Is that necessary?" Juan asked.

The man smiled. "Are you shy? We'll give you back enough to be warm and modest."

Juan thought of the pistol in his pocket as he glanced at Lena. Her expression was impassive.

"We must speak with Tasarov," he said.

"I won't bargain," the big man said impatiently. "You can only give us what's on you."

"Are you sure?" Juan said.

"You're bluffing."

"We've arrived openly, hiding nothing," Lena said.

The convict leader smiled sourly. "That is the safest way to come here. Cheaper to come with things we can steal than to bring an armed force. Be glad I don't much care what happens to you." He shook back his black hair. "There's not much more anyone can do to us. Why Tasarov?"

"That would take a while to explain," Juan answered.

The big man took a deep breath. "I'm tired of this!"

"I'll be honest with you," Juan said quickly. "We may not be able to do much for you, but we can report that you received us well. That's better than saying that you were hostile."

"Not by much. You're suggesting we stay on good terms with all the nice folks back home. Don't be sure you'll get back."

"What will you gain by harming us?"

Laughter followed his question. A few convicts jeered. "Revenge!" someone shouted. "We'll tear you to pieces for the fun of it!"

"Quiet!" the dark-haired man cried, raising his hands. He stepped closer to Juan. "Strip back there," he said, motioning to a partitioned area behind him. "Stay put until we copy your gear."

"What about Tasarov?" Juan demanded. He looked around the dome, at the reclining and squatting mass of humanity that was staring at him and Lena. These were human beings, he told himself, if only in some small part of themselves, hidden behind hard inner walls.

"Your naive honesty is charming," the big man continued. He stepped close to Juan, as if to say something in confidence. A sudden weakness showed in his face. "Follow me right now," he said softly, looking around. "Go back to sleep!" he shouted, then led the way across the black floor to the partitions on the far side of the dome. "Speak softly," he whispered as Juan and Lena followed him behind the makeshift barriers, where he sat down in a crude chair and pointed at two others.

Juan and Lena sat down. "I hold this place together," he said suddenly. "They look to me to decide things between them. We have everything we need to live, but in truth we have nothing. I tell you this because it's plain what you are, and maybe you can help us."

"What are we?" Lena asked, putting her helmet down on the floor.

The convict almost laughed. "Forgive me, but you walked in here like children."

"Why do they look up to you?" Lena asked.

"Isn't it obvious? I'm both attractive and intelligent. That's hard currency here."

"Why were you sent here?" Juan asked.

"I'm Tasarov," the big man said, apparently taking great pleasure in startling him. "I was exiled because I wouldn't submit to my betters. A few of them even stole my work and put it out as their own." He smiled. "I'm a prideful, boasting man, and I make good on my boasts. Men and women both find me insufferable, but they can't keep their hands off me. Now, what is it you two want with me?" He smiled at Juan and leered at Lena. "I really should have had you stripped in full view. You're both very beautiful!"

"Thank you for the compliments," Lena said. Juan tensed.

Tasarov's expression changed. "Dr. Obrion, you can't imagine what an absolute dead end existence has become here. We have everything we need or can duplicate, but it reduces us to our physical appetites, to the games we can play with each other in place of life. It's like trying to swim in a stone sea. We exist and struggle against boredom, inventing ever more trivial matters to quarrel over. I hope very much that you have come to ask me something very important, or at least amusing."

"Has anyone else come looking for you?" Juan asked.

"Soviet? Yes, but he died. I killed him."

"Killed him? But why?" Lena asked.

"He mocked us. We disgusted him."

"And you killed him for that?" Juan said.

"We fulfilled his opinion of us. It cost us nothing to destroy him. What do you want from me?"

"Are you still a mathematician?" Juan asked.

Tasarov nodded. "Of course. It's the single delight I have. I live on it. This may be the ideal place for it. I wander through ideal space within myself, even when I dream. The others sense my joy. They see that I am untouched by our physical plight. It helps them. They don't grasp very much, but I tell them what I can when they ask. They escape with me a little. Do you understand?"

"Yes, I do," Juan said. "How much have you thought about the alien web?"

"I'm sure that it doesn't just connect to this place."

"You're right. It's spread across the known universe. There's no sign of the builders." Juan summarized his experiences, ending with a description of the variant effect.

Tasarov was delighted. He leaned forward in his chair. "And you have observed this effect?"

"Yes. Four of us have drifted away from our prime world. We're here because it was reported you had done some theoretical work that might help us understand movement through both the web and probability."

Tasarov shook his head in denial. "You intrigue me. I want to begin thinking about the problem right away. But I fear that in coming to find me, you have perhaps lost the Yevgeny Petrovich Tasarov who did the work you're after. In this probability, I have not done such work." He smiled. "I seem to remember some thoughts about possible worlds—perhaps I am remembering what one of my other selves knows? I wonder, from your description, if only consciousness is displaced through probability, as in musical chairs—you know the game—or if bodies move?" He shrugged. "What does it matter? Space, time, and matter may be illusory. Only thoughts exist, in a matrix of relationships, in a kind of stage setting, I mean. It's real, as far as it goes, but falls apart if you move between stage sets. You two have seen through the painted sets!" He grinned at them.

"I suppose we have," Juan said, wondering if the man was mad.

36

THE TONGUES OF MEN AND ANGELS

Tasarov turned on a small portable lamp, gestured at a samovar, and offered to make tea. "It's good Russian tea. We've duplicated it a thousand times." He sat back in his chair and said softly, "I would consider it a kindness if you would let us duplicate what you have on you. Do you have weapons? If you do, I would prefer that you keep them hidden. We have not had occasion to duplicate weapons, aside from cutlery. Life is strange enough as it is. I wouldn't want what authority I have here to start depending on weapons. It would destroy the stability we have. Arms might tempt us to try to go back and storm the Amazon terminus."

"Our weapons are too small for that kind of action," Juan said.

"Good—don't even show them to me."

"This Soviet you killed," Lena said, "what was his name?"

"Ivan Dovzhenko. Did you know him?"

"Yes," Juan said, wincing.

"Ah, but he wouldn't have been the one you knew."

"How was he killed?"

"I snapped his neck. I felt ashamed for him."

"That was your only reason?" Juan asked.

"It gave us a moment of relief to see one of our captors die. There was great bitterness here in the first months after our arrival, as we began to see what our existence would be—a very slow dying." He shook his head and said, "We will never see the world we knew again. Can you imagine that? No more sun, green fields, or blue sky. Only this rusty landscape."

"We might be able to take you out of here," Juan said.

Tasarov stared at him in disbelief, then took a deep breath. "I don't think I could go alone. There are people here I love. I could not live while they suffered here. You do mean that I alone would be permitted to leave?"

"Yes," Juan said.

"But what would justify such privilege? I have done no work on possible worlds. They would know I have nothing to give."

"Perhaps you could start some work," Lena suggested.

"Yes, but it would come to nothing. They would want a way to control, or predict, movement in probability, and that is not probable. I'm not being facetious. It would be a compounding of the infinity of probabilities for us to be able to target the world into which we would pass, since probability also guides that outcome. There is no ground on which to stand that would be immune to the workings of probability."

"But I think that human probability is limited," Juan said.

"I would like to hear your reasons, but how might that give us prediction or control?"

"One can find the limited human history that one wants by passing through the frames until that world is found. Our group did so to escape a run of worlds destroyed by nuclear war."

"Ah, yes, of course, but you won't ever be able to do much more than that," Tasarov replied, "or find worlds that are not in the cards for human nature—utopias, for example, which might be found only in futurity. You can't enter the future or the past, can you?"

"No," Juan said, "but we've lost time between variants."

"Good. Time travel into the past or future along one line of probability would shake my understanding of physical theory, though mathematical descriptions of timelike journeys are possible."

"Will you consider coming back with us?" Juan asked.

Tasarov shook his head. "Not alone. I would not be able to return to this same place and the people I care about."

"What if we could take them with us?" Lena asked.

Tasarov smiled. "What would I go back to? Society is made up of interlocking gangs, a system that is more violent, more lethal and abusive of land and people than any criminal acts. And it brands the outsiders, the ones who oppose it for gain or politics, as *the* criminals. Nothing could be more reversed, more false than that. Criminals know what they are and accept it. The social gangs wage war and commit economic violence while pretending to be something better. Their crimes are not as unsightly as rape or murder, but strike deeper, because they are systematic and protected from justice."

"But you're neglecting an important fact," Lena said, "decent people who can only live their lives in a social framework."

"Yes, and they never wake up to the violence that is done against them, in the exploitation of their work. They're prisoners and never know it. All revolutions are merely prison mutinies at bottom. But it's useless. Even though the criminal, like the artist, sees through the playacting of the straights—through their fear of the unconventional, their insistence on courtesy and manners—he is also one of them, in that he strives to shut out his true nature. I have no illusions that the underdog in power would be any better. For me there is only personal honor, personal accountability. All so-called progress is individual."

Juan said, "A social system is only a harness on a horse. It enables that animal to do what it couldn't before, but it's still a horse."

"That is why I will not go back," Tasarov said. "Our human world is fierce and terrible, and tragic. We love it for its poetry, for the clean lines of its suffering finality as it wars with itself. But I have all that here, where I can probe and experiment in my thoughts."

"And do nothing," Lena said.

"What is to be done, dear lady?" Tasarov replied. "The endless reform and adjustment of social systems will never be enough, because they all must rest on power and authority that is external to most of the individuals who must live in them. No man is an island—but sometimes I'm convinced that it would be better if we were each absolutely autonomous. Perhaps people would treat each other better if they could only visit each other once in a while."

"You protest against your humanity too much," Lena said.

"Why shouldn't I?" Tasarov replied with a wave of his hand. "I can be free within myself, see clearly the gulf between what I am and what I should be. Not to confront this gulf, at least in one's thoughts, is to wear blinders."

"I know how you feel," Juan said, thinking of his own

whims, impulses, and stray feelings. They made him feel mean-spirited and tawdry, hidden from himself. Humanity pretended to change the world, but could not change itself.

"Life should be about much more than it is," Tasarov added. "We all once expected more." He looked away. "I shall make tea now." He rummaged around for the burner, samovar, and cups.

"There's a dome here," Juan said, "a kind of alien planetarium."

"Yes," Tasarov replied as he lit the burner with a match. "We avoid the place. It affects us when we're in there."

"How?"

"Things get into our minds. It's obviously an informational storage and retrieval area, but we don't have the minds to match it."

"Have you learned anything else about this place?" Juan asked.

"Nothing. All this alien technology resists basic analysis. It can't be taken apart and studied. Believe me, we have clever people who have tried."

"You can see the future of science in its workings," Juan said. "A profound understanding of the fluidity of nature exhibits itself. The technology gives freedom from material rigidity by using the more basic fluidity of nature. To do this requires the energy of whole suns."

Tasarov laughed as the water began to boil. He put the tea in to steep and sat back.

"So will you go back with us?" Juan asked.

Tasarov stared at the samovar. "An agonizing choice." He smiled. "My mind is convinced, but the rest of me is weak."

Juan said, "Is there anything I can say to help you decide?"

Tasarov sighed. "Say it, then. I don't know what it is." As he gazed at the seated mathematician, Juan realized that here was a potential ally, someone with whom he might pool his discontents and discover a plan of action.

"Shut up!" a sleepy voice shouted from the floor.

Juan peered between the partitions and saw a group of convicts sitting just beyond. They had apparently been listening to the conversation.

"They're curious about what's going on back home," Tasarov said. "I'm afraid they've found our talk disappointing." He leaned over, poured the tea, and handed Juan and

Lena their cups. Then he stood up. "Excuse me," he said as he kicked down one section of the partition. "Now you can all hear better!"

The half dozen seated convicts gazed at Juan with narrowed eyes. Tasarov said, "Perhaps you can tell them something."

Juan nodded to the shadowed faces. What could he say to them? "It's the same world back there," he started haltingly, "the same humankind—"

"Humankind!" a voice shouted. "A fancy word for something that's neither human nor kind."

"—choking cities," Juan continued, "ruined countrysides, growing deserts. The coastal cities are working hard to hold off flooding as the temperature rises—"

"We know all that!" another voice shouted. "When are they going to send us more women?"

"And younger boys!"

Lights began to go on in the dark dome. People were sitting up to listen. Juan gulped some tea and put the cup down on the floor, then stood up and looked around at the faces that were watching him. "We will tell what we've seen here."

"Leave us your woman!" a distant voice cried. "You can have her back next time."

Juan raised his voice against the laughter. "We'll let you duplicate all we have!"

"Let us?" a voice asked. "We can take what we want!"

Juan felt a moment of dizziness. His head was once again throbbing from the blow he had received.

"Quiet!" Tasarov ordered as he got to his feet. "These people are not our enemies. They came to ask me about some work they thought I'd done, nothing more. They'll do what they can for us when they go back. Now get some rest!" He started to raise his partition. Juan helped him set it up again. "There is so much pride here," Tasarov said softly. "We'll never run out of it. You two sleep here."

"Thank you," Lena said as two convicts brought their packs and Juan's helmet.

"We'll dupe your belongings while you sleep," Tasarov said.

Lena began to open their backpacks. As lights began to wink out, Tasarov made his way back between the shapes on the dark floor to his sleeping place.

37

WHAT IS TO BE DONE?

"Juan," Lena whispered.

His aching head told him to keep his eyes closed. Lena touched his shoulder. He opened his eyes. Her head seemed to float in the yellow glow of the dome.

"What's wrong?" she asked softly.

"Head hurts more now."

"We must get you checked," she said. "There's nothing more we can do here. We'll leave everything. Leave your helmet. The shuttle might be there again."

He sat up. "Where's Tasarov?"

"He's still with his fivesome."

Juan struggled to his feet. Lena steadied him. They came out from behind the partition and quietly made their way around the mass of sleepers to the exit. Together, they stepped toward the door. It glowed, and they passed—

—through into the bright alien night.

The silence of the desert landscape sang in his ears. "Can you stand by yourself?" Lena asked.

He nodded. "Let's go." They walked between the domes. He kept his eyes on the ground in front of him, trying to keep his balance. "I need to rest," he said as they came to the tree. A shadow slipped out from beneath the branches, as if detaching itself from the trunk, and came toward him. Juan was about to speak as the man's arm went up, holding something. Lena cried out as the bludgeon struck him across the head; he fell and lay on his back, unable to open his eyes, listening to Lena struggling with the man. He felt bodies strike the ground, and tried to get up. He raised his head, but his arms refused to move. The starry sky was inside his

head. Lena called his name. He forced his eyes open. Red
flooded his vision and drowned him.

He woke up in his sleeping bag. Tasarov was kneeling over
him, his face a mask in the dim yellow light.

"Better?" the face asked.

"Yes," Juan said.

Tasarov leaned back and turned on a standing lamp. "You
cried out at any light during the last two days."

"Two days?"

"Don't you remember?"

Juan tried to think. Lena and he had been asleep. They
had left for the shuttle. A fist closed in his chest.

"Where is she?" he demanded.

"Be calm, my friend. You've a concussion, and must stay
quiet."

Juan lay back and closed his eyes. He heard whimpers in
the back of his head, then silence. He tried to move his
arms, but they were tied to his sides. He lay still and fell
asleep.

Tasarov was sitting in a chair, watching him, when he
awoke. "You seem better," the Russian said. "I hope you
agree." His words seemed dreamlike. Juan felt as if he could
float into a standing position with no effort. "I've freed your
arms."

Juan raised himself to a sitting position against his pack.
"I do feel better."

"Do you recall what happened?"

Juan's chest tightened. He drew a deep breath. "Maybe if
you tell me."

Tasarov stood up. Juan looked around. The dome was
silent. Everyone was asleep.

Juan said, "Tell me."

"The shuttle keeper. He attacked you and the woman by
the tree. She's dead. He broke her neck during the rape. I
heard you both going out, and followed as soon as I was fully
awake, but it was too late by the time I dragged him from
her. We tied him to the tree."

"He's still there?" Juan asked, taking short breaths. He
closed his eyes and saw the void closing in around him.

"He's there," Tasarov said in the darkness, "for when you
are ready."

"And Lena?" Juan asked through clenched teeth.

"We buried her under the tree. Do you object?"

Juan shook his head, unable to weep.

For three days he drifted in a half-waking state, unable to feel or think. Once he dreamed of carrying Lena's body with him through the variants, to keep from encountering her alternates. When he could stand, they took him out to the tree. The shuttle keeper was on a long chain, squatting on the mound of Lena's grave.

"You can kill him now," Tasarov said, offering a knife.

The man under the branches did not react.

"Kill him!" the small gathering shouted.

The shuttle keeper was oblivious, resting his chin on his knees.

Tasarov said, "It's your right here to kill him."

Juan stepped closer and tried to see the man's face in the patches of white sunlight. The man was breathing slowly.

"He cares nothing for your scruples," Tasarov said.

Juan turned away and pushed through the crowd.

"Kill him!" a voice hissed.

"Cut him so he bleeds slowly!" another added.

"Rip his guts so he takes a week to die."

Juan broke out into the open and wandered between the domes. At his right he saw a line slowly passing into the dome which housed the replicator. The men did not look at him as he passed.

He heard a long shriek and looked back. Tasarov's large shape was under the tree, working on the shuttle keeper with the knife. The big man thrust hard into the torso, and the chained figure went limp.

"I killed him for you, my friend!" he shouted as he came out from under the tree. Something in Juan was satisfied, but he also felt shame.

He turned away. Tasarov caught up with him. Juan reached into his pocket. "Here. You might as well have my weapon. I don't think you can do much worse with it."

"My friend," Tasarov said, pushing it away, "you take this too seriously. He wanted to die. I made him want to live as he died."

Juan stopped and saw blood on the other man's shirt.

"What do you want to say to me?" Tasarov demanded. "I will understand."

"There's nothing I can say."

"But down deep you're glad." Tasarov touched his shoulder. "I am sorry about your Lena. The shuttle keeper was never one of us. We knew whenever he came here that he was outside our code."

Juan nodded and turned away. Tasarov did not follow him.

"But, of course!" the Russian shouted after him. "You will see her again!"

Juan quickened his pace. A breeze blew dust into his face, but he marched on, hoping that the shuttle would be waiting. He came over the rise and ran when he saw the sphere, afraid that it would leave before he reached it.

He staggered through the open lock, feeling weak as he went up the winding passage to the drum-shaped chamber. He sat down and waited for the viewspace to come on. It seemed to take a long time, but it finally lit up. The planet fell away as he watched. He felt empty.

Tasarov was wrong. He might not find Lena again. She might not be alive in the next variant, or in the next dozen. In any case, she would never again be the Lena he had known.

The sun grew larger in the viewspace. For a moment he imagined that the vessel would not switch into otherspace, but would run at the star and be consumed. Finally, tears welled up, and he wept.

The shuttle was in final approach to the suncore station when he looked up again. He gazed at it and tried to think. What could anyone have done? He and Lena had taken a risk; she had chosen to come. They might have come back safely.

The great globe of the core station filled the viewspace as the shuttle was pulled into the glowing entrance. Suddenly, he felt a raging hatred of his own kind. Its first use of the alien web was to find a dumping ground for criminals; and Lena, who had not doubted humanity as he did, had paid with her life.

38

SEEKING

◑

He stepped into the frame, emerged into darkness, and moved slowly toward the exit. It glowed and he slipped out—
—into the winding passage.

Hands seized him from both sides and pushed him forward. He staggered and turned to face two soldiers pointing automatic rifles at him.

"Take me to Titus Summet," he said. "I'm Juan Obrion."

The soldiers motioned with their weapons; he started slowly up the passage. "You'll be met at the drop well!" a voice barked after him.

"Sit," Summet said in his office. "You look awful. What happened?"

"How long have I been gone?"

"Four days. Does that agree with your time?"

Juan nodded. "I went alone?"

"Lena showed up with Moede and Rassmussen. They went after you immediately." Juan gripped his armrests. "You didn't run into them?" Summet asked.

"No."

"They thought you might need help. You wanted them along, didn't you?"

Juan asked, "Are you aware of the variant effect here?"

"We are," Titus answered, drumming on his desk with his fingers. "We sent you out to find Yevgeny Tasarov, who might help us learn something about the nature of the effect. What did you learn?"

"Nothing. Tasarov claims he did no work in possible worlds."

"Was he lying?"

257

"I doubt it. It would have been to his advantage to lie about having done the work."

"Are you up to going again? Your friends might need you."

Juan started to tell him about Lena, but his head throbbed as grief and anger rushed into him.

"What is it?" Titus asked.

"I'm very tired."

"So tell me about the prison."

Juan's throat tightened. "It's a reasonable facsimile of hell. They can get everything they have over and over. Death is a mercy."

Titus put his hands together on his desk. "Describe it."

"The economy of your penal colony," Juan said, "depends on the replicator. Available goods are copied. Sooner or later there will be a struggle over who controls the copy dome."

"Why hasn't it happened?"

"It's orderly there now, as I saw it, because they all look up to Tasarov. But it's a corrupt life—no goals, no meaning. Tasarov has an inner life, which is probably part of the reason for his influence. They sense a kind of salvation in him, but they envy as much as admire him."

Titus rubbed his chin and leaned forward. "Extraordinary. Economists warned us about the consequences of using the replicator. If we make the ship a mass production factory, it will unbalance our scarcity-based economies. We're copying essential and costly things—mostly drugs and rare metals." He sat back. "Well, they're welcome to what they can make of their existence out there, and we don't have to feed them."

"It doesn't disturb you, to let it happen?" Juan asked.

"Let what happen?"

"To permit people who have already been stripped of their human connections through prison and exile be further deprived of all human purpose? Do you have any idea of the cruelties that may become possible?"

Titus smiled. "It's all too metaphysical and removed from us now. No one is starving. It's up to them to make the best of it."

Juan took a deep breath and sat back. "Don't you have any personal feelings?"

"They don't count. I do what's possible—second and third best, according to you—to make something from human nature as it is. I choose between immediate disasters and what you find repugnant." He shrugged. "Good will continue to be achieved with the bad. Maybe that criminal society will learn to do something creative with their circumstances."

"Tasarov was right," Juan said, "when he told me that politicians are the best-organized criminal class."

Titus stood up. "But what else can exist! What is to be done? Shall we beget angels?"

Juan closed his eyes as his head throbbed.

"What is it?" Titus asked softly.

"I was struck on the head."

"Why didn't you say so? I'll get a doctor. Can you walk to your quarters?"

Juan stood up and leaned on Summet's desk. The director stared at him as if from a poster. Juan fell forward and tore him down the middle.

He woke up feeling that he was a boy again, when days delighted him by simply following one another, before the fools who named things made everything familiar.

The moment fled as he remembered that Lena was dead. He sat up, realizing that her variant might return with Malachi and Magnus, then lay back again, afraid that he was trapped in a run of probabilities where she would always die.

The door slid open and Titus came in. "Good, you're awake. The doctors say your concussion has healed nicely. Do you still want to try again?"

Juan got up and started to dress. "So you think there's a Tasarov who can give you some basic knowledge?"

Titus sat down in a chair. "I can't afford to ignore the possibility. Don't you want to go after your friends?"

"I guess I have to. They came after me here."

"Did they in your last variant?"

Juan said, "Lena caught up with me just before I reached the frame chamber."

"What—then where is she?"

Juan told him, then finished dressing.

"I'm sorry, Juan," Summet said.

"You forced her."

Titus gave a nervous laugh. "Sure. Here I let you go alone, then sent the others as soon as they got here. I wonder if I'm smarter here." He stood up and said, "You'll need a new pack and headgear. I'll go with you as far as the deep chamber."

"Don't bother."

• • •

Juan approached the shuttle bay with caution; the variant shuttle keeper was also likely to be a dangerous man. Juan reminded himself that this was not the man who had killed Lena, even though the criminal personality would be the same. The two men up in the winding passage had been the same. They had confirmed that Lena, Malachi, and Magnus had come through a week earlier.

He came out of the passage into the bay. The cradle was empty. As he waited for the craft to return, he peered into the exit and entry tube behind the large bowl of the cradle. A soft whine came from the tunnel. The shuttle rolled in. He watched closely and saw that it did not touch the passage. It drifted into the cradle, and rotated a half turn. He tensed as the lock opened and the keeper came out.

"You're alone?" the unshaven man asked; his hair was grayer this time.

"I'm Dr. Obrion. You took three of my colleagues down."

"A pretty woman like that," the man said, "coming here with a nigger and a grandfather. What's it all about? You're not her type either."

Juan went past him into the lock, and hurried around the passage into the drum-shaped chamber. He was sweating as he dropped his pack and sat down on it. The keeper came in behind him and squatted down near the exit. Juan tried to ignore him.

"So you have it for her, eh? We don't see many lookers here."

Juan asked, "Where's the overhead view?"

"It's slow sometimes."

Suddenly the chamber filled with amber light. The viewspace blinked on. The station was receding in the gray otherness. Juan watched the bright exit close in the black globe.

"Is she good?" the keeper asked. "I would have asked her if she'd been alone."

Juan grasped the gun in his pocket as the shuttle switched into normal space and sunlight flooded the chamber. The man was a variant of the same rotten character, he told himself, trembling with indecision, but still likely to commit the same crimes; by killing him now, he might save another victim, even a variant of Lena. The man's innocence of her murder was only a feeble technicality.

"Why are you here?" the keeper asked.

"To meet my friends." He didn't need to reason about this; hadn't he always claimed that rationality was powerless against human nature? The woman he had loved was dead. Shooting this man might ease his pain, and no one would hold him responsible. He saw himself returning endlessly to kill the shuttle keeper's variants, and held back.

"But they went back yesterday," the man said.

"What?"

The keeper nodded. "Guess the guards didn't bother to tell you."

"I'll check anyway," Juan said, even though he knew the man had no reason to lie. The previous variant had not carried over when he had stepped through the frame. The convict shifted his weight and looked away. Juan clutched his weapon and waited for the man to say or do something that would make it easy to kill him.

39

YIELDING

◐

As he neared Tasarov's dome, Juan told himself that the variants of his parents had been all too familiar, and oddly bearable. Finding another Magnus had been something of a relief; but how would he feel toward another Lena? The woman he had known was dead, but she would still be herself, because she would know everything they had shared, except those final moments before the keeper had broken her neck. That Lena was irrevocably lost, but the difference amounted to only a few memories. He and she would meet for the first time, even though they had known each other for years. The gulf between them would be both trivial and significant, but what could it ever mean if he loved her?

He came to the tree where she and Magnus were buried, in different variants. His feelings twisted as he turned away, and he knew that the cruel knot within him could not be untied.

He went slowly to Tasarov's dome. There was no one outside when he came to the entrance. It glowed—

—and he stepped into a yellow space filled with the stench of human beings.

"Another one!" a voice shouted as figures gathered around him.

"I'm Juan Obrion," he said.

"If you're looking for the other three, they've gone," a man answered. Juan recognized him as the one who had clubbed him.

"How long ago?"

"Yesterday."

"Take me to Tasarov."

262

Juan followed him through the sprawling throng to Tasarov's partitioned area. The big Russian got up from a chair and said, "They told me you might come. I can only repeat what I told them—I did no such work, and I won't go back with you." He held out his hand.

Juan shook it. "Your variant said as much to me."

Tasarov nodded. "Dr. Rassmussen explained. It will give me something new to think about." He smiled. "How did you and I get on during our first meeting?"

"One of your men clubbed me. The shuttle keeper killed Lena Dravic."

Tasarov took a deep breath. "I'm sorry to hear it. We must watch him. He's not one of us."

"You killed him for me," Juan said.

Tasarov grimaced. "What will you do now?"

"Go back. Is there anything else you wish to copy?"

"No. Your friends had everything. You don't have anything special in your pack, do you?"

"I don't think so. Do you still refuse my weapon?"

Tasarov nodded. "One of our more lawful impulses." He shrugged. "I'm sure one of my variants will take it from you, if you keep coming back." He motioned to a chair. "Do sit down, Doctor Obrion, and keep me company for a few minutes. Delaying you may spin the probabilities more profoundly."

Juan took off his pack and sat down in the chair facing Tasarov. The din from the floor was louder, but the Russian spoke over it. "You seem about to ask me something."

Juan nodded. "Why are you confined here? I'm curious about what it may be in this variant."

Tasarov smiled and leaned back in his chair until it creaked. "Simple vindictiveness. My enemies were jealous. My name was changed on certain records, and I was shipped out. My enemy wanted to deny me a chance to work, to fulfill myself, at least in the world I knew. The fact that I would suffer, unable to contribute, warmed his heart." He smiled. "The news you have brought me is very consoling. There must be variants in which I'm still there, irritating my enemy! Do you know anything interesting about me?"

Juan stood up. "You're certain that you won't come back with me?"

The big Russian nodded. "How would I be able to live with myself, knowing that my friends are still here?"

Juan said, "I don't know what to say to convince you. Your reasons are the best wrong ones I can imagine."

Tasarov stood up as Juan put on his pack. "I feel you are already a friend." He laughed. "I hope my variants remember!"

"I told you so," the shuttle keeper said.

Juan dropped his pack and sat on it. "Get away from me."

"So polite."

The viewspace came on as the shuttle took off. He tried to ignore the keeper, but the man kept staring at him.

"Do you see this?" Juan said, taking out his automatic and pointing it at him.

The keeper smiled. "I don't think you'll use it. Can't figure you out."

Juan tightened his grip and took careful aim at the man's chest. "What good would it do you to figure me out?"

The keeper's smile faded as he retreated out into the passage. Juan grimaced at the weapon and put it away.

Somewhere, the web builders' civilization was in full flower, fulfilling the dreams of alien imaginations; but its existence required the presence of desolate, ghost-filled continua. Juan tried to imagine why existing objects carried nonexistent twins. Every stone might not have existed, yet each nonexistent made sense as the subject of a sentence. . . .

The nightmare of seemingly reasonable links between ideas was absurd. He knew that he was asleep, but he was not yet ready to break out of the dream. A deeper self would carry him through the chain of reasoning to a subtle conclusion, and he would awaken. . . .

He saw the shuttle keeper hiding in a canyon of nonexistent objects. The man spotted him and leered. "You want to see human destiny?" he shouted from behind massed geometrical shapes. "Watch two people fuck! Nothing's more obviously set up to happen except birth, eating and shitting, and dying! In between, you fuck!"

I'm lost, Juan thought, struggling to open his eyes.

"Not yet!" the keeper cried.

In all the variants open to him, Juan knew there had to be a way to deal with his despair.

"No utopias!" the keeper shrieked. "You can see them,

know what they are, but you can't have even one!" His hand reached out from the deep gorge and grabbed Juan's throat.

He opened his eyes and sat up. Titus stood at the foot of his bed.

The director said, "You seemed to be wrestling with yourself."

"Are they back yet?" Juan asked, remembering that he had missed Lena, Malachi, and Magnus again. They were with Tasarov in this variant, still looking for him.

"No," Titus said. "Better just wait it out. If you go now, you'll only shift things for yourself again."

"But you still want Tasarov?"

"Yes."

"Even if he doesn't have anything for you?"

"I'll put him to work. He's wasted out there."

Juan said, "He'll refuse."

"Then we'll bring him back by force."

"That might cost lives."

"Not if we're careful."

"I won't go, Titus. Send your armed goons and see what it'll get you. The man doesn't know anything, and I haven't heard anything from him to make me think that he'll ever do useful work in variant theory. It's unlikely that anyone can. Do you understand? No one knows a damned thing about how and why all this happens!"

"Calm yourself, Juan." There was something of the keeper's leer in Summet's expression. "You've been under a lot of stress. Your judgment's shot."

"Because I disagree with you?"

"Of course not. Look, you may be right about Tasarov being useless. Maybe he should be where he is, but you could try to be more convincing."

It was unlike Summet to show this much doubt, Juan thought.

"I'm on your side, Juan. I let you go out there because from day one I was convinced that good would come of it."

"And I haven't delivered, have I?"

"Don't be stupid. You helped open the web."

"And it's being used as just another way to avoid problems and help the powerful." He closed his eyes, realizing how much he missed Lena, and how little he had given her.

Titus sighed. "The web is not a tunnel out of life. Forgive us, and yourself, if only a little. It's not over yet."

40

RECURSIONS

◐

"Who are you?" the keeper shouted from the shuttle, his voice echoing insanely in the bay.

"Three people came through here," Juan said as he approached.

"They went back," the man answered dourly, then sat down in the lock.

"When?"

"Hours ago, with a group of armed Russkies."

"Was Tasarov with them?"

The keeper nodded. "Why'd they want him back?"

Juan retreated toward the exit.

"Not very sociable, are you!" the convict cried after him. Juan slipped through the glow—

—and hurried down the passage to the frame chamber.

Again, the soldiers sent him out through their checkpoints in the winding passage. He went up slowly toward the outer lock, wondering what he would find in this variant. Every pass through a frame twisted the cruel knot within him tighter. The only solution, if he could call it that, would be to never again venture across the probabilities. Could he put down new roots?

He heard voices. Three figures came around the turn. Each was in full gear.

"Juan!" Lena cried.

His face stiffened as she came toward him, innocent of what he knew. For a moment he imagined himself standing behind her with Magnus and Malachi, straining to become real.

She stopped before him. "Juan, are you all right? Why are

you coming back?" Her eyes seemed a little grayer, but then she lifted her head and he saw they were the blue he remembered.

His two friends came up and stood beside her. Malachi's broad, dark face was unchanged, and Magnus was the same lean, older man. "We decided to come," Malachi said.

"If you'll have us," Magnus added.

Too late, Juan thought, overcome with regret.

"Well, shall we do as Summet wants?" Malachi asked, smiling.

Magnus dropped his pack. Juan felt a rush of panic.

"What is it?" Malachi said.

"You must know," Juan managed to say, "that I can't be the one you knew."

"We know," Magnus said.

"Lena, you were killed out there," he said, trembling. Her thinning face drew itself into a mask as she gazed at him, and she was a stranger.

"We're fooling ourselves," Juan said in his quarters. He turned on his back.

Lena sat up and hugged the pillow to her breast. "But are we? We're the same people. Am I so different from her, Juan?"

"No—except for a few memories."

She said, "I had a nightmare a week ago about dying on that far world." He lifted his head, startled. "Juan, why did you go off without me?"

"I waited. Titus told me neither Magnus nor Malachi would come. Then Mal called me and said he couldn't go— Dita had just left for Russia, but he was hoping she'd come back, so he was staying on the chance she might. Titus couldn't reach you."

"I came as soon as I got the message," she said.

"So did your variant."

"Mal told me when he arrived that he knew Dita wouldn't come back. I think their farewells were pretty final before she left. She really wanted to go back, and he knew he couldn't follow her."

"I figured as much when I saw he was here."

She put the pillow aside and lay back next to him. "We're lucky to have each other at all. We're not any more confused than most people."

He was silent, unable to answer.

"Juan?"

He reached over and caressed her belly.

"You mustn't give up," she said. "We can't give up. I may seem a substitute for the Lena you knew, but we can start again. It's the same for me. We have that in common."

He said, "You probably still think my misanthropy a defect of some kind."

She looked at him with tenderness. "I couldn't bear to see you hating yourself."

The door buzzed.

"Come in!" she shouted, pulling up the covers over them.

It slid open. Summet came in and stopped as it closed. "There's been an armed breakout, but it was stopped in the winding passage."

Juan sat up. "Was Tasarov among them?"

"No."

"Any dead?" Lena asked.

"Ten. More than a hundred wounded."

"So they copied my gun," Juan said, feeling responsible.

"I couldn't have let you go unarmed," Summet insisted.

"And we don't have Tasarov. Was it necessary to shoot back?"

Summet nodded. "They came through in a suicide wave and overwhelmed the first guards. Then they went up the passage with hostages."

"Which you let them kill," Juan said.

"Standing orders. I had no say in it."

"A suicide wave," Juan said. "Doesn't that tell you anything, Titus? Have you come for our approval? What do you want from us now?"

"I want you to go back to Tasarov. Maybe he'll come out now. I know the variant may not carry over, but I want to try. Tell him he can bring three people out with him."

"Generous of you."

Summet said, "I sympathize with how you feel, but I must think of the larger good, according to what is possible. You want life to be fair, brave, and honest, people to be decent, and for things to always come out right in the end."

"Too much to ask of mere human beings," Juan answered.

"Will you go?"

"You know I have to," Juan said.

• • • •

There was blood in the winding passage. The dead and wounded had been removed, but Juan felt their presence. Was there a variant in which the break had succeeded? It had to be there, however small the chance. He stopped before the large portal to the deep chamber and faced Lena, Malachi, and Magnus.

"I can do this myself," he said.

Magnus smiled. "What's one more variant?"

"We'll stay together," Malachi added, "from now on."

"It may get even more dangerous," Juan said.

Lena said, "Juan, we've all had time to think and discuss it, and we've concluded that we can't ever go back to our private lives. The web is too important, too filled with danger and possibility for our kind. We must devote all our efforts to understanding and using it, and we know you feel the same. Summet is right about getting Tasarov on our side."

"Our side," Magnus said, "is either UN-ERS, in the person of Titus, or the four of us. Arrogant as it may sound, it's up to us to do what Titus can't do, and to take things out of his hands if we can."

"Do you believe he'll sit still for it?" Juan asked, glancing back at the turn, where a few soldiers were lighting up cigarettes.

Malachi said, "In his heart he's one of us."

"But he'll oppose us," Juan replied, "if it threatens his authority."

"Well, that is reasonable, old man," Malachi said. "He can't be pure in his position. Neither are we. He needs us to cut his hair."

"And who will cut ours?" Juan asked.

"No one," Malachi replied. "The cut stops here."

"We'd better go," Lena whispered, "before something stops us."

Tasarov's dome was filled with wounded and dying, but all the copied resources from the replicator could not make up for the lack of medical skills. Juan, Malachi, and Magnus administered emergency aid under Lena's direction. Juan put on antiseptics and bandages, injected painkillers and infection fighters. Sixteen men died and were buried near the alien tree. He dimly remembered Tasarov leading him to the bedding behind the partitions.

He sat up after what seemed endless sleep. The dome was

quiet. Tasarov slouched in a chair, watching him. Lena and the others were asleep nearby.

"Thank you for helping," Tasarov said softly. "The dying has stopped."

"Why did you let them even try?" Juan asked.

"I couldn't prevent it. No one could. They were completely broken and crazed, my friend. The realization that they would spend the rest of their lives here was finally too much. Even visible guards might have helped, by providing some link with the outside. Guards can be mocked, even provoked. But this desert, these domes, and all the endlessly copied artifacts and foodstuffs from a lost home drove these people over the edge. Even more women would not have relieved the futility. They would be a constant reminder of a future that could not be, since no one would condemn children to this place."

"Did you lose anyone?"

He nodded. "One of my lovers is dead, the other blinded."

"I'm sorry," Juan said.

"Could you have prevented it?"

"No."

"Then don't be sorry. Why did you come this time?"

Gunfire sounded from the other side of the dome. "Stay as you are!" a voice shouted.

Juan struggled to his feet. Lena, Malachi, and Magnus stirred and sat up as Juan and Tasarov peered between the partitions.

"ERS troops," the Russian whispered.

41

ESCAPE

◐

Armed figures rushed in through the glowing portal. Two dozen soldiers formed a line and picked their way through the prostrate and wounded.

"We want the UN team!" the lieutenant shouted.

"A variant Titus sent them," Juan whispered, "one who doesn't trust us." They had entered a world, he realized, in which Summet was capable of actions his previous self would have rejected. He glanced at Tasarov. The Russian seemed resigned.

"Lay all your weapons on the floor!" the lieutenant cried.

Juan stood up. "We're over here. Leave the wounded alone." He looked at Lena and the others and whispered, "Don't leave your packs." She gave him a questioning look as he rolled up his own.

"Dr. Obrion?" the lieutenant called out.

"Yes," Juan said, putting on his pack.

"Yevgeny Petrovich Tasarov?"

The Russian nodded as the officer motioned for him to come along.

"We're ready," Juan said, and led the way toward the exit.

The lieutenant hurried to keep up. "Move out!" he shouted to his unit. The soldiers hurried through the exit, and were all gone as Juan reached it. He went through the glow—

—and faced a line of soldiers. Lena, Tasarov, and the others came out and stood next to him. The lieutenant emerged and went ahead. "Quick march!" he shouted, then fell back to escort his prisoners.

"What do you know about this?" Juan asked him as they followed the squad.

"Your group is under arrest, Dr. Obrion."

"What's your name, Lieutenant?"

The soldier ignored his question.

"Has something happened back home?" Juan demanded apprehensively.

The lieutenant was silent as they passed the alien tree.

They were made to wait at the entrance to the deep chamber while the squad went through. Finally, only the lieutenant and his sergeant were left.

"Watch where you point those weapons," Lena said.

The two men pulled back their automatic rifles, and let them hang in their harnesses. "I'll go first," the lieutenant said. "Sergeant, bring up the rear. Everyone, turn on your helmet lights." He waited until all lights were on, then stepped forward and disappeared into the portal's glow. Juan followed him through—

—into the dark chamber.

The others came in behind him. As they faced the frames, Juan reached into his thigh pocket, grasped the automatic, and brought it up near the lieutenant's face.

"Sorry to hurt your professional pride, but your body armor won't stop this from going right up your nose with no trouble at all." Out of the corner of his eye he saw Malachi quickly put his weapon to the sergeant's forehead. Lena and Magnus stepped back.

"What will this get you?" the lieutenant said.

"A good question," Tasarov added.

"Maybe we have to burn our bridges behind us," Juan answered.

Malachi helped him disarm the two officers. Lena and Magnus took out utility cord from their packs. Tasarov collected the automatic rifles and slung them over his shoulder.

"When they find you," Juan said, "the two of you won't know a thing."

"Very neat," the lieutenant said as Lena tightened his wrist cord. Magnus tied the sergeant, who cursed softly.

"Sit," Juan said when their hands were bound. The two soldiers obeyed. "Tie their feet, and tie them to each other, so they can't turn their heads to see which frame we take."

"Are you sure you have time?" the sergeant asked.

"Certainly," Malachi said, squatting down.

Juan took off the sergeant's helmet and put it on Tasarov's head. "You may need the light."

"Thanks."

"Ready?" Juan asked. He pointed to the last frame on the right. Four, Five and Six were the unknowns. "Keep right behind me. Malachi, bring up the rear."

He entered the black field. Lena was next to him as they hurried through. A red glow appeared ahead.

"Is that an exit?" she asked.

He stepped out into the red glow and looked around. The vast floor was the same as in other suncore stations. He turned and faced the exit. Frames curved off to his left and right. There might be a ship at the center of the circle, he thought, remembering the blue station where the frames connected with the string of sun shells.

Lena and Magnus emerged, followed by Malachi and Tasarov. "This is extraordinary!" the Russian said, startled by the openness of the station.

"We'll go through another frame immediately," Juan said. "They might send a squad into all six frames."

"Wondrous!" Tasarov exclaimed. "A variant we can never regain is looking for us."

"They come in runs," Juan answered, "so our escape may carry over. If we were to go back right now, only small details would differ. Therefore, we must expect to be followed, at least to this point."

"What will this accomplish?" Tasarov asked.

"First let's lose our pursuers," Malachi said. "Which frame? There must be hundreds here."

"Where do they lead?" Tasarov asked.

"From a suncore station," Juan said, "the frames probably lead out to various points throughout this solar system, if past experience is any guide."

"You're unsure," Tasarov said. "What if they lead out into a vacuum, or a poisonous atmosphere?"

"It's never happened," Malachi replied.

Juan looked back anxiously at their exit frame.

"Mark it," Lena said. "We may have to go back."

Malachi took out a small medical sticker and slapped it down on the floor. Juan moved off to his left and stopped at the fifth frame. "This should be far enough. Ready?"

Lena came to his side, looking skeptical.

"Step in together," Juan said.

"Shall we hold hands?" Tasarov asked.

"Wouldn't hurt," Juan replied, "but I think stepping in as a close group should be enough to insure that we'll be the same people when we come out."

"Lead in," Tasarov said.

"I hear shouting," Lena said suddenly.

Commands echoed from inside the frame Malachi had marked. Juan took Lena's hand and went through, then hurried forward. In a moment he saw a green glow ahead.

They came out into a vast hollow ball. "Another starship dock," Lena said, looking up at the small fleet of vessels hanging in the shell's great central space.

"This one's different," Juan said as the others emerged and stood at his side. "The ships in the first such construction dock we visited were all globes, differing only in size. Here we have various shapes." He gazed at the linked globes, long sluglike hulls, and egg shapes. One ship was a cylinder with globes at each end.

Tasarov looked back at the lone exit frame. "Can they find us here?"

"Even if they're at the suncore station now," Malachi said, "they'll pick this connection only by chance."

Tasarov laughed. "They'll get lost."

"Look over there!" Lena shouted, pointing at a small globe that was sitting on the green incurving surface.

"Looks like our ship's shuttle," Malachi said.

Juan started toward it. "I'll bet it's set to dock with one of those ships up there! If our pursuers get lucky, they'll find no one here, and with no shuttle they'll have to go back."

They jogged across the inward curve of the shell, but the globe was more distant than it seemed. Juan felt a tightening in his chest as he tried to keep up. There would be no place to hide if the craft wouldn't let them in.

They reached the ball at last. Juan triggered the lock. It opened. They rushed inside and up through the winding passage to a small drum-shaped chamber. The overhead viewspace came on as they dropped their packs into the control circle and sat down; it showed the docked ships in the center space.

"It might not move at all," Juan said, fearful that troops were already rushing from the frame.

The starships pulled close suddenly. Tasarov cried out as the viewspace went dark.

"We've docked with one of the ships," Juan said, getting up. "It wasn't a great distance."

"But which ship?" Tasarov asked.

"We're out of Summet's reach."

"Unless there's another shuttle on the inner surface," Malachi said.

"Even if there is, it might not dock with our ship. They'll have as little control over where these shuttles go as we do."

42

A WAY TO CHANGE

◑

The shuttle lock was open when they came to it. Juan led the way out into a long, straight passageway. The black floor and overhead lights were the same as in the big ships, with oval portals spaced less frequently on each side. This was probably the cylindrical ship with globes at each end.

They came to the end of the passageway and peered through an open lock into a winding passage. Juan led the way up through two turns into a drum-shaped chamber, and stepped into the control circle as the others came in behind him. A forward viewspace lit up, revealing the inner surface of the shell through a magnified hemispheric display.

"There's the exit frame," Malachi said.

"Look, there!" Tasarov shouted. Two dozen figures spilled out from the frame, looking like black ants on the green surface.

Juan turned around. "Quick—we've got to put something in the shuttle's lock. It might return!"

"I'll get it," Malachi said, and sprinted away.

"We'll be trapped if they get up here," Juan said.

"We're trapped anyway," Tasarov answered. "Where can we go?"

Juan watched as the soldiers spread out on the inner surface, expecting at any moment to see the ball of the shuttle whisk toward them.

He heard footfalls in the passageway. Malachi came into the chamber and dropped his pack. "I put a spade across the lock."

"But the shuttle might override it," Tasarov objected.

"Look!" Lena shouted. The squad divided into groups of six and went off in four opposite directions.

"They're thorough," Malachi said, stepping closer to the display, "but it won't help them. I don't see another shuttle."

Magnus said, "If there are others, they're probably set for the other ships."

"I think we're beyond their reach," Malachi replied. Juan took off his pack and sat down on it. Lena and Magnus did the same.

"So what now?" Tasarov asked, carefully laying down the automatic rifles.

Lena stood up and said, "We'll explore this ship until our friends below tire and go away. I'm curious if there are duplicators in any of the chambers along the passage."

Magnus got up. "I'll go with you."

"Be careful," Juan said.

Malachi sat down and looked at Juan. "Are you thinking the same thing I am?"

Juan nodded. "This group of ships may be linked through frames. More than one shuttle isn't needed. But our friends down there aren't likely to find those connections anytime soon, if they exist. We're safe as long as we see them moving around down there."

As Lena and Magnus left the chamber, Tasarov sat down cross-legged on the floor. "My friends," he said, "does this escape of ours have some purpose?"

"It does," Juan replied.

"What do you want, my friend? What are we to do?"

"Explore the web," Juan said, "learn enough to open a way for our kind into a better life."

Tasarov took a deep breath and smiled. "Are you serious?"

Juan said, "If we grasped even a thread of what the builders knew to make all this, we'd be able to remake human life."

"We've come to suspect," Malachi said, "that the builders climbed to some great height and pulled the ladder after them. The old Indian rope trick, you know."

"Intriguing," Tasarov said, glancing at the viewspace, where the sprinkling of soldiers was now at the limits of the field. "I object to my own kind, and so do you, Juan, I think. So why do you want to put even greater power in their hands?"

The Russian's question was demoralizing, but Juan was determined to attempt an answer. "You're right, we're imprisoned by our humanity, despite the fact that we're freer than any creature on Earth. When I saw your prison, all my doubts were confirmed. I had never seen a prison before—"

"There never was a prison like that!" Tasarov cut in.

"—but what moved me was that even in this prison of fundamentally altered circumstances, in which the same old hunter-gatherer was given nothing to do, I saw reason striving to reform its human burden, with little more than custom and force. You'll forgive me, Yevgeny, but you were their holy man, the one who stood apart."

Tasarov grunted. "Go on."

"I sympathize with the impulse to set any plausible law above human failure."

Malachi said, " 'And in their minds I will write my commandments'—expresses the need to internalize law."

"Exactly. Our reason has always known what is to be done, but not how."

Tasarov recited, " 'I know what I want, but I can't want what I want. The flesh decides that.' T.E. Lawrence's favorite conundrum, if memory serves. 'Man can do nothing unaided, but God can do as He will.' "

"The Bible, old chap?" Malachi asked.

"Why not? We're all pilgrims here."

"The world is as we made it," Malachi said. "How's that for guilt?"

"No," Juan answered, "as we were made. All human efforts have dealt with the outwardness of things, with social structures. Education was the closest we ever came to changing our insides, which can't be altered because they're locked up in the body's codes."

Malachi said, " 'If the leopard were offered wings, he would be foolish to refuse them.' "

"Whose words?" Tasarov asked.

"Shaka Zulu, the African leader and warrior."

"I've always admired him," Tasarov said. "When his will found the walls of his world, his vision kept going. He uttered prophecies even as he succumbed to his basest impulses."

"Revolution has to be more than revolt," Juan continued. "It must transform as it sweeps away, starting with our bodies. When we've removed the crippling legacy of evolution's survivalist strategy, then hatred and rage will storm more softly within us, perhaps even become a vital song, as we

compose ourselves for thought, and shed the mystery of our
waking and sleeping selves. Environments shaped our bodies, but we began to shape environments. Finally we must
shape ourselves." He paused and saw Lena standing in the
entrance. Their eyes met and he felt as if he had been caught
saying childish things.

"There are replicators in the first chamber on the left,"
she said and came inside.

Magnus came in after her. "I counted fourteen chambers
along the passage," he said. "The first one on the right has
three frames in it."

Juan looked at the viewspace. The soldiers were milling
around at the edge of the field.

"We should eat and get some rest," Lena said as she sat
down against her pack.

Tasarov said, "My friend, I'll grant you that all efforts at
change have been from outside, which is why utopias fail.
Count the false steps—Christianity's attempts to train the
human will by exhortation while insisting that there is a un-
impeachable pedigree for moral law; military and political
power as the basis for law; eugenic and racial theories. Presumably, you would want to change my humanity more radically. How will you go about doing that? Clearly, the human
world as we know it will never agree to it. Do you know a way
that will not be subverted by our objectionable humanity?"

Juan said, "Before a larger group can see the virtue of an
idea, a smaller group must first understand it."

"Dangerous words, my friend. But where shall we begin?
How will we reach into the core of ourselves, elevate our
best impulses, and seize the organism?"

Juan looked at the big Russian and saw that he understood,
and was not mocking. "We must begin," he said, "however
badly, no matter how hopeless it seems. Perhaps right here
in this vessel, away from the treadmill of human history. In
the web there is all the knowledge we might ever need to
remake ourselves."

"Into what?" Lena demanded.

Juan sat up nervously. "Into a being that will continue to
change. Not instant homo superior, but with small steps over
a long period of time. But we can only begin if we recognize
how pitiable is the progress we can expect from purely political, religious, or educational regimes. Civilization has always

reached a certain degree of civil order, but crimes and violence remain irreducible. We settle for a power pyramid in which everyone is disposable."

"Civil order is an achievement," Malachi said.

"It holds the fort, but the fort always falls, the culture dies and limps on to something else that always forgets its gains. Have you looked at the Earth lately? It's dying. And the alien web waits to be invaded, to become the next terrible arena of death. No amount of law or inner regimen will eliminate homicide, rape, or criminal economics, not to mention the endlessly growing network of personal cruelties, ego-power struggles, and vainglory that we call social life."

"But expansion into the web may also save humankind, such as it is," Tasarov objected.

"Would your decisive changes take away choice, and our capacity to be violent?" Lena asked. "I ask as a biologist, since you're saying there's no progress in being a human being."

"We could be a more humane creature, in whom reason wouldn't teeter on the edge, but would tip the balance. Not perfection, but an organism that would be in control of itself, that would be replanning itself from one generation to the next, aided by mirrors of self-knowledge. The body's history, as we have been given it, is an event horizon holding us in. Knowledge of what we are is fragmentary. We don't possess ourselves. We prize self-possession and knowledge, creativity and growth, but only taste these things. Human history is a shameful gloss on the evolutionary slaughterhouse. Genuine gains belong to an insignificant few who are always in danger of losing them."

"But where to start?" Tasarov asked eagerly.

"Right in this ship. Slowly, we might begin to operate it."

"Familiarity breeds knowledge, eh?" Malachi said.

"More like trial and error," Juan replied. "A lifetime of it."

"Life inside a puzzle!" Tasarov shouted.

Lena was silent.

Tasarov struck the floor with his fist. "I will stay with you," he said, "because I have a taste for ideal forms."

Juan looked at the viewspace. The soldiers were returning to the frame.

"They've given up," Tasarov said.

As he watched the small black figures form a column and pass through the frame, he imagined that he was seeing a virus under a microscope. Superman is a good cry, a superior man had once written, and a good cry is half the battle, but it also breeds contempt for the human.

He glanced at Lena. She seemed lost as she gazed past him. "I don't love humanity in a self-serving way," he said to her, "which is the way it loves itself."

She glared at him. "You want to cut yourself off completely, but you want company! It's been tried."

"Yes, by religious and political groups who wanted to escape human failure by laying down new traditions, new ideals. We can't do worse, and we may do much better. It'll be a long time before small changes produce a new human type. Several hundred years may pass. . . ."

"I see. You will need a biologist, and some more population."

"Yes, when the time comes. And supplies, equipment."

"Who will help you?"

"Titus might, or some variant of him. We'll start by trying to understand this ship."

Magnus said, "Juan, the fact is that we're incredibly stupid when it comes to this alien technology—and we have no way to measure just how stupid. I've tried to envision what you've been talking about, but I just can't see any hope for it. We've never been able to influence these ships one whit. You're off the deep end."

"So what do you suggest?"

"I'll explore with you as long as it seems to make sense, even if I don't accept much of what you've said."

"Will you keep an open mind?"

"I'll do so without much hope."

Juan looked at Malachi. "And what do you think, old friend? Am I around the bend?"

The African smiled. "You've taken a bold leap inside yourself."

Tasarov shrugged. "What can I say, my friend? Life is short, nature very hostile, and man sublimely ridiculous. What have we to lose? When you part the Red Sea, there will be few doubters."

The green inner surface below was now free of creeping black ants. "I wonder," Juan said, "if Summet told them about variants. The poor fools are in for a shock."

Lena looked at Juan anxiously. "Do you think they can reach us through one of the frames in this ship?"

"I doubt it," he said. "Any frame entrance to this ship would probably lead in from another ship. The shuttle may be the only way into this ship. It might not have even occurred to them that we could be out here."

"But there may be frames elsewhere," she objected.

Magnus said, "They don't know what they're looking for, and are unlikely to find it even if they did."

"Just as well," Tasarov said. "What would we do if they somehow found their way in here? Kill them as they came through? And then what would we do? I will serve our dinner," he said as he got to his feet. "Then we must sleep."

43

THE WALL

◖

He was poised to regain his lost youth, to confront death, and to find a new life for his kind. Rooms floated in gray nothingness, each a receptacle of yellow sunlight. What was it about a bright room? Light—matter's fugitive song—trapped in a finite interior. "Where are you?" he whispered across the inner light years. "Why did you build your web and abandon it? Don't you need it any more?" Secrets stood like fortresses around him. Many were small redoubts, hoarding their knowledge, but knowing that loss was inevitable. Larger fortresses held their secrets with pride if not certainty, knowing that loss was possible but not likely. The greatest fortresses were vaults of arrogance, defying all assaults of understanding. No probe would ever reach their infinitely desirable treasures. . . .

Lena nudged him awake. He sat up and saw that the ship was moving directly toward the green surface.

"It may be some kind of spurious movement," Magnus said. "There's no sign of an exit."

"We must use the shuttle," Tasarov said, "or flee through one of the frames!" They all got to their feet.

"Wait," Magnus said. "Look!"

A portion of the shell's inner surface reddened and grew large, revealing the ship's increasing speed. The vessel shot through—

—into the glare of a yellow sun, and seemed to slow suddenly as comparisons were lost in open space. The view shifted to a green planet with two bone white moons. The three bodies grew larger.

"Is that where we're going?" Tasarov asked. "What prompted the ship to leave?"

Lena said, "The large ships also left without warning."

"But why?" Tasarov asked.

Juan said, "We've always suspected that artificial intelligences ran these ships, and that they sometimes picked up things from us."

Tasarov looked puzzled. "You mean thoughts?"

Juan nodded. "At one time it seemed that we were being probed, but it stopped, as if something had seen the error of trying to work with us."

Tasarov said, "Perhaps we're enough like the builders to elicit only a confused response."

The green planet grew larger in the viewspace. A flat side on the larger moon suggested that a piece had been sheared off by a major collision.

"It does seem," Juan said, "that these craft are controlled through mental links that select automatic programs, but our minds don't match the systems, so it's unlikely we'll be able to navigate."

"We can try!" Tasarov exclaimed. "What is there to lose?"

"This craft," Lena said, "may not have interstellar capacity."

"We don't know that," Juan replied.

Tasarov said, "Maybe we should leave by one of the frames."

"We can do that any time," Lena answered.

Magnus pointed to the viewspace. "We're entering a high orbit above the green planet."

Wispy clouds covered the planet. Green and brown land masses wore lakes and rivers like jewels. The oceans varied from dark blue to magenta.

"It's beautiful," Lena said as light glinted off the northern icecap. "I find it hard to believe that in the end all this became nothing to them. They made their manufacturing, medical, and transport systems, and controlled the power of a galaxy's suns. Why wasn't it enough? What happened to them? It must have been a terrible accident of some kind."

Juan looked to the stars beyond the planet. All their discoveries had occurred through blind luck, but he could not accept that this would remain so indefinitely. Sooner or later they would learn more, and have that knowledge confirmed. He wondered if the ship's sudden departure had been an answer to his silent pleading.

Lena gazed at him calmly and said, "Do you think the builders became what they wanted, what you want, powerful and knowing, and it wasn't enough?"

He was silent, feeling inadequate.

She gazed longingly at the planet. "Let's see what's down there."

"If the shuttle will take us," Juan said.

"Should we?" Malachi asked.

"Why not," Tasarov said. "We don't know what we're doing. Let impulses lead us."

"We'll go," Juan said.

"Too late," Magnus said. "We're moving again."

The planet fell away to their right as the ship accelerated, and Juan felt that a clearer purpose had taken hold of the ship.

"What now?" Tasarov asked, gesturing at the stars that now filled the forward view.

Juan said, "It's accelerating toward a jump."

Juan sat on his pack and watched the stars blue-shift in the forward view. "Maybe one of the frames connects with one of the other ships back at the dock."

Magnus said, "It's likely the ships were linked together from the outset. In any case, the dock holds the only way we know that leads home."

"We might not be able to get back down to the inner surface of the shell," Tasarov added. "As far as we know, the shuttle attached to this ship is the only way. We'd be trapped aboard one of the other ships."

"But we have three frames here," Lena said. "They may lead to a station from which we could go home."

"That might take a lot of trial and error," Magnus replied.

Juan felt uneasy as he gazed at the blue-shifted stars. The center of the field was fading into black only three hours after they had left the dock.

"There's something different about this voyage," Lena said. "Do you sense it, Juan?"

"Yes," he answered without looking at her, afraid that she would see his crowded, confused thoughts. "I feel the ship's attempting to take us where it thinks we want to go."

"And where might that be?" she asked.

The viewspace flashed.

"We've jumped," Magnus said to Tasarov.

The flash came again. A thin scattering of stars appeared in the viewspace.

"No target star," Malachi said.

Juan tensed as the view flashed a third time. Nothing showed ahead.

"A malfunction?" Tasarov asked.

"We've never seen this," Lena replied.

"Are we still moving?" Tasarov asked.

Magnus said, "We've entered a different kind of space."

Lena stood up and peered into the blackness. "There's something ahead. I feel it," Her voice trembled.

They watched the viewspace, as if awaiting a revelation. Juan felt detached. Are you somewhere here? he asked the darkness.

"There!" Lena cried.

He saw a faint red sphere. It grew large suddenly and filled the viewspace, masking all evidence of forward motion.

"Are we landing?" Tasarov asked.

"It seems solid," Lena said.

The surface flashed, as if reacting to the ship's arrival.

"It's not a star," Magnus said, "either in normal or otherspace—but we're in some kind of otherspace."

"I don't think we're moving at all," Lena said.

"Is it natural, or a construction?" Tasarov asked.

"Maybe the ship can't enter," Lena said, "and we're expected to use the shuttle."

44

THE EXALTED PLACE

◐

They went up through the shuttle's winding passage and entered the drum-shaped chamber. Juan stepped into the center. The viewspace came on, showing the red enigma before the ship.

"We're not moving," Magnus said after a moment. They waited. He shook his head. "And it violates everything we know if we're not orbiting. It's as if we've come to a wall of some kind that appears to us as a sphere."

"Why won't the shuttle take us in?" Lena asked.

"Maybe we're not welcome," Tasarov said.

"What do you think this place is?" Juan asked him.

"My friend, I would guess that this is where they are, the ones who built the web."

"But where is it?" Lena asked.

"Not in any space we know," Magnus said.

"Why did the ship bring us here if the shuttle won't take us in?" she asked.

"Another accident," Magnus answered.

They went back into the ship, dropped their packs in the control chamber, and sat down. Juan looked up at the red glow that filled the viewspace, feeling that something was holding them at arm's length.

Tasarov looked over at him and grimaced. "Suppose, my friend, that this is the place where the builders now live. Perhaps they didn't all come here at once. Some came first and others followed. This ship brought us here, as it might have countless others over time, until none were left, their empire abandoned."

"But what's here?" Lena asked.

"A place to live," Magnus said.

"Yes!" Tasarov exclaimed. "But what is it, hidden behind a wall? I don't think that's a solid surface. It's only what we can see."

"I see what you're getting at," Magnus said. "Is this a sealed-up area, a pocket, inside our universe?"

"Perhaps," Tasarov said, "but I think they were more ambitious than that. Once they learned how to escape into superspace, which is where I think we are now, they realized what could be done. They could free themselves of the universe from which they had sprung, from its physical laws. The web is the engineering infrastructure of an abandoned universe."

"Why abandoned?" Lena asked.

"It may be," Magnus said, "that they grew tired of working within the nature we know. Everything we've seen is a heroic attempt to overcome distance, biological limits, material scarcities. All are prosthetic solutions to the problem of entropy, ways of cheating the universe, by stealing energy from one place and using it in another, to make it do what you want, to help you survive, learn, shape. However successful such a civilization would be, it would still have to face the singularities between the cycles of expansion and collapse. Why not escape the pattern of birth and death completely, and build a universe that is not so hostile to the survival of intelligence? Once the starcrossers entered superspace, in which all universes exist, they realized that they could start from scratch, free of the realm that had bubbled up from some insane unconscious."

"How did they do this?" Tasarov asked.

"They brought a ball of false vacuum—a region of densely packed material—out here into superspace, where they worked on its internal specifications, then let it inflate into a new universe. There may be countless such offshoots of our universe out here. All universes, ours included, materialize as quantum fluctuations in empty superspace, whenever that space contorts itself into an isolated space. There may be two kinds—those that occur naturally, and those that are engineered by highly advanced intelligences."

As he listened, Juan realized that his war with himself, with his kind's history, with nature itself, might end. A creative divorce was possible.

"We have come out from an evil land," Tasarov said, "inside the gates of hell."

Lena asked, "Do you truly think that?"

"Of course! Consider our universe, its limits, its heart-breaks. It's *against* so much. I find it rational that the star-crossers went and built their heaven rather than continue to renovate the mortal treadmill of our space-time."

"Yes," Magnus said, "but they were good at it. Just imagine what it took to build the web. To start, they probably removed a wormhole from the quantum foam and enlarged it to classical size, using the energy of a sun. Then they lengthened it, learned to transmit energy and later themselves through the lines. The jump ships operate on an intermittent use of wormholes, which don't last, but get a ship from point to point. They realized that wormholes implied time travel, which led to an understanding of how natural laws might be suspended. That enabled them to exit into superspace, where they designed their new universe."

"But we never encountered any time travel effects," Lena objected.

"They had no need of it," Magnus replied. "It was the violation of the average weak energy condition that was significant, because it meant that physical law could be remade, albeit in a suitable context. Time travel within our universe would have given them dominance over their own history, but to what end? The remaking of themselves and the creation of their own sealed-off universe in superspace was a much nobler task."

"And that's where they are now," she said, "in there."

"In there is a literal way of putting it," Magnus replied.

"I'm a biologist, Magnus. Say what you mean."

"The universe beyond that horizon may be infinite," he continued. "If they created it, they might also be masters of scale. Their universe might have been no larger than a walnut and still be infinite."

"They must have known," Lena continued, "that others would find what they left behind. Not just us. How many other races might our universe contain?"

"That might explain," Juan said, "why we've run into so many visual operating manuals. Perhaps they wanted us to have what they outgrew."

"But if all this is true," Lena continued, "then they're telling us that it's no good trying to adapt to a given nature. I wonder if they had to abandon our universe because they damaged it in some way. By opening up pathways between variants, they might have created an intolerable condition."

"Variants are probably a feature of all universes in superspace," Magnus said. "Interesting to think it might have been some kind of accident."

"How can we confirm any of this?" Malachi asked. "It isn't exactly obvious."

"Maybe we've had help and don't know it," Juan replied.

The red field disappeared from the viewspace, and was replaced by what seemed to be a grouping of flickering stars.

"Those may not be stars, or distant galaxies," Juan said. "If we're in superspace, they may be entire universes."

The view pulled in closer, revealing a circular area filled with a gossamer patchwork. "Our universe, perhaps," Magnus said, "as seen from outside."

It flickered as they watched, and seemed to Juan that it might disappear. He felt a moment of agony, as if at any moment something would come from the darkness and devour this delicacy. "They know we're here," he said calmly, "and we're being instructed. Once in a while, there had to have been other escapees from the natural creations. They must expect it if they left us the means."

"I wonder if we interest them at all?" Lena said.

"Why not?" Tasarov replied. "We're probably their children, one way or another. Perhaps we're an offshoot of life they might have seeded, some colony which went off on its own and never developed sufficiently. We may be all that's left of those who have not gone into their exalted place."

"Their technology cared for them," Magnus replied. "We've seen it do the same for us, as much as it was possible, given that we're probably very different from them. This ship responded as if it was bringing out more immigrants, from those who stayed behind, but now wanted to join the others."

"But they won't let us in," Lena said.

"Perhaps we don't know how to knock."

Tasarov, Juan noticed, was entranced by the flickering universe in the viewspace. "The mathematics of it," he whispered, "the divine mathematics . . ."

"How do they live in there?" Lena asked. "What could it be like?"

Malachi said, "One thing worries me. Superspace, if it's a permanent, infinite plenum, must be the one thing that's beyond them. It can't be remade, and its laws may take precedence over what happens within the isolates. I wonder how they feel about that? It would worry me if there was even the possibility of a realm around my own that might intrude, however insulated my universe might be from its laws. Perhaps superspace isn't infinite, and comes to some kind of end, following a vast cycle of its own."

"I'll bet," Juan said, "that the universe of the starcrossers can survive, if it comes to that." He looked at the other patches of light around the flickering universe, and wondered how long they had existed.

"Do any of you truly believe any of this is true?" Lena demanded.

"We have the evidence of their abandoned works of cosmic engineering," Tasarov replied, "and the fact that nowhere, not even in variants, have you found the starcrossers. Only their echoes remain in their empty works. I reason thus: After working to reshape the universe we know, after trying to bend it to their will, they gave up. We don't find them in our nature; therefore we must look outside it. And here we have an event horizon, in a place outside. We find ourselves in a preponderance of suspiciously systematic circumstances."

"So you admit," Lena countered, "that this may still all be wrong?"

Tasarov stood up and stretched. "That would be a great pity! Our universe is only a few steps beyond birth. It can't make up its mind, but splits endlessly, suggesting that it is a natural growth. It defines the very nature of choice, for us, its creatures. Every time we choose, we enter a new world. You have seen the naked stage works of its flow and branching. Do you think, Juan, that the builders have abolished variants inside their new cosmos? Have they escaped the sum over histories and now live in only one?"

"We can't know," Juan replied.

"Economical chaps," Malachi said, pointing to the viewspace, "in what little they choose to present us with. We spin a web of reasoning and remain uncertain. Lena is right. This could all have other explanations."

"Let's assume it's all true," Lena said. "What can it mean? What's in it for us unless we can go back and be of some help to our own kind, most of whom can't start over somewhere else?"

"We may not be able to return," Juan said.

"You may not mind for yourself," she said gently. "But whatever happens to us, our kind will spread through the web, for better or worse. If we go back, we can influence how that happens. Maybe we need to run through our own mistakes. We'll change, socially and biologically, but I hope it won't happen out of self-hatred. I don't want to see humanity further divided against itself, into supposedly lesser and more advanced types. I'd rather we all went ahead together, to keep faith with all the billions who lived and died so that better times might come. Perhaps one day we'll come out here and make a new place for ourselves, but not yet. For now, it's people like Titus who are coming to grips with things, who are trying to work through the failure around them. We're out here because Titus gave us the chance. Bergson may have been right about universes being machines for making deities, but we're not those deities yet." She paused. "So what do we do?"

"It may not be up to us," Magnus said softly. "We may be a sample, lured here to see if there was anything original in the seedlings. They may not let us go home."

45

NEVER COME HOME

◑

What was there to go back to? Juan asked himself as he lay awake. They'd wander again through the runs of human variants, seeking a haven, and find only the usual inner constraints producing unwanted outcomes. Future ages might bring utopias, in which humankind would remake itself, but an infinite universe would always escape control. Its laws would always rule, ineradicable, hiding in the conscious craft of remade bodies and singing psyches. For his kind to soar, to escape its inner torments, a new nature was needed, not merely a new rapprochement with the old. To battle the weary variants would only yield the same comedy.

So why did Lena want to go back? Out of pity? To reproduce and die? He imagined his colony of ever-changing transhumanity, each generation reaching deeper into the beast to clear away evolution's stubborn residues, and himself wandering across the colony's variants, an estranged Moses crossing and recrossing the river Jordan, always hearing something different on a changing Sinai.

He looked at the universes in the viewspace, and wondered if they were merely some odd optical effect. If this was superspace, then its different laws might even express the old Aristotelian notion of regions at absolute rest, with each fixed universe a dynamic creation within the rigid frame.

He thought of what lay beyond the red wall, then imagined himself back home, in his boyhood bed, dreaming of the red limit, where the light of fleeing galaxies winked out as they approached light speed. He had wondered about the space into which they sped, still too unsophisticated to accept that space itself was expanding. The question of what lay beyond an expanding space had tantalized him, in the same way that superspace did now. Superspace made no sense unless one accepted it as eternal and infinite; it was incapable of not existing, unlike the things within the quantum fluctuations that were its universes, which existed contingently. There was no logical problem in imagining their nonexistence, but superspace *had* to be infinite, or it could not serve as a proper basis for the existence of contingent universes. It existed necessarily, because genuine nothingness was impossible; a mere absence, a vacuum, could always be filled, and made sense only if surrounded by substance. The infinite universe of superspace, therefore, existed as God might have, not needing a beginning. There was no logical difference between an eternal universe and an omnipotent deity; they both served the same role in explaining existence. Religious mythologies simply rode piggyback on this truth. There was no way to avoid an infinite existence, but at the same time it was infuriating, and unimaginable. Or was it possible that another superspace enclosed this one, and another beyond it? Was it superspaces all the way up and down, with no final up or down, and fixed dynamic space-times in each? Was one kind of infinity preferable to another?

He sat up suddenly, and wondered if the frames on this ship were still linked with the home universe. They would have to stretch across superspace to remain functional. He imagined a torn-away wormhole, trailing after the ship, leading nowhere, but he knew it could not happen. Passages were anchored at each frame, if this was in fact the model for how the frames worked.

He turned his head and saw a dark shape rise up against the universes in the viewspace.

"Magnus," he whispered to the figure, "where are you going?"

The dark shape beckoned for him to follow. He got up and followed it into the straight passage.

"To try these frames," the older man said. "I may not return."

"Why do you think that?" Juan asked.

"I may not want to, more likely, than not be able to."

"What is it, Magnus?"

"I think one of these frames now leads into the red sphere. It would explain why the shuttle didn't work."

"You think it's a new link, set up for us to use. Could it have existed before, when the ship was still in its dock?"

"No, not if we've left our universe, but who knows what's true any more? I'll know, at any rate. Do you want to come?"

"We should all go. I'll wake the others."

"I don't think we should all go," Magnus said.

"What more can we risk?"

Magnus smiled and leaned closer. "I'm an old man, Juan, with nothing to lose. I look forward to being surprised by what I find—something more than the life that's given to us by an unfriendly universe. You should appreciate that. Take Lena back and be human, however small that may seem to you now. Promise me that's what you'll do that if I don't return."

"What about Yevgeny?"

"Take him back with you. He's suffered more than he shows, and deserves a place where he can relax and do his mathematical dances."

He turned away and approached the oval entrance. It glowed and he slipped through. Juan hurried after him—

—into the harshly lit chamber. The gray-haired man stood poised before the three frames.

"Magnus—" Juan murmured as his friend hurried into the blackness, then took a deep breath and stepped back, feeling that he had just witnessed a suicide.

Magnus suddenly stepped out of the frame, looking surprised. "What is it?" Juan asked, tensing.

"It doesn't go through to anywhere, just turns back on itself." He faced the next one.

"Magnus, wait!"

"Maybe it goes back to the dock." He stepped through, and in a few moments emerged again. "Another circle." He sighed. "At least it suggests that we're outside normal space-time." He confronted the last frame.

Juan grabbed his wrist. Magnus pulled free and said, "One of us has to play things out to the end. We've strained all the old limits of human life, Juan. You're selling a vision that would abandon most of our bodily history. I feel the weight of possibility, and at the same time it seems there's nothing left. Good-bye."

Juan grabbed at him, but Magnus pushed him aside with surprising strength and fled into the frame. Juan stood back and waited, hoping that there was no place for his friend to go.

46

DANCING MINDS

◑

Blackness pressed in around Juan as he stepped into the frame, squeezing him forward through slippery textures. Deaf and blind, he was drawn forward.

Gradually he saw that he was slipping through a red plenum of shapes—round, oval, long, and thin—all soft and transparent with other forms inside them. He slipped between them as if he knew where to go. Joy stirred within him, but it was not his own. He looked around in panic, saw a bright open area of yellow, around which the shapes circled, and swam into it.

As he looked out from this storm's eye, he noticed that the organisms not only circled, but also danced in short, jagged fits—up, down, and sideways—and shook once in a while. He felt this motion within himself.

The swirling mass around him parted, and he saw distant spaces, around which galaxies of orange, yellow, and green shapes also did their kaleidoscopic dance. Suddenly they entered each other, radiating a great sense of pleasure and satisfaction. Alien joy burgeoned within him.

Magnus appeared next to him, looking gaunt and pale. Juan's anxiety banked the invading joy. He tried to speak, and failed; but Magnus seemed to understand.

"They constantly reshape themselves," he said, "to please each other, and find this satisfying. All that we surmised must be true."

Juan gazed at the alien creation around him, trying to grasp how it could be fulfilling.

"Entropy is constant here," Magnus said. "The gamelike, goal-oriented aspects of life are nonexistent. Only play exists, if we can call it that."

"Are they aware of us?" Juan asked.

"They perceive our longings, I think, our unfilled states."

"And you want to stay?"

"I will lose all that I am, all caring for what we have been. I'm not sure if it's right or desirable, if that means anything here."

"It's a heavenly host!" Juan cried out with sudden fear.

Magnus turned in the bright space, smiled, and said, "We can't judge. We were made to be empty, then to be filled, emptied and filled. We don't know, then we do. We forget, and remember. We learn, and need more knowledge. We're a two-position switch, or a sieve which longs to be full. Satisfied, it would miss the longing." He twisted and looked directly at Juan, his face contorted by pain. "We're not made for all this. If we resist, we'll suffer in the transition. . . ."

"Magnus!" Juan cried. "Don't let go!"

The gaunt face seemed unafraid as it gave him a questioning look.

"Magnus! If superspace contains both natural and deliberate universes, then you don't have to settle for this one. We can find others, see what they offer!"

Magnus nodded as he turned end over end. "You want to go and find them?"

"Yes," Juan said, feeling a new passion kindling within himself.

"You will always be going."

"Come with me!" he shouted, looking around at the vast merry-go-round. Their free space shrank as the shapes closed in. Were these what was left of the web builders? Was this their reward—nothing more than a deep pleasure? It had to be more than that.

A black frame appeared in the distance behind Magnus. Lena, Malachi, and Tasarov shot out. As they drifted nearer, he realized that they might all be trapped here forever. The creative effort of the starcrossers was a failure. Even though they had escaped their origins, they had made what seemed a mindless heaven.

"Go back!" Juan shouted, trying to swim toward the frame, willing himself to move, but it felt as if an invisible gelatinous mass were impeding him. The shapes seemed to be singing a silent song, a mix of ragged calliope and blissful Mozart. "Let us go!" he shouted, clawing his way past Magnus, who now seemed beyond reason as he closed his eyes and tumbled. Juan heard him say, "Hold up the shell / And hear the secret sound of childhood / The sea within! / Blood pouring

through / Your heart and mind / As you contain / The salty
mother / From whom you swam."

Juan turned and gazed back at him. Magnus's eyes opened
wide and he said, "Our souls are small / But we know
infinity / With every longing." He smiled and added, "We
must sit from time to time / And think about being / How
life is lived / What might be / If we shaped it." He nodded
and closed his eyes, apparently satisfied.

Juan turned away and motioned again for the others to go
back. "Leave Tasarov!" Magnus whispered after him. "He
will know what to do with this place."

Juan was moving faster now, even though he had no idea
of how he was doing it.

"What shall we do?" Malachi demanded as he reached him.

"Go back!" Juan shouted, looking at Lena's sleepy expression. She seemed to be slipping away.

"What about Magnus?" Tasarov demanded.

They looked at the older man. He beckoned to them.
"Tasarov!" he called out. "Come!"

"Wait!" Juan shouted as the Russian moved off, laughing.

"What can we do?" Malachi asked as Lena tumbled
over end next to him. He reached out and steadied her.

"Leave," Juan said, looking toward Magnus and Tasarov.

"What about them?" Lena asked lazily.

Juan replied, "We're losing them."

"Do we go get them or not?" Malachi asked.

"I'll go," Juan said. "Get Lena out."

"Right."

Juan swam toward the two men. It was slow going as he
flailed his arms and kicked with his legs. After a moment, he
was moving with no help from his limbs. He glanced over
his shoulder. Lena and Malachi were nearing the frame.

Magnus and Tasarov embraced and tumbled together as
he reached them. He came up between their heads and
grabbed their shoulders.

"We must go back!" he shouted, turning with them.

They looked at him sleepily. "You go back, my friend,"
Tasarov said. "I'm beginning to see what they do here."

"What?" Juan asked.

"Pure mathematical ecstasy. I have already solved all the
insolubles I have known in my life." He smiled. "But Magnus
is far ahead of me."

Juan asked, "Are you serious?"

"Of course he is," Magnus answered. "Go spy on God in your own way."

Juan glanced back and saw Lena and Malachi slip through the frame. "You'd better let go," Magnus said.

The shapes turned a dark green as they closed in. Tasarov pushed him away. "They will only hurt you, my friend," he said.

As Juan kicked away, one of the egg shapes drew near and absorbed the two men. They became motionless inside the transparent mass, still holding each other. The shape rejoined its school, and in a moment Juan could not tell it apart from the countless others who seemed to be circling a hidden center, a central mind. For a moment he was transfixed, realizing that this was as close as he was ever likely to get to a Godlike being. Then he felt revulsion; even here, he thought, minds were drawn to power. Idolatry was as attractive a state for the idolator as it was for the object of idolatry. All that was needed was for the idolator to be convinced that the object was worthy of worship; but even if such worthiness were possible, the genuinely worthy being would not degrade lesser beings by requiring adoration. Only powerful, unworthy entities demanded worship.

Sadly, he turned away and willed himself toward the frame. He shot in horizontally and crawled through on his hands and knees, emerging into the harshly lit chamber.

Lena and Malachi sat on the floor. They got up and helped him to his feet. "Are they coming?" Malachi asked.

"No."

"I knew they would stay," Lena said. She seemed awake and herself again. Juan felt empty.

In the drum-shaped chamber, they sat down and tried to picture the dock from which they had started, hoping to trigger the ship's return.

Juan looked up after a few moments, but the viewspace still showed the red wall. As he watched, it changed to show the universes of superspace, then switched back to the red wall.

"We're confusing it," Lena said. She looked at him accusingly. "It's probably you. Some part of you doesn't want to go back."

"I do," Juan replied.

"And you?" she asked Mal.

"Ever so much."

They waited. Finally, the viewspace went blank.

"I think we've jumped," Juan said.

47

THERE IS A DOOR ...

◑

They waited like sleepwalkers as the ship returned to its
dock. When finally it slipped through the glowing lock and
resumed its position among the other vessels, Juan felt like
a rejected toy being put back in its box. He walked toward
the shuttle as if alone. Lena and Malachi avoided his eyes
as the sphere whisked them down to the inner surface.
Silently, they made their way back to the big ship in the
suncore station and passed through the frame back to the
ship in the Amazon. The way was clear of troops when they
came up the winding passage.

"I hope it's not another ruined variant," Lena said at the
final turn.

The open lock was guarded. They identified themselves,
were shown to a jeep, and driven down to Summet's dome.
A corporal ushered them into the office.

Juan glanced at his companions as they all sat down before
the large desk. "What should we keep to ourselves this
time?" he asked.

"Nothing," Lena answered. "What's there to hide? What
have we learned?"

The door slid open and Titus came in.

"Welcome home," he said as he hurried behind his desk.
"I see you're all here," he added as he sat down.

Juan said, "So Magnus didn't go with us in this variant."

"He got here just after you three left."

"And Tasarov?"

"We brought him in just after the riot. He helped us close
down the prison. We let them use the frames to settle an
Earthlike world. Their colony is accepting regular immigrants. You'd approve, Juan."

"How long have we been gone?" Malachi asked.

"Thirteen months. What happened?"

"Well?" Juan asked when he was finished.

Titus smiled. "It's all very interesting, but you haven't given me any assessments. What's it all mean, and what's in it for us, if I may be crass?"

"As far as the web is concerned," Lena said, "we've dealt with a vast, impersonal system of transport, manufacture, and medical care, abandoned by its builders. It responded to our presence, to our needs, as well as it could, according to how well it could match us with its programs."

"We had some success," Juan said, "in operating one of the smaller starships. We think we were able to make it bring us back."

"The abandoned web," Lena continued, "was an attempt, we believe, to lay the foundations of a second nature, to be superimposed on our universe, using the energy of countless stars."

Summet said, "But they went elsewhere."

"We think so," Malachi replied, "but I fear that we may never fully understand what we saw. Either the builders made a botch of their final development, or they succeeded. Or we've got everything wrong."

"Maybe we'll go back to their realm one day," Juan continued, "and be able to learn something from them. Our Magnus and Tasarov stayed behind."

"What?"

"They were taken by the place," Malachi said. "Nothing we could do but get ourselves out."

Summet sat back. "You've called it a universe. Do you mean literally?"

"Possibly," Malachi replied. "No way to measure, actually."

"I believe," Juan said, "that they designed the laws of their new universe."

Summet shook his head. "From what you've told me, ours may be a deliberate creation, perhaps bungled by some fledgeling god!"

"Why think that?" Lena asked.

"Because the builders abandoned it."

Malachi said, "They probably left a natural cosmos, rather than a wrong job."

"What is this . . . superspace?" Summet asked.

"Just a word," Juan said. "Think of it as the real universe, in which all others are merely local regions, with varied dimensional structures."

"And it's infinite in extent, not just lacking an edge or boundary as ours does?"

"We can't be sure," Juan said, "unless we could measure its curvature, if it has any. It does provide a background from which to derive our universe. An infinite universe avoids the need for an omnipotent and omniscient deity, if you will."

"You sound unhappy about it."

"I don't like infinities, either in a deity or in nature."

Malachi said, "There's always that nagging thought of something lurking outside."

"But not outside an infinite superspace," Summet said.

"Yes," Juan answered, "but you could never get to the end of an infinite superspace to know if it was infinite or not. If curvature is unmeasurable for superspace, you'd have to be convinced of its infinite expanse on purely rational grounds."

"Which are?"

Juan shrugged. "A secular ontological proof. Informally speaking, it asserts that a zero-field, or nothing, is logically contradictory, as well as being physically and psychologically impossible. We can't think it and we can never offer up an example. What we call space is a full plenum. On that basis, something must exist necessarily, meaning it doesn't depend on anything, never came to be, and will never disappear. It exists eternally and infinitely. God, never having come into being, is nothing more than a psychologically primitive metaphor for this fact, known intuitively long before we were able to defend it rationally. The old religious ontological proof put forward by Anselm is exactly this, except that he conveniently identifies that which exists necessarily as the Christian God. There's no need to, because everything needed to have a universe is already present in an infinite necessary existence. By Occam's Razor, God is one entity too many, a technical extreme of language which we've mistakenly personified."

"Ah, yes!" Titus exclaimed. "But can you have a very large necessary existent, your superspace, and have genuine nothingness outside, an infinite nothingness?"

"The word has no meaning. It would involve us in a lot of contradictory talk. Nothingness outside superspace would end up being something, which would reduce our superspace to a function of that something, and we'd be off into an infinite regress of renormalizations. You can define nothingness all you want, but you can never find any."

Titus smiled. "And you can't ever put your hands on infinity, either."

"This is all well and good," Lena cut in, "but we can only be sure of our space-time and what we've seen nearby."

"She's right," Juan said. "Whatever our universe is, we'll have to keep developing in our own way, through all our variants, using whatever comes to hand, following whatever interests us. Maybe somewhere among the other universes of superspace we'll find a culture that might have an idea of what's going on."

"Why so sad about it?" Titus asked.

"I don't think I am," Juan answered, feeling tired and knowing that his thinking was scattered and inadequate. He needed time to organize his thoughts and impressions.

Lena said, "Titus, we'll help you do as much as possible with what we're learning, but we must widen our group. We may be able to run these starships."

"Yes," Malachi added, "we must make sure our kind survives."

Juan said, "In our own way, not that of the builders."

"So you'll throw us a bone once in a while, eh?" Summet said.

"I deserve that," Juan replied. "I've looked so hard for the better that I forgot the ordinary, which still needs to be tended."

Titus said, "We haven't done very well with what knowledge has come our way, not in my time or before." He stood up. "Look, Juan, I don't want to see you down like this. You go for the long shots, and just promise . . . to help a little with the nearer targets. I can see you've stared all this in the face without flinching, reasoning your way through conclusions without fudging. Don't stop. Take some time to record your thoughts while they're still fresh."

Juan felt his sincerity. "Thanks," he said, sure now that he had never given himself a chance to know the man.

"Oh, we'll disagree. Count on it."

48

... TO WHICH WE HAVE NO KEY

◐

There are gods out there, Juan thought as he showered. Large aggregate beings moved through superspace and occasionally tried to create something *other*. They might have been made in some infinite past, or had grown to awareness from natural space-times; during their endless existence they had learned everything except the answers to one or two possibly unanswerable questions, and had become confused, perhaps even startled anew by their own being, and tried to *do* something. . . .

He watched the water running out at his feet. They were leviathans, these swimmers in the vastness, minds as large as universes, left with nothing to do, because doing flowed from desire, and desire was a function of lacking; it kindled in them only when they remembered the few mysteries still beyond them. . . .

He had once hoped that humankind was alone in the universe, with no competition, not just an isolated child. Now distant others waited, and there were no clear common parents from whom to win favors. Countless universes swam in superspace, some of them the creations of large minds; but even though the relationship might resemble that of God and Creation, these stand-ins were not omniscient or omnipotent. . . .

For months he had worked in his house, struggling to assemble his notes for *Another Region of an Infinite Universe*, but had found no easy way to organize the mass of his ideas, arguments, impressions, and suppositions; yet he continued to set them down.

Either the universe was infinite and contained regions at

differing levels of development, or endless finite universes grew in an infinite superspace. The first model had no need of a surrounding superspace; all regions were open to each other, even though logic required regions that would be at an infinite distance from each other, governed by the same laws. Such a universe required no creation in some distant past. . . .

There would always be time in an infinite universe to escape a dying or collapsing region, and go where the stars were young. It was a simpler infinity than one requiring local spaces set in superspace. The space-superspace model was only the single-infinity universe expressed with more terms.

If this was true, then the alien ship had only jumped across a vast space to reach the red sphere, and the web builders had not escaped entirely; they had only walled themselves off from infinity. Their universe might last forever, but no intelligence would ever be able to remake an infinite existence. Its reality was transcendent, an arrogant citadel of secrets which could never be stormed. Supercivilizations might transform whole galaxies, populate the silence of space for a billion years, and still not touch its infinite otherness. . . .

There was no secret behind this infinity; it simply existed, had always existed, and would always exist. Nonexistence was an impossibility. . . .

It maddened him. Finite universes were tidy, but they required an outside space to contain them. Infinite space, like the notion of nothingness, was incomprehensible to common reason, which claimed that it couldn't be imagined, only defined and insisted upon. For Aristotle it had been an absurdity, a word that stood for nothing, since infinity could not be had. On the face of it, both finite and infinite universes were an affront to rationality . . .

To prove that the universe was infinite in all directions required difficult measurements. The attempt itself exposed the finite bias of the human mind—to measure infinity and make it a verifiable fact, even if it could not be encompassed. Reason depended on limits, which meant that infinities were not rational, or that a finite creature took its own limits as the model for rationality. . . .

The varieties of infinity escaped the intuitive grasp of his kind, yet they insisted on talking about a God in those terms. So why not simply accept an infinite, uncreated universe as the central fact of existence?

An infinite, uncreated universe was unimaginable and terrifying; but an all-powerful Deity was even more terrifying—especially if It might reach into finite beings and speak. Perhaps that was why God preferred to whisper in a still, small voice that human beings could easily mistake for their own conscience. . . .

Deity would be an insoluble mystery to Itself, never having come into being; in Its presence, finite creatures would be nothing. . . .

Hopes for afterlife clung like barnacles to archaic human notions of Omnipotent Deity; but these afterlives were banal systems. If true, they would be a tyranny imposed on finite beings, who had been created to be tested for moral worthiness, in which the exercise of free will decided the game—except that everyone had to play.

Without afterlife, it was argued, life would be degrading; but an additional life could not make life fair, since it would also be imposed, not chosen. So why did human beings cling to Deity and afterlife? Tasarov had been right—to preserve the appearance of an unquestionable pedigree for ethical norms.

It seemed more reasonable to accept the growing evidence for an eternal existence in which the growing freedom of intelligent beings was a central feature. Humanity was on its own, responsible for the discovery of its own humane norms as it strove to transcend itself. There might be fellowship with powerful others, also struggling, by degrees, to comprehend a transcendent universe, but no prior, omniscient God. It had been a case of mistaken identity to attribute the features of an infinite, fecund nature to an omnipotent being. . . .

Ethical rules had grown out of religious justifications, but could now stand on their own. Deity's insisted-upon enforcement of ethical norms was only psychologically necessary—but this made them no less real, since ethical norms could not help but grow out of historical needs; they could never be arbitrary, even in a Godless universe. The price of transgression had never been God's wrath, but social damage. . . .

Juan imagined an eternal Deity lying down in the void to create a finite universe of passing things, then watching Its creatures test themselves against Its moral laws and physical mysteries, and finally plucking the worthy for what—an unequal, enforced fellowship?

Only an uncreated life offered true freedom, he realized,

because it steered alone through an open, infinite universe that offered a true test of freedom, because it did not consciously impose purpose. Humankind was free to work against natural limits and find its own way. Personal death, with nothing after, was a terror for only the vain and egocentric. A godless universe, infinite in all directions, including time, was the best state of affairs imaginable. Religious imagery presented hoped-for states that would one day be attained. . . .

At the edge of life's shore, the arrogant fortress of infinities rose before him, but he knew now that it was uninhabited, and there was no key to its gates. Order arose from chaotic process, which could not help but produce order, given endless time. The unpredictability of process did not make it acausal, only opaque before the fact. This was the secret of all creativity. Too much order was uncreative and totalitarian. Biosystems, with their plasticity, seized the regions between order and chaos. . . .

Job's answer to God's cruelties was that he would obey and be faithful. But God's test of Job made sense even in a Godless universe—humanity still had the chance to shine or fail before temptation and adversity, to choose a human morality over lawlessness. . . .

Juan could not imagine a nobler freedom as he stepped out of the shower and remembered the boy who had loved attic spaces—the more irregular the better—and had crawled into them in search of strangeness. We're drawn to small, narrow spaces, he thought, to places filled with odd individual things that revealed how far the universe had come from its hot, early uniformity. Humankind was one such oddity, organizing to be an enemy of entropy. . . .

He turned off the water and stood at the center of silence, realizing the fragility of insights that lived in isolated moments. He and Lena needed a time of private spaces—kitchens, bedrooms, sitting rooms and backyards—a collapse into the human scale of things. Was he so tired, to think such docile thoughts?

She had gone to pick up Magnus at the airport. Juan was looking forward to telling him the story. One day they would all visit Tasarov on his distant green world, even if it meant braving another variant. The Russian had remained loyal to his community, and had secured a better life for it, even as his variant swam in mathematical ecstasies.

He dried himself in a rush of hot air, put on his father's

long red robe of Spanish silk, and went up to the attic. The
steeply set oak planks did not creak. He reached the top and
saw faint daylight filtering in through the drawn shades on
the three small windows. He pulled the chain on the old
Edison industrial bulb. The irregular filament glowed in the
clear glass, casting a harsh light into the gables and distant
corners, summoning into being a universe of brittle cardboard
boxes, old night tables, footstools, broken chairs, rolled-up
rugs, and two old closets, on which sat an assortment of
empty cake and cookie tins—all travelers from the past,
trapped here in the stillness of dry wood.

He imagined protons decaying in the house beams, forcing
the structure back into chaos, and wondered about this attic's
variants.

Feeling warm, he took off his robe, hung it on an old brass
hook set in a beam, and began to move boxes. Sweat ran
down his back, and he coughed from the dancing dust. He
smiled as he imagined Lena and Magnus coming up and
finding him here like this, obviously out of his mind.

What contingencies, he wondered, had arranged the objects
in this attic? He saw endless pages scrolling up on a screen,
listing in minute, economically phrased steps the actions of
countless people, all leading to the deposit of one article after
another under these beams, throughout the infinity of
variants. . . .

He caught sight of himself in a partially covered mirror. An
olive-skinned biped with a large head peered back at him, as
if it had just pulled back the old sheet from the other side and
been surprised to find him here. He stepped closer and covered up the old mirror. This place, he realized, made him
happy, and wondered if Tasarov was fulfilled in the distant red
universe.

Voices echoed downstairs. Lena and Magnus had arrived.
He marveled suddenly at the intimacy of the social world, at
the way it blacked out the universe around it, arranging itself
for the exchange of simple needs, making strangers of those
outside the circle.

Disoriented, he put on his robe; in another moment he
might have slipped through an event horizon and scrambled
up on a new shore of understanding. It always seemed that
way, when the world dragged him back into commonplaces.
Kafka was right, he thought; at every turn we need an ax to
break the frozen sea within us. The scheme as given, to live,

reproduce, and die, was a sorry thing for an intelligent being to bear. Mind should live as long as it pleased, pursue knowledge, and love profoundly.

"We're here!" Lena shouted from below. His heart skipped a beat as he recalled her other self calling to him, and remembered how they had slowly drifted apart. Her death was still within him, forcing him to admit that he had failed to achieve fellowship with his kind. He was closest to Lena, who had turned him away from self-hatred.

The aliens in their entropy-free zone attained fellowship by dancing and swallowing each other. Did they also mix and remix their thoughts? Was the vast swirl of their red heaven a system for processing a finished body of knowledge—in the hope of extracting something new from it?

"Juan, are you here?" she called as he started down the attic stairs, thinking that probability was a form of divine hesitation. God was reluctant to lose anything, so He let it all happen. No joy or sorrow could ever be avoided; the best and worst embraced in the infinite sum of histories.

"Be right there!" he answered, but stopped on the landing, fearing that he would not live to see what would become of his kind, even though the alien technology might offer life-extension along with its other secrets. Titus had put Lena in charge of a team of biologists to work in Earth's suncore station, where the medical mode of the alien technology had revealed itself most obviously; Mal's British facade had slipped when Lena told him that Dita would join the group. Together with Malachi and himself, Magnus would lead a group of physicists and systems analysts in attempts to gain control of the starships. A map of the web would be made.

He turned left, hurried into his bedroom, and dressed quickly, overwhelmed by the thoughts of how many working lifetimes would be swallowed by the web; but its treasures would be earned, after all, and that was better than wallowing in an alien inheritance. In time, humanity might transform itself, and pass on to a realm of its own making. The nature of that existence was unforeseeable, but it might free his kind from its inner torments and fulfill its deepest longings. Then humanity would be ready to start its dialogue with the leviathans of superspace.

He finished dressing and sat down in the gable. Early spring sunlight warmed his face, reminding him that the web had already bettered the chances for human survival, through

Tasarov's colony, for one thing. Summet had found the right way in this variant.

He heard footsteps and turned to see Lena, Magnus, and Malachi in the open doorway. The sight of them flooded him with recognition, and he swam through their most private regions, liberated beyond himself with a new gift of childhood.

His friends were here and it was time to play.

ABOUT THE AUTHOR

George Zebrowski's twenty-six books include novels, short fiction collections, anthologies, and a book of essays. The late Terry Carr, one of the most influential editors of recent years, termed him "an authority in the field." Zebrowski has published more than fifty works of short fiction and nearly a hundred articles and essays. His best known novel is *Macrolife*, which Arthur C. Clarke described as "a worthy successor to Olaf Stapledon's *Star Maker*. It's been years since I was so impressed. One of the few books I intend to read again." *Library Journal* recently chose it as one of the hundred best SF novels, and Easton Press reissued it in its "Masterpieces of Science Fiction" series. His stories and novels have been translated into a half dozen languages; his short fiction has been nominated for the Nebula Award and the Theodore Sturgeon Memorial Award. *Stranger Suns* is also published in Easton Press's signed, leatherbound "First Editions" series, with illustrations by Bob Eggleton.

From two of science fiction's greatest storytellers
comes the stunning tale of a civilization
facing its greatest fears and its impending doom.

Isaac Asimov
& Robert Silverberg
NIGHTFALL

In 1941, Isaac Asimov published a short story about a
world whose six suns set simultaneously only once
every 2,049 years. When nightfall comes to the world of
Lagash, its people -- who have never seen the stars --
must deal with the madness that follows. The tale,
"Nightfall," named greatest science fiction story of all
time by the Science Fiction Writers of America, remains
a landmark of the genre.

Now, two of science fiction's greatest names join to tell
this story in all its immensity and splendor with a novel
that explores all the implications of a world facing
ultimate disaster. When academics at Saro University
determine that 12 hours of darkness are coming, a
group of religious fanatics called the Apostles of the
Flame begin to capitalize on the event, preying on the
fear of the general populace by "saving" converts and
damning non-believers. Both groups -- in conflict for
centuries -- know that the coming night will mean the
end of their civilization, for the people of Lagash have a
proven fear of the dark, and in the wake of unspeakable
horrors, must rally to save the fragile remnants of their
world.

Now available in Bantam Spectra paperback.

A dramatic new series of books at the cutting edge
where science meets science fiction.

THE NEXT WAVE
Introduced by Isaac Asimov

Computers, the space shuttle, biogenetics--what was once the domain
of science fiction is now business as usual. Developments in science
and technology are propelling us forward so fast that only a few dare to
speculate where we might go tomorrow.

Each volume of *The Next Wave* contains a fascinating scientific essay,
followed by a complete novel about the same subject. And every
volume carries an introduction by Isaac Asimov.

Volume One
Red Genesis
by S.C. Sykes
The spellbinding tale of a man who changed not one but two worlds,
with an essay by scientist Eugene F. Mallove on the technical
problems of launching and maintaining a colony on Mars.

Volume Two
Alien Tongue
by Stephen Leigh
The story of contact with a startling new world on the other side of a
newly discovered wormhole in space, with an essay by scientist and
author Rudy Rucker on the latest developments in the search for
extraterrestrial intelligence and the possibilities of first contact.

And coming in November, 1991
Volume Three
The Missing Matter
by Thomas R. McDonough
with an essay by Wallace H. Tucker

Look for the first two volumes of *The Next Wave*
on sale now wherever Bantam Spectra Books are sold

AN288 -- 7/91